A Behind-the-Curtain History of 20th-Century China

HOPE AND LIFE

Volume 1

Hu Xuewen

New Classic Press

2023

HOPE AND LIFE

Written by Hu Xuewen

Translated from Chinese by Joel Eric Batchler

First Published in China by © Jiangsu Phoenix Literature and Art Publishing Ltd., 2021.

This English Edition Copyright © 2023 by New Classic Press

This edition is published by arrangement with Jiangsu Phoenix Literature and Art

Publishing Ltd through the agency of Veritas & Mercurius Publishing Co., Ltd.

All rights reserved.

ISBN 978-1-915865-15-1

Printed in the United Kingdom of Great Britain and Northern Ireland

10 9 8 7 6 5 4 3 2 1

The publisher's policy is to use paper manufactured from sustainable forests.

TABLE OF CONTENTS

Chapter I

Zunai[1]

<hr>

1 The term Zunai is generally used to indicate a father's paternal grandmother. In this publication, however, it implies a revered mother goddess, viewed by many to be she who created life's many miracles. (All notes in this book are added by the translator.)

1

One foot was already in the grave, but my ears could still make out a pin drop. I could hear the chirping of male insects enticing their prospective mates, the wings of sandgrouse flying across the sky in winter, the babble of the village, and the sighing of the night wind. While my body was worn and tattered like a piece of petrified wood and my eyes had lost that spark of life, my ears and nose were still as sharp as ever.

That morning, the first ray of light climbed into the room, and the hairs on the side of my neck suddenly pricked for some reason. It wasn't a spider. Neither was it a centipede.

An ant!

Of course, I cried out in surprise, but only to myself. Nothing was audible.

In northern China, April still had that nip in the air. The snow atop Naobao Mountain had only just melted. How could there be ants? Insects' lives are here one second, gone the next. Most keep huddled up even in the warmest of times. Ants, though? Didn't seem likely.

It was just Maixiang's hair. Poor woman was always losing it. Slivers of firewood seemed to attach to her clothes like iron on a magnet, and she didn't seem inclined to brush off the ever-accumulating dirt and grime. She never was the careless type, but when her mind was off somewhere, she would sweep crumbs under my folds.

After giving things a moment's thought, the strange prickly feeling on my neck started to shift direction.

It really is *an ant!*

The thing made its way from the nape of my neck to the trunk of my ear before curving toward my eyebrow for a few seconds' rest. It seemed to be studying my salt-and-pepper eyebrows, wondering if it was worth the shot, but then it made another turn toward my nose and started on a beeline for the corner of my mouth.

I wondered how my karma was holding up. Was it my time? How would I weigh in the balance? I was tired of living, and like I said, one foot was well set in the grave. Just like a brown leaf waiting for that last push of wind to separate me from the branch, I was ready.

But why was my heart pounding?

"Maixiang! *There's an ant!*" I cried, hoping that Maixiang, who was busy in the other room, would hear at least the faint echo of my voice. This was to no avail, though. I could attempt to scream myself hoarse, but it wouldn't make much of a difference.

The aroma of fresh milk and millet porridge wafted in. In normal times, my nostrils would expand most greedily. Maixiang did what she could to help me out in her day-to-day affairs. She would give me a warm sponge bath every evening, make sure my clothes were clean, comb my ever-greyer hair every morning, and switch out my pillow-side sachet which she had sewn herself on the daily.

Wheat, corn, naked oats, buckwheat, soybeans, wormwood, elm, osmanthus … I was already lying down, but it was as if all four seasons were swimming in my nasal cavity. When I didn't get enough water and rice, she gave me three, flavour-filled meals each day, and so things went.

Breakfast was milk, rice porridge, and eggs. For lunch was stew. I could make out beef, lamb, pork, chicken, white radishes, carrots, winter melon, pumpkin, potatoes, eggplant, beans, cabbage, and celery from the fragrance. There was just one thing I couldn't tell for sure. She told me she also had bamboo shoots, which she procured from Luo Bao's restaurant in spite of the recent argument the two of them had. I had a feeling she swallowed her pride on my account.

For dinner, she only stewed bean curds and occasionally mixed some kelp. Bean curds and kelp helped with calcium deficiency. During one of her rantings, she talked about how she wished I would inhale more of each batch. As if the added calcium I'd get would allow me to jump up from the heated brick bed and become a midwife again!

The ant was scurrying. I gave up on shouting and waited for Maixiang to approach.

The door squeaked, and Song Pin stepped in. He had been a

secretary for nearly twenty years by that point. One leg was long, the other short, but the condition was nothing serious. Few people ever noticed it, but I did. I delivered him, just as much as I had delivered Maixiang and many other young souls in Songzhuang Village. I noticed it the moment he came out. I wouldn't call it a defect. It was barely noticeable in his gait, but the way both feet hit the pavement was different. One foot was heavier than the other, and the effect was even clearer when he broke into a run.

Song Pin was always the first one to come to the door. It had to be because he wanted to visit Maixiang. Those two … Alas, what could I say?

Sure enough, Song Pin moved into the room and groped Maixiang, who was caught off-guard. Maixiang was surprised.

"Hold on! I haven't wiped Zunai's face yet."

"That can wait until someone else comes by."

Song Pin's voice was hoarse and deep, and his throat always had a frog, it seemed. That wasn't always the case, though. He drank a whole pint of booze that one night. At least, that was what he told me. Others said it was a quart or better before he got behind the wheel of that car to come back from the county seat. His eventual wife, Wang Dacui, and her sister, Wang Xiaocui, were passengers. A mile or so away from the village entrance, the car fell into a ditch.

The reason they were out and about was for the sisters, particularly Xiaocui, to go on a blind date with a man. The man was a distillery worker and looked decent enough, but his legs were an issue. If it weren't for this problem, I wouldn't have gone wife-hunting for him in the countryside. The middleman and Song Pin were drinking buddies. He opened a grocery store in the town. The date was for the middleman's brother. He gave Song Pin the nudge to start looking for prospects, and Song Pin immediately thought of Wang Xiaocui. The sisters' temperaments were rather different. Wang Dacui was hardworking and capable, while Wang Xiaocui was lazy. She spent most of the year with Song Pin's family because the food there was much better than her mother's. Song Pin felt that Heaven had opened its stores of grace, allowing Xiaocui to find her future husband's abode and be less of a burden. The first date was smooth. The man's eyes honed right in on Wang Xiaocui, who was more beautiful than Wang Dacui because she'd never had an honest day's work in her life. Her skin was also nowhere near as sun-tattered.

Xiaocui, on the other hand, was hesitant to go, but Song Pin had a way about him that convinced her to take the leap of faith. He gave her a fat, red envelope packed with cash to ease the tension. Song Pin was in a good mood, and the man's liquor was also of repute. He definitely enjoyed it that night.

No one would accuse Song Pin of being a teetotaler. He could down a quart in a single sitting and a cup in one gulp. He also was a capable driver, having been behind the wheel for more than a decade by that point. He was certainly more experienced than Wang Dacui, so neither of them were worried that night.

Disaster struck. Wang Xiaocui's young life was immediately

extinguished, and a withered bush did a good job of tearing Song Pin's neck up. That was when his voice changed, after the reconstructive surgery. Wang Dacui's face had two gaping holes that needed patchwork with sixteen horrendous stitches. She never really recovered, so she donned an ever-present scarf, no matter the season. Only Song Pin had seen her take it off.

The porridge wasn't quite done yet.

"You're barking up the wrong tree!" Maixiang shouted.

The stool fell. Song Pin stopped trying to woo her. There was a loud smack, presumably from Maixiang.

"Let me turn down the stove!"

Song Pin didn't respond, save for his wheezing.

The ant was scurrying.

"Hey! Stop that! I just sewed this button!" Maixiang exclaimed. "You crazy? Now?! But the door! Let me close it."

Song Pin had covered her mouth by this point, and Maixiang's cries got louder, even to the point she began wheezing just like him.

"Stop! Zunai will hear!" Maixiang pleaded.

"And? What's she going to do about it?"

The ant was scurrying.

Maixiang suddenly began begging for him to close the door.

"Please! Don't do that to her!"

The door slammed and almost rocked me. I lived by my ears, though, so a simple door couldn't block what I heard.

The ant was scurrying.

2

One evening in August, my mother sat on the semicircular stone at the door. The stone was maroon-coloured, with a white band in the middle that seemed to hug it.

My father, Qiao Quanxi, had picked it out and showed it to my mother. It was a curious thing. Mom couldn't believe it was a stone. Dad admitted its mysterious nature. Mom said something along the lines that stones couldn't be ground to gold. Dad asked her what shape she thought the stone took. Mom's eyes fell on the stone again, and she blushed when she looked at it. She brushed Dad's dark face. He observed her with a smile. Mom's cheeks turned even redder.

"I've always thought you to be a prude," she said.

She turned and walked into the house. Dad went after her, grabbing her waist from behind.

"You do this with all the women you're with?"

Dad laughed. "If I was that type of guy, how could I still put money in your hand?"

"Fair point," Mom nodded, turning to meet his glance.

For two whole years of marriage, my mother was barren. She took all the medicine offered to her. She even went to the temple to pray and burn incense. Nothing.

But just a month or so after Dad had found that mysterious, brown stone, she conceived. When she told my father, he was overcome with tears of joy. He thought he had misheard for a moment, so he made sure she said it nice and slow just one more time.

Dad thought the stone brought good luck He kept it clean, brushing it, washing it, polishing it with his hands, unable to keep his eyes off it. Mom never questioned him on his beliefs. She respected the situation so much that she thought it improper to sit on it like on a stool. Dad reassured her that it was a stone from Heaven but not a god in its own right. It just had a godly nature to it. Whatever child was in her womb would gain strength just by being in the nearby vicinity. Thinking it over, Mom gained a newfound resolve.

From then on, the stone became her stool. She would take it out and bring it back in with her. Its normal place was right before the centre of the square altar. Sometimes, she would strike a match and burn some incense there.

Mom would sit on the stone, but she wasn't lazy about it. She would sew clothes, work on shoes, cut fresh and tender beans into strips, or roll cigarettes and hang them on the hanger-like nails of the courtyard wall. That one day, she used her old clothes to sew a pair of baby pants, pink with white flowers. She was on her fourth set. It was August 1900, her unborn child due in one month's time. The "melons and fruit" in her were already ripe, but if there weren't enough milk, then the batch would come out in a mush. At least, that was what her mother told her.

Every now and again, Mom would abruptly lift her gaze and stare off, obviously tense about something. My parents had a moderately-sized, shallow pond out front that was infested with toads. They would be submerged during the daylight hours, but in the evening, they bobbed back to the surface, croaking away well into the night, as if competing for who was the loudest. South of the pond was a patch of grassland with sweet wormwood, pure-blue ladybells, pink-hued magenta plants, and fork-shaped geraniums. Beyond that was a thicket. Flocks of birds would soar high, dip, dive, and soar again. The main path leading out of our village was through a zigzagging, snake-like trail through the bushes. Mom was waiting for Dad. He was a tinker, leaving at the crack of dawn and not returning until dusk had settled. Basins, bowls, dishes, plates, pots, jars, baskets, long seams, and short seams, after being repaired by my father, were watertight. Should anything crack or rip again, it would never be where he had mended. He worked practically every single day, but it was a long haul to get to and from his stations. Regardless of how many villages and towns he passed and no matter how far he travelled, though, my father would return on the same day. Once Mom was expecting a new child, he would make absolutely sure to be home for her, even if he left half his work unfinished, just to make the whole hike back the next day to finish whatever pots and jars remained.

That particular evening, Mom kept her eye out more than usual. Dad was tall and had long legs. The bushes could never hope to conceal him. Mom's vision was so eagle-like, too, that she could spot him in a hot second if she ever needed to. Still, that night, there was something different about that gleam by her pupils. She saw Dad coming and bolted upright, but just as she did, he and the bag he was carrying seemed to vanish into thin air. This happened more than once, and Mom was all in a panic. She whisked the brown stone inside, shelved the pair of baby pants she was half done sewing along with the sewing kit of a wicker basket she had on hand, and planted herself at the doorway, her eyes peering out into the distance. The pond and the bushes issued wisps of light-pink mist in the light of the setting sun. The path was just barely visible, but Mom was sure she could see my father. The whites of her eyes were very much visible, but in the end, all she saw was a mere illusion. The glow was swallowed by the twilight, and the silhouette of the pond and bushes was lost to shadow. It was difficult to make out anything then. The croaking of the toads came and went in ceaseless waves, akin to the wild beating of gongs and drums. The toads were most lively at such an hour, but there was just something different about that one evening.

My mother cradled her womb without even noticing she was doing so as if the noise of the croaking would terrify the child within her. She could see the ground shifting. The toads were making their way on land, hopping and skipping about, rustling all the while in their frenzy. Mom had no fear of toads, but these ones were particularly unbridled and boisterous, enough to agitate a saint. Perhaps if they were just one notch quieter, she would have refrained from kicking at them. She didn't really want to hurt them; she just wanted to scare them off. Still, her efforts were in vain. Her bound feet kept her from doing much to them, and in the end, she just ended up on the ground herself, her body squashing a good seven or eight of the poor beasts. Mom rolled over. The toads underneath jumped to safety, but her weight crushed the others. Mom kept still, though, making sure that her hand remained firmly over her unborn child. Even when she fell, her first move was to cover her belly. A fall like that, though, was nerve-wracking. After a short gasp, my mother got up, unable to tell anymore if she lost her worry about her missing husband or if the worry that she had for the little life within her superseded it.

My mother patted the dust off her clothes and brushed off the green moss on her sleeves, which was smeared on by the toads. After taking a few deep breaths, she carefully unfastened her pants and looked for signs of her baby with a now inexperienced eye. There was nothing really unusual out there, but Mom didn't let up. She downed a bit of water and gently sat herself down. A moment's thought later, she reached out for the brown stone and set it in the corner before plopping back on her seat. "Breathing air by stones brings strength to children's bones." My father's words were like scripture to my mother. Her eyelids drooped a little, but her hands remained firmly planted on her abdomen, one of her ears listening for signs from her baby-to-be, the other waiting for my father's footsteps.

Dad finally made it back around midnight. Mom had already succumbed to her drowsiness and was leaning against the corner, her hands still around her abdomen. The oil lamp had gone out, and the room was dark. My father didn't dare enter. Instead, he stood at the threshold, calling my mother's name several times. Mom finally woke with a start. At first, she was delirious, wondering where she was and whether the voice she heard was real or from her dreams. Dad spoke again, and Mom realized her ears hadn't failed her. She uttered a reply. "Just stay there," Dad said. "I'll get the oil lamp going." Mom wanted to move, but her legs were aching. Using her hands as a guide, she managed to find a safe route from atop the stone to the ground.

Seeing my mother lying on the ground, Dad's mouth was frozen in a half-open gape. Mom, on the other hand, seemed more in shock than he was. My father had slipped a sleeveless tunic over himself. Many sizes were too small for him, the sheet was covered in bloodstains. His face was a terrible shade of bluish-purple, as if someone had taken a paintbrush and swiped him with it. It was a good thing my mother didn't venture to stand after he arrived, as the horror before her would have been enough to knock her off her feet. The two of them were three strides apart, but there they were, staring blankly at each other. Dad asked her why she was on the ground. My mother, suddenly mute, raised her hand, at first in a gesture to accept his, but then curling the fingers inward except for the forefinger, which hung in the air as if unable to decide whether the bloodstained sheet or her husband's face was the most upsetting of the two. The sleeves had at one time been present, the hanging threads evidence of this.

Only at this moment did my father look where his wife was indicating. "Nothing to worry about," he said, his voice the same tone and pitch.

My mother was no dim-witted soul. She didn't believe him at all. My father picked her up and placed her on the bed. Mom grasped firm hold of his hand all the while, refusing to let up her grip. Her eyes seemed to dart an invisible thread, and as they looked her husband up and down, left and right, it was as if he had become bound by her gaze, so tightly, in fact, that he lost the ability to breathe until he confessed.

My father was lucky that day. When he arrived in town, he was called away by the Hou family, the richest around. The ancestors of the Hou family used to be high-ranking officials in the imperial court, but they were in their twilight era by this point. Still, they had thousands of mu of good land, a silk store in Yucheng, three courtyards, hundreds of houses, twenty or thirty servants, and even soldiers at their command. My father, of course, knew well of their legends. The man of the household had three wives, and he would drink a pound of fresh human milk at dusk. My father never thought he would ever walk deep into their abode like he did when following that thin-faced man. It was an exciting treat, but it was also rather unnerving. Could he lay eyes on the grand master? What did a man who drank human milk every day even look like?

At the door, the thin-faced man told my father to look down. Dad knew that this was to prevent him from looking at the man directly. My father was a decent one. Although he was full of curiosity, he still held back and only followed the heel of the thin-faced man before him. A few minutes later, the two walked into a small house. On the table of the hut stood a porcelain vase with a large belly and thin neck. The mouth of the vase had a chip missing, and there was a long crack trailing down its body. The chip was on a plate atop the table.

The thin-faced man asked my father if he could handle a task like this. "No problem." My father offered a price, which of course was a little more expensive than the going rate. The thin-faced man didn't even bat an eye. He told my father to do his best and not to leave without permission. Dad instantly regretted not having pushed the price up even more on the first offer, but that twinge only lasted a second.

The thin-faced man left, and my father worked with fullest ease. After a while, an elderly woman sent my father a pot of water, but no one came back after that. The yard was quiet. My father heard one or two birds singing, and he wondered how such silence could even be possible with the dozens of people living on the property. Again, the thought was only momentary. He couldn't be distracted from his task of drilling holes and applying staples. This was a task for the Hou family. One false move, and not making money in the future wouldn't have been his only worry.

Suddenly, there was a horrendous shouting that flooded his ears. Curses, sounds of someone being beaten, screams. My father was just wrapping up with the task at hand, so close to being finished. He shook himself and took a deep breath. His skill was impeccable. He never once took a break. Still, that voice was getting louder and closer. It soon became evident that the voice was from within the compound.

My father applied the last staple. He stood up and hesitated, listening for any sign of the thin-faced man. A dozen men and women with sticks and spears rushed into the space in front of the hut. Two of them were holding white bags. Dad poked his head out and drew back. "Got another!" someone shouted. My father was hit in the head before he could figure out what was going on.

When my father woke up, he found himself lying in the yard with his clothes stripped off. There was a dead body lying two steps away from him, and the blood underneath it was dry. Dad climbed into the hut, and the porcelain vase that he had just spent two hours mending had been shattered into pieces. The box was kicked over. Fortunately, his staples were still in good condition. Father dared not stay long, so he snatched his toolbox and fled.

There were several dead bodies in the yard, one of which looked like the thin-faced man. On that day, hundreds of hungry farmers rushed into the Hou compound and plundered it from top to bottom. The farmers mistook him as one of the family members. He left with barely his own life, let alone any earnings.

The previous year, several rich families in Huaxian County had been ransacked. My father heard about it, but he was sceptical about all the seemingly exaggerated details. Less than twelve months passed before he personally experienced such a raid at the Hous'.

Of course, my father didn't speak with my mother using such vivid detail. He omitted huge sections of it even. The blow to the head was not even mentioned. Finally, my father said that the world was about to change, but he comforted my mother all the while.

"As long as this toolbox is by our side, we don't ever have to resort to such barbarism."

My mother's hand slowly loosened; her eyes having lost their trail of invisible binds. Her face, though, still looked pale. Dad thought it was because of the lamp light. He told her to sleep in peace.

"It'd be a miracle if you survived a disaster," he joked. He forgot the blood on his face, and his smile made him appear even more menacing. Mom cried out. "You all right, there?" Dad asked. Mom said she was just frightened, concealing the fact that it was her own husband that terrified her. My father bent down. "I'm right here. There's no need to be afraid." My mother asked my father to wash his face and asked him if he had eaten. "You just stay right there," he replied. "I'll take care of it."

My father washed his face and soaked up some leftovers from

a bowl. After eating less than half, he heard my mother moan. He rushed to her and grabbed her with both hands.

"What's the matter?"

"It hurts," was her sole reply. She didn't explain where she hurt, but her hands over her belly told the tale, making my father's head spin.

"Wha—" Dad panicked.

Mom managed to squeeze out two words. "Go get …"

In the time it took for most families to eat a meal, but my father practically carried the midwife through the door. The midwife was in her fifties, her legs still strong. Dad couldn't handle how slowly she walked, though, and whisked her off her feet. Dad later said that Mom first had him wash his face for fear of scaring the midwife into the next plane of existence.

Mom was crying out in pain, her forehead covered in sweat. My father couldn't handle the screams. He kept on asking the midwife if his wife's incoherent words were a sign of anything. The midwife, however, was as calm as a spring breeze. She simply asked my father to undo his wife's pants and had him boil some water. "But she, she's n-n-not due," Dad stuttered.

"*Just get that water going!*" the midwife chided.

He relented, the midwife's words barking sense into him.

The midwife had ten solid years of experience. All the shouting was like the buzzing of mosquitoes by this point. She lit a fire under a pot to get some smoke going and emptied the ash into a bowl. The ash had its purpose after the umbilical cord was cut. Every midwife had a secret magic weapon. Dad poked his head in from time to time, but her words quickly got his face out of the picture. After I became a midwife, I quickly discovered how cold such words had to be. Relenting for just a moment could mean the difference between life and death.

In the morning, Dad's raging seemed to cool off, and Mom's water broke. At the midwife's behest, she was just barely able to shove two eggs down her throat. The midwife obliged by finishing off the other three. She then washed her hands in preparation for her time in the spotlight. My parents had three hens and one rooster. Dad was told to bind their legs. The point was for no one to have to be out catching chickens as her price when things were all said and done.

The midwife laid two bamboo chopsticks across my mother's mouth and told her to bite down. "Might be able to use these again someday if things go smoothly. Don't get too worked up. This is your first one, but think of this like picking beans and melons like you do. Just listen to my words, and soon enough, you'll have a melon at your breast that you can feed and nurture."

The midwife's words felt like a lifeline, but Mom had a problem listening to each command as time went on.

The midwife looked at Mom's bent legs again, and her face suddenly changed. Mom, who was too weak, didn't notice. A foot, not the head, was on its way out. One foot meant the other was on its way. This phenomenon was called, "Hitting the ground running." The midwife had only encountered the same one time before, and both mother and child passed away. She didn't manage to "take the chick," and instead lost both chick and hen. "Get another midwife in here," she told my dad. He didn't understand at first, but in reality, she just wanted to get as far away as she could. The midwife said something about Zhangji, the town, and my father grabbed her by the arm. "There's no time for that!" The midwife's face looked like a twisted batch of dough. Dad probably was an inch from killing her by that point.

"I, I'll try, but I'm afraid that …"

"*Please!*" he begged, releasing her arm.

The midwife wiped her sweatless face. "We'll do this together." Dad nodded. "I just can't promise though."

Mom screamed. Dad was terrified. "Enough of this!" he cried.

Dad and the midwife walked into the inner room. The chopsticks in Mom's mouth snapped in two.

3

Maixiang let out a sigh. The porridge was burnt in the pot. I could tell by the smell of it through the door. I couldn't say anything about it, though. It was all Song Pin's fault. Maixiang complained about how he was like a skinless, faceless monster so early in the morning. She lived by complaining. Even if the batch were saved, she would still find something to complain about. She had a chip on her shoulder, which I knew all too well, but it was no use complaining to the chief complainer. That'd only lead to more hairs falling out.

Maixiang was washing the dishes.

The ant was scurrying. Song Pin didn't answer. I heard the sound of a lighter. Maixiang barked and audibly seized something, presumably the lighter.

"Hey! That's mine!" Song Pin's voice was hoarse but dignified. It wasn't rehearsed. It was like cooking porridge. After applying a bit of heat, the taste would naturally be brought out.

"You think Zunai's lungs haven't had enough?" Maixiang was so worked up that her lips turned blue like they always did when she was worried.

"Come now," Song Pin said, his voice lower.

"Can't you go outside and smoke?"

"Whatever. Just don't yell at me like that," Song Pin said, much calmer. "I only allow the mayor and Qiao Shitou to dare approach me in that tone of voice."

"You just threw me in bed. Wham, bam, thank you, ma'am. Didn't even look my way as you pulled up your pants."

"Hey, hey, hey! Don't forget I took that job for you. Qiao Shitou has something over you."

The ant was scurrying.

"What do you think Shitou would say if I said you disrespected Zunai like you just did?"

"Respect? You mean by praying and offering incense?" Song Pin sneered. "Don't think I don't know. I'm just one on that long list of yours."

"You dare?"

"Want me to name them all?"

The ant was scurrying.

Maixiang paused for a few seconds. "I've come to terms with it. I'll make it up to Zunai later."

"How? How many times can she eat?"

"She can't eat or drink. She just inhales the aroma of food three times a day. Costs an arm and a leg."

"Qiao Shitou's wages could easily pay for six times."

The ant was scurrying.

I didn't know how much money Shitou left, but I knew Song Pin was telling the truth. Sure enough, Maixiang was left reeling before she mustered a sob.

"I thought you coming here early this morning was because you needed me." Another sob. "Story of my life, being bullied by both men and Heaven above. I thought that you might have been different. Now I know. Go ahead and call Qiao Shitou. Tell him what I did to Zunai. If he kills me, then all the better for both me and your happy self."

The ant was scurrying.

"I would never do that," Song Pin said. "I was merely joking. Don't cry like every other woman does. I would never tell Qiao Shitou."

"You talk as if I did something abominable to Zunai," Maixiang snorted.

"You're a good person, brimming with respect."

The ant was scurrying.

"Everyone I know respects her except for you."

"I'm a secretary. I command my own respect. What number of kowtows are most respectful? Respect is something that blossoms from within the heart. Zunai brought me into the world. I would never scoff at that."

"So your idea of respect is to smoke in her room?"

"Did I actually light one, or was I just toying with a lighter? Just look at you!"

"You're rotten to the core."

The fresh aroma of porridge wafted in again. Maixiang opened the door, and the fragrance became heavier layer by layer, falling on my face, just like a sponge, and drilling into my nostrils, feeling like ripples of water.

The ant stopped scurrying. I don't know whether it got knocked out by the fragrance or whether it finally found my grey hair.

Maixiang came close to me and wiped my face with a warm, wet towel. She was used to wiping from the forehead, then the sideburns, eyebrows, cheeks, nose, nostrils, corners of the mouth, chin, ears, and side of the neck. The second time, she opened the net-like folds, and every dust mite hidden could not escape her hawklike eyes. The third time, she used cold water. This was how I was personally used to doing it, and Shitou filled her in on the same. The whole process was over after wiping, wringing, and dabbing. All the added steps to me were over the top. Just rub some cold water and apply some cream. The ointment that Maixiang put on me varied on occasion. In the morning, I could smell roses, mint, and almonds. In the evening, I could smell licorice and chrysanthemum in addition to some kind of medicinal material that I couldn't distinguish. I thought I overheard Maixiang saying that she used what I used. My nose told me otherwise. With the change of the pillow-side sachet, the morning wash was over.

Maixiang didn't leave. Was she in a daze, or was she double-checking my face? Where did that damned ant find a place to hide? It had no hope. Maixiang would still eventually find it.

"I'm headed out," Song Pin said, walking in. "I have to go to the town for a meeting today."

"Eat something first."

"Can't. Dacui made some flatbread and soup," came his hoarse reply.

He didn't need to be so blunt. Maixiang became irritated and sneered.

"Right, right. I was just an early-morning fling. You still got your woman out there, or maybe she's just the big man's cook."

Maixiang had disregarded Song Pin's chastising so brazenly. Song Pin would not be ridiculed, especially when it came to Dacui. Sure enough, the hoarse voice was angry.

"Best hold your tongue, Maixiang. What's she ever done to you?"

"Ah, I see. Her Royal Highness's name is of highest taboo!"

"Don't be like that."

"Why are you defending her? What do you think it'll prove? Come on at me in front of Zunai. See what that'll get you."

"Are we *really* going there right now?" I could imagine the cold light in Song Pin's eyes. It wasn't sharp, but it was enough to make the wheat smell cold. "Some nice parting gift you have for me there." Maixiang began to cry. After seven or eight years of friendship with Song Pin, she still couldn't scratch the surface of what was going on between those ears. "Anything else?"

"I'm just getting started."

"I'm out, then."

Song Pin's footsteps could be heard going farther away.

Maixiang grabbed my hand. "You hear all that, Zunai? A man who took advantage of me turned his face around when he said that I was just like an ant and everyone wanted to step on it." It seemed that Maixiang's words were magical. My ears were tickling. The escaped ant came back. Maixiang would finally be able to see it. "I wish you could do something to help me, Zunai. You would if you could." Her grip tightened. The ant was scurrying. "Just open your eyes." She was practically barking. "Haven't I been praying enough?" She put my dry hand on her face. The woman of thirty-seven or eight years had long lines in her eyes. She was unhappy. That much was clear. She thought she had had a hard time. I also knew that, but she was not the most unfortunate person in Songzhuang Village. What happened to her? If I could enlighten her, if I still had the possibility to speak, I would tell her my experience. It probably scared her, and I was scared myself. Still, I never thought my fortune to have depleted so.

One obstacle after another, one difficulty after another, so was the price of living. I had delivered countless children, none of whom came out with a smile. Crying signals the onset of life. Maixiang had never had a child and couldn't feel the beautiful sound of crying. It was the most beautiful music for parents and for midwives. Yes, infertility was her curse, one of many. She wanted me to help her. I wanted to help her, but I really couldn't do anything. I was not the god in Maixiang's heart, nor the god in the hearts of men and women who bowed to me. They thought otherwise, but I knew better. I was just a dying midwife, one foot in the grave.

"Zunai, what did I do in my past life to make me suffer like this? To think a man could so heartlessly keep a mistress like that! That bitch is expecting again. She thought she could rely on Song Pin, but he only covered her face and his own heart. I was just a leftover tea. He remembered to have a drink and kicked me away after downing it." Maixiang's bitter tears could fill a glass. The bitter water in her heart was more than that in the Yellow River. The ant was scurrying. Maixiang's sight was skewed from the raging outpour.

Footsteps sounded, and Song Pin returned. Maixiang didn't notice until he actually entered the room. "What?" Maixiang was half surprised and half pleased.

"There's an ant."

"What ant?!"

Song Pin bent down. "On her face."

"Ridiculous! You must be seeing things."

"I'm not. Look!"

"Ants at this time of year? You know what month it is."

"This is a house, not a field."

"I just finished washing her off. The clothes are new. You smell the powder. How could there be ants? You're losing it. Why are you here, anyway? Come to have a laugh at my expense?"

"Qiao Shitou's coming back. I just got a call from him."

Maixiang stopped. "Why?"

"What's the matter? This is his home. Zunai's his

grandmother."

"I didn't mean that. It's just … strange."

"Doesn't mean it's right to monitor his movements. Just wanted to let you know he was coming."

"You didn't … say anything … did you?"

"Just do what you're here for!" His voice had changed.

"I'm here for Zunai."

"If he sees an ant on her face … Just saying you should check, as in you already should have."

Maixiang's hands were trembling when she started to undo my clothes. She unfastened the cloth buttons one by one. "Anything else?" she asked after the first one.

"Let me check for you."

"I'm the one who's supposed to."

"What are you waiting for? You afraid of me watching?"

"Just … go!" She finally barked an order at Song Pin, who took a step back.

"Well, that was something."

"I wish to change Zunai, Mr. Secretary. I request that you leave at once."

"I'm already out the door. Just please … look her over carefully. I, I can't—"

Maixiang took off my grey jacket, exposing the cotton vest embroidered with a peony pattern, which was easy to put on and take off. Black cotton pants. A red cotton jacket embroidered with "Forever and Always." Maixiang would tell me the style, colour, and pattern. Although she was flustered, she was still suspicious. I knew because she kept talking.

"How could it be possible? How could it be?"

4

Before I became Zunai, my name was Qiao Damei. Some people also called me Zupo, Ms. Midwife, and Master Qiao, and even earlier, others called me Qiao Dajiao. There was a bit of mockery to those terms, but it was a fact. Of course, there were other appellations, like the Missus, Nana, and other familial terms. But one salutation gradually fell into oblivion. In 1976, my fifth daughter and my ninth child left me, and no one called me Mom again. As for my sister, she had disappeared like the gazelle of Naobao Mountain. Who's plan on Earth was it for me to live so long?

Before becoming Qiao Damei, when I first came to the world, I was just a pink foot. I was the babe who hit the ground running and almost killed my mother. Mother had fainted twice, and the midwife was ready to turn tail and run. Of course, she had no real chance to. At dusk, the toads' croaking made the windows rattle, and out I came.

"Heavens' mercy!" panted the midwife. "A girl!"

Dad held Mom's head and shoulders, called her by her name, and let her open her eyes to see "our child." My mother stayed awake this time. She couldn't speak, but she offered my father a faint smile.

Dad and the midwife found my "issue" at about the same time: my mouth and eyes were closed. The midwife grabbed me and slapped me on my half-green, half-pink rear three times. But I didn't respond. The midwife's face turned greenish-white. She stole a secret glance at my father, touched his red, hot eyes, and immediately withdrew and slapped three more times. Nothing.

"No," came my father's weak voice. "Please …"

The midwife had seen many scenes like this or even worse, so she quickly recovered her composure. She changed hands to make things easier. A dying horse was the best doctor for yet-to-be-living foals. Once the midwife had become determined, her strength seemed to follow suit.

Slap, slap, slap!

The toads got louder and even seemed irritated. The dusk belonged to the toads, and their croaking harmonized the moment. The midwife didn't stop, as if some horrid memory came to her and she was trying to beat it into submission. From outside, the house would have seemed to be crackling, and the toads were singing in unison, like a grand ensemble drowning out Mom's faint moans. She fainted again.

My father gave a shout, and the midwife stopped. My rear was covered in bruises. Two tears trickled from Dad's eyes, and he hung his head, unwilling to see me suffer. The midwife put me down carefully and said, "Fortunately, your wife is fine. She is so young. Another baby is sure to come.. Dad said that the rooster was at the door. The midwife sighed. "Keep it. You need it to help you recover."

The midwife picked up the scissors and the ash pot and was ready to leave.

I suddenly coughed. No … I didn't cry. My cough was the signal that I had entered the world.

My father was so surprised that his tongue thickened. Instead of saying "alive," the word came out as "alive." He uttered it twice.

The midwife had never seen such a scene before. She was dazed for a long time before finally muttering, "Heavens above!"

She still ended up taking the rooster, but only because Dad forced her to. As she left, she mentioned just how fortune-filled the baby's life was. She probably wanted to say more, but in the end, that was all she could muster. Dad was immersed in joy, like in a pool. Nothing else mattered. I was alive, and that was enough. His cries, however, were mixed with all sorts of emotions that he only later was able to express. "You almost killed your own mother."

When I was four years old, my father was hit with some litigation. According to him, he was swindled. The house was gone, and the deed was gone, which had been earned by my father with each staple he had secured to porcelain. In less than a year, all my belongings could fit in my pocket, a heavy pocket, but all the same. In sum, we had tools, luggage, pots, pans, two low stools, an umbrella, a shovel, and the brown, round stone.

My father carried the burden, and my mother carried me.

Sometimes, my father would hold me while carrying the burden. Most of the time, with my mother weak and frail, we stayed in Yucheng. After all, it was more convenient to find food in my hometown, not to mention the troubles of my mother's bound feet. Even if Dad had taken me on top of the burden on his shoulders, he still had to stop to wait for Mom to catch up. She picked at the blisters on her small feet, and she lamented my own large feet. How could I ever hope to get married? I heard her talk to Dad several times about this. Still, she never put my feet through that torment. Living was more important than getting married. Of course, she understood this simple fact. My father later said that he was going to buy back the mud house near the pond without needing to leave Yucheng, but nothing ever came of it.

During the day, he went from village to village. Every time we came to a community, my father would shout at the top of his lungs, saying that he mended pots, bowls, and vats. The acoustics there were excellent. Soon, a head stuck out of the courtyard wall, or a black dog jumped out from an alley, barking and following us. At that time, my mother and I would cling to my father. In fact, my father's hawking seemed to come naturally. Otherwise, his voice would have become hoarse at the close of every day. Practice makes perfect, just like drilling staples into porcelain. The shouting wasn't harsh, but soft, with a rhythm and beat close to singing. Dad closed his mouth, his voice still floating in the air. It seemed that the whole village had an echo. A few shouts were enough. Dad put down the pole in the centre of the street and lay his spread on the open shelf. Then a young or elderly woman would come over with a pot in her arms. Those who talked a lot also had a chat with Mom. If the vat was too hard to handle, my father would do home visits, but often at the end of the day. There were also children who came attached to their parents' hands. They would occasionally become my playmates. Although it didn't last long, it was a very happy time for me. My mother kept watch over me while chatting. If I got into a fight with a playmate, my mother would slap me on the bottom and scold me for not being sensible. I really got into it one time. A boy taller than me said he pushed a girl down. My mother was stunned, slapped me hard, and barked how I should have helped her up instead. It was my father's business principle to go out and pay respect to others. He passed it on to my mother, and my mother gave it to me in her own way.

At night, we slept in the corner, mill house, yard, or idle house that had been unoccupied for a long time. Sometimes, we were under a sturdy Chinese parasol tree. The quilt with patches, which was too dirty to make out the original colour, and the one we had with grey and blue cloth were exclusive to my mother and me. My father often used the straw mat to lie down, fully clothed. The temple was a good place to live. Of course, larger temples were inaccessible. We spent the night in small rural temples, such as the Guan Gong Temple, the Kitchen King Temple, and the Medicine King Temple. We even lived in the Dragon King

Temple, where only two people could live comfortably. My father's legs poked out while we stayed there. Just before dark, I saw the Dragon King's red face, black eyebrows, bulging eyes, towering nose, and black beard, which trailed almost to the ground. My mother held me, but I was still afraid. If I could burrow back into her womb, I certainly would have. We also lodged with others.

In autumn and winter, the weather was cold. We couldn't stay in a house with only one wall and no coverings. We were never lazy, though. If someone's pots and bowls needed to be mended, the master could invite us to live in their house as payment. If someone let us stay the night without needing something to be taken care of, my father would leave whatever mites he could on the table as we left. There were times my mother was spared having to make a fire to cook when someone treated us as friends and invited us to have dinner together. The deepest impression was in Zhao and Wang Villages, where we came across a blacksmith who had a broad face and small eyes that seemed unable to open fully. A pig's head, peanuts, pickled fish, moonshine, and noodles: that was what my mother was able to prepare for us. It was the richest meal I could remember. The oily pork head melted in my mouth, and the noodles were so sinewy they needed to be chewed into a pulp. Mom hadn't made noodles for a long time by then, so I just know she enjoyed herself that day. She rolled the noodles so hard that they tasted like a beef tendon. The blacksmith couldn't get enough servings and told her as much. Not long after I fell asleep, my father picked me up and rushed me out for some reason, Mom following close behind. We didn't stop until Mom injured her knee.

My father was never one for words. His trade as a craftsman meant he always had to be on the alert. If he ever became distracted, his skilled hands would suffer. When there was no work, my father barely uttered a single phrase. Things like talking about love, for instance taking the brown stone back home, were rare, perhaps only brought up a few times a year. After my mother and I had accompanied him for a time, my father suddenly talked so much that my mother complained of him having become a chatterbox. After staying at the blacksmith's house for half a night, however, he fell silent once again for half the next day.

That year was special. I was ten years old. The imperial court took over the emperor's role. It was said that the new emperor was only three years of age. The advantage of visiting households in the countryside was that I could hear legends from far and wide. Of course, it was hard to tell the truth from falsehood. My father's eyes sparkled because Mom was pregnant again. He linked my mother's pregnancy with the new emperor and thought it to be a great omen. "It's a sign of something," he kept saying as he caressed her lower belly. My mother seemed to love hearing him mutter such things, even echoing him at times. I had become my father's apprentice by then. Mom objected at first. How could a girl be a blacksmith? Later, my father convinced my mother that there were many circus girls who played with monkeys, rode horses, and went to Mount Dao to learn how to jump through hoops of fire. My mother and I had seen such a spectacle before, but learning how to mend pottery was far from as daring. It was a pity that I didn't seem cut out for this line of work. Either the holes I drilled were skewed or the staples were rammed in too hard. A pot that had only broken in two would become four or eight by the time I was done. Thank goodness those were only practice shards, discarded waste at best, never anything official. Dad would rap me upside the head every time. From the time he heard about the young emperor, he kept comparing me to him. Three years old, imagine! I couldn't even drill a hole properly at ten. I had no chance of meeting the emperor, but I still blamed him for causing me twice as much aggravation than if my father had never heard word of his existence.

If only I knew what was waiting for me.

Since March, the Dragon King, the legendary king of water, had been asleep without a drop of rain. Fireballs rose and fell day after day. The earth cracked open like a parched mouth. The leaves withered before they were stretched. The trunk was bare. The roads were full of people fleeing from famine. Some fled westward, past Shangqiu and Kaifeng, and went further inland. Some fled south to Fuyang, in Bozhou. At first, my father had the desire to weather things out. He wanted to repurchase our old earthen house near the pond. He wanted to hold on till August when his hope was completely extinguished, and finally, he joined the army to escape from the famine. My father chose to go north, in the direction of Shandong. There was a cousin in Shanxian

County. When I was young and my house was still around, the same cousin came to stay for a night. Not unlike those aimless refugees, my father had his own plan.

One day, supposedly in August, our family of three headed out. In later years, I wondered if it were really July or September. August wasn't really a good month for my mother. My father was still carrying most of our belongings. I carried a quilt on my back and helped my mother, who found it more difficult to walk. The sun was scorching, and the dust was flying. Every face I saw was either black or grey. Groans echoed through the air, and howls pierced the skies from time to time whenever people fell somewhere up front or behind. Those who died alone couldn't be buried, so there they lay under the brutal sun's rays, rotting and then drying up. Mom kept retching, heaving three times in the span of an hour. Her hair was messy, and her face turned sour. She had to keep stopping as we went. Dad would put the brown stone under her as she sat. Indeed, the stone was much more comfortable than the hot sand. Mom didn't do it for herself, though, but for the unborn child she was carrying.

That was when I saw the bird. I wasn't the only one who saw it. It was bigger than a sparrow and smaller than a magpie. It flew low and slow. Its breast was white, its wings were black, and its head was bright red. I thought to myself how difficult it must have been for it to keep itself airborne.

The moment I thought that, it fell.

I gaped. Dad ran up to it. Another figure, a ragged woman,

was faster than my father, although she was farther away. Dad was tall and had a bowed figure. The woman looked more like a hawk herself. She fell on the ground and grasped at the bird, much to my father's surprise.

Dad pounced, his former chivalrous self a mere memory. The woman was much thinner and smaller than he, but she had a fierceness that towered over his. Dad almost broke her hand, but her teeth went for the ear. Howling, Dad let go. The woman rolled and bounced. In the distance, a boy my age just stood and watched. The woman grabbed the boy's arm and ran off into the dust.

Dad had a missing earlobe after that. I didn't know whether it was swallowed by that woman or fell into the hot sand. My father's face was stained with blood, making him look like depiction of the Dragon King, but his eyes weren't as rounded. My mother said nothing as she looked at my father. Her expression was dim, but whether she was appreciative or disapproving was anyone's guess. Dad slowly extended his hand, his palm holding the bird's head and stained with the creature's blood. The gesture seemed to indicate that he wanted to convey his best effort, but Mom had just thrown up. The sight made her gag yet again.

In the afternoon, several black clouds rose in the northwest sky. Dad muttered something to the effect that it didn't look like they were coming our way. Mom didn't even raise her head, too weak from all the vomiting. Around mealtime, the wind picked up, the clouds denser. Dad hunched his back. I grabbed

Mom. Dad threw his arms over me. Sand, dead leaves, and bird droppings blew overhead. When the wind subsided, the dark clouds had already drifted far away. The sky and the earth were clear. Dad looked at the parched land and asked Mom if even a drop had made it to the ground as if only she could know the answer. Mom licked her lips. Dad saw a speck of mud around her eye. He wanted to touch it, but he seemed to recoil at the thought. He managed to point at it, though, muttering something to himself.

Somehow, a few drops had fallen.

My mother could not stand up. Dad and I had to support her. After seven or eight steps, she stood up again, and her waist gradually unbent.

"What's up?" Dad asked.

"Pain."

My father's face immediately changed and helped my mother sit down. "How bad is it?!" Mom shook her head, but her twitching face gave her away.

A few minutes later, she managed to get up. Specks of mud were starting to gather over her cheeks, but this was from sweat mixing with the dirt.

"I can't … I just can't," she kept saying. My father's eyes turned red. It wasn't a mere flare-up.

My father was still calm and knew how to act this time. He quickly unfolded the mattress, lifted my mother up, and undid her pants. I was also able to lend a caring hand. When my father looked at me, I would immediately hand over the right thing. Mother's cry gradually became bleak, like an awl piercing the sky. My father let me caress my mother, and he acted as a midwife. My mother was in so much pain that I couldn't hold her. My father would bark orders at me. As time went on, his frustration mounted. His barks became shrieks akin to hers, his voice echoing through the dust.

"Help! Someone *help*! My wife's in labour!"

The woman, that same woman, the one with the bird, appeared like a phantom. Dad grabbed her by the arms. "*Please!*"

She brushed my father off and rushed toward my mother, who by this point had passed out.

The woman took the role of midwife. Dad wrapped his arms around Mom, squeezing her so tightly that she woke back up. The woman knelt on the ground and tried to separate Mom's legs. I stood to the side. The woman kept yelling to keep Mom's attention. "This ain't your first go-around! Come on!" But her orders ceased the moment the blood started. It went from stream to full-on gush, soaking the mattress and flowing into the sand.

"I … This isn't going to work," she breathed.

Dad almost pounced on the woman again. There wasn't a head; neither was there a foot like last time. Just blood. Dad took off his coat, wanting to plug the stream, but it was of no use. He began to howl and embraced my mother like never before.

I didn't cry or anything. My eyes were on a group of birds with red heads and black wings. The birds bumped off one another, feathers falling to the ground on occasion.

I wondered when the woman left. After the birds had dispersed, I saw my father wiping my mother's face. He wet his fingers with his mouth and then extended them to my mother's face, getting all the mud off it until her cheeks were smoothed out and clean. My father didn't speak, and I didn't dare make a sound. My father and I watched my mother in silence. After a long time, my father's mouth finally moved.

"Stay."

He took his shovel and walked away to a point before he started to dig.

I sat motionless. It seemed that if I stayed quiet enough, my mother would wake up.

An ant came out of nowhere. It came up, its antennas waving before the sand stained with my mother's blood. Another one approached. Then several, making a pack.

The scorching sand didn't seem to affect the ants at all. They were all black, but white and red ones also came along. It soon became like a thick and mighty army. They scurried between my mother's thin arms, her protruding belly, and her blood-stained legs. I was in a daze a long time before I mustered up the wherewithal to wave my father's clothes at them. They scattered, but they came back together soon enough. I began to yell and swing like crazy.

My father didn't know what had happened and rocketed up like a monkey. He was obviously horrified, too, seemingly on the verge of asking something, but nothing came out. He took off his sweat-stained vest and joined me in the frenzied fight. Insane as we appeared, we still were unable to disperse the colony. Dad threw away his vest, picked Mom up, and ran. He fell down after a few strides. Mom's limp body wasn't nearly as cooperative as before. Dad hoisted her on his back again, and I ran after him, grabbing my mother's legs to keep them from catching on my father's feet. The hole was dug, but it was horribly shallow. Father scooped up the sand and threw it over her body. I put my hands over her. The ants scurried around, but before they could escape, they were buried in the sand just like my mother. When the earth was finally heaped up, my father straightened his back and inhaled sharply. That was when it hit me that I would never lay eyes on her again. I lost it.

A dark night had fallen.

5

Still warm and wet, the towel in Maixiang's hand wiped my body from the neck down. Her hands then moved to each shoulder, once heavy laden, in turn. Four sons, five daughters, and three husbands had already sucked at the breasts. The hole was dug, but not deep enough. When she got to my feet, she spread my toes one by one and then turned me on my side. She put her leg against my back and hips, where there was a mole. Maixiang was afraid of being too rough with me, so her hands were extremely gentle. She took my clothes off and put new ones on for me, telling me all about how today's vest was embroidered with a water lotus. A purple velvet jacket with two rows of buttons. Red cotton socks with circular, bright, and shimmering old-fashioned Chinese characters meant to arouse blessing and fortune.

Song Pin was at a loss. "Where's the ant?!" Maixiang said my body was unfit for being seen by men. Otherwise, she would let him search. Were it not for his wife, he would take advantage of her, she told me.

"I didn't fall in love with him because he was a secretary, Zunai. I need a man to love me. He's a good character. Yes, he has a temper, but he has the village's weight on his shoulders.

He needs someone by his side. If only I bore a child for him … Zunai, what's wrong with my body? Can't you help me with this?! Please!"

Maixiang grabbed my hand again. Her own man never touched her. Maixiang not only wanted to conceive Song Pin's child but also worried about private affairs. She thought the whole thing got on my nerves. Every time Song Pin left, she would ask me for forgiveness. The moment she received payment for her "services," she always backtracked and became repentant.

The phone rang. Maixiang got up and went out.

I'm all clean with new clothes on. It's okay, dear. It's just a strange, little itch. Just an ant on my face.

Maixiang failed to wash my hair. She always takes care of my head, face, and body separately. The ant must have taken cover and survived the storm.

The ant was scurrying.

"Absolutely!" Maixiang shouted.

Song Pin was worried. He had never been such a fuss. Maixiang grabbed my hand.

"Even if Qiao Shitou never comes back, I'll keep watch over her. Isn't that right, Zunai?"

The ant was scurrying.

Maixiang was only a foot away from my face.

Can't you see the ant scurrying? Alas, I couldn't remind her of anything.

"I had a strange dream last night, Zunai."

Maixiang never kept secrets from me. Every dream, every argument she had with Luo Bao, that little fling she had before she married him, I knew it all. Sometimes, she would even fill me in on all the gossip. With rain, wind, or snow, she would never get bored and talk all day. She had this advantage. Depending on her mood, those men who flocked to "see" her form near or far might score a chance to have an hour or two of conversation, or she would shoo them away before they could even close the window. Most craned their necks to see me in front of or just outside the gate. I was just an old midwife, but that game of telephone had a way of deifying me into a Zunai. Maixiang said that I had sealed Luo Bao and some god-forsaken whore within a glass jar. No matter how much they wailed and pleaded, I paid them no mind and even kicked the jar from its stand. Apparently, this happened while we were on the roof, for some strange reason or another, and when that jar fell, I fell with it.

The ant was scurrying.

"Something wrong, Zunai? Why should I stay with Luo Bao?"

6

I only remember two things about Shanxian County: mutton soup and the memorial archway. My father rewarded me with mutton soup when I had finally grown up. I could drill holes properly and patch things by myself. The only thing I couldn't do was hawk with the right voice. Dad said that last bit wasn't as important. Only later did I come to understand the meaning of my father's words. One evening, just as we arrived at the edge of the city when coming home, we caught a whiff of something close to our hearts. It was wafting out of the Old Meng Sheep Soup Restaurant. I lowered my head in a way that would get the smell locked into my nostrils. Dad couldn't see my "wavering" stance, but we ended up eating there anyway. When he said we were stopping, I thought my ears deceived me, but in we went.

One room, four tables, the edges of which were so badly scraped they could have been chewed at. The bowls placed on top were entrancing, white porcelain with blue patterns. The peppers had just been fried, their red as bright as a newlywed bride's traditional dress sans veil. Dad asked for a bowl of mutton soup for me, only getting water for himself, though he sampled some pickles and four sesame cakes.

My father was very happy that I did my best that day. In the outer port of the Dragon King Temple, my father and I met a tinker in his fifties who was sharp-tongued. The first to the street typically had the prime spot, but that tinker thought otherwise. Dad raised his fists, and the man nodded begrudgingly.

Dad whispered to me that the man was using a leather drill, making him a native to Shandong, where we were at the time. My father and I used bow drills. Dad said that thallium drills were used more in Zhili, but no matter what drill you used, you couldn't do anything without curium staples. The key was to make sure the pots, pans, and bowls were smoothed over after the staples had been applied.

Dad tried to keep my mind focused, but it was elsewhere, focused on the other tinker. I wanted to make a good impression, but he was cold as ice. He came over to Dad and me, saying something about how porcelain could handle leather drills, showing us his stash. He just stood there for a moment before finally turning away. Dad told me to ignore him, but I just couldn't hold back. "Bow drills are just as good!" The man stopped, turned, and stared.

A woman about the same age as my father came over with her two children, who were my age or so. She seemed to be pondering, wondering if what I said was true. "You capable?" she asked.

"Course! Been in the business a year, maybe even two by this point!"

The man hissed in disdain, which clearly made the woman come off the proverbial fence in my favour. A crowd started to gather, interested in the young female tinker before them, something they had never seen before.

When I was done with the lady's porcelain, she looked it over and over before finally saying, "I have more." We went to her home.

That was how I came to be drinking that soup, after earning money from that gig of course. Dad sat there, his face growing longer before saying, "I'll have some, too."

There are more than one hundred memorial archways in Shanxian County. The largest one is Hundred Lions' Square, carved with a hundred stone lions. People said it was given by the Qianlong Emperor. My father and I used to rest under the archway.

One day, Dad touched the mane of one of the lions and sighed. He was probably thinking of his cousin. His cousin drowned in a bog some three years back. They never found the body. No sooner had his widow finished her mourning when she took her child and married a man who made steamed bread.

I later remarried myself. What would Dad have thought if he knew from six feet under?

My father and I were in Shanxian County for the time being. Dad said Shanxian County's people were easy to get along with, but more importantly, we had found a place to live. His cousin had passed, but the house was still there. It was better than nothing. We could sleep well at night. When my father and I left early one morning, an old man approached, asking us in dismay whether we knew the house was haunted.

"I'll fight the ghost off," Dad retorted.

The old man began to recount the tale, but Dad started walking faster, forcing the man to stop mid-way through the plot.

"Pay him no mind," Dad told me, but I wasn't afraid. We had slept in many a temple by then. My fearlessness was taller than I was.

Two years later, my father and I left Shanxian County and headed north. We earned a living every day, but it was impossible for us to buy back our old house near the pond, even if we could return to Yucheng. My increasingly exquisite skills gave my father an idea, though. Actually, while his apprentice, I came up with the thought myself: to become a royal pottery mender. The menders out in the streets were the ones who did the most basic repairs, but those of the royal court handled the most intricate facets of the trade. Working on the street made sure you had three hots and a cot, but a seal of approval by the royal court was enough to earn a lifetime's income in less than a decade. There were legends and ballads about such craftworkers. My dad was great at the basics, but the finer details eluded even him. The ones most capable were those who began as children.

Dad's eyes had a new spark to them. I remembered the emperor, who ascended the throne at three. Perhaps I might lay eyes upon His Majesty. My eyes didn't have my father's sparkle, but my heart felt as pure as the most precious diamond.

One afternoon the next spring, my father and I stayed at the Yuelai Inn in Gaobeidian, said to be less than twenty miles from the capital. I was caught in the rain, and my clothes were soaked through. I couldn't stop sneezing, but that wasn't why my father decided to stay there. I had been caught in the rain before and baked in a fire-stoked oven at night. I was strong enough not to fall ill because of some rain.

The moment we checked in, my head was buzzing with curiosity. The room was small, with two beds and a square table. It was all very simple. A clothesline was hanging. There were spare clothes at the bottom of our case. We got changed, one after the other, and my father looked me up and down.

"We're going to have to get you something new. Can't go like this …" He paused. His poise reminded me of what it must have been like to be a woman being selected as a future concubine by some esteemed pot mender of the royal court. Still, I didn't care what he thought. It was rare for him to be so generous.

"You thinking of getting something today?"

My father glared at me reproachfully, saying that I still hadn't even learned to hold my own breath for two seconds despite my age. My father had always instructed me to harbour the utmost respect for the court pot menders and said things like how he was afraid the callouses in his ears were thicker than the soles of his feet. I half expected him to say the same then, but he didn't. Instead …

"Get some rest. I'll see what I can do."

I wanted to lie down and fall asleep. If it weren't for the birds singing outside, I would have slept until dark. Before my father came back, the room suddenly felt much emptier. The birds were still calling, their voices like soft whistles. I opened the window and looked around. Nothing. They seemed to be coming from another yard. A weeping willow was three or four steps away from the window. The trunk was rather thick and had palm-sized cracks throughout. The bright yellow leaves were still unfolding like hanging needles. A willow catkin floated over, and I stretched out my hand. It ignored my gesture and instead landed on my shoulder. I gently tore it apart, blowing its remains back into the wind, where the pieces drifted away.

I was about to grab a second one when the door opened. Dad stood by the door, his face as grey as death, his eyes grieved. Of course, it wasn't this that surprised me, but the fact his braid was missing. His tattered hair suddenly made his head look much larger. I almost didn't recognize it.

My father seemed to be in a daze. I called his name twice before he snapped out of it, closed the door, and then sat down on the floor against the door plank.

"His Majesty … has been taken."

I squatted down, grabbed my father's arm, and tried to pull him up. He told me how the court was in shambles. I asked him to get up, but he ignored me. After a while, he said he lost all will to stand. I couldn't move my father, so I sat beside him.

Sure, becoming a royal pot mender would have been nice and all, but that would have meant separation from my father. I slowly stretched out my hand to smooth his messy hair, but he pushed me away before I touched it.

"What's the *point*?!" he shouted, covering his face with his hands.

I didn't know what to do but stare.

After a long time, my father moved his hands away, his eyes bloodshot but with no tears present.

What brimmed in them instead was a mighty fire.

"Did I frighten you?" he asked warily. I shook my head. My father was clearly in shock. "Finally made it here, but one step too late." He looked toward the capital. "We came so far. When will it stop?" When I asked if I would go to the capital anyway, my father smiled bitterly. "There have to be people to mend for. When no one's around, whose pots can we mend?"

"Then why can't we go back home?" The question stunned him, as if he didn't understand what I was saying. I looked at the clothes hanging on the line. "Let me put them outside. It's dry in the morning."

Dad still hadn't quite come back to Earth. He asked me what we should do next. Ever since that day I showed my hand before the other tinker, he started asking me for my opinion on things. "What say you, Damei?" he'd say. It seemed that I had become his backbone. Of course, he still made the final decision. It didn't really matter what I said.

This time, though, I had to keep positive. I asked if one bite of the sweet ice-sugar gourd in Beijing really could last up to three days on the palate. His mood remained unchanged.

"Don't know. Just some fantasy I made up."

When I woke up in the morning, my father had already packed everything up. "Us having come so far couldn't have been in vain. Where we are is whither we went and whence we came, so they say. The world never stops changing, and even the best pots have cracks. Fortune, whether good or bad, never stays that way. What say you, Damei?" he asked as I jumped down to stand by his side. I sided with him.

Twenty days later, my father and I went to the suburbs of Beijing. Worldly bowls and basins, as Dad said, would inevitably need repair. Those days we were up north, I did a lot of work. I stayed in each town for two nights. One day, Dad heard someone say a single sesame cake could buy someone a mu[1] of land beyond the Great Wall. He overheard that in someone else's conversation, but that didn't matter to him. That seed wasn't meant to be planted in quiet.

The villages in the suburbs of Beijing were no better than those along the way. In fact, some were even worse off. Only a few places were covered with grey tiles. The rest had mostly clay walls and mud roofs. On the edge of one village were low shacks. A woman was nursing a "baby" by one of the doors, but the babe

---

1 A mu is the Chinese acre, equivalent to 0.1647 Imperial acres, or 7,176 square feet. It is currently bound to SI units of measurement, with one mu being 2/3 of a hectare.

was mere cloth, the woman's breasts as black as charcoal. At the door of another shack was a man, sprawled, motionless. Dad called out to him a couple times, but to no avail. When he finally reached out his hand to turn him, the man suddenly shouted for him to go away. Dad apologized and obliged, leaving as quickly as possible.

That village was about an hour away from the Yongding Gate. Those big, small, tall, short, dog-house sheds were built by beggars, acrobats, and other craftworkers like my father and me in the capital. They worked in the capital during the day and returned to the sheds at night. There were also thousands of people who came to Beijing to offer up their grievances. They had no money to stay at inns, so they also set up camp there. A warm-hearted monkey entertainer said that some shelters were empty. Those who left did so without tearing them down. He asked Dad if he could ascertain which were empty, teaching him the telltale signs. The monkey squatting on his shoulder scratched both sides back and forth, making for a comical sight.

I finally found a room without an owner. The place was about to collapse, but it still provided some shelter. There was also a cushion on the ground that was warm to sit on. My father built a makeshift stove to light a fire, and I followed others' instructions to carry water. My father and I ate at the door. I realized why those people liked to sit and lie at the door, not because the sheds were too narrow, but to announce their shed as occupied. Someone passed by. It was easy to see from his eyes that he was a newcomer. At that moment, it was really like celebrating a victory.

At night, my father and I lay on our backs. My feet ran into the shed, while my father kept pacing to and from the door. He couldn't get our case into the shed, so he had to keep checking on it each time he came out of his doze. I hoped to have a nice dream that night. Dad and I would be entering the city the next morning. If I met someone selling ice-sugar gourds, my father would definitely buy them for me, especially since no money was spent on new clothing. This "home" took our worries about spending nights in the capital far away. So far, the capital had been good to us.

The shouting woke my father and me, and a dark figure stood at the door, yelling that this was his shack. My father was confused. "How's my roof now yours?" he asked after a while.

"This has been my place for the past two weeks."

"Prove it."

"Got something shoved up under the grass mat."

Dad was incredulous at first, but he checked. It was there.

"That's my whip."

Dad was no unreasonable fellow. He tried to negotiate with the shadow that he had no money to go elsewhere and that he had his daughter with him. He begged for this simple favour. His sincerity touched the shadow, who sighed about how leaving at this time of night would make things more difficult and that he could manage. The shadow came in and squeezed against my father. The already narrow shack seemed to shrink even more.

There was no snoring. After a while, the two men who couldn't sleep and couldn't see each other began to talk. The man asked where Yucheng was, and Dad also asked the man about the scenery outside the Great Wall. Slowly, their discussion intensified. The man asked Dad why he ran to the capital to mend pottery. My father didn't hold anything back. Perhaps it was because they couldn't see each other. This was the first time that he ever told his dream to a stranger. Perhaps his long-settled boredom moved his lips for him. He asked why a sheep driver had nothing to do with the capital. "Why?!" The man suddenly choked. "Fate's turn was rough on me, much more so than you. Beijing's known for its high-quality hot pot. The quality comes from the good meat. The sheep all come from Zhangjiakou, freshly slaughtered. The sheep-driving business is booming. They ain't mine. I'm a sheep just like them, you could say. I'm out here ten times a year. We were to bring two dozen this time around, but some soldiers caught us before we got here. We were lucky to save our own skins, let alone the sheep. Soldiers, humph! They're just nicely dressed bandits, if you ask me!" He was angry. His companion turned tail and fled. The man tried to find justice at the barracks, but he was denied entry. His only option was to go to the shack, watch the entryway during the day, and find a place to lay his head at night. Dad asked why the man was kept from going in. The man said his only chance was to set up camp at the entrance and wait for those responsible to go in or out. Dad asked why he didn't go home. The man scoffed, saying his employer would skin him as payment for the two dozen he'd lost. Dad said it wasn't his fault. "Would you let me go if you were in his place?" Dad sighed something about the state of the world. "Have you been to the city? Practically everything's shut down." Dad said he could still earn as a mender and that his diamonds were immune to burglars.

"That girl of yours ain't too young, you know."

"She's thirteen or so." My father shivered for a moment, and I could feel it.

"Sorry. Couldn't help but ask."

After a moment of silence, my father asked, "I heard that one sesame cake outside the Great Wall could be exchanged for a sixth of a mu of land. That true?"

"Depends on the place."

"The worst plot is also a plot. The land I bought in Yucheng wasn't good, but I made it work through blood, sweat, and tears."

"If you ever head beyond the wall, could you give a message to my brother in Songzhuang Village? It's in this town called Yingpan, less than twenty miles from Zhangbei, the county seat. I don't think I can ever go back there. My name's Li, Li Gui. My brother is Li Fu." Dad seemed to nod in agreement. Li Gui continued, "He was always the responsible one and was quicker witted. Had I listened to his advice, I'd be married and settled by this point."

"If I ever find my way there …"

"Just give him my thanks. As for you, this shack is always

open."

I don't know when I fell asleep. When I woke up, my father had prepared a meal. I didn't see the man named Li Gui. The conversation the previous night was more like a dream. I asked if the man had gone. My father said that he got up in the dark. His fate was really worse than ours. I picked up the whip, shook it, and then put it down. "Put it under the straw mat. It's his mark."

After dinner, I asked my father if he was still in town.

"What say you, Damei?"

7

At over eighty years old, my legs and feet were still strong, and I could walk miles without rest, but I was not as agile as I was when I was young. In summer, I went to dig up vegetables for the pigs. The basket would always weigh fifty pounds or so. I switched the load from shoulder to shoulder on my way home. In winter, I went to the market in Yingpan to buy some drum-shaped rattles and small mirrors for new-borns. I was used to doing it. Back in the day, I would present a copper coin, a beautiful feather, or a smooth, round stone. Blessings can't be measured. If you think something's important, it's important. If you don't things too seriously, a mountain is also light as a feather.

My eyes were still sharp. I would often help women in their fifties and sixties thread needles when passing through the street.

One time, I was in the neighbouring village during a time when the lying-in woman was having a breathing spell, I said something to the man bringing me sugar water about some scorpion I had seen in the corner.

"Your house is too damp," he said, his head spinning to where I indicated. He was standing on the ground while I was resting on the kang[1]. "A scorpion? Really?"

"I swear I saw it."

The man looked around, scrunching his shoulders for fear of being bitten.

Alas, it was true. Naturally, this matter became legend and turned more mysterious with time. I was just an impersonal oracle by the time it metastasized to the state it ended up being. Truth be told, I was just a midwife, far from divine. Some things seem simple, but there is nothing we can do to prevent others from adding insult to injury. We can control our own mouths, but we can't control the tongues of others. Such was the case with this man.

Of course, with age, change is inevitable. Eyebrows become thinner as they blossom. Wrinkles on the face grow longer and deeper by the day, like ploughs running through the soil. I also liked to bask in the sun. I would just plop a mazha[2] down when free. Compared with a stool, chair, or sofa, mazhas were most comfortable to me. I would lean on the door frame, close my eyes, and pat my face under the sun. With my eyes closed, the sound of falling leaves was notably loud. Every time someone passed

---

1 Kang, or heated adobe bed, has long served as a common feature of northern Chinese living rooms. People traditionally place a mat or quilt on the top. Chimneys trail upward to let the smoke out beyond the rooftops. Even the imperial palace was fitted with them. The palace in Shengjing has many, with several in a single room. This allows for more living comfort, with Kang the perfect winter couches, beds, and tables, and rooms retain heat much more easily this way.
2 Mazhas are much like campstools and are common Chinese seats. Their simple nature allows for easy folding and unfolding, with a stretch of canvas serving as the seat proper. They are viewed as aesthetically pleasing and known for their portability.

by, I could tell who it was from the speed of their steps. The eight chickens would gobble and cluck, but each had its unique differences. Some called quickly, while others were slower. Some called twice and then would busy themselves looking for food. Some were afraid and seemingly cried for help.

One afternoon, when I was bathing in the sun, I suddenly heard several shrieks from outside the village. Recognizing the direction, I hurried out. I almost passed out from standing up so fast and went blind for a moment, but I didn't stop moving. Some busybodies were sitting on the stone in the middle of the street. I called for their help, saying someone had fallen into the mud[1]. No one doubted me. Er Bao, who had just come back from a stint in the city, was still quite youthful, and thereby a fast reactor. The moment I finished shouting, he jumped on his motorcycle in the corner.

When I arrived at the edge of the lake, Er Bao had pulled the boy out. It was Ma Da's grandson, six and a half years of age. Ma Da's home was nearest the mud. When his grandson fell into the water, he was weaving baskets in the yard. The poor child choked in a few mouthfuls, so nothing serious. Over the years, the mud had become shallow, its perimeter inching inward. Had this happened a few years back, the chance of disaster would have been graver.

Ma Da's wife scolded him out in the street for being deaf and having long, white ears. She didn't know that the key to the

---

1 The term "mud" here is a nod to the Mongolian word for lake.

sensitivity of the ear was the heart. Best to have a clear mind and bright eyes paired with a quiet heart and crisp ears. Everyone knows that, but few honour it.

This house was specially built by Qiao Shitou for me, with large windows on the floor so that I could bask in the sun without going out. I didn't agree, but nothing I did could convince him otherwise, just like nothing he said could stop me from digging up vegetables for the pigs. The apple didn't fall far from the tree. I went to Yingpan Town and came back to find the old house in ruins. Alas, I was left with no choice in the matter.

After my body could no longer move, my ears often heard about "forced demolitions." People often uttered these two words, the tone behind them heavier each time, jaws clenched in spite. The ears could hear much, but the substance between them was often at a loss.

At first, I wasn't used to the new look. What was that bright window? I still liked to lean against the door. As the days passed, I grew fond of the new addition. Wind, sand, or ice couldn't keep me from the sun's pleasure, especially after I lost the ability to move. Because of the big window, I could still feel the heavy touch of the sun, and the many "faithful" who stood out in the yard could make out my figure from a dozen feet away. I was just an old face, though, nothing to admire. Alas, I could do nothing to shy away.

Maixiang was talking about taking precautions in the courtyard. It was the third time already that morning.

"Put that cig out! Talk about disrespect …" she chided, her voice suddenly sharp.

The ant was scurrying.

After all that time confiding in me, she still hadn't found the culprit on my face.

"Can I get a better look? Just want to get a clearer shot."

"You're close enough. Don't plaster yourself against the glass. Zunai can hear every word you say where she is."

There was a sudden silence.

The ant was scurrying.

"Just pray for your heart's desire right where you are."

"Should we go one at a time?" Still that timid tone.

Maixiang's words were patient. "You're fine."

The sound of footsteps went away. A moment later, someone came back and whispered to Maixiang. "Sure!" she said. "Whatever you give will be used toward her needs. Zunai doesn't eat or drink, but whatever food she gets she can still smell."

I would have told Maixiang a thing or two if I could. She shouldn't have kept going like that, but she'd gain a guilty conscience and come begging for my forgiveness later. I knew her prices. She always told me, though there were times she would think I knew already.

The woman followed Maixiang into the room. She was full of woe. The voice was strange. It sounded like she was in her forties or fifties.

"Do I need to kneel?" The woman was near the bed. She

should have seen the ant from where she was.

"Kneel, sit, as long as you're sincere. Zunai won't mind."

"I heard she was over a hundred. She doesn't look so old."

"Come on! She's well over two by this point."

The ant was scurrying.

I sighed. Where on Earth did Maixiang catch the disease of nonsense?

"I just thought …" the woman whispered.

"You think that's not Zunai?"

"Can I touch her hand?"

"That's pushing it. Don't reach for a yard after taking an inch. Hands off."

"I got up at three and walked all the way here. Not even a touch?"

Maixiang was clearly moved. "Oh, all right."

"Th-Thank you," the woman uttered her gratitude.

"Your hands are clean, aren't they?"

"Washed everything before I left."

The ant was scurrying.

"Let me fetch you a bowl of water to be sure. Stay there."

The woman washed her hands and gently took hold of mine. My palms were covered in callouses from all the labour I'd done throughout my life.

"Time's up."

The hand retracted.

"What do you want to say?"

"Can … can I speak with her alone?"

"Course. Just don't touch her again."

Maixiang withdrew, and the woman leaned against me. The smell of her sweat was strong.

"Zunai, my name is Chi Xiaofeng. I came here from Datong, Shanxi, for marriage. My parents-in-law and husband were all three delivered by you. My husband's nickname is Huansheng. His legal name is Li Aiguo. Do you remember?"

I'd delivered countless children and walked every path of all surrounding villages. How in the world could I remember a single one? Some were simple. Others were turned. Some were born with shrills and shrieks. Most came out shrivelled like raisins. They blended together in my mind. Their unique features could only be better distinguished as they aged. Some became county mayors, others professors, others scavengers, and some travellers. There were some good ones and bad ones. There were some who became great figures and some who rotted behind bars. Such were their fates post-birth. All were the same that moment I slapped them on the rear.

"My two children were not delivered by your hand. Li Aiguo and I moved to Datong when we were six months pregnant. My father's grocery store succumbed to a fire. He was badly burned. I went back to take care of him. Last year, Li Aiguo and I moved back to Xisanpo. Something happened. We couldn't stay in Datong. We thought we could hide away when we moved back to our hometown, but …" The woman began to sob. "Zunai, I beg your help!"

The ant was scurrying.

I couldn't "help" but sigh. This woman must have listened to those horrid rumours. Granted, after praying to me, some people's fortunes indeed changed for the better. That was all because they dumped their unfortunate experiences, the pain of being abandoned, the despair of being in trouble, and the thoughts of dying like discarded waste. Their hearts became calm. When the heart calms, outlooks change, and the whole person becomes transparent. Truth is, nothing really changes, though it seems like all has. When seedlings are dry, heavy downpours are sweet dew for those out in the field, but the same could spell disaster for the sick along the road. Such is the logic of things. Of course, there are also some coincidences. A barren couple once became pregnant after praying, but I had no say in the matter. If I could inspire miracles, why was Maixiang left childless? I prayed for Maixiang hundreds of times. Lo, though named an oracle, Heaven heeded not my words.

"You see …" The woman was about to pour her heart out, but hasty footsteps were on the approach.

There was the sound of crying. Seemed like Ruhua.

"What's the matter with you, Ruhua?!" Maixiang exclaimed. "You get into a brawl of some sort?"

"I want to see Zunai!" Ruhua was typically mousey. This wasn't normal.

"Shh. Someone else is in there with her."

"How long's this going to take?"

"I'll tell her to hurry up. What's up? Why's your collar torn?" Ruhua repressed her sobs, like a kitten with a foot over its neck. Maixiang put something on a shelf. "Speak. Else you won't get in there."

Ruhua gave a sob, seemed to choke on her tears, and exclaimed, "Qian Yu was shot and killed by Mao Gen!"

Chapter II

Ruhua

1

While Ruhua was giving the perennial begonia some water, the plant snapped at the stem, and the flowers hung, their faces pointing down. Tears streamed down Ruhua's face, and she froze on the spot. She was never one to cry or yell or do anything impulsively. When she cried, she meant it. Her chest was heaving. It was clear she was trying to keep herself from breaking down. She was always wary of upsetting others, so her tears were soft. Though she refrained as much as possible, in truth, she was all right with crying itself. Actually, when she cried, her tears doubled that of anyone else's. Her mother figured she must have been an absolute cry baby in her previous life.

The flowers died. No one would blame her for crying over something like that. It was a distressing sight, more painful than if she were to break her own neck. Ruhua was fond of flowers. She would stop anytime she caught sight of any. She had a green thumb, but that same green thumb was laced with poison, it seemed. Perhaps she'd inherited it from her parents.

Her father was by definition a mighty rumble of thunder. His voice was booming, and his temper was insatiable. He bought a radio in town once. Turning the dial left would get some talk show. Turning it to the right would hone in on a music station. After he brought it back to the village, turning it left brought static. Right was also static. He lost it. Instead of taking it back to town to exchange it, he threw it on the ground and stomped on it, but that wasn't enough to still him. He grabbed a stone to finish the job. Drinking made him worse, and his chest would puff before horses and cars alike. Drivers honking horns at him set him off. He'd step right in front of the grill and tell the person behind the wheel a thing or two, swigging all the while, egging the driver to run him over. No one heeded his beckoning. Most gave up and turned away.

Her mother could be defined as an unquenchable fire. She could ignite at the drop of a hat. She was a fast walker, as if someone were always chasing her. She was also a fast worker. A plot of farmland took no time to finish handling. Boiling chicken took a fraction of the normal time, though this usually meant tougher meat for her husband to nearly break a tooth over and half the water still standing in the pot when "done."

Thunder had a way of setting off in the heat of fire. Ruhua's parents might get into it one day, get worse on the third, and ready to kill each other on the fifth. No one would back down. Hands-on involvement was the way to go. Her mother had a way with her fingernails over her husband's lips. The husband, when drunk, would pucker a lot to make an easy target. He, on the other hand, used his hands to grab a fistful of hair. Ruhua's mother once had a pair of big pigtails, but later cut them short in male fashion, but her husband could still grab hold. The two would also like to throw things to keep life spicy. She threw a plate; he tossed a bowl. She grabbed a glass; he smashed a pot with a stone in hand. Ruhua's flowers were also added to this mix. The pot of cyclamen, which had been nurtured for three years, was used by her mother as a weapon. Naturally, the pot was broken, and the golden blossoms were used as a whip over the face by her father. Orchids, lilies, narcissuses, none were spared such a fate, save for a vermilion, which Ruhua defended from the rage. Still, after her father drank himself to oblivion one night, the pot seemed a good place to relieve himself. Somehow, the flower seemed to enjoy it and became even more beautiful than before. The caveat was that a horrid smell persisted thereafter.

Ruhua cried so hard that her mother was left confounded. "Just some flowers. The world over now?" Ruhua ignored her, tears still flowing. "You'll be 25 soon and still have eyes like a tap. It'd be some rarity of a man who'd want to hook up with you." Ruhua leaned against the cabinet, shoulders shrugged. "Just let it all out already. Don't hold back, for Heaven's sake! You'll hyperventilate if you don't. Take after me for once! You see me sitting idly by? Who'd've thought I'd give birth to such a withered seedling?" She got out a chopping board, cut up some meat, and prepared to make dumplings. Her anger sped up her already rapid pace.

After chopping the stuffing, Ruhua's mother calmly told her to wash her hands. Ruhua stopped crying before her mother put down the kitchen knife. "Xiaowu didn't mean to do it, you know. Why do you have to be like this?" Ruhua had rolled up her sleeves and was about to wash her hands, but her mother's words reopened the tap of tears. No wonder her parents used the flowerpots to vent their anger, but Xiaowu wasn't known for doing so. Ruhua was closest to Xiaowu in their family. He knew that she loved flowers and always helped her protect them, but he was the one who snapped the begonia. That was why he ran out in a rush after she came back in. He was guilty of plant slaughter.

Ruhua kept shedding tears while working, though she wiped her face with her sleeve from time to time. "Can't you turn off that faucet?" her mother grunted. "You're really the odd one out in this family. The Dragon King, the granter of rain, would find better use for you." Ruhua didn't say anything in defence or otherwise. It was the same old, same old. Her mother would either be unhelpful or passive aggressive. Neither happened that day, so it was still better than most. The worst words had yet to leave her lips.

Ruhua didn't eat the dumplings. She didn't mean to be so "off," but she just couldn't eat. When they ate, Ruhua was trying to save the begonia. Not even the remains could be arranged nicely. She was filled with regret for not having been there to keep it safe. She wrapped the flowers in a strip of cloth and tied the ends with some twine. Xiaowu came to help her. He offered an explanation before resorting to flattery. Ruhua couldn't be angry with him, but she still didn't want to say anything. Xiaowu begged her to eat, but she shook her head in response.

After she was done with the binds, a spark of hope ignited within her heart. She couldn't get a good night's rest. Every dream had something to do with begonias. She'd open her eyes, squat before the plant, but sigh when seeing nothing had changed. The petals were still bright, though. The colour of the root was a little lighter, but such was the case when the flowers bloomed. The yellow stamens were like a tightly waisted shy woman, and the leaves were still green, the dark red stems and leaves varying between thick and thin, same as before. Her binding seemed to be successful at first, but in the evening, she found that the petals were losing their red hue. After a day, the withering began. Another day, the pistils collapsed. After a few more days, the petals were dry, the leaves yellow. Their final farewell to Ruhua was being bidden.

The flowers' suffering tortured Ruhua. The reason why Ruhua was angry was because of their torment. It took a toll on her own body. A while was needed before she could even think of beginning a new batch of flowers.

Ruhua found this instance to be one less easily forgotten. The pot of flowers symbolized a stake, a low stake, but a special stake nonetheless.

In late autumn, Ruhua went to the salon in Yingpan to get a perm. This was her mother's idea and was something she kept urging her to do, even going to the point of threatening to push her through the door. Ruhua liked her hair natural, black and shiny as it was, but all the young women in the village got their hair permed. The most fashionable even went for some dye. Ruhua knew what her mother was doing and that she wasn't joking in the slightest. She thought it to be the quickest way to land a husband. Ruhua sucked it up and decided to go, especially because she didn't want her mother taking her there herself.

After shampooing, she looked into the mirror and froze.

"What's it going to be? Perm for you?"

She nodded without a word. Her hair wasn't wavy or anything after the rinse, but it seemed like a congealed mess that had exploded like a bomb.

She spent ages looking at all the pictures hung on the wall, found one she liked, and pointed it out. Her stylist was a fashionable man with dangling earrings.

"Big hair is too old-fashioned. Frizzle is the rage now." Ruhua could make out by the way he talked that he was a homegrown local, save for the non-local extravagance. "I'll give you one for fifty, but just know these are going for three hundred in Shanghai."

Another girl came in and was immediately taken away by Ruhua's frizzles. "Ooh, can I have one just like *that*?!" she asked before the stylist even said a word.

Ruhua said nothing as she took out the money.

After she left, she had only taken a few steps before lowering her head to shield herself from all the turning heads. Upon crossing the street, she stopped right in front of the Flying Sky

Photo Gallery. She swore she saw some green. Well, maybe she didn't actually *see* it, but she felt it. She tilted her head.

Sure enough, it was a pot of begonias sandwiched between a dustpan, rope sleeve, broom, sieve, and basket. The leaves were covered in thick dust.

Ruhua was rooted to the spot.

She squatted down and gently flicked the dust on the blades.

"Flower girl, huh?"

The phrase was common enough, but to Ruhua, with the parents she had, it felt like a bullet ripping through her insides. "How do you reckon?" she responded, holding back her trembling.

"I don't reckon. I just know. Call me surprised," the man said with a smile. "It's all over your face." His teeth were white, eyebrows thick, smile natural.

Ruhua didn't like taking compliments, but in that moment, something stirred within her. "You're just trying to get me to buy it."

"It's been waiting for the right girl to come along," the man winked.

No, it wasn't a bullet, but the sharpest arrow. Ruhua couldn't move and paused for the longest time. "How much?" she finally muttered.

"I don't know. Don't sell flowers." Ruhua blushed, feeling deceived but not saying a word. The young man pointed to the basket and broom. "That's my thing. The knot on the rope is my doing."

"So why the flower?"

"It's been with me for four years. Haven't really done much with it. Needs a new owner, I suppose."

"Why don't you sell it, then?"

"Not sell. I'm okay with just giving it away."

Ruhua's heart thumped. "Were you waiting for someone to give it to?"

The young man shook his head. Ruhua felt a wave of disappointment. The young man pondered for a moment. "No, but here you are." Ruhua felt nearly strangled by some unseen force. She didn't want to just … pop the question. "The moment I saw you looking, I knew fate had called for this little fella. Take it. It's yours."

"Take it?" Ruhua hesitated. "Just like that?"

"I mean, I'm not opposed to money if you really feel the need."

"How much?"

"Ninety-nine hundred."

"You're joking."

"I tried just giving it to you, but then when I do, you ask for a price. I give a price, so now I'm joking?"

"You having fun?"

Someone wanted to buy a rope. The young man got up to handle it.

When the customer left, the man turned back to the

indecisive Ruhua. "Just treat it well."

"Thank you," Ruhua breathed.

"That's all, then?" Ruhua was stunned. Were there any conditions to this deal she just made? "What's up with you? Your nose is brimming with sweat. I told you to just take it. What's your name? I'd like to know who's this begonia's new owner." Ruhua hesitated for a moment, but she eventually gave in. "Ruhua?! 'Flower-like'? Talk about a fitting name!" He extended a hand. "Qian Yu, from Songzhuang Village."

"Mom took me to see Zunai there. She was me and my parents' midwife when we were all born. When I came into the world, she found a marigold by the roadside. She's the one who chose my name."

Ruhua held the begonia in her arms, knowing that her way home would be a smooth one, but she felt that she still owed this Qian Yu something in return. "You think it'll bloom?" She had raised many flowers, but she'd never raised a begonia. She felt comfortable in front of this young man and lost all pleasantries before him. "I … I don't mean anything by that, of course."

"Stop," he said. "Let's make a bet."

"I was just thinking aloud."

Qian Yu ignored her attempt to skirt around the topic. "I'll say it'll bloom by this year's end. If not," he looked at the store nearby, "I'll get you a bike."

"Words just slip out sometimes. They tend not to come out the right way." Her face was hot and bothered.

"I'm not trying to scare you off. What's with all the shyness, anyway?" Qian Yu's words pierced right through her.

"If it blooms, do you want it back?"

Qian Yu stroked his chin, as if he had grown a long beard. "Nah, but you'll have to man the stand here for a day. Fair?"

The stake was low, so Ruhua agreed. She never gambled, but she was up for the new experience. All she knew were flowers and her parents' arguments.

"Just don't let me down," Qian Yu said as she left.

Ruhua had become the new owner of the begonia. From that day on, though, her heart was divided. Sure, she loved flowers, but part of her felt lifted up like a balloon that had long floated away, as if it would be all right if they didn't bloom. Of course, it would be great if they did, but still. The bicycle was nothing. She had one at home. Technically it was Xiaowu's, but she could use it whenever she needed. Her words got even more convoluted. Nothing seemed clear anymore.

The bud began to pout. The verdict was in. The dust had settled. Ruhua's heart was finally at peace. Watching the stand for a day would be fine. Her parents almost never went to town. What would they care if she did that for a single day? A bet was a bet. She had to honour the gift Qian Yu had given her.

But with the begonia gone, her past sadness became burdensome and hard to handle for the first time. How could she bear telling Qian Yu the horrid truth? Perhaps he wouldn't want to hear her explanation, but she didn't know if she could offer one anyway. She should have thought of her other flowers' fate before bringing this one back with her. How could she even begin to explain if he asked what happened? She debated saying that it indeed had bloomed but ended up dying in the end due to her sour hand. He had already put this much faith in her. How could she lie?

She decided to conceal the whole truth, to say some but hide the rest. Perhaps he would say he had forgotten all about the bet, but Ruhua couldn't get her thoughts straight. She was uneasy for an entire day just pondering. It was as if a hare were trapped in her throat, scratching and biting to get out. Nothing would soothe it.

A few days before the Chinese New Year, she made up her mind to tell him.

2

Life in town was much more lavish than that in the village. Merchants piled mountains of boxes of Chinese baijiu and drinks at their doors. Clothing vendors lined their shelves by the entryways. The stalls along the road were being fitted and opened for the day. Some had small stalls, but their voices accounted for the disparity. They sounded like trumpets, declaring all the best they had: lamb feet, heads, and entrails; black or red dates; frozen persimmon. "Step right up!" over and over they cried. "Don't be shy, or it'll pass you by!" Passers-by would carry small or large bags but were sure to take extra, just in case. They would weave among each other, squeezing their ways through. Cars and bicycles didn't stand a chance.

Ruhua stood eight or nine yards away from Qian Yu's stall. She didn't see the dustpan or anything. Chinese New Year couplets lay at his feet and were weighed down with stones. Qian Yu squatted down and stood up. It was cold, but he had nothing over his head. Still, he managed to don a smile. Occasionally, he would shout a hello to the young man beside the stall when he was too busy. The young man wore a cotton hat and carried a thick book. Hearing Qian Yu's cry, he put the book under his arm and followed the buyer's finger to get whatever was demanded, couplet or otherwise. Then he sat down until Qian Yu called for him again.

Ruhua waited until it was just her there. "Which pair for you?" Qian Yu stuffed the pastry he had bitten into his cotton coat pocket. Ruhua's heart fell. The cake must have frozen through. She lifted the hood of her down jacket, Qian Yu smiled so widely she could make out every tooth. "Which pair?"

"Why the switch to couplets?"

"Thought it to be a good idea for the end of the year," he replied. "My brother Bao wrote this one. You like it? It ain't too bad, I think. He won an award at the county level for his calligraphy. Choose what you want, and I'll discount the price on account of him not using jacquard. I think he forgot to paste it on."

Mom has already bought the couplets we're going to use, so there's no point in that. Did he completely forget about the flower? Why hasn't he said a word about it?

Seeing Ruhua hesitating, Qian Yu spoke up. "This set's one of the cheapest."

"I'm not here for couplets."

"Oh, you're here cause of the flower, right? So? What's the verdict? To bloom or not to bloom?"

Ruhua couldn't hold back her tears any longer, and they fell like rain drops. Qian Yu was caught completely off guard. "D-Don't cry. What's up?" Ruhua wiped her face a few times, almost as if she were wiping a stain that wouldn't go away. Her tears fell silently, but everyone around noticed. Qian Bao's nose had been buried in his book, but even he looked up. "It's the bicycle, right? That ain't nothing. I'll get it. Promise. Just don't cry. This is where I do my business. You'll scare people off!" Ruhua got up and left. Qian Yu called for her, but she didn't stop. She had affected his business, which made her even more upset. She wanted to say that the flowers were blooming. She could help him watch the stall for a whole day, but she didn't say anything. Her tears were endless. Perhaps she shouldn't have come.

The day after New Year, Xiaowu went out with his friends. Ruhua's mother didn't know who to lay all the neighbourhood gossip on. It was a whole bunch of vague somewheres, somethings, somehows anyway. She was hoping to talk about something that happened on a street corner or beside the grindstones. Some woman came across another and said something she shouldn't have. Perhaps it was about something wrong with the other's sweater and how to sew a lapel, or perhaps it was about how fast the other was walking. Whatever. Point was, they got into it, and a third and fourth even joined in. It was like a theatrical performance. Ruhua's dad got riled up whenever his wife gossiped like she did because she would always forget to put dinner on the table when she was supposed to.

Ruhua stayed at home with her father, who had passed out from drinking. She had nowhere else to go. The other young women her age had already been married off and mothered their own children long before. The children in the neighbourhood were still very young, and to them, Ruhua was considered old-fashioned with that hairdo. They always raised a brow the moment they saw her. Ruhua suddenly got very itchy, and nothing could satisfy the prickly feeling. Her mother was agitated by her loafing around at home. "You'll get fat." Ruhua ignored her words, though she would cry the next time her mother decided to throw a harsh word her way. In the end, she walked outside, unwilling to lend an ear to all the gossip. As she went, she kept her head down and eventually ended up outside the village. She found solace in the fields, woods, and grasslands. The moment she set foot out of the community, she was able to take in a breath of fresh air. Even with the snow on top of the snow, she was happy. She closed her eyes as she walked, and the crunching below her feet was soothing. She was in her own paradise. She uttered nary a word, but the footprints that zigged and zagged in her wake were enough to tell the tale. Such was her way of venting her frustrations to Mother Nature. The bitter wind sliced at her face, turning it purple, but her eyes were wiped clean, able to reflect the blue sky overhead. One time, when she was out in the woods, she came across a sparrow that fell unconscious and landed beside her. She cradled the poor thing in her arms until it woke up nearly half an hour later. There was another time when a crow seemed to be following her, flying from one branch to the other. The crow was trying to say something to Ruhua, but she didn't speak crow. It was only after it left her that she realized it must have been hungry. The next time she went out to the woods, she took a small bag of corn, but the crow was nowhere to be found.

Eventually, Ruhua's mother caught up with her. Ruhua assumed the gossip train concerning her whereabouts made its way to her mother's ears. In a word, her mother was furious. Something about how she would end up like some woman in a neighbouring village who got possessed by some fox demon when wandering out all by herself in the woods. The whole bout ended with her forbidding Ruhua to ever go out alone into the wild again.

So, there Ruhua stayed indoors. She was looking forward to the day the ice would melt and the snow would recede. At least then, she knew her mother wouldn't forbid her from working out in the garden, tilling the land, and handling the vegetables.

She heard her name suddenly. She sat there, stunned, her ears attentive. It happened again. The ice on the glass had just melted. The trails it left made it difficult to make anything out at all outside. She got flustered, grabbed her coat, and fumbled about trying to get a single arm in the right sleeve.

The courtyard walls to her home were about waist high, so when she finally stepped beyond the front door's threshold, she saw Qian Yu standing outside the gate. Again, he wasn't wearing a hat, but this time, he had on a pair of earmuffs. His slender neck was red due to not having a scarf or other covering over his bare skin.

"Thought you weren't here for a minute." Qian Yu was

straddling a bicycle that he had obviously ridden there. One foot was on the ground. He was smiling, of course, and his teeth seemed so white that they appeared freshly brushed.

"How'd you know where I lived?" Ruhua was so nervous that she couldn't walk properly. Her two legs seemed latched to the ground.

Qian Yu laughed. "I have a mouth. There is only one person named Ruhua in all Nanxiaomiao Village."

"But … why'd you come to see me?" Ruhua felt a blush coming for her supposed silliness.

Qian Yu took off his earmuffs and hung them around his neck. He squinted, but his eyes were still crystal clear. "Not you. I'm looking for Ruhua. Have you seen her?"

"Wh-What?" Ruhua's heart began to race.

Qian Yu licked his lips. No words. Just savouring a swallow.

Ruhua looked behind her, half expecting someone to be spying on them. The blush finally came. Her father was snoring, true to his thunder-like self. She didn't want Qian Yu to lay eyes on him. Or … perhaps she would ask for a walk with him outside the village. The house, particularly that house, brought out the worst in her, making her stiff as a wooden board. She was more herself in nature. She wanted to be her real self with him there. Such was the desire in her heart.

"Relax. I'm just kidding around. I won't barge in," Qian Yu said. "I wanted to see you before the holiday, but I was glued to my stand."

"What's … up?" Ruhua was careful with each syllable, but she already knew.

"The flower didn't bloom, right? I hated seeing you cry. This bicycle here is practically off the shelf."

Ruhua was too nervous to breathe. "Are you for real?"

Qian Yu smiled. "Course. I can take a loss. It's my end of our bet. Fair and square."

Ruhua had no idea what her face looked like. Her voice was small, like the buzzing of a mosquito. "But … it did bloom."

Qian Yu's gaze was like a magnet that forced her eyes up to meet his. "Figures. Someone who has a thing for flowers is like that extra pinch of fertilizer, you know? Looks like I'm going to have to ride this bike all the way back, then."

"Hmm."

"You owe me one."

"Mm-hmm."

"I'm just kidding! Really, if you can't take a joke like that, people will start to think I'm berating you. It's clear you're not inviting me in, so I'll just be on my way!"

"I'll go with you." Ruhua insisted, regardless of Qian Yu's urgings otherwise. She wanted to go. Her heart was full of things to say, but nothing got sorted out on its way through her throat.

Her mother appeared. Ruhua wasn't able to duck away in time.

"Friend of yours, Ruhua?" she asked, sizing up Qian Yu. He was quick to respond.

"Happy New Year, ma'am! Just came to wish Ruhua the same."

"You're not leaving, are you?" Ruhua could hear the twinge of regret in her mother's voice. She thought her face appeared similar in texture to a cockscomb. Qian Yu seemed to catch on.

"Gettin' late, I'm afraid."

The appearance of her mother completely foiled Ruhua's plan. She had to go back home the moment Qian Yu left the village. Her mother pummelled her with questioning the whole rest of the day before waking up her husband. Ruhua confessed everything in bitter detail. "So it all happened the day you got your perm?" Ruhua nodded. "See what I told you? That perm really was the magic wave that found you a man." Her voice was filled with both surprise and dislike.

Ruhua was no stranger to blind dates, having gone on nearly two dozen of them by that point. Nothing, not a single one, had any promise. Her mother did all the picking, but no one she selected took a liking to Ruhua upon meeting her. She was too thin to work, and her hips and glutes didn't seem capable of bearing children. Still, her mother continued to search as easily as foraging through two rows of wheat, filling prospective mates' ears with nonsense they could never believe. If Ruhua cried, out the door they most certainly went. No one wanted that. As they left, her mother would say the men were blind, but in the same breath, she also chided Ruhua. Ruhua seemed to be the embodiment of everything her mother disapproved of. She was very pushy in her dealings with husbands to be, with not a polite bone in her body. "My daughter hasn't found a husband yet. Why should she just serve as a godmother to everyone else's children? No one's filed for divorce last year, and all the other women her age have a child or two by this point. *They* don't suck off the teat of their parents anymore." Ruhua had yet to give her hand, and Qian Yu, a man, had just come to their doorstep. Her parents were quite understandably interested, not really confused, but wanting to get to the bottom of every last detail.

Fire and thunder were able to join forces rather unexpectedly and with surprising efficiency. In less than three days, they found out everything there was to know about Qian Yu. His father died young, and the older uncle, Qian Zhuang, opened a shop in the village. Qian Yu lived with (or more like offered his home to) his younger sibling, Qian Bao, who failed the national college entrance examinations four years in a row. The stress of studying had sent him to a mental institution for a whole year, and upon release, his mental fortitude was rocky at best. It wasn't like PTSD from battle or anything, which was a relief, but it was too much book smarts that clogged up his brainwaves. Qian Yu was twenty-seven and *still* without a wife, but the weight of the world on his shoulders could explain that away. Nonetheless, the whole situation would put a burden on Ruhua should she take his hand in marriage. After ages of Ruhua's mother's hmms and her father's uhs, their hearts seemed to settle in favour of the whole situation, at the very least because their daughter would no longer be on the verge of wasting away like a rusted scrap of iron. Ruhua had been the source of her mother's woes for quite some time. Of course, marriage is no vain matter. A dowry was in order. Thirty grand seemed fair.

Ruhua's mother told her about her decision, and Ruhua felt that she was going to burst. Her anger would well up and roll around in her belly, but never did it gush like a geyser in her mother's face. In total, she had only met Qian Yu three times, and the words they shared were few. Who knew if Qian Yu was even considering courting her? Her mother said that Ruhua was a lump of elm. If Qian Yu had no interest in Ruhua, he would have never come to her in such cold weather. "Do you like him?" she asked her pointedly. Ruhua didn't know how to answer. Qian Yu's smiling face was certainly attractive. Her quiet self always wanted to at least say something when she met eyes with him. Perhaps that was what she liked, that he made her come out of her shell. "Do you hate him?" Ruhua shook her head. Her mother hammered the point home. Ruhua conceded and said she would see where things went. "And you'll drown him in your tears when you do."

Fire and thunder began to work hard on this matter. When the matchmaker came to the door, Qian Yu was stunned. A proposal for marriage in such strange fashion as this? The matchmaker turned to leave, but he reached out and grabbed hold. Hearing about the 30K bride price made him waver, but he agreed that he would at least talk to Ruhua about it. The matchmaker made it seem like 30K wasn't much compared to the normal 80 or 100, but his family was poor. Marriage was a big affair, though. The matchmaker kept pushing how much Ruhua liked him. "It's not that," he replied. "I just want to see her."

In Nanxiaomiao Village, Ruhua met Qian Yu, who grinned when Ruhua came near. Ruhua was extremely nervous, not knowing why Qian Yu had demanded to see her, her being so undependable as she was.

"Is it true, Ruhua? This whole marriage business?" he asked, his mouth agape.

Ruhua understood that he was as insecure as she was and suddenly relaxed. She didn't answer him directly, but asked back, "What are your thoughts?" She was surprised the words came out.

Qian Yu's eyes seem to pop out of his head. "I thought I was going to die the first time we met, God as my witness."

Ruhua's worry about what would happen in the bridal chamber was all for naught. A two-and-a-half-year-old was leaning against the door, and Qian Yu stuffed the sugar bag that had been prepared for them out the crack. No one returned for more. Qian Yu tied the courtyard door shut before coming in. Ruhua felt relieved. Her palms were dripping in sweat.

"Well, time for business, I guess." Qian Yu's face was serious.

"Have you eaten? It's easy to forget on a day like this."

"Not really."

"I'll get you something," Ruhua said as she plopped herself on the ground.

Qian Yu grabbed her, "I've got something to eat right here." Ruhua paused, confused by the statement. Joy seemed to pour from Qian Yu's eyes. Ruhua's flowery face was starting to turn both red and purple.

"I'm not afraid," she said in a low voice.

Qian Yu got closer, his eyes brushing over her like a broom. "You're the stuff of dreams."

Ruhua's eyes grew wide. "Really?"

"Course. Wanna bet on it?"

"You can stop beating around the bush. I see where this is going."

Qian Yu hung his head and winked. "Tired yet?"

"It's still early," she whispered, nearly inaudibly.

"Let me get a good, long look at you."

Ruhua felt a flush coming, her breath uneven. "You could scare someone off with a look like that."

"Then close your eyes."

Ruhua obliged.

Qian Yu held her face and kissed her forehead. His lips were cool, and they moved down toward her eyebrows, eyes, and then nose. She felt like an itchy, crisp, yet still soft flower submerged in a flowing liquid.

Tears began to flow. Qian Yu stopped. Ruhua wanted to tell him not to stop, but no words came.

"You'll never suffer in my arms," he said, taking a loving bite at her ear.

Ruhua's tears intensified.

Girls should cry when they get married. Those that don't wish they could. A girl in the Nanxiaomiao Village had once fainted from crying. This was Ruhua's specialty. People in Nanxiaomiao Village said that Ruhua, the definition of a teardrop, should be careful of crying too much when getting on the "Just Married" wagon, but what happened surprised everyone, even Ruhua. Not a single tear. Her mother was humiliated, jerking at Ruhua's arm so much that she cried out in pain. Still, not a single tear.

Instead, it was her mother who dabbed at her eyes, though it was questionable whether there really were any tears in them. To cry or not to cry … That was Ruhua's worry. She feared that Qian Yu would look down on her for it.

"You look better when you cry!" Qian Yu said. "It reminds me of dew on petals."

Ruhua smiled. Qian Yu hugged her.

Upon becoming Qian Yu's wife, Ruhua had transformed into someone she didn't know. In the past, she was confined in a cage, tied at her hands and feet. The cage had disappeared, and her binds had vanished. She was still shy and would blush without reason when talking to others, but she had nothing to block in her heart. She didn't have to hide her opinions anymore, and she became rather vocal in voicing them. She was able to "gauge" how she felt, and Qian Yu didn't even try to stop her. To the contrary, he even encouraged it, and pretty much every affair between him and Qian Zhuang were handled on the politest of terms anymore.

Ruhua let her obsession with flowers take off. She got married in May, the right time to sow the fields. She scattered broom plum seeds on the ridge of the field and sunflowers over the potato, naked oat, and wheat fields. There was a garden in the courtyard. In the past, there were several rows of onions, like a lot of other families still had, and there was even celery, leeks, and water radishes. The whole place was transformed into a flower patch, with only half the garden for vegetables. Passionflowers and chrysanthemiums took the other. Ruhua also planted flowers in the front and back of the house and on the side of the wall, where there was soil. The house was also a flower sanctuary. Qian Yu bought two dozen flowerpots for her, which contained pretty much every species locally available for purchase. Cyclamens, summer chrysanthemums, roses, lilies, narcissuses, Chinese perfumes, vermilions, and moth orchids. Every day was a festival of flowers.

In July and August, broom plums, centennial chrysanthemums, marigolds, summer chrysanthemums, sunflowers, and helianthuses would begin their blooming season, and the bees and butterflies danced. Qian Yu and Ruhua worked in the field, their spirits constantly uplifted among the beautiful colours. Placed anywhere blindfolded in the village, they could find their way home by the smell alone. If outsiders asked about Qian Yu's household, the villagers would point, and visitors would see the grove called their courtyard.

Ruhua was not only good at planting flowers, she was spectacular at it. The strength of her inner bean sprout was allowed to grow to its fullest potential. A hundred-pound potato bag over the shoulder? No problem. Her needlework also improved, so much so that she could rival Maixiang. Of course, only Qian Yu was more skilled in this area. Ruhua's figure was on the thinner, frailer side, but her breasts were full. She would get shy and don a constricting bra all day, but when released from their cage, out popped Qian Yu's eyes at the newfound sight. Her thin bones began to pack on muscle. Her growth spurt had ended long before, never getting her to her father's height. She was even shorter than her mother and Xiaowu. Still, for some unspeakable reason, she grew three quarters of an inch after only three months of marriage. Qian Yu never had anything less than praise for his beloved wife, and her confidence swelled. Him telling her how much he treasured her banished the doubt that had previously settled in her heart.

Songzhuang Village, however, saw things differently. Ruhua wasn't perceived as a woman with a lot of common sense. Many in Song thought she was growing flowers to sell on the market, but not even a couple pounds of meat could be scored for her whole lot. This misconception branded her as an incompetent ignoramus. Qian Yu wasn't all sunshine and rainbows upstairs either. He got married in his late twenties, and his cherished baby of a wife could get a bit difficult to hold in his arms. He also wasn't the brightest star in the sky. He made a wind-powered turbine, but the electricity it produced couldn't even light a bulb. He additionally endeavoured on this fantastical flying machine, the semi-finished product of which his uncle sold as scrap. The surface of this couple's pristine life, once scratched bit a little, revealed some far-fetched and hare-brained delusions, though it could be explained that these were traits passed down from their ancestors. And Bao, Yu's brother, the one who never made it to college, wasn't all at home either. Saying more about it would be a waste of ink on this page.

Qian Zhuang, Qian Yu's uncle, decided to come knocking

when this family's oddities came to light. Handling flowers was really no job at all, and inner-family madness was concerning at best. But the lightning? Something had to be done after that day.

Ruhua liked lightning and saw it as flowers from Heaven. Although fleeting like orchid cacti, it could illuminate the whole earth. She didn't dare express her thoughts on this before, but after marrying Qian Yu, she told him all, save for one hobby. When the dark clouds rolled over, her heart was summoned, ready to move, and she leaned against her window. Upon seeing lightning, she would go out into the courtyard or even lie flat on her roof. Qian Yu happened upon her one time, and it turned out he liked it just as much. "I'll show you a good time under Heaven's flowers." Out they ran into the field, having donned raincoats and boots. Sure, it was a bit crazy, but not asylum-worthy. Still, Wu Tai, a cattle herder, saw them gallivanting. Everyone in the village knew by the following dusk.

Qian Zhuang and Qian Yu were talking outside, and Ruhua was waiting silently indoors. For some strange reason that Ruhua couldn't explain, Zhuang gave her the shudders. He always had a smile and never seemed to be demanding, but something was behind those eyes. Still, he was the one who raised the brothers until they could live on their own. He also was the one who paid most of the 30,000 bride price, so his words carried weight. When he sold Qian Yu's half-finished flying machine, the latter didn't say much of anything except to himself. His uncle always told him to be more practical, but on that particular day after the thunderstorm, something seemed to snap. Qian Zhuang called the couple crazy, and Qian Yu bit back, something he had never done before. Words flew.

"I didn't come here just to get the dust kicked up in my face," Qian Zhuang said.

"Not everyone is the same. If they were, they would all be mindless machines."

"Can stiff-winged birds fly?" His uncle was angry at this point. "There's this thing called order, you know."

"It's not like I stole anything. Just had a bit of fun in the field. What harm did we cause?"

"You harmed our good name."

"I can always change it to get out of your hair."

"You would go against the grain in spite." The anger was now fury.

"Don't let your blood pressure get too high, now."

"Are you turning against your own flesh and blood?"

Qian Yu seemed to take a direct hit from that. "I understand Qian means 'money,' and 'money' runs in our blood."

"Just turn a new leaf. Otherwise, it's like stabbing me in the back."

"Don't preach. I know very well you like to rub salt in wounds."

"And don't you try to ambush me. Your smirky daydreaming gets you nowhere. Think of your brother. He depends on you. I raised you, so now it's your turn to pick up the torch."

"He still eats, doesn't he? He can enjoy life with his nose in his books."

"And you would be just fine with him never marrying?"

"Fate is Heaven's decision, not mine."

Qian Zhuang sneered. "Pfft. Fate. Better decisions are made through hard work and money, our namesake." Again, these words from Qian Yu's uncle made him falter. Qian Yu would normally be considered a content individual, but that wasn't always the case, like in this situation. "If you're still a Qian at heart, then take care of your brother. That's your responsibility."

Qian Yu began to hunch. "I swear he'll have a wife before the day I die."

"Just make sure you don't go off to find 'one for sale' like they have in Sichuan. I can't stand the mentality behind that."

Ruhua heard every word. It was clear that Qian Zhuang wanted her to. Qian Yu came back to her, all smiles. He had backed down and taken the fall for her. She couldn't sit with herself at that moment.

"What's around the corner for us?"

Qian Yu bopped her on the nose. "What do folks know but to eat and drink? Tell me. What sound do flowers make when they speak to you?"

Ruhua's eyes were dry, but her heart felt plunged into a pool of clear water, the bubbles fizzing toward the surface. Her husband was guilty of aiding and abetting her insanity.

By fall's end, Qian Yu had set up a stall in the town square.

He didn't have much to offer, and what he did offer was out of season, meaning he earned very little. Still, he didn't give up hope on living up to his name. Ruhua stayed at home to tend the flowers. Winter meant no pests but lack of water. Her job was to loosen the soil, speak to each individual plant, and sing soothing songs to them. When flowers are in the wild, they have the wind, butterflies, bees, ants, and moths to keep them company, allowing them to cheerfully sway. When indoors, they had the tendency of going numb and stiff. Alive, but stunted. That was why Ruhua did what she did. Back when she was with her parents, she could only whisper to them, but in her home with Qian Yu, she could have full-blown conversations. Qian Yu even recorded her conversations so that they could be played back to save her voice. There were different tapes for different moods. Ruhua would sometimes go with Qian Yu to help him set up shop. She also let her perm fall. She hated the way it made her look. It was like her head was fitted with a dusty awning. Her mother complained, saying that that was how Qian Yu had met her in the first place, but Ruhua paid her words no mind. The Shanghai-influenced stylist, when he saw her, sighed and groaned about how she'd destroyed his masterpiece of a do. Ruhua could barely hold back from chortling, making her stomach hurt and forcing her to hit the ground once he was out of view again.

A month before Chinese New Year, some heavy snow hit the area, and the roads were covered in six inches' worth. The clouds hung low, threatening to have another go. Ruhua still hadn't brought the rice to the table when more flurries began. Such heavy snow signalled a bumper harvest to come, so everyone in the countryside was high-spirited. There wasn't a single firecracker, no chatter, not even the chirping of overwintering birds. The sky was silent, and the ground was quiet. Still, 'twas the season to be jolly. The air seemed alive, bouncing off the rooftops, flowing over the streets, and jostling through the snowflakes. Ruhua was going to ask Qian Yu to join her after dinner for a stroll, but she couldn't help herself and popped the question before the food was ready. "Fine, steal the food right out of my stomach," he replied, pleasantly surprised.

They left the village, facing north. The road was covered with snow, but they weren't headed toward the main road. They were used to the road. Northward, beyond the woods and fields, was grassland, where they rarely trod. The sky was boundless, and a couple of birds finally decided to sing. They couldn't find where they were singing on a day such as that, but still, singing. Inspired by their chirps, Ruhua suggested splitting up and rejoining later on in their walk. Qian Yu said he couldn't stop his wife from turning into a white fox and sprinting away from him. Ruhua said he could join her in her transfiguration. "I feel more like a crow." Ruhua brushed him off and decided to be the first to move forward. Ten yards, then twenty. Eventually, the two lost sight of each other. Ruhua called for her husband. Though neither could make the other out, each knew of the other half's existence.

"Marco!" Ruhua liked the wilderness. Her voice could be

as loud as she wanted without her having to shyly hunker down afterward.

"Harken? What now?" Qian Yu was obviously playing. Ruhua laughed.

"Miss me? Come find me if you can."

"I'm good. Want to hear about a dream I had last night?"

"Don't make one up on my account!"

"I don't sell counterfeits."

Ruhua suddenly cried out. Her foot had hit a mole hole in the ground, and she lost her balance. She tried to jerk it out, but it didn't budge. Down she went. Qian Yu burst out into laughter. "Talk about karma, casting doubt on my honesty!" But no response. Neither was there a blurry figure still before him. He suddenly bolted toward where the figure once stood. "Ruhua! *Ruhua!*"

Qian Yu snatched her up and rushed back to the village. Ruhua felt something wet on her legs, something flowing like a stream. She couldn't see the scarlet rose petals dripping behind her and Qian Yu as he ran.

$$4$$

Qian Yu untied the grey and blue cloth bag, which had obviously been made from a worn-out pair of pants or coat and faded from countless washings. Inside this shoddy bag was a satchel made of light-green velvet tied in red silk. The velvet was also worn, possibly from the red silk tie, but more so from having been shoved in another bad for so long. There was a sense of mystery about it. Ruhua asked what it was, but her husband remained silent and he opened the satchel and poured its contents onto white paper. Flower seeds! They were as big as rapeseed but dark violet in colour. One made a run to the edge of the paper, as if to escape, but Qian Yu's fingers snatched it and put it back where it belonged. Ruhua knew these weren't any ordinary seeds, and she tried to ask Qian Yu what they were. His response wasn't with a smile. "You'll find out soon enough." Ruhua asked if he bought them. "I didn't steal them, if that's what you're asking."

After Ruhua had a miscarriage, she wilted like a frosted flower. Qian Yu quickly hailed her mother, and the moment she arrived, she laid in on Qian Yu. She yelled at him for being as reckless as her own daughter. She heard all the neighbourhood gossip about the two of them and assumed them to be causing more trouble than she could have ever bargained for and needed a stern talking-to. She went into the door and looked at Ruhua, who was leaning on the kang. She said nothing to Ruhua directly and asked Qian Yu to take out the noodle roller, but she had no intention of making noodles. Instead, she pulled back hard and took a swing at Qian Yu, who dodged. This made her even more angry. Qian Yu eyed the chopping board, his only defence against the potential onslaught. In the end, though, she thought better of it, slamming her hand down on the pot lid before her. "I'll crack your skull like an egg should she get hurt under your care," she warned. Qian Yu replied that he would take care of that himself before she had to. She stormed into the living room. Qian Yu scratched the back of his head in dismay.

Ruhua was her next target. "What brain is in that head of yours when out in the middle of nowhere like you were? A human's or dog's? At least a bitch knows how to take care of her young!" Qian Yu couldn't bear listening any longer. He poured a glass of water to distract the pointed fury, but he was deterred by her yelling. It turned out that after all this, Ruhua never once shed a single tear. Tears on her face were once reminiscent of a leaky faucet, but no longer. At first, it could have been explained by her simply being in shock, but as her mother kept going at it, it became clear that she had neither inclination to defend herself nor a speck of regret in her heart. Ruhua didn't have any biting comments to return, but her mother also viewed that as not taking the situation seriously. "You hear me, girl?" she roared.

Nothing. Ruhua heard, but she didn't want to talk to her. It was like she wasn't even there. Ruhua was sad, but it had nothing to do with her mother, which stung the latter like a horrible wasp's malice. "Look at the kindness I've shown you! What do you have to show for it?! You're married, but you're still my daughter, mine, Yang Meirong's!" Silence. Her mother couldn't handle it anymore, threw a fifty on the table, and charged out of the house, pouting. Qian Yu came over to console his wife, but he didn't bring up anything his mother-in-law had just said. What was it? Pride? She felt like one of those legendary Robin Hood-like bandits of Mount Liang, self-righteous in their cause. She shrugged Qian Yu off, saying how he didn't need to serve her hand and foot.

Ruhua was physically okay, but her heart felt shattered. Qian Yu was desperate to make her happy again. One thing he knew could be the key, and Ruhua knew he strained his brain to do just that. Thinking of this, she was able to shed tears for the first time in a month. "It's all my fault," she whispered. "I'm sorry." Qian Yu held her in his arms, saying how she didn't need to blame herself and that it was the child's choice not to come into the world. "Do you hate me for what happened?" she asked.

"I'm just grateful you didn't turn into a white fox and leave me behind."

With the advent of spring, the darkness began to fade. Wheat, naked oats, flax, potatoes, beans, celery, and cabbage were waiting for them. Of course, there were also those mysterious seeds. During the winter, Qian Yu prepared several varieties on the ridge, behind the house, on the barren slope, and Ruhua even scattered some seeds. The extra-large, dark-violet seeds had a special place by the naked oats. Qian Yu was the one who picked that spot out. He said something about them being a delicate type, worthy only of his and Ruhua's eyes. Ruhua didn't think much about it. She thought that Qian Yu was just trying to cater to her imagination. Given her way, she would plant flowers on the roof.

There was nothing special about the violet seeds when the stems first appeared. They were slow growers, far worse than broom plums and even worse than chrysanthemums, but after a span of time, their unique traits became apparent. There were two branches one day and three the next. The buds soon came, yearning to wake up to the world. Ruhua recognized the buds, but there were many, many more than the three to five found in other people's gardens. Qian Yu equated this type to a wild display of fireworks.

They were poppies, something highly illegal to own. Qian Yu, wondering what Ruhua would say, quickly said how they were hidden among the naked oats in a place no one would discover. He also said they would wait just long enough for seeds to come before pulling them out by the roots and taking them inside. Ruhua paused, wondering if it was all right to go along with the idea, but Qian Yu comforted her by saying it was much better than waiting for just the right strike of lightning to bloom. The lure of seeing the grandeur of poppy flowers was well worth the risk.

The first poppy was scarlet red. The branches and leaves were still greyish green, as if they were parched, but the petals were brilliant. Perhaps their brilliance came at the expense of the branches' nourishment, but it wasn't the colour that was most magnificent. It was the flowers' pose. Something about them was just entrancing … bewitching even. Their grandeur could catch anyone's eye from afar. From a single patch, it was as if the whole land was dyed red and drunk from the majesty of their presence. But, like any flower, they began to wither and fade. Ruhua had half a heart to pitch a tent in the field and retire for all time. Qian Yu said something about how it would attract unnecessary gossip, and Ruhua relented.

Alas, though they were careful, their fate turned for the worse. The petals were withering like an old woman, and the flowers were to be pulled the next day. Still, while Ruhua was at home cooking Qian Yu's lunch, a police car pulled up. She arrived in the field with the lunch box, but by that time, Qian Yu was in handcuffs, and the poppies were no more. Ruhua knew the elder of the two policemen, the one with a long face and hawk-like nose, his eyes like cymbals. His surname was Yan, his nickname Hell. She knew how he solved some big case in Nanxiaomiao Village before she got married in Songzhuang Village. Many rumours surrounded his name, and "when Hell came knocking," things always turned downhill. Thieves were said to wet themselves just at the thought of him. Some bandit stabbed him once, maiming him, but he still lobbed a shoe at the perpetrator so hard it knocked him clean out. So the stories went.

A frightened Ruhua stood rooted to the ground, but she told the officers that she was the one who planted the flowers. Hell looked her up and down. "Take him in for questioning." Ruhua begged him to take her instead. She didn't know where she got her courage. Hell didn't seem ablaze in fury. It was just that the car couldn't hold two detainees. He told her he'd be back for her. She only later realized that the officer was well-intentioned, but her mind couldn't process anything at that moment. The patrol vehicle left, with Qian Yu and the poppies in it. She stumbled after them. It was only after a while of this that it occurred to her to ask for help.

Qian Zhuang knew what was up before Ruhua came to the door. "Whose idea was it?" he asked coldly before she even opened her mouth.

"*Please.* You have to do *something*!"

He waited for the beer to finish brewing before he finally uttered, "You think I'm a magician or something?"

Ruhua was on the verge of a flood of tears. "There has to be some way."

"What about Bao? He involved?" Ruhua shook her head. "Two knuckleheads and a half you three." He then stopped and sighed. "I'll see what I can manage."

Qian Yu came back the next morning. Ruhua was scared, tossing and turning all the night prior. Her lips were parched and cracked. Her eyes resembled a bed of weeds. "It was just questioning!" he said the moment he saw her in such a state. "Just questioning! No need for all this!" Ruhua wiped away her tears, looked over Qian Yu, wondering why she didn't see bruises or lash marks. Nothing was there. She was incredulous. She asked whether they hurt him after interrogating him. "I wasn't on trial. Only the worst scoundrels are beaten. All we planted were flowers." He then told her that in addition to the poppies being pulled out, he had to attend something like a "public awareness" course. Ruhua's suspicions were high, but Qian Yu didn't want to say anything further for fear of scaring her. "Just happy I'm back." Ruhua told him about how Qian Zhuang's face looked ready to tear them to shreds. "It was worth the risk, though, if you ask me. Addicted yet?" Qian Yu asked jokingly.

Half a month later, for no reason she could tell, Ruhua miscarried again. She had fetched some water for her face and suddenly come down with horrible cramps. Qian Yu was out working in the field, sickle in hand, the harvest right around the corner. Ruhua kept silent and slowly moved toward the kang, which dampened the pain. She lay down for a few moments before getting up to cook, but something strange began to slither between her legs. That was when she finally cried out for Qian Yu, who wanted to carry her all the way to the hospital, but it was too late. The child couldn't wait inside that long. After a few days' rest, Qian Yu took Ruhua to the town hospital to grab some medicine and prayed before Zunai's bed. Zunai was said to not only deliver babies, but also treat barrenness and other childbearing issues. Ruhua and Qian Yu didn't see these miracles personally, but the anecdotes were everywhere. Wu Daqiao's wife had had similar issues, and having taken Zunai's protective medicine, she was able to give birth to a healthy babe the fourth go. "I only had to take three doses!" she said reminiscing of the same. "By that time, I was so desperate. I didn't even feel worthy to be called a woman. My husband couldn't even look me in the eye." She then kicked Wu Daqiao, who was squatting at the door smoking as she recounted the tale. "Ask the old geezer yourself. I relied on his every move, but he treated me like a wasteful hedgehog." He grinned and nodded without protest. Qian Yu and Ruhua asked what was in the medicine. "I honestly don't know. Some powder of some sort. Bitter as hell." It was a shame that Zunai had only recently become bedridden. The only thing Ruhua could do was stand before her and beg her blessing. She told Qian Yu she wished she had been born a few years earlier, but Qian Yu smiled.

"Your precious flowers would have been plucked by someone other than me, then."

The first swipe of the sickle had to be done with care. By tradition, it was done with two people holding the handle. The result was a predicter of how things would turn out for the year. The two holding the sickle could be brothers or father and son, but the best pair was husband and wife. It was the proper balance of Yin and Yang. Qian Yu's first thought, though, was to go it with Qian Bao, but Ruhua remembered how he wasn't able to finish the entire row, even going as far as to slice his hand in a few places. She insisted on taking his place. "You sure?" Qian Yu asked. Ruhua replied by saying she wouldn't fall apart like a tower of mud and that it was only for the first swipe. Qian Yu said nothing more.

The first swipe came and went, but Ruhua didn't feel like stopping. In fact, she found herself happier than Qian Yu at the task. He just let her do her thing. Ruhua wasn't known for being headstrong, so she didn't see much of an issue moving forward. She was a good judge on just how much her body could handle. She felt like a beached fish when indoors all the time, unable to catch her breath. Outdoors, however, she was back at sea, swimming in utter delight.

When time to rest, Ruhua lay over Qian Yu's legs and looked up at the sky. Wild geese were honking, and the white clouds were drifting toward the horizon. The vast sky was worthy of ponderance. "I wish I could plant flowers up above," Ruhua muttered. The words escaped her mouth without her knowledge. To her, lightning was a type of flower, and so were the clouds. If the sky had just one more variety, then it would be filled with colour. She wondered these things, but just as one would consider the steps to becoming emperor, the sentiments meant nothing, went nowhere, and were utter nonsense.

"Why don't you?" Qian Yu's words were as if from the most natural speculation. Ruhua, who was used to Qian Yu's against-the-grain nature, continued by saying that if she were a white cloud she would plant herself. "There's no need for transformation. Want to bet on it?" Ruhua gave him a gentle pinch, calling him a thoughtless gambler. Qian Yu didn't put money down on card games, but he always made even the simplest ponderance an offer.

"What are the stakes?"

"Don't scold me when I tell you."

Ruhua wasn't much of a worthy opponent, and even though it was a game of words, she felt a trickle run down her spine. "You're bad."

"Your word."

"Fine."

"I'll take twenty lashes from you should I lose."

"I suppose the same the other way around?"

"How could I bear to lay a hand on you? No, if I manage to plant flowers in the sky, I'll just cash them in for a fair exchange."

Ruhua thought Qian Yu to be just like her. On the evening after the fall harvest, they put the sack into the cart, and Qian Yu asked Ruhua to close her eyes. His voice was shrouded in mystery. Ruhua looked around first. "Here of all places?" Qian Yu laughed and told her to heed his words. She couldn't guess what Qian Yu was going to do, and her heart was like a sprinting doe. When Qian Yu urged her, she still stared at the sky. Qian Yu ran over and half grabbed her. A fireball bounced from the court into the air.

Zing!

The streamer was as bright as a meteor. Ruhua didn't know when or how Qian Yu got the fireworks. Nine spherical flowers exploded one by one, some like chrysanthemums, others like peonies, still more like pink lotuses. Although the excitement was short, it was enough. No wall is unbreakable. Ruhua's eyes began to swim in tears. No sound escaped her lips.

Before bed, Qian Yu made sure to cash in his flowers for a fair exchange. Ruhua's cheeks flushed. She patted him on the chest and closed her eyes like in the yard.

The next day, Qian Yu laid out his plan. He didn't want to set up a stall anymore. He was going to work with Hao Zhu. Five or six years before, someone in the village had moved out. Qian Yu didn't care at first. His first priority was Qian Bao. Second, he felt that earning money outside was far from easy to earn. What would the purpose of earning money be anyway? Qian Yu was not short of happiness, but his financial reality started to hit home. The money he borrowed from his uncle remained unpaid. It was hard to avoid being upset, but where does being upset get anyone? Qian Yu didn't pay much attention to money, but the world operates on money. Fireworks cost money. Had he more, he could have planted extra flowers in the sky. Some happiness could be bought with money. For those who left the small town for the big skyscrapers, their eyes and tone said it all. Although Ruhua was reluctant, she didn't object to Qian Yu following suit and only asked when he would come back. Qian Yu said by year's end, no matter how much or little he made. He promised more flowers in the sky on Chinese New Year's Eve. Ruhua suddenly realized that Qian Yu was doing this for her and instantly said that seeing fireworks was just fine the one time. Qian Yu said that no one called the police over which flowers were planted in the sky and that she should wait for him and take care of Qian Bao.

A few days later, Qian Yu left the village with Hao Zhu. Ruhua didn't know that Qian Yu wasn't going to the county seat. Instead, he went to some factory or construction site like so many others did. He chose the place where he could earn the most money. After Qian Yu arrived, he called Ruhua and said that he would plant flowers in the city. Ruhua asked what kind of flowers could be planted in such a season. "Potted plants indoors are fine for any season. The indoors here are warmer than at home." Ruhua was able to breathe a sigh of relief and even yearned for one day owning a house of flowers like Qian Yu spoke of.

If only she knew that that was adieu.

5

Qian Zhuang and Xiaowu were accompanied by Ruhua, who's father was under the table by that point and whose mother had a duster in each hand but stood motionless. When Xiaowu had come back, his mother appointed him to the task. He worked in a repair shop and was already covered in oil stains. His mother yanked off what he had on and had him dress into something more appropriate, but he came out still reeking of oil. The leather shoes were blotchy, and the laces were stiff as boards, reminding Ruhua of her own father. Ruhua didn't mind the whole adventure, though. Honestly, if it hadn't been for the woman in the row in front of them who had to change her seat because of it, she would have forgotten the stench emanating from her brother's pores next to her.

The train wasn't due to leave until half past nine. Qian Zhuang led Ruhua and Xiaowu into Lanzhou Pulled-Noodles and asked for a bowl. Qian Zhuang said that he needed to eat but feared that the time wasn't enough. He sat opposite Ruhua and Xiaowu, looked at Ruhua, and then looked away. On the wall were pictures of various noodle-filled bowls and cold dishes. Qian Zhuang's eyes seemed drawn to them like magnets. For just a moment, Ruhua was consciously aware of just how heavy her head was on her neck. It was as if she was being directed by some puppeteer that whole day. "Did he really go to the coal mine?" she asked Qian Zhuang, but Qian Zhuang's eyes were locked on the images on the wall. Her own eyes fell on Xiaowu's face, who just grunted in response. "Why did he go to the coal mine?" She stared at Qian Zhuang, but Qian Zhuang ignored her. He didn't turn around until his bowl of freshly pulled noodles came to the table. He scooped a tablespoon of chili powder and motioned to Xiaowu. Xiaowu shook his head, and Qian Zhuang dropped the spoon's contents into his own bowl.

"I like it hot."

This seemed to open a floodgate of words to Xiaowu from the previously silent Qian Zhuang. He asked Xiaowu how much money he made, how his boss was treating him, and whether he had found a special someone. Ruhua couldn't get a word in edgewise. The dark cloud on Qian Zhuang's face began to lift, and she could breathe in silent relief. The coal mine had collapsed, but perhaps it was like Qian Zhuang said. Perhaps Qian Yu was barely affected and only came down with a small bout of whatever it was that he was supposedly "sick" with.

There was someone assigned to pick them up when they arrived in the morning. "Where's Qian Yu?" Ruhua blurted out before anything else.

"You need to eat something first," the thin man said. "You couldn't have rested well on the way."

"We're fine. Ate before."

The thin man looked at Qian Zhuang. "We'll head out in a bit."

"We're ready now."

"Sooner the better," Qian Zhuang said.

Xiaowu pulled at Ruhua. Ruhua remembered that it was Qian Zhuang, her uncle-in-law, who was in charge in this situation.

Breakfast was very rich. Steamed buns, fried dough, rice porridge, noodle soup, eggs, and several small dishes. Qian Zhuang and Xiaowu were starving and had their fill. Ruhua put down her chopsticks after drinking half a bowl of porridge. She hadn't eaten much the evening before. She stared at Qian Zhuang and Xiaowu, hoping they could pick up the pace. Xiaowu dodged Ruhua's eyes, but in doing so, he lost his grip over his chopsticks, the fried dough plopping back down onto the plate it came from. Qian Zhuang used his own to manoeuvre the dough back to Xiaowu and told Ruhua to eat some steamed buns. Ruhua promptly refused, but Qian Zhuang "insisted," using it as a condition for their departure. The thin man piggybacked on the words. Xiaowu passed a bun to his sister. Ruhua's head bowed.

They arrived at the county seat at noon. Ruhua thought she was going to see Qian Yu, but the car drove to the hotel instead. Qian Zhuang, Ruhua, and Xiaowu were each given a room. Ruhua asked about seeing Qian Yu. The thin man said that he would be arriving any moment, that he was en route, just heavy traffic. Ruhua asked if her husband was in a car. The thin man just told her to wash up and relax. He would knock when Qian Yu had gotten there.

Ruhua had only sat down for less than a minute when there was a knock. So fast? She jumped up and rushed to the door, but it was only Qian Zhuang and Xiaowu. Ruhua craned her neck to see if she could see Qian Yu behind them. Qian Zhuang went straight into the room, sat on the chair by the window, and tightly grasped the handle of the chair, as if afraid that the chair would break and send him crashing to the ground. He asked Ruhua to sit down, but Ruhua did nothing. She heard a strange thumping in her chest. Xiaowu came over, half hugging and half supporting her by the edge of the bed, his hands on her shoulders.

"I hope you're ready for this," Qian Zhuang finally said. Ruhua's breath got caught in her throat. "Qian Yu ran into some trouble." Her head began to buzz.

"So, he's not sick? What happened? What do you mean by 'some' trouble?" she asked, trembling all the while.

"More than just some."

"We talking a cup or a gallon? Or a barrel?" It was as if she were being strangled by some unseen rope. She stood rooted to the spot.

"You see … he … Xiaowu, get your sister some water!" Xiaowu offered, but Ruhua shook her head.

"Zhuang …" she uttered, her voice pleading.

"It would be better if you went about your life acting as if he's long gone."

Ruhua's head began to roar. "How far gone?"

"Beyond the horizon." The words were like a bomb, and once the vocal cords stopped, the room was as still as the calmest waters.

Qian Yu left her!

Qian Yu abandoned her!!

Qian Yu went farther than the horizon!!!

It was quite some time before she could breathe again, but there was still a spark of hope that managed to survive. Why wasn't he back? Why did he leave? Qian Zhuang lowered his eyes. It was as if he had died. Confusion ruled the moment. To think of it like that made her head spin but with a large stone between her ears, a stone that eventually plummeted to her stomach. She finally understood that she would never see Qian Yu again. She didn't faint. She didn't know that Xiaowu was holding pills at the ready. She didn't howl either. Tears streamed from her eyes. She slowly sat herself to keep from startling anyone, but it was as if her entire body, bones, limbs, vital organs, hair, everything was completely paralyzed, like a statue placed on the bed and hoisted over the dark purple carpet covered with stains, concealing the blurred patterns and the holes burned by cigarette butts. Her body was one long flow of stillness, head to toe. She didn't faint. She just flowed.

Qian Zhuang said that it was not time to cry, that that time would come once they had made it back home. Rather, business had to be taken care of. A spark again ignited. She began to stutter. Qian Yu was gone, or so Qian Zhuang said. He no longer dodged Ruhua's line of sight.

"I asked about how much it would take to calm things down. Damages seem to be in the range of 200 to 400 thousand. I say even more is in order. Of course, they're trying to chew us down. What do you think?" Ruhua didn't say anything. Xiaowu had to speak up before she realized the question was meant for her. She was at a loss for words, but Xiaowu said it was all up to her.

"I … I just want Qian Yu."

Qian Zhuang and Xiaowu looked at each other. "So do we, but a single tear is like shooting the boss of the coal mine 200 times in the heart. Nothing can be done. He's not coming back. Anger has no place in this moment. He won't come back. Only conditions can be set to appease the coal mine's situation. What's your condition, Ruhua?" Ruhua shook her head. "Then I'll take the stand."

Staying in the hotel for five days, Ruhua had never been so free. In the morning, Xiaowu knocked on the door and called for her to eat. She said that she couldn't, so he had to basically spoon-feed her like a reluctant child. He began to lose his temper, which shot her anxiety through the roof and forced her to comply by following him downstairs. She was highly unwilling to move a single muscle. Just smelling the wafts from the pots of food made her sick, but Qian Zhuang called for her anyway. He said his negotiation process was far from smooth. Being with Qian

Zhuang was on a fiery edge, his voice hoarse. He kept reminding her to play her due part, at the same time asking her bluntly if he hadn't played his. Ruhua shied away from him. This time, though, she got up in indignation. After dinner, Xiaowu escorted Ruhua back to the room and then sat on the chair and stared at her. Ruhua's eyes were open all night, tired like lazy waves during the daylight hours. When Ruhua lay down, her eyelids were pasted open. At noon, Xiaowu woke her up, and she followed him downstairs for lunch. Same thing for dinner. In the evening, Qian Zhuang came and sat down and reported the progress of the negotiations. For the first time, Ruhua heard Qian Zhuang swear.

On the big day, Qian Zhuang and Xiaowu both downed a glass of hard liquor. Qian Zhuang's face finally cleared up. He and Xiaowu talked about the local weather and how to properly cook braised pork with stewed eggs and chicken feet with stewed mushrooms. Ruhua listened silently; their conversation was both near and far from her. The next day, the boss of the mine didn't show up, but the skinny man took the agreement and asked Ruhua to sign and press her red-inked fingerprint. The compensation and funeral expenses added up to 320,000. After signing, they went to the bank for payment.

After ages of being manipulated and coerced by the fat cat and thin pawn, there was an empty urn in Qian Zhuang's embrace. It was over. Ruhua would finally "see" Qian Yu. Was Qian Yu still the same as before? Ruhua recalled her memory of Qian Yu over and over again. It was originally clear, but the finer details had already become blurred. It was as if Qian Yu were angry and didn't want to be mentally painted by her mind's brush. Ruhua bowed her head in despair.

The car stopped by the river. The thin man led them through the winding path and stopped in front of a pavilion. There were several black spots on the frozen river. Ruhua couldn't make out what they were exactly. The thin man pointed to the endless sky of black and grey across the street. "There."

It took that long for Ruhua to figure out that Qian Yu was still at the bottom of the mine, somewhere deep in the endless mountains. Only then did she howl. The thin man took a step back and carefully and rightfully said that they had signed an agreement. Xiaowu hugged her tightly as she wailed. Ruhua's tears couldn't flow anymore. She was shaking like a bunch of dried firewood, completely out of control.

Two days later, the three returned to Songzhuang Village. The urn fell in her hand, and she grasped firm hold. That was her husband, the ever-smiling Qian Yu. The box contained a shirt and a pair of underpants belonging to him, but her husband had become an urn.

Qian Yu was buried, and Ruhua served as Qian Zhuang's shadow. In just a few days, she became accustomed to Qian Zhuang's arrangement. At the entrance of the village, Ruhua saw her mother holding herself and her father with swollen eyes. Beside them was a three-wheeled car. Her mother wanted to take Ruhua back to rest for a few days. Ruhua looked at Qian Zhuang.

Her mother gave her a gentle push. Qian Zhuang said that it would be better to go back and stay for a few days, as it was and always would be her home. Her mother thanked Qian Zhuang and invited him "home" when he was free, saying that they were still a family. Before Ruhua sat down, her mother had her father get behind the wheel. As the car bounced and banged along, Ruhua unexpectedly fell asleep. It was far from sound rest, of course. She heard her mother mutter under her breath, saying she couldn't put a ball and chain on her own daughter for the rest of her life.

Like in the hotel, Ruhua only ate and slept. Day blended with night, and her body simply existed in the moment. No one forced her to do anything. Fire and thunder didn't fight, at least not that Ruhua could hear. The first night, Ruhua finally sat up like a human being. She asked her mother what it was she heard going on outside. It was firecrackers. Ruhua knew it was New Year's Eve. She washed her hair and wanted to help her mother prepare, but her mother wouldn't let her lift a finger. Ruhua watched for a while, then leaned against the glass and remained motionless until her mother called for her.

The next morning, Ruhua said goodbye to her mother, who was shocked and asked where Ruhua was going. Songzhuang Village. Her mother said that she was already "at home." Ruhua lowered her head and didn't argue. "That place doesn't have anything to do with you anymore. If you need to grab anything, just let your brother do it or ask your father to go with him. You're in no state to do that. You need your rest." Her mother dropped her voice, but Ruhua was resolute. Xiaowu held her back, saying she had to eat first. She didn't object. Why bother objecting? After eating a dumpling, Ruhua put down her chopsticks.

After dinner, her mother continued to try to convince Ruhua and even got into how life's dishes were often served cold with spare pinches of spice. It was clear she was worried about Ruhua. Ruhua understood this, but she was determined. Her own mother might not have known why. She didn't want to tell her mother that Qian Bao needed her care; neither did she want to tell her that it was Qian Yu's final request to her. Ruhua was Ruhua, but Ruhua was no longer a tearful bubble. Her mother used her trump card, sat down at the door, and said that Ruhua would have to physically force her out of the way. Ruhua jumped onto the kang, opened the window, and jumped out. Ruhua heard her mother shouting behind her, but she couldn't make out the exact words. She fell to the ground and ran away.

When Ruhua entered the yard, she shouted to the interior. Qian Bao didn't respond. Ruhua knocked on the door, pushed it open, and shouted again to make sure whether Qian Bao was there. She then opened the door of the main room. When she married, the main house belonged to her and Qian Yu. The fragrance of the flowers was like a wall that caused her to fall into a marvellous trance. The pots of clivias, pendulous golden bells, roses, and red such-and-such flowers she had long forgotten the proper name for were neither dead nor frozen. They were green, and the perennial begonias were in full bloom. Ruhua's head was in the clouds. Qian Yu? Could he be back? Inside? Outside? Ruhua stared for a long time and opened the clay stove. Warm, as expected. Because Ruhua liked to plant flowers, Qian Yu changed the iron stove into a clay stove. The furnace could keep warm all night. Only one person could take care of the flowers for her, though. Ruhua knew who it was.

Ruhua suddenly entered the house, and Qian Zhuang and his wife Song Lihua were moderately shocked to see her. Qian Zhuang reacted quickly and urged his wife to cook dumplings for Ruhua. Being met by the icepick-like eyes of her eldest brother-in-law and his wife, Ruhua suddenly felt her heart in her throat. She lowered her head and said she had eaten. Immediately, she raised her head again and looked directly at Qian Bao, who was seated at the table.

6

After a long time, Ruhua still didn't want to believe that Qian Yu had left her. Qian Yu couldn't have been serious. He might have been playing around with her, or this was another strange bet of his. Only Qian Yu's shirt and underwear were buried under the earth in the bag. Qian Yu himself had to be hiding somewhere. He promised to plant flowers in the sky. He never failed to hold up to his promises. What about this time? He just wanted to surprise her.

Sure enough, Ruhua heard Qian Yu call to her. With one sound, she woke up immediately. She looked at the wall, the corner, and the flowerpots again and again. Qian Yu was playing hide-and-seek with her, and he hid as soon as she looked at him. Ruhua walked out into the wilderness and the woods once again. There were constant calls around her, but every time she turned around, Qian Yu disappeared again. Sometimes, Ruhua would ask Qian Bao for confirmation. She asked him if he could hear his brother. Qian Bao looked puzzled. "When did he come back?"

"Never mind. Just eat your food," she replied, though she mentally chastised him for not being able to hear his brother's clear voice.

Ruhua suddenly became afraid of people coming. Those people were of all kinds, visiting, persuading, comforting, some beating around the bush, some being more direct in their words, saying things like death is final and that people can't come back from the dead. They constantly confirmed and solidified the idea that Qian Yu had gone to another plane. Ruhua felt torn between Qian Yu's calls and the "kind" words calling her back to reality, like being bathed in warm water and then thrown into an ice cellar. Ruhua was eager for warmth. She ran into the wild to avoid those people, but sometimes, it was unavoidable, such as when her mother came over. She had no choice but to follow.

Song Lihua, Ruhua's sister in-law, came most often. She was most unlike Qian Zhuang, who towered over her by more than a head. The two of them were like comparing apples to oranges. Qian Zhuang was similar to Lv Bu, that famous general from the times of the Eastern Han dynasty often caricatured in plays and operas. Song Lihua was rather ordinary, though she did have peculiar freckles that bespeckled her nose. In terms of shrewdness and competence, however, Song Lihua was a worthy competitor of Qian Zhuang, though she was still blackened by his shadow. Song Lihua was low key on the whole. She never failed to come back from the field empty-handed, holding either a bundle of grey cabbage or a bag of jelly-ear mushrooms. If she didn't bring supplies with her, she would take off her coat and bind the cuffs with fur and grass to form a makeshift basket. The upper part of the cabbage would be used for dumplings, while the lower part would be fed to pigs or rabbits. The jelly ears were dried in bunches and sold to fungus dealers together with the ground-picked mushrooms they had. At the exchange meeting in Yingpan, other people used detached bicycle frames as on-the-spot mazhas for watching opera, while Song Lihua would be carrying a paper tray containing buckwheat powder she prepared earlier as well as small capsules of vinegar, some of which had a mighty nip to it. She didn't enter the centre of the theatre. There were just too many people there. She was always about ten yards away from the theatre itself, selling powder and watching from afar. Being short was no disadvantage from such a distance. Those who purchased her wares were mostly outside the main hub as well, so it was easier for her to get to her clientele. They basically threw money at her, and she did the same toward her savings. She'd contributed quite a sum to Qian Zhuang, whose shop was set up not only for selling goods, but for entertainment. Two tables were there that people could freely use to play cards or mahjong. Song Lihua would whip up most scrumptious delicacies, like lamb broth pork, cow's head, and horse chittlins. The aroma would flow from the establishment and pour into the street, and with that, the entertainment room became a restaurant. No money? Start a tab or offer some grain. Better yet, sell the grain to the town mill and bring back the earnings. Rations for the village were growing short, so people began to flood the distribution centre. Qian Zhuang had Song Lihua see what she could get. What she could procure was adequate to make a meal, but Song Lihua turned her nose up at it. Instead, she ran to the bridge and waited for everyone to stop eating. There really was no rhyme or reason to it all. She just felt like that was the thing to do. One thing led to another, and while everyone at the distribution centre went home empty-handed after gorging, she was able to get an extra bag with two piglets at fifty yuan each. She sold both for ninety a pop two weeks later. Everyone got their meal. Song Lihua got eighty yuan to pad her pocket. A fortune teller once said her face was a money magnet, able to bring great fortune to her husband. Qian Zhuang kept an eye on her. He needed to keep the gears well oiled.

Song Lihua always came at night, often "just passing by." She rarely did, though, when Qian Yu was around. Qian Yu and his uncle had starkly different temperaments. Ruhua and Song Lihua were far from the same. Ruhua would get nervous if Song Lihua came around, but Song Lihua wasn't as harsh as others. What she said had nothing to do with Ruhua at all, so Ruhua welcomed new chatter that didn't affect her.

That day, Song Lihua came in and said something about being parched, pouring two large bowls of freshly boiled and slightly cooled water down her throat. Ruhua was puzzled and asked what caused her to be so thirsty. Song Lihua said that she had just come out of Wan Liu's house. Wan Liu had taken out five pounds of meat on credit the past year during the Dragon Boat Festival. He perhaps forgot all about it, but the tab remained unpaid. Wan Liu and his wife were famous for saving face, and Song Lihua had a way of not getting to the point. She tried to enlighten Wan Liu and remind the couple using roundabout words, but they had truly forgotten all about the ordeal. In the end, Song Lihua had to just come out and say it. She also carried the account book for Wan Liu to read. After a lot of talking, her mouth felt like cotton. Ruhua asked Song Lihua what happened in the end. In truth, it really wasn't the biggest deal. They genuinely forgot, but Song Lihua felt so embarrassed for speaking so directly that she feared what the couple might be saying behind her back. Ruhua just sat there, uncertain of how to respond. She didn't know how to comfort others, so the only thing she mustered up was a, "You shouldn't think that way." That somehow seemed to work. Song Lihua spoke on how relatives don't think that way and that her good standing didn't come from nowhere.

Ruhua was honest but not dim-witted and saw how things were coming to light. She chided herself for not having seen it coming. She told Song Lihua that she would help to pay the tab the next day. Song Lihua had the look of having just been slapped across the face, a look that soon turned to unease and annoyance. "So that's it then? That's why you think I'm here? Don't worry, Ruhua. I won't darken your door in the future." Ruhua's face started to burn. She tried to say that she only felt like offering. "It's fine," Song Lihua replied. "Just let it go. You're one of the few that Zhuang knows hasn't skinned me alive yet." Ruhua replied by saying she wouldn't tell Qian Zhuang. Song Lihua sighed. "What more can I say, Ruhua?"

The next day, Ruhua went to return the 20,000 Qian Yu

had borrowed when he married her. She almost forgot that she still had a card with 320,000 on it that she got because of Qian Yu's passing. She had the money sent to Qian Zhuang himself. After a while, Qian Zhuang came to the door and asked if Song Lihua had asked for it. Ruhua shook her head. Qian Zhuang's demeanour relaxed, and he muttered how that was a good thing. He also said that if Ruhua had no money, he would never request the 20,000. Although it was borrowed by Qian Yu, he accepted that it was money long gone and told Ruhua not to think much about it. "I know." Qian Zhuang said that the rest could be deposited over time with higher interest. "Mm-hmm." Qian Zhuang glanced over the crowd of flowerpots and gave a heavy sigh.

Ruhua went into town again and liquidated the card. Ruhua saw the card as something foreign, but the numbers on the bills did something to awaken her. The numbers were voiceless, but their effect was stronger than the most persuasive speech. Qian Yu was gone forever, but his likeness was expressed in the numbers. Though he had become numbers, those same numbers could not turn back into Qian Yu. Qian Yu had become numbers on her account. Qian Zhuang had no idea about how his brother was able to plant flowers in the sky. His glance across the flowerpots was like a whip. If he had known, perhaps his gaze would have been more like a knife.

Qian Zhuang ended up tilling the land for Ruhua, who finished planting in a few days' time. She refrained from going toward the ridge, and she also avoided the front and back of the house. Instead, she focused on the small plot originally dedicated to gardening. The packet of flower seeds was put into a bag and buried in a corner, but she really didn't want to let them go. Her feelings on this were so strong that she dug it all up again two days later and hid the sack and its contents in the cabinet.

One night in the middle of June, Ruhua heard Qian Yu call her. This wasn't a game of hide-and-seek as before. He squatted in the flowerpot, smiling, but his face was black, like coal.

"When did you get back?" Ruhua asked.

"It's been some time."

"Why is your face so black?"

Qian Yu winked. "Guess."

"I can't."

"To plant flowers in the sky, of course, like you guessed before."

"How can you plant flowers in the sky if I don't plant anymore?"

"Want to make a bet?"

Ruhua shook her head. Qian Yu stood up. "Are you leaving me?" she asked.

"I never left." With one arm, Qian Yu flew up, turned into a crow, flew around the room, and soared out the window.

Ruhua woke from her dream. Everything was so vivid and lifelike. She looked left and right and suddenly jumped down and ran out. There was a crow squatting on the branch at the door. It was dawn, so the light made everything clear. "Is that you, Qian Yu?" The crow cackled, started from the branch, and flew north.

Ruhua bolted from the yard, crossed the street, and chased the crow. After running through the fields and woods, Ruhua stopped. On both sides of Butterfly River, hundreds of crows stood and perched on the grass, as if holding a grand meeting. Ruhua wept with joy. Qian Yu had come back as a crow. She didn't know where Qian Yu was, but she knew he was in the middle somewhere. He was just playing another round of hide-and-seek with her.

Ruhua's soul finally felt at peace. With Qian Yu, everything was the same as before.

Still, she would never think that during that bitter October four years later, Mao Gen would brutally shoot and kill her man-turned-crow of a husband.

Chapter III

Zunai

1

My eyes leaped over the dusty mugworts and the shy white and purple potato flowers and skipped between the broad leaves and slender stalks of corn. I didn't see any cobs, but I knew they were hidden among the dense foliage, not yet fully formed, but like milk bubbles, their sweet aroma more than just attractive. I grasped hold of the toolbox and took in a whiff.

I looked back and saw that my father hadn't quite finished relieving himself against the tree. He redid his pants, his back against the road. The way he went about it made it seem like he was nodding to the dead poplar in front of him. He always had a strange way of doing things, sitting up in the middle of the night and asking things like, "Why isn't it dawn yet, Damei?" I didn't care, at least not particularly. The corn field tempted me, and I was a little anxious. After a while, I looked back again. Dad still stood in front of the dead tree, motionless, as if frozen. Something was up. I shouted, but my father didn't answer. I let go of the toolbox and jumped into action. My father was only about twenty yards out, but I rushed toward him as fast as I could go, almost headbutting the dead tree in the process. Dad reached out and blocked me from the certain collision. I almost cried out. "Don't move!" he exclaimed, his voice not loud, but serious, nervous, and somewhat mysterious. I felt a chill creep through my spine, and the tip of my head went numb. Dad wasn't staring into the depths of the forest, where the worst of the worst happened. Instead, he was staring at the trunk of the tree. The bark was still rough and dark, though without water. "Are we looking at a cash cow?" I wondered why my father was speaking such nonsense. I muttered a grunt-like response and traced his gaze with my own eyes, landing on a black ant struggling to climb its way up the trunk. The chills intensified throughout my body. Black ants, fire ants, and termites often visited me in their dreams, monsters to be slayed. When they appeared, however, no matter how much I fought, I could never win against the mighty colonies dragging my mother away. I was bitterly weak each time I woke from one of those. It was as if I were fighting in a war. Yet my father was interested in this very ant? "I thought I drowned the thing." Turned out he aimed directly at it with his stream. The hole his urine had carved in the bark was still there. He began to do his pants in a statement of victory when he saw that the ant had somehow managed to survive, as if resurrected. What's more, the critter decided to try to climb the tree. Dad could have strangled the ant, but instead, he remained still, unable to believe it alive and able to run. From his viewpoint, he was staring at a real-life miracle.

My father and I looked at each other and covered the ant that smelled of urine. It was a small but mighty lone warrior, trudging through the wind-blown scars in the bark as it fought its way up. Two branches up, I noted the hole leading to the anthill. Streams of similar-looking ants were entering and exiting. Dad kicked the trunk. "Go on home, then. Live another day."

If it hadn't been for the sheep driver Li Gui whom we were supposed to meet, if it weren't that very season, if that ant had slipped past our glances, Dad and I would have never placed our roots in Songzhuang Village. What was fate, anyway? The question seemed to always linger in my mind, but the answer was never truly clear.

The mud took the shape of two semicircles that looked like a butterfly, and the streams were like its antennae, twisting and turning until converging a couple miles off. North, north again, then southward, but strangest of all were the real butterflies flying along the banks. Their tan wings were half the size of one's palm. There were pink ones, too, and the two colours could remind one of poplar leaves. The dark blue ones were like beanstalk flowers. The blossoming golden lotuses formed in clusters, like gold ingots from Heaven.

I immediately liked this place. Nothing foreboding seemed to linger in the air, and my mind had steered clear from that direction anyway. I was young, after all. I didn't know then that the more I wanted something, the greater said thing would end up costing me. But in this world, who could bear going day to day with nothing to show for it? Giving up in and of itself was no easy task. To give up often cost more than paying the fair price.

The village was on the west bank of Butterfly River, and to the west was Naobao Mountain. There were hundreds of families living there. It was said that it was the largest village outside the Great Wall, a village that existed during the reign of the Qianlong Emperor. There were two willow trees in front of the village, one of which had a thick trunk like a human's waist, curly branches, and a huge mushroom crown, making it grander than the one I'd seen at the inn in Gaobeidian. The other one, shorter and thinner, was born from an old willow tree. People in Songzhuang Village called the two willows mother and child.

My father and I stayed at Li Fubo's house. Li Fubo, his sick wife, and his three children lived in the main structure, which had two rooms. The inside was more than a foot underground, making it seem like entering a cave. The first time I went in, I almost fell over. My father and I were placed in a side room, which was even lower than the main house in terms of elevation but didn't have such a stark contrast between the interior and exterior landings, making our lodging more comfortable on the whole. The only disadvantage was that the door hinges were harsh and heavy, and the latch was tighter than the strongest bite. It wasn't all for nothing, though. My father was able to earn our abode, keeping this side of sure disaster. Bean curds, pig's feet, and tobacco were all bought for and offered to Li Fubo, calico and locally procured medicine for his sick wife, a grindstone for the eldest son Li Dawang, hair ties for his second child, a daughter named Li Erni, and sesame candy for his youngest, a son with two extra digits. Naturally, Li Fubo's plates, bowls, and vegetable jars passed through my father's hands, and all of them were soon watertight.

There were many lands outside the Great Wall, but with them came their owners. Qian Guangwan owned the most, with thousands of mu that he accumulated by purchasing a dozen or so whenever he could over the years. Those lands were of good soil quality and suitable for farming. Still, the idea that one sesame cake could be exchanged for a mu was not laughable, but the mu in question were on the side of Naobao Mountain that was the most rugged and debris-ridden, meaning backbreaking work to just get a single plot. Li Fubo's six mu of land were gnawed out in this way. It took him five years. You had to get out all the gravel and rubble, dig deep, carry away the larger stones, and then screen the soil with a coarse sieve. If the soil was shallow, you needed to carry more in from the shore of Butterfly Lake. Then you would have to build a dam to prevent the water from washing away the fine soil. Pig, chicken, and sheep droppings would then be dried, crushed, and mixed into the soil. Locals called the final fertilization process "feeding," a nod to the idea that the soil would find its way into your stomach, allowing you to become one with the land. The final step was cultivation. After planting a crop, the land would absorb the fragrance of the plants and exude life and virility.

Dad frowned. Things appeared much harder than mending a bowl. Li Fubo said that some people didn't want to spend the effort and would rather rent land for a large amount of money, but he himself thought it would be better to have his own land. He could come and go as he wanted that way. This remark touched Dad's heart as well as stabbed it with a hidden blade. He couldn't forget the acres he had in Yucheng, as if they were still named after him. Still, my father hesitated. Li Fubo said that if my father made up his mind, he could ask Dawang to help. Dawang had nothing else but strength. After talking it over with me, my father asked Dawang to take me along as he went out to mend. My father said that if we couldn't bear the hardship, we could leave at any time. The world was so big. Surely, there were other places to live.

The second time my father climbed Naobao Mountain was one month later. Dawang and I had carved out a piece of land about the size of a bed, but we had yet to do any screening. Only the first two steps had been completed. Dad grasped the clay, twisted it in his hand, smelled it, put it in his mouth, and chewed it. His eyes suddenly became teary. He later said that he smelled Yucheng. The smell was mixed with wheat, corn, beans, and perhaps the sound of the frogs in the pond. My father was finally moved. He heard the sound of seeds falling and sprouting. He and I were the two largest seeds. We just needed planting to turn this village into our home. Dad looked up. "What say you, Damei?"

I was surprised at my response. "Standing here, I can see a golden lotus."

Li Fubo was a bright bulb. One day, my father suddenly

realized that Fubo's head was in the stars, which set off this huge, gnarled knot in Dad's heart, but not then. Li Fubo said that the land could not be reclaimed in two days, let alone fed. The top priority was to build a house. He made it abundantly clear that it wasn't that he didn't want us living there over the winter; it was just that overwintering was a difficult feat. He didn't say how difficult, just that it was. There seemed to be something hidden behind the words. This would only add to Dad's complete list of grievances against him when all was said and done.

With the help of Li Fubo, my father began to build a house just to the west. Finally, we would have a house beyond Yucheng. Dad had a spark in his step, often getting up at the crack of dawn. There were stones at the southwest end of Naobao Mountain. The sod used for building the house wall was shovelled from the grass. The soil bearing weeds wasn't good for brickmaking, but it was still waterproof. My father's toolbox contained silver at the very bottom. He used it to buy rafters, make doors, and build windows. Like Li Fubo's home, ours sank deep into the ground. I only later understood why these homes had their cave-like appearance.

My father, Li Fubo, Li Dawang, and I were the four brains and eight hands behind the project. There were times, however, when Li Erni carried something our way. We also hired professionals when it came to some odd jobs like setting doors and windows. Later on, I detailed the whole ordeal to Qiao Shitou, who yawned the whole time. Chronicle-like tales were such a bore to him. His life was much different than before. I heard word that the mayor had to make an appointment to see him. I understood why he wouldn't have found any interest in the tale, but this was my life's first major project, something I could never forget.

My father and I were immersed in joy. We had no idea that disaster was looming overhead.

2

The ant was scurrying.

3

When my father entered the courtyard, I smelled the aroma. It wasn't any ordinary incense. The strings of various odours lingered in the air, just waiting to hook both nose and tongue of anyone passing by. This particular one had me looking around for its source, though. When the water boiled, I threw the noodles into the small iron pot that followed us from Yucheng. We stayed at Li Fubo's house, but we ate separately. The stove was set in the corner of the western room. I scooped out the noodles, and my father picked up his chopsticks. I turned to the toolbox again, not even trying to hide my gaze. Father buried his head and said nothing. After dinner, my father slowly opened the box. Although it was wrapped in paper, I still recognized that it was a stewed pig's foot. "Smells nice, doesn't it?" Dad asked. The gift was undoubtedly for Li Fubo. My father let me admire it, but he didn't send it off to the family right away. There was calculation involved in his generosity.

I had been in and out of the main house many times, and every time I felt like falling into a hole. Those in Li Fubo's family had just finished eating and were licking their bowls clean, even the sick mother of the household. Li Fubo had a long tongue and would make a large swipe before picking at the remnants, like a grain of rice or half a cabbage leaf. Everyone had the habit of turning the bowl on its edge. Better for the tongue to reach in, especially in Li Fubo's case. There was also the added benefit of checking on the others to make sure they'd left nothing behind.

The ceremony was in progress, wrists held high. It was all automatic. When I went in, they looked at each other, including Li Fubo. Then I heard a clatter. Li Sanbao's bowl fell. Li Sanbao had one extra finger and one extra toe, both of which were longer than their counterparts. In total, he had eleven fingers and eleven toes. The extra finger and toe not only didn't help, but also made him clumsy. He couldn't run like other children. He walked like a duck. Li Sanbao didn't drop his bowl because of me. I guess he was shocked by the smell of the pig's foot. His father didn't scold him. Li Sanbao was a sick child like his mother. Li Fubo couldn't bear a harsh word, but Li Erni's mouth did the job for him. "Nincompoop!"

I was greedy, but I didn't want to drool. That night, the pig's foot had somehow become Li Fubo's, and the scent's hook was still scratching at me. Would the pig's foot be kept until the next day or eaten that night? It'd be a pity to eat it that night. You could smell it all night if left for the next day. The aroma was both a comfort and a malice. The foot couldn't be divided, but even if it could, Dawang would certainly have gotten the scraps, naïve as he was. Even if he were granted more, Erni would be able to coax some out of him. Sanbao would certainly have gotten the most, probably with their mother's share to boot. And Erni? She was nothing in stature compared to Sanbao, who was the most loved of the three. Erni was sly, though, and her stomach would have surely ached at the sight. When it came to starting a fire, cooking, washing the dishes, and cleaning the pots, Erni was the one who handled it all. Should she up and strike, Li Fubo's family would be in an uproar. I knew all this after living in their western room for less than two weeks. I became worried about Li Fubo's decision. Should and could he divide the pig's foot?

The shouts and cries from the internal struggle caused me to run back to the main house with my father in tow. I thought Erni must have scratched at either Dawang or Sanbao, but I was wrong. It was worse than I could have ever imagined. Erni succumbed to the temptation to snatch the pig's foot, and Sanbao caught her in the act. Erni was unable to swallow the whole thing in time, and the meat got stuck in her throat. Li Fubo was furious, but the red anger turned into green worry when he saw Erni's face turning blue.

Dad came up with the idea to use chopsticks, but it was in vain. Dawang twisted her by the arm. Li Fubo tore at her jaw and upper lip. Her tongue flapped around, allowing Dad to get the chopsticks down there, but Erni shied away at the sight. Instead, Dad grabbed a sharp hook, but he couldn't see the foreign object lodged within. He had to trust it by feel alone. In the end, though, Erni retched, and Dad patted her on the back. "There, there."

Many years later, I became a midwife and gained another skill. Without tools, I could remove foreign objects from any throat. I found this out by treating pregnant women. No one taught me, except for perhaps God on High. Still, many people's lives were saved by that skill, Erni included.

With the meat out of her throat, Erni squatted on the ground, crying and spitting blood. Dad, covered in sweat, breathed a huge sigh of relief. After all, he was the culprit. He had reason to worry. Li Fubo didn't know what to do and said something like, "Where are all the smiles at?"

The next day, Li Erni crept up on me. I thought she was trying to get close. She was neither as enthusiastic about me as Li Dawang nor as curious as Li Sanbao. From day one, she was hostile. Her looks were fine. The people of Songzhuang Village called her "upright," but her gaze never met people in the eye. Instead, it would fall somewhere by the corners. Back then, I didn't know that Li Erni would be such a pest for so many years. My father saved her. You would think that would have made her want to get closer, but what she said stunned me. Her voice was hoarse from the accident, but it still stung like bitter cold. "Aren't you going to say anything?" I shook my head. "I told Sanbao that I'd tear him a new one if he ever spat nonsense out of his grill." I had never been so directly threatened. I looked at the girl who was the same age as me, but much shorter than me. "So are your pretty lips going to say anything?" My gaze drifted. I had to maintain some level of dignity. I was living in their home, after all. I swore to myself not to think of Erni's eyes as being any different. "We friends or what?" I nodded. "Cool. Fair trade then." I asked what she meant. "Secrets. Got any?" I hesitated. Li Erni's lips curled. "I know you got some." To win her trust, I talked about stealing corn. "That's it?" she asked, disappointed. "Right. That's one. Fair trade." Then she told me in a hushed voice that Li Sanbao wet the bed every night and was as timid as a mouse. I asked about Erni herself. "Two for one's not a fair trade." Then she left in a twirl.

The pig's foot incident was just a rehearsal. A bigger mishap was waiting as we built our home.

On the day we were to finish our roof, a ton of people came, all of whom were uninvited. Li Fubo said in advance that it was a Song custom to eat cake when a roof was done. Those who came didn't need to offer money. They just had to bring cake. Li Fubo was busy, and Dad was out and about. Yellow rice noodles and sesame oil were bought a few days in advance. Bean curds were bought two days prior and were ready to be stewed with the potatoes. Of course, Li Erni and I were too busy. We invited two adult women to cook. The first half of the day was relatively smooth, and things were jubilant outside the house. Erni bit off some bean curd from time to time, and I stared at her. My cravings dwelled in the heart, while hers were always in her mouth, especially when it came to bean curds and onions. I couldn't help but remind her that onions left horridly bad breath. Li Erni's corner of her eye immediately twitched straight up. "Everything's strange to people living under a rock. So much food now that empty stomachs aren't a thing. You know, Damei, it's always best to avoid building a house if you can't afford to finish it." Her statement was so off the cuff that it seemed deliberately provocative. "Upright" as she was, I didn't know how to respond. Just then, firecrackers went off, and I ran out as an excuse. Some random village people were hanging a red couplet on the excess sandalwood. The moment the sandalwood fell off, the house would be christened.

The smell of fried cake was no less powerful than that of pig's feet. The cake itself was usually too difficult for anyone to eat. Some can't even manage to swallow a bite during Chinese New Year. Such a delicacy, once earned, was often let go because of this. Li Fubo asked my father to buy more yellow rice noodles to prevent empty stomachs, but the way it came out gave Dad the impression that it was unlucky to be short-handed. My father wasn't stingy, though a migrant. He viewed the whole thing as an opportunity to make a name for himself, so he bought loads. Two women whispered that the mender was an awfully generous fellow. I was secretly pleased when I heard it. Even so, I still stared at Li Erni. Why did things turn out like they did? Even later, I never could tell. Although she slipped a lot of food into her mouth, Li Erni still seemed to have enough hunger to last years. Was she afraid of choking again? Honestly, it was probably for the best, since Dad wouldn't have been able to hook a piece of heavy cake out of that gorge of hers.

Alas … someone fell to the ground. Not Li Erni, but Wu

Kui.

The scene was shocking, especially with the festive air lingering. Four middle-aged men quickly picked up Wu Kui and went out of the village toward the shore. A group of people followed, some adults but mostly children. Seven or eight dogs were barking after them. The four men were placed two in front and two behind. Wu Kui's head was pitched forward over his knees in an attempt to relieve his cramping stomach. He had eaten thirty-seven cakes. I never caught who said that. The four kept moving, grabbing toads, worms, and other critters to shove in Wu Kui's mouth to make him sick enough to vomit. Such was how the people of Song treated those who ate too much. From the mud shore, the four men turned and worked on Wu Kui, trying to keep him conscious. There were fewer people chasing behind than before, but there were more dogs. They weren't barking, but their long tongues were out like on a summer day.

I was always one who lagged behind. While escaping famine, I saw too many people fall to the ground due to hunger and become covered with loess. It was my first time seeing something like this, though. Of course, I wasn't that much worked up, perhaps at first a little bit, but fear took hold soon after.

Wu Kui opened his mouth wide, but nothing fell out except a string of saliva. He stopped breathing before making it to the bottom of Naobao Mountain. Wu Kui's personal mantra was never to die from starvation. He got his wish.

The cake was stuffed by Wu Kui himself. His "criminal

record" made it easy for his father to just let things go. His family kept things on the hush, but he was still the relative of some official. Li Fubo led Dad to the Qian Family's courtyard. Qian Guangwan negotiated with him. Dad lost a large sum of money before he was pacified.

A few days later, my father took me to their door to thank him. We worked in the Qian compound for three days and even repaired the lid of the seasoning tank. One catastrophe avoided, another buried.

4

Ruhua had long gone, but I could still hear her desperate cries ringing in my ears. What in Heaven's name could be said about this child?

Ruhua came to see me several times. The very first, she was escorted in by her mother at the age of twelve. Such a shy soul, like a flower in a crack on the wall. Her mother asked her to call me Zunai in a voice that reminded me of a kitten. There was no way for me to remember every child I had delivered. Only the most special engrained themselves within my mind. Ruhua was one. She seemed like a natural birth, but lo and behold, the umbilical cord was strangling her. Her face was a strange blue, and that plus her striking eyes really gave her a pitiful appearance akin to a pouting flower. I beckoned her forward. She stopped halfway. Her mother, in a frenzy, shoved her into my arms. I hugged her tightly. "There, there." Her mother only sighed and said Ruhua lost spirit often, crying at the drop of a hat. "People and plants have all sorts of natures. Wheat's wheat and can't become a tree, no matter how much you want it to." Her mother didn't take my words to heart and went back to scolding Ruhua as they left.

The second time was when she got married in Song and came with her husband, Qian Yu, to my door, asking for my blessing. I was catatonic by that point, one foot in the grave. What could I do? I knew of all sorts of regimens for protecting children *in utero*, but my mouth could say nothing. The third visit, she told me about how Qian Yu had become a crow. Her tongue seemed bent as the words escaped her lips.

She said this to me at great risk. Even in the most ancient of days, none could tolerate nonsensical words. Still, regardless of whether Qian Yu actually became a crow, flower, bird, crop, or bug, what was most important was Ruhua's conviction. Belief equates to truth; unbelief, untruth. Believe the day to be good, and so it is. The opposite is also true. Same with gods and whether they be lingering near to one's heart or mere fantasy. Qian Yu could have become a crow, but her belief in it allowed her turmoil to drift away like vapor. This was most fortunate for her soul. Her heart beat once again. Her demeanour did have an effect on others, but no one despised her. Her quirks never hurt anyone. Calmness ruled. Songzhuang Village opened its arms to her, or perhaps it simply honoured its ties to Qian Zhuang.

Mao Gen had a grudge against me. All in Song had been by my bedside save him. I couldn't blame him. Honestly, I felt guilty instead, but his and my issue remained between us. Should he wish revenge, there I was, but why shoot Ruhua's crow husband? I hoped it wasn't on purpose, out of hatred. Even so, would Ruhua's solace return?

"Zunai, lunch," Maixiang whispered. "Are you tired after the morning?"

The ant was scurrying again.

5

The winter descended with a bang, and suddenly, violently, there was no time to prepare. The night before, Li Erni and I were out dancing in the moonlight. Li Erni's attitude toward me changed a lot after I entered the Qians' courtyard. Later, I learned that it was an honour. Not everyone had the opportunity to enter and leave the Qian Family abode, especially children of my age. In the early morning, the north wind cut the face like a knife, and white steam swirled around the mouth when speaking. When water splashed on the ground, the ground sizzled as if fried, but instead of grease came ice, slippery ice that was dangerous if one wasn't careful.

My father and I were fully equipped that day, having donned a dog-leather hat and cotton-padded overwear, pants, and shoes. I also had an extra lambskin vest. Thanks to Li Fubo's warning, we prepared our winter wardrobe in advance. "The first winter is hard; the next is better after experience," Fubo chanted. At the end of autumn, my father and I returned to going out mending, but after the whole ordeal with Wu Kui, our funds were depleted. The clothing was effective. I even began to sweat. I told Dad I needed a break. He said we shouldn't for fear of getting hungry and not being able to move farther forward. Some villagers allowed us to mend things in their homes, but others ignored my father's offers. We ended up setting up a stall in the corner of our shelter. Dad didn't complain. He said that people let us in out of sympathy, with nothing to be said if they didn't. The distance between the villages outside the Great Wall was very far. For more than one village, my father walked fast. Fortunately, I had a pair of big feet. Mom refused to bind them, so I could easily keep up. One day, we went super far, and Dad suggested we stay in the county seat, but after sunset, we turned back anyway. Staying at an inn cost money. Returning to Song was more profitable. Dad speculated that my hormones were acting up and said it would be more comfortable to stay at home, where I could sleep the day away, but I never, ever slept in. He of course woke me before dawn. Was that truly more comfortable? Perhaps it was the new house, but I always felt that things were damp. I was comfortable, yes, for I didn't need to live under the dragon king's downpours and gusts in the middle of the night, shaking me out of a good slumber. My father and I had been sleeping in the open for many years. Those two low rooms were not the only places to sleep; there were others. I was a little unhappy, but the dying moon was hanging in the middle of the sky, and I was pushed away by desire. I had never felt this way before.

One night, my father and I lay down early, and my father began to snore. My father didn't let me carry the toolbox. He said that my bones had yet to thicken enough to bear it. It was a heavy thing, even without anything else in tow, and we always walked a long way. One day, my father was sore all over and fell asleep mid-word. The wind blew white, and its voice was melancholy and miserable, like the cry of a hungry wolf, as they said beyond the Great Wall. I didn't view it as a wolf, though, but dozens or even hundreds of horses, which seemed to be on the roof, the chimney, and the windowsill, also in the corner. The room was still warm, although the humidity was heavy. This was the advantage of the cave house. Those who couldn't afford to build a house dug a cave for the winter, put branches and firewood overhead, and erected a ladder to climb up and down. Outside the Great Wall, such was termed a mouse hole. Li Erni passed by. She curled her mouth and tilted her eyes, saying she really didn't see any notable difference between such our room and a proper mouse hole.

I couldn't sleep because of the howling wind, which sounded urgent that night, but it wasn't enough to scare me. But in the howling of the wolf, I heard other noises. After becoming a midwife, my ears developed extraordinary abilities. At that time, my ears seemed nothing special. But I heard it, clattering, broken, and hurried. I couldn't guess what kind of beast it was. Bigger than the wolf, but more agile. It was approaching. The earth seemed to tremble.

I couldn't help but rock my father and call him awake in a low voice. He was in the middle of a good dream in which he carried my mother to Songzhuang Village. They would have arrived in just a few more moments. Dad asked if it was time to get up, but I said no. He then asked what was up, and I told him to listen. "It's just the wind," he said. "Stop making something out of nothing. Tomorrow's an early day. Get to sleep." I disagreed. "Are you losing your good nerve?" I was silent. Perhaps it was just a passing fright. Perhaps it was just another type of wind. Dad turned over, and his snores returned. I eventually dozed myself. The rickety racket didn't fade, but it became something to chase in a dream.

The Qian Family abode was robbed that night. My father and I got up early but made it out of the village. None in Song could enter or exit. There were many bandits that year, including outside the Great Wall. There was one named "Hell Frozen Over," another called Ma Wuge, a third known as "One-Eyed Wolf," a fourth said to be Er Gedan, a fifth paraded as "Whirlwind" Liu, and some woman named Sai Xishi, who was known for being well-kempt but bitterly ruthless, pretending to be a good girl who only wanted to earn an income as a cleaning lady, just so that she could get her eyes on all the prospective loot. Each man that touched her, though, never touched anything again with the same hand. These bandits each had their calling card, marking their territory. Once a place was ransacked, there was no need for a second go, for the mark they left was clear. Large families would always send their goods and money to warehouse-like locations to keep them all safe from sneaking hands. The bandit who went after the Qian's was different, though. No calling card, and there was a mask worn. There was even a beeline made straight for Qian

Guangwan's sterling silver chamber pot. No one was hurt, but a lot was taken.

Dad and Li Fubo squatted face to face and smoked a bag of pipe tobacco away. Dad picked up the habit soon after our arrival in Songzhuang Village. Fubo told him the harrowing tale amid the plume. I couldn't tell if the story was exaggerated, but I could tell he was bursting at the seams wanting to get it all out. He seemed to know them. Dad grew wary, and Fubo changed the subject to calm him down. Bandits only wanted things from large families. "You two are slim pickings and have nothing to worry about, unless ..." he stopped, looked at me, leaned in, and whispered, "you get on their bad side. But if there's no provoking, it's all good." My father must have heard something else from Li Fubo's pause. Even I felt it.

When Li Fubo left, Dad stared at me. "That thing last night you heard," he said, "that was real?" I nodded. My father's eyes stiffened and went slightly bloodshot. His tone deepened. "Never speak a word of that. If anyone asks, play dumb. Your ears were deaf to it all." I understood, but only so far. "*Got it?!*" I had never seen my father upset in such a way, so I shouted out in dismay. I was frightened, frightened of my own father. Perhaps it was my pale face that softened him. "Sorry. It just came out of me. Just ... don't make me worry about you. Your mouth is to be sealed at every moment. Ignorance is bliss here and won't run you afoul."

My father's worry seemed to be unnecessary. Nobody questioned my father or me. The next day, we picked up the toolbox and went on the road again. The robbery of the Qian Family seemed to have become a distant memory, but two days later, as my father and I were out, we were stopped by uniformed men and thrown onto some carriage. Another carriage was close by, a triple-length. The driver of ours ordered us not to speak. We were being taken in. Li Erni used to show off the fact that she had ridden in a carriage once. She had the ability to fill me in on anything she had eaten, worn, seen, played with, or heard. Sometimes, it was enjoyable to hear. Other times, I couldn't stand it, especially when seeing her eyes twist the way they did. I always wanted to board a carriage. My wish was granted, but I should have been careful what I wished for. My father was nervous, but he still talked with me, or rather warned me, with his eyes. I answered him in kind. The two of us were equally nervous, but I also had a spark of curiosity. I closed my eyes and remembered Erni's words to see if the feeling matched. "You can just close your eyes and tell when it turns." Her showing off wasn't just make-believe after all.

Later, I learned that my father and I were escorted by the police of Zhangbei County. It was my first time to that particular county, and it was also my first time at a police station. Dad and I were initially put in the same cell, with nothing inside but straw, not even a bed or mat. It was like an ice cellar, so the two of us had to keep moving and stomping to keep warm. Eventually, Dad was taken out, and after what seemed like ages, it was my turn to be escorted to another building with a moonlit door right smack in the middle.

The room was dark, perhaps because of it being cloudy, but it was much warmer. The man who brought me in made me sit on the stool beside the wall. My nose kept running, so I had to keep wiping it with my sleeve. It was indecent, but what could I do to keep it from pouring into my mouth? Opposite was a big table with a chair behind it. After a while, a stout man with a face like a wax gourd came in, and the man who escorted me called him Sergeant Lu. Later, I learned that this Lu was judge and jury of major cases; minor cases were all tried by his subordinates.

"You cold?" Sergeant Lu stopped in the middle of the room. I hadn't recovered from the turbulence and panic, and his words seemed abrupt and unexpected. He didn't wait for me to answer or nod, but ordered the person who brought me to pour me a bowl of hot water. I looked at the door and asked where my father was in the smallest whisper. "Another room. You'll be rejoined soon enough." The sergeant sat down behind the table with a smile on his face that I couldn't fathom. When I held the hot water bowl, he waved his hand, and the man who saw me in backed out.

"It's all right," the sergeant said slowly. "Just bringing you two in to ask a few questions." I was about to put the bowl down. "You can finish that. It's okay. They didn't hit you, did they?" I shook my head. "That's good. I told them that you were craftworkers, not bandits. Go on." I carefully drank the water that had cooled down and wondered what he would ask.

"I've already had a few words with your father," he said, still smiling. "He told me everything. Just want to make sure your story lines up." I kept my feet together to hide my nerves, but he caught on. "It's all right. I don't beat answers out of girls like you." The sergeant was about forty years old, and his face was green and oily. "Just be truthful. If you lie, well, it'll be freezing in a few hours' time. There was this one bandit that we hung up on a tree. After he said nothing, we poured some water over him. His body was hard as a rock in no time." I shuddered. "Come. I'm reasonable. There's nothing to be afraid of. Just tell the truth. We clear?" I nodded.

The interrogation surprised me. It had more of a get-to-know-the-new-neighbour vibe. I was asked about where I was from, why I had come to Song, and why the cold beyond the Great Wall seemed so appealing. Wandering from famine, shaking in the suburbs of Beijing, dreaming about becoming a court mender, one plot of land for a sesame cake, all of it. I didn't expect that my memory would be so good that even the ice-sugar gourd promised by my father did not fall by the wayside. The sergeant slightly pulled at his lips. The drum of my heart was still beating. This man seemed to have thorns for eyes.

"Have you ever been to the Qian compound?" the sergeant suddenly interrupted me, and the drum burst with a roar. I nodded mechanically. The sergeant asked me to talk about the process, every day, what I did, what I saw, whether my father was with me, and whether I ever left alone. "What about you? Have you walked around the place?" I shook my head with a jerk. The sergeant seemed satisfied. He kneaded his greasy chin. I never thought in a million years he would ask such things. Who would have expected that his face would turn so suddenly? "Where is the meat drying room? You really haven't been there?" I almost fell off the stool. Li Erni once asked me if I met Qian Guangwan's aunt. People said that she was as thin as a tea bowl. After I shook my head, Li Erni was extremely disappointed. The corners of her eyes shook, and she seemed about to burst. The sergeant then asked me if I had been to Qian's meat-drying room. Perhaps I was being ostentatious, or I lied to her because I felt uncomfortable seeing the slanting corners of her eyes. Li Erni's eyes didn't droop, but they shook violently, as if they were covered with strips of meat. I had to continue to make things up. Li Erni kept wiping her mouth with her sleeve. It was Li Erni's saliva that was fuel to my fire, and the lie was also very enjoyable to form.

My gaffe never escaped the sergeant. He stressed that there must be a price for not telling the truth. He disregarded everything about the meat drying room, and Li Erni said what I said to others. She couldn't miss a chance to show off. Although it wasn't her experience, she always had a way of turning things in her favour. I could almost imagine the tone of her voice. I said I hadn't been there. The sergeant said that someone could testify that I said the opposite with my own lips. I spoke on my lies to Li Erni and why. In those three days, I didn't leave my father's side by half a step.

The sergeant did not press on this matter, but instead asked me which villages my father and I had visited and who we had seen, especially the days before the Qian Family incident and everything about that night. I thought of the clattering sound in the howling wind. I heard it. I remembered Dad's stern warning to keep my lips shut. I supposed he wouldn't have fessed up, so I officially never heard anything. Everything spoken to the sergeant was truth. Just the bit about that noise was concealed.

"Your father really intended to send you to the imperial court as an official mender?" came the sergeant's cold words, which threw me back a moment. Why the sudden change in tone? "It's a yes or no question." All softness was gone. I whispered my yes. The sergeant laughed again, and the wax gourd face became more swollen. "At least he didn't go for a concubine." Serious again. "Are you better than your father?" I didn't respond. Instead, I stretched out my hand and raised it. My fingers were very long and thin. Anyone who saw me mending any bowl would notice. There was one house where a woman grabbed my hand and prodded it, saying that it was the longest and softest hand she had ever seen in her life. Seeing me embarrassed, she finally loosened her grip.

The sergeant said there was a way to verify whether I was lying, but he didn't say anything. It was getting late. He asked someone to take me out to another room. It wasn't cold, but it was still uncomfortable, laid with straw like the cell, but there were beds and tattered quilts. Everything was dark, so I could barely make out a thing. I never knew what had become of my father. Was he in my same situation, or was he under the gavel? Nerves defined the night.

The next day, they sent the toolbox to my room, and at the same time, they sent a blue porcelain plate with a white background cracked into two pieces. They wanted me to fix it. Is this what the sergeant meant? I mended it in two hours. Then I took the plate and was brought to the sergeant again. He raised his plate and looked at over time and again, noting the quality of the stapling.

What happened next was more confusing. My father and I met again, but we weren't free to go. Instead, we were confined to a large home in the east of the city. Saying "confined," though, shouldn't really imply that we had other restrictions. We just were unable to go beyond the threshold of the courtyard. There was an iron stove and a bed, and the bedding was old but clean. We got two meals a day, which was delivered at certain points during the day. The food was still hot when we got it, so I could only assume that it was prepared right next door. My father and I were to mend together, given plates and vases. Dad warned me to be careful because of how old the porcelain was, but I would have been careful even if the porcelain were newer. The sergeant came once a day to check the results. He wasn't as gentle with my father. Rather, his face was always stiff. Dad asked softly if the work was good. The sergeant merely replied with mm-hmm.

We stayed there a total of nine days. The moment we were finished, the sergeant finally smiled and praised both my father and me, saying that he would let the carriage take us back to Songzhuang Village. Dad said nothing in response. We were told the carriage was waiting for us just outside. The sergeant then took out two silver coins, one of which slid out between his fingers and hit the table with a heavy thud. The other one he stood on the table and spun like a top before he slapped his hand down on it. I looked up. "Your pay. You two shouldn't work for nothing." I heard a purr in my father's throat, and his waist bowed a little.

"I can't possibly, sir. Please don't jest."

The sergeant's smile seemed to freeze. "I said that you two shouldn't work for nothing." Dad was trembling. I don't know whether he was more excited or afraid.

"I ... can't possibly, sir."

The sergeant's eyes were cold. "Are you finished?" Dad gave a heavy nod. "Better be. Just be sure your lips utter nothing. We clear?"

"Sparkling."

The sergeant's eyes slid toward my face. "Clear," I spat out.

The sergeant pointed to the porcelain that had not yet been removed. "Do you know what this is?"

"What is it?" Dad asked.

The sergeant beathed in satisfaction and waved at me. I walked over, and he handed me the silver. "Your hands ... are truly something else. You can go. Ride's waiting."

6

The fragrances trickled into my nostrils and swam toward my heart. One could say I'd become a foodie of sorts. The people of Song said as much about people who could actually eat, so no one really ever called me one personally. Indeed, I was treated as a goddess. Heaven as my witness, I never hinted that they should ever do such a thing. How it all came to be was anyone's guess. I delivered them all, though, ushering them into this world. More or less, I'd been showered with gratitude by all, but it couldn't be for just this reason that I became deified. You had maternity wards in hospitals, all well-staffed. But here I was, a midwife turned goddess. They prayed, meditated, whispered in hushed voices to each other, and admired before my feet, but I couldn't stop them. Just like this fragrance … I couldn't keep it from swimming through my system.

I "kicked my own bucket" half a year after my broken body lay down. There was cause. The grandson of Yang the blacksmith fell into Wu Dayong's fishpond and drowned. Wu Dayong was meant for the water and had a thing for breeding fish. His ponds weren't far from Butterfly River. There were three in total, with different fish in each. Yang asked for Wu's life to compensate his son. Wu bluntly declared his hands to be clean. He wasn't Yang's grandson's keeper. He also refused to pay reparations, instead only offering two hundred. Yang wouldn't have any of it. He bludgeoned Wu's mouth and knocked out two of his front teeth. Yang had been forging iron half his life. Although old, he still had brute force. The two teeth couldn't quell his inner fire, though. His eyes rather lay on Wu's twelve-year-old granddaughter.

Did this have anything to do with me? Of course. Yang came to me to vent his frustrations. The day before he set out to kill Wu's granddaughter, he paid me a visit. "My knee is bent for Thee, O blessèd Zunai. I, Yang, blacksmith of nearly sixty suns, behold Thy grace." I knew something was up by these strange words. "O blessèd redeemer, how I have toiled with shovel, hoe, sickle, hook, and spade as my blade, killing poultry, swine, ox, and lamb, but ne'er once has a man lost the light of his life under my hand. Wu Dayong now forced it to oblige. My grandson's departure left me without meaning. My heart is beyond all consolation! Wu's disregard is my ill regard. Oh, how I long to offer him the same bitter cup, his granddaughter for my grandson. O blessèd carer, my heart is without beat. In my mind is but one thought. Zunai, O mother of mercy, bless my soul. Forsake me not!"

Imagine all that. Me bless such an atrocity? A fire ignited within me. My heart shattered. How thoughtless. Oh, how mindless! I wanted to jump up, yell at him, stop him, and stamp out the horrible flames within him. Alas, not a muscle twitched.

I couldn't even breathe heavily. There I was, his words piercing my aged soul, mentally tearing me limb from limb. Sure, he had many a piece of iron in his hands and slaughtered livestock beyond measure, but he was still afraid of killing someone. He asked for my blessing, but I knew it was to give him backbone to finish the horrid deed. Humph. Who was I? Yang was becoming a murderer under my nose. Did that make me an accessory? An accomplice, even?

The murderer-to-be had no clue that I was boiling within, so the words in my head were for me and me alone. I couldn't speak. There was no use worrying. Over time, my heart settled. He couldn't hear me, but I had much to say. Silence ruled, however. I couldn't stop what was going to happen, but that was certainly not for lack of trying on my part. My regret remained unabated, the same with my guilt of having given this man the spine. I could do nothing.

Yang, how could you be so reckless? Wu Dayong didn't dig the pond just so that your grandson could drown. An accident was all it was. You are blind, and so is Wu. Even if the fish lover were guilty, Wu would be the only one to blame. His innocent granddaughter, what does this have to do with her? How could one lay a hand on such a pure soul? Even if your heart were made of iron and you didn't care about the life or death of a girl, would you still have a mind for your own kin? Your son lost his son. His tears form a river to his own, sorry grave. Shall he lose his father, too? He wouldn't be able to shed the same tears then. And your stroke-stricken wife still needs your help

These were my thoughts, and Yang was weighed down by his own. Every word he said lashed me, but nary a word of mine bit at his ear. There was nothing I could do.

"And now I part, O heavenly watcher." He stood and bade me farewell. His legs had to have fallen numb, for he fell over soon after. I couldn't quite gather his expression from the sound of things, but I was sure his eyes must have been glowering with evil intent.

I couldn't stop blacksmith Yang; neither could I tell Wu Dayong. I was disappointed and filled with utmost despair, so I thought of ending it all for me. If I had disappeared from the world, blacksmith Yang would have never come to my side. The lack of courage he had then might have staved off the act. She was just a girl, and I was just an old woman with one foot in the grave, nothing more.

I held my breath for as long as I could to do myself in. My life was lingering on a thread, but my breath remained. Perhaps it was my "food," the wafts of it at least. That had to be it. Without it, I'm sure my broken bones would have well turned to dust.

I failed in my plan, of course. I hadn't the strength to hold my breath. I couldn't muster it. No matter how much I tried, the food's fragrance kept entering my pores, my nose, my mouth, and my hair. Such a waste I was; I didn't even have control to end my own life. The smell … Did God have something against me?

I had delivered countless. Was I without merit? What sins had I committed? Why was Heaven sentencing me so?

The next evening, the blacksmith came again. Maixiang refused to let him in. He bade many good tidings. I thought the murderer wanted to tell me about the bloody process because he said he would thank me, but I didn't expect him to say that I saved him. He got it right.

His fall the day before had given him pause. He pondered and thought that I was trying to stop him. Zunai won't let him kill. Would he still? He wanted to talk to someone, but he didn't know whom to talk to. He didn't sleep all night. He said as much. Instead, his hatred kept him going, and he even darkened the gates of the school, waiting, knife at the ready. But then, suddenly, he heard my voice. It grabbed his heart. The bell rang, and off he ran. He finally realized that regardless of his issue with Wu Dayong, his granddaughter was off limits.

There was a wave in my heart, and then I was very happy. I thought my silent words had magically found their way, or perhaps God Himself stepped in. Whatever the case, the murder never happened. Hatred still burned, but as long as the fire wasn't fed, it would die.

I never thought of suicide again. I let it be. Calm I remained ever since.

Well, at least until the ant started scurrying.

7

That winter, many things happened in Songzhuang Village. A man named Er Manzi got drunk in Yingpan and left going the wrong direction. The next day, he was found on the shore, frozen. He squatted down to warm himself by a fire, but there were only a few egg-sized stones in front of him. They all said that he was hallucinating and used the stones as fire pots. Some speculated that he was visited by spirit fire, which acted like siren songs to the lost.

A family living in a mouse hole was careless one evening and didn't cover the entrance of the home in time. A gazelle fell in looking for food. The family was too poor to build a house, but they ate enough meat that winter. The smell of meat wafted out every three to five days. On windless days, the white, cloud-filled air often attracted eagles. Those with shotguns ran out when they saw white air, but none of them ever scored an eagle.

The most surprising thing was that "Little Man" Song, son of Song "The Kidnapper," opened up a shop outside Dajing Gate in Zhangjiakou specializing in leather goods. "Little Man" Song travelled by camel between Zhangjiakou and Kulun. Because of his short stature, he was often teased that he was finally as tall as two humps on humpback, the shape of this leading to his other nickname, "Three-Piece Meat Hammer." Leading camels was a hard job, and his size made it even more so. He never married, though he was already thirty, so to think that he would become the owner of Wanlong Yong and eventually marry the daughter of another shopkeeper who was engaged in the tea salt business shocked all. It was said that the girl was as beautiful as a fairy. Even Qian Guangwan couldn't set up a shop in Zhangjiakou. "Little Man" Song became Songzhuang Village's pride and joy. The family of Song "The Kidnapper," who had always been ostracized, suddenly became buzzworthy. Some wanted to get a job in the shop, and some wanted to ride on a camel. They asked "The Kidnapper" for advice, but his stony face warded off anyone who dared. The man had no face, but no one disregarded him.

The robbery of the Qian Family was also a big event in Songzhuang Village. Many legends came of the matter, and it became difficult to distinguish truth from fiction. Dad and I should have remained on the side of the protagonist, but ever since we were taken away, there were rumours that we were moles. No one expected the two of us to return, but once we did, the rumour finally died. Li Fubo was also surprised, thinking that my father and I would never return. That night, the two men held long pipes and smoked until midnight.

I asked Li Erni if she had told anyone about me being in the Qian Family compound. She denied it. I knew that she was lying through her teeth. Although she lifted the corners of her eyes as if I had insulted her, her heart was empty. It was her look that told me. Li Erni didn't turn her back on me because of my questioning. On the contrary, she approached me in a variety of ways. She was eager to inquire about my experience in the county seat. I didn't indulge per my father's instruction. Erni tried to exchange two secrets with me, and then added three, one of which was her own. She stole frozen lard and had diarrhea for several days. "That do?" She looked at me expectantly. I said that when I got into the carriage, I fell asleep and couldn't remember what happened after that. She didn't buy it, of course. "Slept in a carriage for days on end? Stop twisting my leg." I said it was up to her whether she believed it. She desperately uttered another secret about having dreamed that she had married Qian Guangwan and that she had his sausage while Guangwan enjoyed her melons. She woke up when his teeth clamped down hard on one melon's stem, but it was Li Sanbao who sneaked up on her and bit down on her in her sleep. She whipped him good for that one. He cried. Her mom and dad thought some otherworldly force was at play. Li Erni glared at me. "Now spit it out," she demanded. I was shocked at her thick skin, but I didn't let up on my word to Dad. "You're a cheat," she said. "Stole all those secrets, and what do I get? You're not worth my friendship." The next day, though, she came at me again, and I was ready to crawl out of my skin.

The winter was long, but spring finally came. Overnight, the earth offered green buds on the soil, corners, and potholes. The dandelions were soon ready to present their seeds. Prepping our new home became a thing again. Dad spent his time evenly divided between working in the various villages and going up Naobao Mountain. Li Dawang often came to help me, but Dad didn't like him wasting effort on things that weren't his affairs. Li Dawang replied by saying his father would scold him if he didn't and that Dad should talk with him. If he said it was all right not to go, then he would gladly keep his distance. Li Dawang's voice was so low that he seemed reluctant to say all this. Dad shook his head helplessly. Upon discussion, Li Fubo called Li Dawang a good worker, though sulky, and that since he had so much bottled-up energy, he would do well helping out. It ended up that Li Fubo said that Dad could reward his good deed with a meal. From that point on, we put out an extra set of chopsticks, just in case.

One day, after our stomachs were filled midday with dried food, a hare crept over. In front of the hare was a blooming dandelion. The hare was tempted to eat it, but because of Li Dawang and me, it hesitated. Li Dawang felt for a stone and tossed it. The creature became frightened and darted away like an arrow. Li Dawang chased after it. I almost laughed. How could he hope to compete?

Li Dawang was often called Li Dumb-Dumb. He wasn't a fool, but his simple and honest demeanour caused him to be teased in such a way. One day, someone on the road told him that there was a frozen yellow sheep on the shore that he could fetch. Dawang asked why he didn't get it himself. The man said he wanted to pick it up, but it was too heavy to carry. He then asked him to bring the poor beast back and requested a leg as payment for the tip-off. Dawang went there and searched till dusk. He went back and called the man a trickster, but the man said he had to have been blind not to see it. The tale swept across the village in a heartbeat, and people chided Li Dumb-Dumb for his supposed stupidity. He worked hard, and it could be said he worked the most. He never slacked. Those who worked together with him shook their heads, saying even a mule knew when to take a break. Dawang insisted that he wasn't tired and that he would stop if he ever felt so. "Two mules equal one Li Dumb-Dumb," someone said. Li Erni filled me in on her brother often. She liked to play tricks on him, which fit her personality.

Li Dawang never caught up with the hare, but he came back with his hands filled with these white-stemmed, green-budded plants, the thickness of each being slightly more than a chopstick. "They're sour willows." He deskinned them and handed some to me. I took a bite, and my cheek started burning.

"God!" I cried out.

"Don't you like it?" he asked with a bit of sudden urgency. His face fell a bit.

I was never one to mess with people, but I couldn't help myself and allowed a sinister spirit to take hold. "How could I? I dare say you're off to kill me." I jumped up and toward him, and he fell back in shock, the sour willows sprawling across the ground.

"I … I didn't mean to!" he rushed to say.

"Your heart is like a stone!" I said, scowling.

Li Dawang's nerves made him stutter. I was almost bursting with laughter inside, but I contained myself, picked up a sour willow, and peeled it. Inside was crisp and tender. The tanginess had a slightly sweet taste to it. In fact, it was rather refreshing.

Li Dawang's eyes turned to my face, full of confusion.

"I'm kidding. Honestly, it's really good."

"R-Really? You're sure?" I laughed. "Y-You …"

"Can't you take a simple joke, Dumb-Dumb?"

He smiled as if I had just given him a trophy.

I ate half. Li Dawang said that the sour willow we had would don another flavour after three to five days. Li Dawang couldn't describe it. I wanted to know what the other taste was. I asked Li Dawang to stay for dinner. Because of the day's episode, I planned on making some flatbread. Just after scooping up some noodles, Li Erni came in. She never knocked at the door as she barged in. The sour willow was on the windowsill at the door, and Li Erni grabbed it, like collecting stolen goods, under her armpit. The whole thing was just weird. "I never got the chance to try the sour willow this year, and here you are having stolen it from me."

"What are you on about now?"

"Tell her. Haven't you given me all the willow leaves you pulled in the past?" Dawang was obviously unwilling to answer, but he still said yes in the end. Erni put her hand on her hip as if having just claimed the throne. "This here is mine, but here it is in your home. Say it wasn't stolen! Hope your teeth decay." I didn't want to argue with her, but I couldn't stand the way she was acting.

"That was all previous years. New things happen, like finding out frozen lard causes diarrhea."

Li Erni's face turned a horrid blue. "You're a witch."

"Throw some water on me."

Her eyes twinkled with tears, as if she wanted to escape, but she didn't move. "The willow's mine."

"You planted it. I pulled it. This has nothing to do with Dawang." I immediately realized that this was something that was best left unsaid. Sure enough, Li Erni's once paralysed fighting spirit swelled up again. She stared at Dawang and asked him who pulled it. Knowing that Dawang couldn't utter a lie, I piped up. "It was me, I tell you!" Li Erni pressed more aggressively.

"Do you have lips or not? Who?!" Dawang looked at me and looked at Erni. The whole thing was just too frustrating. It was little wonder why people called Dawang Dumb-Dumb. The haughty Li Erni continued to coax. I couldn't let her win.

"Say he did pull it, he did it for me, right, Dawang?"

"Yeah ..."

Li Erni just about blew a gasket. She tore the willow out from under her arm and slammed it down. "That's always been *our* thing. Why give it to someone like *her*?" she scoffed before pivoting and flouncing away.

Li Erni's blatant pestering vexed me, and Li Dawang's

performance made me even more disappointed. I left the idea of flatbread behind and just heated the previous night's leftovers into some soup. When Dad came back, he, Dawang, and I sat together. Dawang drank a bowl and put it down. Dad asked him why he only had one bowl, to which Dawang just urged us to continue minding our own bowls. A fool with a fool's brain. He clearly saw that there wasn't enough for everybody. Father only took one ladleful. "Don't mind him. Let him wait if he wants to wait. His funeral. His mind is full of mischievous ideas," I said. Dad gave me a light kick. I couldn't bear the situation and put down my chopsticks. Dad said he was full, too. I pushed the basin over. "Have at it. Just don't choke as it goes down." Li Dawang didn't hear my sarcasm and said he was fine. When he left, Dad first scolded me, and then he suddenly laughed.

"He really is dim, huh?"

The next day, Li Dawang and I worked at reclaiming the wasteland, as was usual by then. Dawang talked to me, but I didn't answer him. He felt my apathy and focused on his work. After a break, I took out the dry food prepared in the morning and asked him to eat some. Dawang rubbed his hands and shook his head, saying what was mine was mine. I went to find the sour willow. It turned out that he was thinking about the same thing. I said that we should eat before going. He sat down hesitantly. I asked if the willow only grew on the slope. He said that there were more flatlands and that he knew of several places. I asked him if he could take me with him. I hadn't seen the willow actually growing on the ground, after all. Dawang was startled. "You really want to go?" I nodded, though I really didn't care. Still, Dawang couldn't figure out whether he was nervous or excited, but he was certainly trembling.

Li Dawang took me to the flatland on both sides of the river, which belonged to Qian Guangwan. The willow had a long stem, but the leaves on the ground weren't large. They were somewhat similar to mugworts in early spring, making them a chore to find. Of course, Li Dawang had a keen eye just for these. He gave me a tight hug from excitement, and I sat down on the spot. After a full meal, I couldn't close my jaw. My happy appearance infected Li Dawang. He said that there was a "killer" herb that grew on the shore and asked if I wanted to try it out with him. I had no idea what he meant by "killer," but curiosity killed the cat, as they say. I asked if it was far. He said it was but that the journey could be made before dark. I bounced to my feet.

"Well, let's go, then!"

Li Dawang had a special skill, which I found out about later. He knew of every sour willow, killer herb, and fungus. Nothing could escape his radar, and his memory was excellent in this regard. Using his own words, each type had a "nest." He mentally mapped everything out, even caves. I asked him how he did all that, but he didn't have an answer, saying that it was just something he could do.

The so-called killer herb was similar to that of wild leek, but it had neither the same nip nor fishy taste. It was about a span long, with leaves and stems on the ground. Although the land outside the Great Wall was barren, Heaven showered its blessing upon it. I liked the sour willow and killer herb, both of them sour and tangy. Li Dawang said that he would take me out once in a while. I asked him if he ever brought Erni. He shook his head. I asked why. He gave me a firm look, clearly trying to see what I was getting at. In the end, he bowed his head. "She's just a homebody." I didn't expect that. There was no telling where that came from.

We met a whirlwind on the way back. When living in Yucheng, I saw a whirlwind, like a huge mushroom. My mother said that the whirlwind would take away people's souls. The solution was to spit three times. Li Dawang said a tornado was brewing and that we should head back quickly. I looked behind me and saw that the whirlwind was still in the sky, only a few feet above our heads. I didn't care. I wanted to show off the solution when the twister came, so my feet were slow. Li Dawang slowed as well, but he was obviously flustered a bit. I thought him a bit of a coward in that moment.

I looked back, and my nerve was completely blown away in an instant. The whirlwind whipped into the sky and became enjoined with it. It was difficult to tell whether it was strong wind that rose from the ground toward the clouds or the dark clouds that hung upside down and aimed for the earth. We could only see the whirlwind running, like thousands of troops. It became like a cylinder and a steel cone. The sounds were mixed, seeming like roaring, drums beating, shouting, crying, and swords clashing. Before we got close, the sky and earth went dark, and ten paces forward was obscured. I wanted to run, but instead, I sat, incapable of urging my legs forward.

Li Dawang dragged me to squat under the achnatherum splendens, saying that people would never make it by running through a whirlwind. He told me to hold on to the grass before taking off his coat and putting it over my head. He sat down and pressed against me, clasping my other arm. With ear-splitting roars, the whirlwind swept over us. It was as if the whole world were sound or wind itself. I felt like my body was fit to fly, but my hands grasped firm hold with every bit of strength. The coat left my hair, and hail-like crackling swept over both head and face. I closed my eyes, hunkered, and clutched the achnatherum splendens with all my might.

The wind finally started to get weaker, and there was a voice in my ear. Li Dawang! His words were crisp and clear. "Don't let go!" After the time it takes to smoke half a bag, the sky grew much brighter. Both Li Dawang and I were covered in soot-like debris. Dawang's coat was long gone, and willows and killer herbs were strewn about. I was told such an occurrence was super rare. Li Dawang spoke of one man who got sucked up by one and was never seen again. The two of us were lucky. The thought of what could have happened shook me to my core. Mom's secret weapon was nothing against such unimaginably brute force. Li Dawang comforted me and said that he would fetch us some willow and killer herb another day. I nodded.

I had no idea we had gone so far away. The sun was setting, but the village was yet to come back in sight. That was when I saw the wolf. That day was really special. The wolf followed Li Dawang and me as if it were our dog. Li Dawang was experienced and said that it was best not to walk fast when accompanied by a wolf. If you ran, it would think you were frightened. He also mentioned not moving straight but turning at jagged angles. Wolves darted forward and were not easily able to turn on a dime and pounce. He had dodged one before by doing just that. "Were you alone?" I asked, my voice trembling. Turned out he was with his father at the time. Dumb-Dumb wouldn't have been so brave.

The village finally made its appearance, but everything was shrouded in darkness, making me shudder. Li Dawang let me go ahead of him. I didn't know what to say. Li Dawang said that the wolf would go for him, the bigger of us two. Unless the wolf was starving, I supposedly had nothing to worry about. His words would have been funny, but in the moment, they were more like a thunderbolt.

8

Maixiang was on the phone. "You think your business is more important than Zunai's? You're my cousin. Blood helps out blood. I wouldn't leave half a step if it weren't for this."

The ant was scurrying.

After a while, Song Hui, Maixiang's cousin, rushed to the door panting. "I ran the whole way. I'd be here quicker if I had wings."

Maixiang responded with a chilling voice. "Keep it down. Zunai's sleeping."

Song Hui usually spoke loudly. It was really difficult for her to lower it, actually. "Where's my head going? I completely forgot about her nap after lunch."

"If you can't remember her simple daily routine, what can you remember?"

"She wouldn't hold it against me, would she?" her voice was tense.

"You think she's one to chide?"

Song Hui breathed a sigh of relief. "You're right."

"Your memory needs some work, though, or else you can't do well covering for me."

"I'll remember her affairs, even at the cost of losing mine."

The ant was scurrying.

"Listen up."

"I'm all ears."

"No one, and I mean no one, not even God Almighty, is allowed in this home."

"Not even local villagers?"

"*No* one. Capeesh?"

"And Song Pin?"

"He's at some meeting in town and will come back after dark."

"Got it."

The ant was scurrying.

"You also can't go near Zunai. let alone touch her hand."

"I've already washed them."

"So?"

"Mm-kay."

"Don't burden her with your troubles. She's already spent two hours listening to others' woes. Just do your normal thing some other time. Clear?"

"I hear you."

"I've peeled and chopped some apples and pears. At three o'clock sharp, you're to take them out of the refrigerator and simmer them, but not too long. Don't boil them dry. Place them and let her absorb the fresh fruit."

"Can I put a piece in her mouth?"

"Nitwit. Ordinary people swallow food. You dare compare Zunai to a layperson? You're driving me crazy, here."

"I just thought," she began, her voice timid, "it would be nice for her, you know?"

"Is there anything between your ears? Talk about inconsiderate."

"All right, then."

"You'd better remember everything I just said."

"You'll crack my head open if not, I assume."

"As if there's something to crack."

"Right. I'll be careful."

The ant was scurrying.

"And don't even think about going anywhere. Don't even take half a step out."

"How could I give up such an opportunity?"

"I mean like last time."

"I forgot to lock the d—"

"Not a thought. You dare leave again, and you'll be in for it."

Song Hui promised that even if her house caught fire, she wouldn't dare leave. Maixiang asked Song Hui to recite these five requirements. Song Hui was nervous and got things wrong three times. Maixiang corrected them one by one.

"You're going to Luo Bao's?" Song Hui caught on by the way Maixiang was acting. I couldn't help but sigh to myself.

"What business is it of yours what I do?" Her intonation was sharp. "Just mind your own and take the task of looking after

Zunai seriously." Song Hui was the only person who let Maixiang treat her like that, though Maixiang never really dared chide others. I felt bad for Song Hui.

The ant was scurrying.

The same thought must have also struck Maixiang, who fell silent for a moment before continuing in a low voice. "There's also something else that I haven't told anyone."

"What?" Song Hui asked, suddenly interested.

"Qiao Shitou's coming."

Song Hui was taken aback by the shocking news. "*What?!* When?"

"Doesn't matter. He's just coming back. Not a word."

Song Hui was so excited. "It's a secret?"

"You think he has to sneak his way back? Is his name so bad? No, I'm just afraid you'll fill others in, making rumours spread to the point people who don't even know him flock to his door. He's far from as well-tempered as Zunai. Don't poke at the hornet's nest.

"Why's he coming back?"

"What am I, the fly on his wall? How should I know?"

"Better to be a fly on his wall ..." came the yearning-filled response. Maixiang's face fell.

"Talk about a backhanded comment."

"Sorry. Came out wrong, honest to God."

The ant was scurrying.

I believed that Song Hui really didn't mean for things to

come across that way. Honestly, she didn't have a way with words and coming up with that took some verbal skill.

"Whatever. I'm done with your nonsense for the day. I'm out."

The ant was scurrying.

Maixiang was back after only a few minutes.

"You decided against it?" Song Hui's voice was filled with unspeakable surprise and disappointment.

"Forgot something, I think."

"What?"

"Can't remember."

"At least you can think while you walk."

"Can you bring that voice of yours down a peg?"

Song Hui tried, her words coming out garbled. "Kay."

"I just got flustered all of a sudden."

"Maybe it's because you're approaching that horrid woman?"

This incensed Maixiang. "I'm his wife. You think I care for that ogress?"

"Came out wrong again."

"There's really no cure for that head of yours."

"Probably not."

"And you'll forget everything I instructed you on."

"I swear I won't."

"I'll take you at your word this time."

9

I never knew how others cultivated the wasteland. Perhaps a horse and a plough were enough. My father and I didn't have much to do. It wouldn't be right to say we "tended" it. Really, it was more like we gnawed at it. For four years, we did the task in irregular bits, but the total accounted for just over three mu. That land, though, wasn't ever really "ripe." Some plots were ready in a couple years. The fertilizer was mixed with grass and our sweat. Dad planted various vegetables, heeding Li Fubo's suggestion to let the ground get acquainted with the plants, accept them, and later become one with them so that tilling became easier with time. In addition to wheat, potatoes, and flax, naked oats and millet were also planted. Naked oats fare well in cold. Mixing their powder with rice would make anyone's mouth water. I wasn't used to the taste at first, but then I couldn't bear to live without it. Dad said that drinking a local area's water made one more capable of eating the land's produce. The millet we used was colloquially termed "big yellow rice." Wu Kui died from eating too many rice cakes mixed with it.

There was plenty of rain that year, and several plants had a good harvest. My father was so happy that he couldn't close his gaping mouth. He stopped mending for a time, instead waking up early just to rush off to Naobao Mountain and coming home after dark. He said that Li Fubo helped him a great deal, that most of the ideas applied were his. Thanks had to go where credit was due. "Dawang, too," I said. Dad nodded and said how generous Li Fubo's family had been. "Not Erni, though." Dad scolded me, talking about how Erni and I were becoming women and shouldn't talk like little girls. After all, with Dawang pitching in, Erni was the one who was left at home to take care of the chores. I never mentioned how Erni came after me about the carriage situation, making her mouth spit fire. Rarely did I argue with my father, and in this instance, I saw his reasoning. Erni indeed wasn't worthless.

Dad and Li Fubo began to part ways while thanks were being offered.

I prepared that meal carefully. Stewed pork with bean curds, fried mushrooms, fried shredded potatoes, and fried cakes. It was something I'd picked up. Erni offered to help, but she of course pilfered bits into her mouth like always. The spirits poured were of fermented naked oats. Dad had bought a bottle while in town. Ms. Li was immobile. I scooped some up for Erni to take out. Fubo, Dawang, Erni, and Sanbao were all together in our home. After eating, Dawang's brothers and sister left. Only Li Fubo remained, downing the liquor with Dad, the two of them talking about the village and Zhangjiakou. In the end, Li Fubo said he couldn't handle any more of the booze. Dad insisted on pouring another round. "One more. Happiness like this is hard to come by."

"You know, it isn't something our family does, talk about another's business, but …" Li Fubo's tongue was flopping around, "there's been something on my mind. I've been waiting for a more formal occasion, but I just can't hold back anymore. I just don't know how to put it out there."

My father feigned vexation. "I feel an insult coming. Let's hear what you've got to say. I won't hold you back."

"You sure you want to hear this?"

"What are you, my mother?"

"Well, you see … it seems my Dawang and your Damei are growing up. Life's next stage seems on the horizon. I was thinking about contacting Hua Erniang."

Dad froze. "Dawang and Damei …?"

"Sitting in a tree."

"You can't be serious."

Li Fubo smiled. "You don't see it?"

"You're joking."

"How can I be?"

Father shook his head slowly. "I just think they're … incompatible."

"Why not? Dawang, Damei. It sounds like a family. I've also checked their signs. They're a perfect match."

"How'd you find out when Damei was born?" Dad was

obviously surprised.

"Erni. She asked, and Damei doesn't lie."

Dad's voice chilled. "So you took it upon yourself to consult the stars?"

"That's a rude way of putting it. The time of one's birth isn't something to keep secret. Why the long face? Sure, Dawang has issues, but he also has a shining bright side to him. Should he marry Damei, he'd be like your other half. You wouldn't have to worry about whether to work at home or—"

"Stop. Just stop."

Li Fubo looked smacked in the face. "Just like that?"

"I said stop. Just go. I can't. Let's just act like this whole conversation never happened."

"Is it really that bad? You're making it seem like it's a massive personal insult or something." Li Fubo's voice was deepening.

"I just can't. Please go."

Li Fubo snorted. "The bridge had been burned."

"I said *go!*" Dad had obviously had a bit too much to drink. He wasn't so feisty on most occasions.

Li Fubo didn't recoil. "Are you going to come at me?"

It was a good thing Dad was able to keep on this side of sane. "I've never struck anyone. Today would be a horrible time to break that trend. But … hear me when I say this. Marriage is a voluntary affair. I'll never force anyone's hand. Heaven has its way. People know what they want for themselves."

And that was that. Li Fubo didn't retaliate. He just

jumped up, left before his shoes were on properly, lost a shoe in the process, picked it up, pounded the sole a few times, and disappeared beyond the threshold.

"So now we know why Dawang's been around so much," Dad muttered to himself. "The stars were in alignment for him from the get-go."

My father and Li Fubo quarrelled, and I went in and out. I wanted to listen but was too afraid to. Neither of them minded my thoughts. It was as if I didn't exist, but everything they said was related to me. Li Fubo noticed me when he left. He smacked head-first into the bellows, and I gave him a hand up. It was at this time that my father remembered that I was there and added that though Dawang was honest, he was too silly and unworthy of me, his daughter. My silence made my father nervous. "Are you telling me you're fond of this fool?" I said Dawang was no fool. "So you're saying I'm the fool?" I lowered my head. "If you like, I will jump over the wall. Would that suffice?" I didn't answer. "He'd be all right for a son, but he's not good enough as son-in-law. Damei, you're meant for better, someone more financially capable."

That night was torture to me. I remembered many good things about Dawang. He was really good to me and had even saved me. The day we came across that wolf, he walked behind and would have let the wolf charge at him first. If Li Fubo hadn't come to look for us, he might have served as the wolf's dinner. Although Dawang was simple, there was something cute about him, and his strange abilities seemed specially tailored for me. I could never say

I was in love with Dawang, however. There was perhaps a twinge, but it was far from long-lasting. I never imagined my husband-to-be to be quite like him, so when Li Fubo mentioned the proposal, I was no less surprised than my father. Still, my father's decision made me feel both at ease and disappointed. The whole thing was a burning, melancholic contradiction.

The next day, when Li Fubo saw me, he immediately turned his face, as if I were a lost star. Although he turned fast, I could still see the wounds on his forehead and cheek. He fell more than twenty times. When I met Li Dawang, he also lowered his head. I called him, but he ignored me, and Li Erni, always dependable for spicing things up, spat at me three times. She even spat when she didn't see me. She made noises each time she passed my door. Although I didn't leave the room, I could hear. There were some rumours going about the village about my father and me, courtesy of Li Erni. Her brilliance outdid itself that time.

My father was no more relaxed than I was, although he kept saying that melons couldn't be twisted open, especially after Li Fubo raised the courtyard wall next to my house. Dad would leave earlier and come back later. I should have gone with him to do some mending after the autumn harvest, but since this bitter relational mishap with Li Fubo, I was kind of trapped where I was, with no way out.

The long winter was coming, its sudden and arrogant face turning our way.

Many things also happened that winter, but only two things

are worth mention. One is that my father promised my hand to Zhao Jinyuan, the third son of Beer-Bellied Zhao, who owned a steamed stuffed bun shop in Yingpan. Jinyuan had part of his ear bitten off by a mouse when he was young. The half-eared man still had a whole brain, and he did well helping out his father. When married, I would be able to gorge myself on as many steamed stuffed buns as I wanted. Dad said he hoped wedding bells would be due for us by year's end, but Beer-Bellied Zhao asked for our fortune to be taken. The fortune teller said autumn would be best, meaning we had to wait for the year to pass. Dad did a lot to comfort me as we waited, but it wasn't I who needed comforting.

The other is that Ms. Li died one morning. When she woke up, she asked Erni to wash her face. Erni dumped the used water outside the door leading to the street and returned to the house to find her mother had stopped breathing. That same day, Li Sanbao joined her. Sobbing, he held his mother's body close, and his father couldn't console him. Half an hour later, that was that. It was said that the mother and son were two peas in a pod. Where one would go, the other would follow. Did this soothe or strike Li Fubo? None could tell. He showed no acute reaction. My father and I went to help. Dad was afraid that I wouldn't be able to handle the sight and drugged me up with medicine beforehand, but it wasn't needed. Since my betrothal to Zhao Jinyuan, I was always on the agitated side, as if mice were gnawing at my heart. Li Fubo was in a sorry state, and it was hard to tell what could be done. He didn't drive Dad away. Rather, he gave each of us mourning cloth. Dad put it on his sleeve. I donned it on my head. Not a word was exchanged between the two men. Two caskets lay in the courtyard, one large, the other small. Li Erni was terrified seeing them. Her eyes were red and swollen, but I could still make out the fear. Sure enough, that evening, she asked me to sleep in the same bed with her and was too scared to even go out to relieve herself. I nodded without hesitation. On our journey from Yucheng to Song escaping famine, my eyes had seen many a corpse. I wasn't afraid.

Li Erni talked to me the most at night. She was afraid that I would fall asleep, and she was only calm when she heard me speak. Once in a while, I would doze, and she'd bump me with her arm. My job was to cheer her up.

Li Fubo never spoke to my father. Li Erni and I were inseparable. When I left the yard after the funeral, Erni was still reluctant to let me go.

One spring evening, she stopped me just outside the family's property. "Hold it right there, Damei!" Her harsh tone shook me. Three days before, she had asked me to fetch some sour willow. "You almost had me," she said most provocatively. I asked her what she meant. "I'm motherless and less a brother." I asked what that had to do with me. "Both of them had a grudge against you. If only you had married Dawang, they would have never left."

"*What?*"

"Dawang almost died that night because he wanted to save

you. Instead of repaying his kindness, you want to marry the steamed stuffed bun seller's son?" I had to concede. I indeed told her that Dawang saved me that evening. There was fire in her eyes. This wasn't just a whim. She had been saving this for a while. Anyone her rage touched made it nearly impossible to meet her gaze thereafter. Still, it wasn't as if it had been years since I decided not to expose her and those many words she spurted that night we spent together.

"What formal declaration was there that I just had to marry Dawang?" I asked, smiling a bit.

Li Erni choked a bit. "You're *inhuman*!"

"If that's the case, why should I marry into your family? What's that say about you?"

Li Erni was shaking with anger. "Murderer!"

"How do you reckon?"

"I never knew you to be so shameless. Faceless, even."

"Don't need a face. As long as there's skin, but look at you. You have one, but it's all bones." It was true, she had high cheekbones and a thin face. She herself even spoke on how it all felt like bones. I didn't want to rip the scab off that old wound, but what she said forced me to play my hand. The words struck hard, and she snapped up.

"I'll rip a new one if you say any more." But I wasn't afraid. She was shorter than me and wouldn't be able to hold up a finger against me.

Dad came back from outside, and Li Fubo ran out of the

house. My father shouted and I stopped. Li Fubo stopped Erni, too, but she continued to hurl insults. Goblin, whore, soleless shoe, anything she could think of. Li Fubo gave her a slap. This stupefied her for a moment, but then she burst into tears.

Three days later, Li Fubo came to the door with a bag of tobacco leaves. Dad and I had just had dinner, and the dishes had yet to be cleaned. Li Fubo's sudden visit stupefied my father, and it took him a moment to regain his composure. I placed the square stool he had for Li Fubo, who put the tobacco on the table and said that he bought it in town during the day, thinking Dad would like it. Dad said that he didn't like how Fubo was spending his money on his account. He ignored my father and remarked that the tobacco was the "golden leaf" kind. He had tried it himself and loved it. "You would know," Dad said. "If you say it's good, I believe you." He immediately called for me to get him his pipe. Li Fubo drew his own from his waistband, and the two men packed together. Fubo stared, pushing for Dad's impressions. Dad took a drag, then another. "It's good!" he said, nodding heavily. Fubo was pleased.

There was a sudden silence, and the two men buried themselves in smoke. My father coughed and spattered until the smoke blurred his face.

"What's up?"

Li Fubo was a little hesitant. "'Bout that day ... I drank too much, you know? Said some nonsense. Don't take it to heart. I immediately regretted it."

Dad was clearly moved. "I'm sorry, too. Me and Damei are indebted to you."

"People should help each other out. I was born with a selfish heart, though. When both their deaths hit … you know, I thought about many things over the winter. Absurdity lasts a lifetime. Sanity, too. Looking for absurdity, on the other hand … well, how absurd is that? Best thing is to live with a clear conscience, free from future turns left or right."

"Don't beat yourself up."

"Who said I was? Don't worry about me. Everyone has their own life to live, their own blessings to receive. Can't force hands, you know?"

"Damei's been through a lot, too, much of it with me by her side. There's nothing left for me in this world. I just hope she won't worry about the clothes on her back or the food she'll eat. When I finally join her mother, my departure may at least make a positive difference."

"Got a point."

"Dawang is a fine young man. Don't stay up at night worrying about him."

"What's the use of worry? Worrying is as worrying does. Just go with the flow, you know?" Li Fubo asked in a way that was almost laughable.

Dad didn't know how to respond, so he just changed tune. "Hear anything new recently about Li Gui?"

Li Fubo shook his head in dismay. "War's hell. I'd thought

that he … might send something back by now …"

Dad tried to say something to console him, but his efforts were futile.

The war became the new topic. Li Fubo mentioned how many places were in upheaval. Dad was surprised to hear that he knew so much, never having been the wiser travelling back and forth on mending treks. Li Fubo talked about how the blacksmith was complaining about how the price of iron was skyrocketing and how he had to follow suit. Horseshoes doubled in a year alone, from two dimes to four a slab. All for the sake of making firearms for battle. Li Fubo said that he had bought a donkey the previous year and was grateful it wasn't a horse. Otherwise, he wouldn't have been able to tack it properly.

My father and Li Fubo made peace, and whatever it was that was stuck in my chest suddenly disappeared. Li Fubo was at relative peace. Li Erni's anger soon died.

One day in June, my father took me to purchase my trousseau in Zhangbei County. Beer-Bellied Zhao's family wasn't rich, but they had a good name and background. Sights had to be set high. Dad said it was expected to go slightly over the top. Otherwise, the family may not look so kindly on the offer. After half a night's consideration, we went out to buy bracelets, earrings, clothes, shoes, and socks for me, fox fur hats and sheepskin coats for Zhao Jinyuan, and small items for his parents. In order for me to eat steamed stuffed buns every day for the rest of my life, my father spent every last cent he had. The best food in Beer-Bellied

Zhao's steamed bun shop was the pork and carrot kind. I had eaten it twice before. I raised an objection.

"If you never listened to me before, listen to me now," Dad said. "An abacus should play its role. Wrong calculations aren't part of its makeup."

It had been years since the overthrowing of imperial reign and the Republic of China was declared. That particular day would embed itself in my memory. When my father and I went out, Li Fubo was collecting half-dried donkey dung at the door. When he heard that my father was going to buy my trousseau in Zhangbei County, he was upset that Dad hadn't said anything beforehand. "How far you two going?" Dad said we wouldn't be back for at least a day. "Mind your feet." When Dad and I were out mending, walking was never an issue. Li Fubo insisted, however, that I ride his donkey this time. "I couldn't offer her our hand, so this is the least I can do. Don't object." Li Fubo pressed so hard that Dad couldn't even if he wanted to.

"What say you, Damei?" he asked as always.

"I think we should listen."

Li Fubo smiled. "Glad to hear I'm still on your good side."

The donkey wasn't tall, a chestnut with a grey back. I mounted too quickly, and the poor thing spooked. Dad fortunately snatched the lead rope in time, and I didn't fall. "It's all right. Good listener, that one," Li Fubo said. I caught sight of Li Erni from the corner of my eyes. She had to be unhappy. I had never seen her straddle the donkey. Still, I didn't care, and I straightened my back.

Such was how I left Song that day. I didn't know what future lay before me.

10

Song Hui opened the door and stood, obviously looking around. I knew why. She was hesitating, worried about Maixiang's return or concerned about pestering me. Song Hui was quite devout. The biggest photo she had in a frame was of me. Before my body gave up on me, she wanted to join me in my walk. She stood there, breathing heavily. After a while, she came over, her feet as light as straw. Indeed, she never was a heavy walker. The breathing became heavier and heavier, and I could even hear her heartbeat, like bean seedlings beaten with a flail. She didn't get close, settling down a few feet away from me. Maixiang's warning worked. I could feel her eyes wandering from head to foot and from foot to head.

The ant was scurrying.

It's okay, my dear. Just get that damn ant while you're at it! I cried to her in my head. She couldn't hear me, but my mental voice was nearly screaming. Who knew? Perhaps they would meet her like they did the blacksmith.

She didn't come closer, deaf or blind to my request. There she waited for a whole quarter of an hour before withdrawing somewhere else.

The sounds of spring, summer, autumn, and winter are all different. The same with the smells in the air. Two-fold if counting day and night. I knew this, not only because of ability, but also because it added a spark of fun to my life, judging what time of day it was. The sun began to crawl with strenuous effort. I figured it was around three in the afternoon. Aha! The fruit was on its way.

Song Hui entered the room again. She moved to the bed little by little, and her strong desire drove her to forget Maixiang's words.

"Zunai, I couldn't let Maixiang keep me from you. It's been several days since our last meeting. I just had to come see you again." Her voice was trembling a bit.

The ant was scurrying.

"How sweet and tender you appear. Not a single change has befallen you. I know now why they call you an immortal."

I couldn't help but sigh. Nonsense. Tender?

Child, the wrinkles on my face would make good rags!

Song Hui reached out, touched me, and immediately retracted. "Forgive me. I overstepped."

The ant was scurrying.

"Last time, I talked to you for a while. My head was clearer then. I ate and slept well. Now, though, my chest is heavy."

Song Hui's early days were all right. Yang Bacha, a mighty fine dancer, was a tractor driver in the village and later opened a flour mill. Song Hui was capable of ploughing and tending more than half a mu of land a day, though she was ill adept at other labour. Once the mill began to go under, Bacha began hitting the bottle. When he was drunk, he took out his anger on Song Hui. Song Hui's howls could be heard throughout the village, but never once did she utter the word divorce. She would be beaten and go back out to the field to till before her tears dried. Some said that Bacha got used to living that way because of Song Hui's reaction. She could do half the field and hurry home, and if anyone asked why she was in such a rush, she would say that she had to get back before Bacha awoke. Otherwise, he'd bust the furniture. Not only did she never hide; she was almost asking for a swing. Thus began her silly reputation. I never thought her to be an imbecile. It was just that people didn't understand her or comprehend the pain she was in. Men vent, and she found her way to vent her frustrations alongside one. To each their own. Song Hui's method was special and possibly silly or even weak-minded, but it suited her fancy.

Yang Bacha was unable to block the tides of Song Hui's heart. He didn't play her same game, but his rudeness could be said to have eased the tension of Song Hui's ever-present depression due to her son, who caused so much pain that others just couldn't possibly understand. During one of her manic phases, she begged Yang Bacha to hit her, but he fortunately hadn't had enough to drink for that. When sober, he was like a wilted flower. Still, because he wouldn't honour her wishes, she spat in his face, which incited him to carry on with her request. Song Hui never complained about Yang Bacha, only about her son.

"Zunai, my breathing's out of control. I'm going crazy." I heard Song Hui's impatience. I couldn't help but listen. I wanted to tell her not to worry about Maixiang potentially catching her and to just say what she needed, but alas, she continued to hesitate. "Should I even say it? I'm at a loss. I've even broken two bowls with my mind the way it's been." I was shocked, but she couldn't tell, of course. I wondered what was wrong with her son. "All right. I'll say it. Zunai, this is for your ears only. Mao Gen and I got into a bit of trouble." Her voice lowered, obviously nervous, slightly timid, and somewhat secretive. "Zunai, please, if there's anything you can do to help …"

I was screaming in my head.

What's the matter, child?! What's befallen Mao Gen this time?!

Chapter IV

Mao Gen

1

The neon lights came on soon after sunset. That's when Mao Xiaogen would cry, "Look! Eyes!" in utmost delight. Mao Gen had to correct him countless times on the matter.

"Lights. Ne-on lights."

"Eyes!" came the stubborn response. To him, all coloured lights were eyes. There was a time he only referred to the sun and the moon as such. Naturally, he preferred the brighter over the darker. At sunrise, Mao Xiaogen said that the sun "eye" was open. At sunset, Mao Xiaogen said the moon eye was closed. When dark clouds covered the sun, Mao Xiaogen became rather agitated. When the moon rose, Mao Xiaogen's countenance fell. To him, the moon wasn't nearly bright enough, and then it would grow as thin as a seam from time to time. Should there be no moon present at all, though, he would grow afraid, for to him, the moon had been stolen. He dared not sleep or speak loudly until the sun eye opened. Mao Gen tried to explain that the two of them had one pair of eyes each, like cats, dogs, chickens, pigs, cows, horses, and sheep, with one left eye and one right eye. "The sun and moon are the eyes of the sky," Mao Xiaogen replied upon hearing this. "The sun is the left eye, and the moon is the right eye." It became so difficult to explain things to Mao Xiaogen that Mao Gen couldn't talk any clear sense to him and realized that their conversations were going nowhere.

If it were just semantics, then that would be an entirely different issue. The problem was that Mao Xiaogen donned strange habits due to these understandings he had. He was fond of the bright left eye. When it was open, he could sleep in peace. Although he didn't like the hazy right eye, he was also worried something might steal it away. He wouldn't sleep at all should the left eye remain unopened. He would sleep soundly for up to seven days straight, but then he would stay awake for up to three. His circadian rhythm was completely at odds with Mao Gen's and that of Songzhuang Village, and it caused pretty notable issues. Mao Gen worried whenever he would sleep both day and night away, but when the opposite was true, a headache ensued. Mao Gen even had to go as far as to raise their courtyard wall and insert glass shards to keep his child from wandering. He also erected a row of steel spears upon the iron gate. Xiaogen was clever, though. He climbed up a ladder, removed the glass, padded things down with a sack or cloth, and then hopped right over. Heaven only knows how Mao Gen caught him in the act. With no other option, he attached Xiaogen to an iron chain. Song Pin caught sight of this two days later, told Mao Gen off for what he called abuse, and threatened a lawsuit. As quickly as it came, the iron chain was gone, as was the idea Mao Gen had hatched to build an iron cage.

The question of sleep wasn't the biggest problem, however. The most disturbing thing for Mao Gen was Mao Xiaogen's eating. When he went on his week-long slumber, he wouldn't eat or drink a thimble-full. Mao Gen, of course, became worried at this, but it later became clear that his worries were unfounded. Whenever Mao Gen eventually arose, he would always have food on the brain, to the point that his stomach seemed to be an abyss. At first, Mao Gen was afraid that Mao Xiaogen was eating too much, but again, this fear was baseless. Never once was he filled to the brim. One wouldn't even say satiated. He was a very capable eater, but he never gained a pound and was still lean with some muscle even.

Mao Gen intentionally starved Mao Xiaogen once in an attempt to remedy the situation. It was no easier to be cruel than to tie an iron chain to him. No matter how Mao Xiaogen cried during this bout, Mao Gen would never let him eat, let alone smell the food. In the end, though, Mao Gen had to relent, especially when Xiaogen was nibbling at anything he could: the bean cakes for the cows, the bran flour for the chickens, peanut shells, whatever. Even buttons or coins, though they couldn't truly be adequately consumed, would just sit in his mouth, though he did swallow some, which fortunately came out eventually. The branches and leaves of the two elms in the yard were gnawed bare, and even the bird feathers lodged between the branches became his food.

Mao Xiaogen definitely caused a ruckus when he attended

school those two years. He ate others' cookies, candy, and erasers with abandon. One time, some of his classmates decided to mess with him by putting raw potatoes into his backpack, but the joke was on them when he thought them to be stupendously delicious. While he slept, some would put branches in his hair, while others would tug at his ears. He didn't do anything to stop them, though. In fact, it was much more boring to do anything to him while he was sleeping. The principal called his father in for a meeting a couple of times and asked him to take Xiaogen home.

Mao Gen brought his son to the hospital, where he was admitted. The first time, he was there for a week. The second time, it was nine days. Nothing resulted from their efforts, though, and it was as if money were being thrown down the drain. Mao Gen became irritated when the doctors told him that his son needed time to heal. Mao Gen didn't have much faith in medicine anyway. The only reason he went in the first place was because he was running out of every option to keep his sanity intact, but again, nothing.

The third time Xiaogen was taken to the hospital was because of Song Hui's persistent nagging. Her house was adjacent to Mao Gen's. She was a kind-hearted woman, and Mao Gen often asked her to take care of Xiaogen. Unlike other people, Song Hui didn't treat Mao Xiaogen as a freak. She always talked to Mao Xiaogen in a loving tone and was willing to give him food. She bought more things for Mao Xiaogen from Qian Zhuang's shop than Mao Gen did. "Symptoms have to mean something. What if he has worms?" she'd often spout. Mao Xiaogen's awkward tendencies became legend in the village, which naturally spread to Mao Gen's ears. Mao Gen's lips curled at the thought, but his general unhappiness was so ever-present that he couldn't ignore it and was finally able to incline his ear to Song Hui's kinder words. She then asked around for the best hospital to look into Mao Xiaogen's condition, and when she found the right one, she pressed him so much that Mao Gen realized that doing otherwise would be like a massive slap in the face. One could say that he took his son to the hospital as a way to thank to Song Hui. He didn't think it would really amount to anything.

First off, the doctor was a female whom Mao Gen related to Song Hui, although he really couldn't put a finger on why exactly. Xiaogen picked up on the same thing and wasn't as resistant when answering her questions and following her directions as he was with the other doctor visits. Mao Gen didn't once have to answer for him. Afterward, he was surprised he remembered her name, Dr. Zhao You'an. The other doctors' names he'd forgotten long before.

Secondly, Dr. Zhao instantly knew what was up with Xiaogen, something called Prader–Willi syndrome. Mao Gen asked questions, and Dr. Zhao was always ready to answer, with not even a spark of annoyance. The condition, abbreviated PWS, has telltale signs of fatigue, gluttony, and abnormal behavioural patterns. She felt Xiaogen's forehead before sending him up to be admitted. After the boy was gone, Mao Gen asked the doctor for more info. Turned out there was this guy from the UK named something-or-other Hilton who was conked out for a year straight. He underwent bloodletting and heat treatments, but nothing seemed to suffice. Then, all of a sudden, he woke up. Another case was of an eighteen-year-old girl who was out cold for six months. "If no needles could rouse a person with such a condition, why admit them?" Mao Gen asked.

The doctor smiled. "Medicine is always getting better. Who can say something won't work if we don't try?"

Third, Dr. Zhao mentioned potential causes. No one in the medical field has come to a concrete consensus, but it was certain that it had nothing to do with the gastrointestinal tract. Doing anything in that regard would be fruitless. Instead, it seemed to be neurological in nature, which would explain the brain's strange need for sleep and resulting raging hunger. Mao Gen suddenly thought of when Zunai helped welcome Xiaogen to the world. He then startled the doctor by collapsing to the floor, gasping and clutching at his chest. What if she were right? What if his son had some brain deficiency? "It's like a wire that's not functioning properly," Dr. Zhao tried to explain. "It's not as if his whole brain is the problem. There's no necrosis of the tissue, but we'll get to the bottom of this." Comforted by her determination, Mao Gen nodded, making out a slim beam of light at the end of the long tunnel.

On the third day of treatment, it seemed that Xiaogen was doing better. He wasn't scared of the night anymore, but Mao

Gen later realized it was because of the neon "eyes" that lit the city. The sun never shined its rays into the room he was in, and the window overlooked an intersection, where neon lights were most plentiful. Since the night was rather bright because of this and the sun never really illuminated the room directly, Mao Xiaogen could actually fall asleep until the next morning. By the ninth day, he wasn't eating as voraciously, and Mao Gen was able to quietly store leftover sesame cakes, pears, and steamed buns in the bedside cabinet.

Whenever there was a slight adjustment in Mao Xiaogen's patterns, his father headed straight to the doctor to tell her the news. Mao Gen was both excited and upset. One night, Mao Gen almost called Song Hui, but his hands were shaking so badly that he kept entering the wrong number until he eventually gave up. Later on, he chided himself for being so bold. Had he succeeded in dialling, Song Hui would have been on the receiving end of his woes.

On the evening of the fifteenth day, there was an unexpected power failure. At that time, Mao Gen and Mao Xiaogen were standing in front of the window. Mao Xiaogen stepped on the stool and was pointing out which eye was round and which was flat. The sudden darkness frightened Mao Xiaogen. He cried out in alarm and nearly fell down. Mao Gen caught him in time and got him to the ground with one hand grasping his shoulder. "It's all right. There, there," Mao Gen said, his voice empty. He didn't know why, but he was also taken aback. After a while, the light in the hospital came on, while the neon lights of the intersection were still off. Mao Gen asked the nurse about the lights on the street. The nurse said that the hospital had its own generator. The streetlights were on the grid. Mao Gen told Mao Xiaogen that the street's eyes must have gotten tired from being open so long. He asked Xiaogen to lie down on the bed, but his son resolutely refused. He stood on tiptoe, his chin against the windowsill, and waited for the eyes to open. Mao Gen didn't dare drag him away. Instead, he just let him be. If Mao Xiaogen didn't sleep, he couldn't sleep. This was a 22-story building with windows which, though shut, forced him to be more mindful.

At dawn, Mao Gen was at his wits' end. He dozed for a few minutes, maybe even more than ten. Suddenly, jarred from his nap, he lunged at Mao Xiaogen, who had decided to take a bite of an IV line. Thank goodness for the boy's gag reflex. Otherwise, he would have swallowed the whole thing. Mao Gen grabbed his collarbone and pulled the tube out of his throat. Perhaps he moved too quickly or too violently, as there was blood on the end of it, indicating a laceration somewhere in Xiaogen's esophagus. A frightened Mao Gen immediately called for the nurse. After a round of questioning, Mao Xiaogen admitted he'd taken the line from a nearby cart and had at least the good sense to remove the needle. Had he swallowed that, well … The nurse, now also thoroughly alarmed, decided to hail the doctor.

Dr. Zhao chided Mao Gen for not having followed her instructions of checking his son's pockets and not sleeping if his child also couldn't sleep or at least calling for a nurse to keep watch while he got some shut-eye. Mao Gen hung his head and didn't make any excuses. The doctor noted the tears hanging in his eyes. "Come on. You're a grown man. Suck it up for his sake, all right?" He nodded and hurried away.

The tears were in his eyes out of frustration, not sadness or despair. He'd honestly thought things were going better under Dr. Zhao's care, but it became all too obvious that it was the neon lights that were helping. The sudden power outage revealed the harsh reality. Although Dr. Zhao looked like Song Hui and she really had some skill behind her white coat, her will outweighed her abilities in this case. To stay would just be a waste of money.

Mao Gen had somehow made it through the difficult day and night that followed. The next morning, the nurse informed him that the deposit for hospitalization had run out. Mao Gen was relieved. He finally had a sound reason for leaving the hospital. As he expected, Dr. Zhao opposed Mao Xiaogen's discharge, saying that she had just finished the first course of treatment and that he needed at least two more. She had sent Mao Xiaogen's information to experts in Beijing who had yet to reply. Mao Gen was forced to say that these hospital visits broke his bank. Dr. Zhao paused for a few seconds, counted out a thousand yuan from her bag, and asked Mao Gen to use it, no questions asked. Mao Gen didn't expect that Dr. Zhao would be so resolute. Seeing Mao Gen stunned, Dr. Zhao got up and put it in his hand. He suddenly snapped back to reality, stepped back, and shook his head, saying something about how this would eventually rob him of everything he had. Dr. Zhao's temper was being tested by this point. "This is your son we're talking about." The tears almost broke free from their ocular prison.

"You're a good person, Dr. Zhao, but I ... I just can't."

"I'm a doctor. I took an oath."

In the end, Mao Gen grabbed the money and walked out, feeling dizzy and staggering as if he were an old man, not yet forty but going on eighty.

The next day, Mao Gen regretted his decision. The money was leaving so fast it could burn a hole in anyone's pocket. Would Dr. Zhao still pay for it? Even if she were willing, the question was whether he should accept it. If Xiaogen could really be cured, then money wasn't the issue at all, but everything pointed to all these efforts being in vain. He spoke with Dr. Zhao once again, and she bore down on him for not acting like a father. "Where's his mother? Perhaps she can understand sense."

"She can't hear anything now. Not since the day Mao Xiaogen ..." Mao Gen couldn't finish and instead gave a long, drawn-out sigh.

"Sorry," Dr. Zhao apologized. "I see now. You're taking on two roles at once. All the more reason to be more sensible. Don't worry about money. Fundraisers are a thing, you know."

It was clear that Dr. Zhao wasn't going to let Mao Xiaogen go without a fight, but Mao Gen also had some fight in him. Fundraising? That was equivalent to making Mao Xiaogen's disease public, hanging a slogan, and shouting from a mountaintop. The family's troubles were well-known in Song. There was nothing to be done about the villagers knowing every humiliating detail that befell Mao Gen, his son, and his son's mother ("Lady Chub" as some said). Still, why let the whole world know? There was something else, though, something that not even Dr. Zhao knew. This "something" was nagging Mao Gen, especially with all the fruitless stays at hospitals.

The next morning, Mao Gen and Mao Xiaogen fled.

2

Mao Gen's grandfather was a stutterer. To what extent? He said each word separately, and it took a long time for him to manage a word, which made his face red and neck thick. One day, he approached a man for a favour. Saying, "Could you lend me your," took so long to get out that the other man was practically done filling and rolling a cigarette. The next word was horrible. The other person, who honestly thought he was trying to borrow his sash, tried to preempt the word at the "sa." When seeing he wasn't being understood, Mao Gen's grandfather got frustrated and started to stomp. He was told to sign it out instead. Seeing a barebacked horse, he lifted a hand and slapped so hard on the poor beast's spine that the horse was startled, bucked, and sent Mao Gen's grandpa flying. The hard landing got the final oomph out of the word "saddle." The hilarity became legend in Songzhuang Village.

Although Mao Gen's grandpa stuttered, he was the best hunter in Songzhuang Village. His marksmanship was on point. He didn't shoot when his prey was quiet and still. If a hare or a gazelle didn't move, he never fired. They had to be running before any pressure was applied by the trigger finger. The other was that he hunted both day and night. People couldn't see beyond a few steps in the dark, but Mao Gen's grandpa honed in by sound alone. Should someone in Song ever start to boast in their own skills, stories of his prowess would always be added to the mix to shake things up. In the middle of winter, the furs of all kinds of animals, such as foxes, gazelles, and hares, were hung on the wall both inside and outside his grandpa's house. On the night of the Mid-Autumn Festival, Mao Gen's grandpa suddenly drowned in a puddle. The puddle wasn't even as big as a mat and was only half a foot deep. He was found face down. It was more like suffocation than drowning. People and animals have souls. Mao Gen's grandpa had killed so many animals. He could very well have been lured into the puddle by their ghosts. How could a puddle where not even a hare could drown kill him? Of course, there was nothing to substantiate this claim, but many believed it.

Mao Gen's father was also a hunter. *His* father had only carried his shotgun when hunting, while he carried it even when nature called. However, Mao Gen's father's marksmanship was inferior. He could fire at the target a hundred times and not have one round hit its mark. People often saw Mao Gen's father wandering in the fields and grasslands from morning to night and from night to dawn, leaving empty-handed and returning empty-handed. That year, wild geese became a nuisance and often destroyed crops. The captain said that if Mao Gen's father killed a wild goose, he would give him a moon cake, but he couldn't even scrape up a feather by the time winter came. The captain scolded him for being useless and not reaching the level of Mao Gen's grandfather. Mao Gen's father had a good temper and didn't get angry when he was scolded. Instead, he became more determined to get a goose one day. "You'd have more luck getting pecked by a goose, carrying that thing around your shoulder all day like you do." Mao Gen's father didn't bat an eye, saying geese were yellow-bellied and would be scared by the mere sound of a round going off. The whole thing became the talk of the village. When discussing Mao Gen's grandpa, people would mention him by name or his nickname One-Gun Mao. When talking about Mao Gen's father, however, few people called him by his name. Rather, they would say things like "that boy of One-Gun Mao's," or "the guy who fathered Mao Gen." At the end of his life, his name faded into oblivion. After he was gone, it quickly became hard to remember what his name actually was. Not only that, but most couldn't tell whether his death was from illness or accident. The only thing that stuck was the saying, "Startled me half to death like hearing the news that that guy who fathered Mao Gen was going hunting."

Mao Gen had been in close proximity to the shotgun since he was a child. Still, there was nary a chance for him to touch it, let alone hunt with one. His father walked with the shotgun and ate with it slung around his shoulder. Because of this, his mother often quarrelled with his father, and even when his father slept, he'd put his shotgun by his own pillow. Mao Gen got up at midnight one time with the intention of just seeing "what it felt like." Mao Gen wanted to touch it, but the chill that spread from the palm of his hand to his arm and then to his whole body was like ice. Suddenly, the chill became a burning flame. He held it up in the dark room as if aiming at imaginary prey. He accidently bumped into the chamber pot, and the clatter woke both his parents. His father didn't punish him. To tell the truth, Mao Gen couldn't remember a single time he was ever punished by his father. Since that night, however, Mao Gen's father became more and more paranoid and began to attach the shotgun to a bell when he slept.

When Mao Gen's mother was seriously ill, his father went to the wild whenever he was free. He wanted to hunt a hare to bring home to his wife. At that time, there was nothing but the bare walls in his house, and they couldn't afford to buy more than three pounds of meat. Hunting didn't require money, only skill, but Mao Gen's father never succeeded before his wife passed away.

Mao Gen's dissatisfaction with his father began after his mother died. The shotgun failed to bring any honour to his father. The only thing it did bring was humiliation. Mao Gen was going to die of shame, but his father had no sense of shame. Mao Gen thus became completely downtrodden. One day, when his father was cleaning his gun, Mao Gen snatched it from his hand. His father was so anxious that he shouted in alarm, but Mao Gen ignored him. His father jumped up, and Mao Gen stepped back, aimed, and said, "Not an inch! I'll do it!" His father's face went pale. That year, Mao Gen was seventeen years old, and he himself was startled that those words escaped his lips. Should his father really have stepped forward, there certainly was a chance that Mao Gen would have lost his nerve. He'd never know for sure, though, because his father was too frightened to do anything. His father's fear made Mao Gen's heart suddenly cold and brave at the same time. His resolve hardened to the point that the potential for losing his nerve was shattered. In the end, his father didn't do anything except rub his thighs in anxious terror.

Mao Gen exited the yard with the shotgun on his back, and when he returned, he threw two wild hares that were still warm at his father's feet. His father couldn't believe it. Mao Gen didn't believe it himself. His first day hunting was a complete victory. It seemed mandated by Heaven.

The second thing Mao Gen did was seek vengeance on Wang Bao. In those years, there was only one place to sell pigs: the food company in the town. Two people weighed the stock, and Wang Bao was one of those at the scales. Wang had a unique ability. He could scan a pig's belly with his eyes and know how much the owner had fed the beast. In the haggling process, something like three or five pounds would be deducted. If the owner refused to go that low, Wang Bao had the pig stand to the side to see if the pig had been fed a lot before arriving at the company. If it hadn't, it would eventually lift its tail and defecate normally. If it had, it would excrete undigested naked oats, wheat, corn, salt blocks, or whatever else. Pigs are timid animals, especially when being sold like that. The smell of the slaughterhouse alone seemed to scare the you-know-what right out of them. No pig could stand Wang Bao's test. The mere act of defecation itself meant the pig would lose weight. Perhaps not up to five pounds, but weight nonetheless. Should an owner see that Wang Bao was on duty, said owner, no matter who, would sigh at the soon-to-be loss of profit. This situation was so well-known that people would say, "Meeting Wang Bao's rotten luck. Pigs that see him run amok." This saying would even be used to talk about rotten luck in general, not just among pig owners. If they lost a card game or hit someone while driving, they would say that they were unlucky that day because they'd met Wang Bao.

When Mao Gen was ten years old, he went with his parents once to sell a pig, which usually ate wheat bran, potatoes, and wild vegetables and drank the leftover water typically used for washing pots. That morning, Mao Gen's mother fed it processed corn and naked oats. She scratched the pig's right ear while feeding to make it more willing to eat up, but there was still feed left when it was done. Mao Gen's mother wouldn't take no for an answer, grabbed the nape of the pig's neck, and shoved its snout right in, practically shoveling the food into its mouth. Mao Gen's father was out waiting, having already started the truck, calling for his wife to just let it go and load the animal. "This is the thanks I get for giving you the meal of your lifetime?!" she scolded the pig.

Wang Bao was on duty that day. Mao Gen's mother sighed when she entered the food company courtyard, but Mao Gen's father was confident as could be. He whispered to Wang Bao, "We both come from Songzhuang Village. I don't need more talk about us at home, if you catch my drift. We've been waiting in line for an hour, you know."

Wang Bao cast a gentle glance at the pig. "You want to weigh it or just shave a few pounds off the asking weight right now?" Mao Gen's father smiled and handed Wang Bao a cigarette. Wang Bao took it and put it behind his ear. Both left and right ears were already occupied, and Wang Bao didn't pick them up when they fell to the ground. He never refused an offer for one, though. Mao Gen's father said that his wife was in poor health and couldn't wait around. "Then shave now, by all means." My father leaned forward, about to whisper to Wang Bao. Wang Bao's eyes fell on the shotgun strapped to his shoulder as if he had only just noticed its existence. "That thing go with you everywhere you venture?"

Mao Gen's father smiled and said, "It's kind of a habit."

Wang Bao suddenly laughed. His was a malicious smile, but Mao Gen's father didn't see it as such. Wang Bao pointed to a chicken looking for food and said that if he could hit it, he would weigh it right away and deduct nothing. This was a trap. It was clearly set to make a fool of Mao Gen's father right on the spot. Mao Gen's father shouldn't have answered, but he did. "Chicken is ol' Wei's," Wang Bao emphasized. "Nothing he'll really miss." Lao Wei was Wang Bao's assistant. Mao Gen's mother didn't stop her husband. Maybe she thought it would be no problem for him to shoot a chicken a few yards away. The result naturally ended in maniacal laughter from Wang Bao, who was bobbing so hard his chin almost fell off.

Mao Gen's father had to pull the pig aside and tell off his wife for feeding the pig just beforehand. She then put her arms around the pig's neck, but it was uncertain to those around her whether she was tired or wanted to comfort the animal. The latter was true. Mao Gen sat on the ground, bored. The sun was like a pool of dung in the sky, without any luster. The pig was still in good spirits. It only had to urinate a small bit that whole afternoon. When it was time to weigh, though, the pig couldn't hold it in any longer. Mao Gen's mother almost beat her chest in dismay. She knelt on the ground, shoveled pig excrement mixed with naked oats and corn into a waste bin, and carried it to the truck. At least it would feed the chickens.

Many years later, Mao Gen remembered this very scene, and it stabbed him like a knife wedged deep within his heart.

Wang Bao only moved back to Songzhuang Village from town after retirement. Those his senior who raised pigs seldom made contact with him, while those his junior had nothing to say to him, so Wang Bao made few friends. He always stayed at home and occasionally went to Qian Zhuang's shop. When Mao Gen came to the door, Wang Bao was both surprised and happy. "What's with the shotgun there, nephew mine?"

"Just had my first go with it."

"That so?"

Mao Gen paused. "The basics at least."

Wang Bao laughcd. "Think you're at your father's level?"

This made Mao Gen wince and smirk at the same time. "You would know, Uncle Bao."

"How so?" Wang Bao chuckled in high spirits.

Mao Gen pointed to the chicken in the yard. "How 'bout I try on them chickens o' yours?"

Wang Bao got the hint that something was up and shook his head. "Why would you do that?"

"Let's make a bet. I'll get three in one shot. If I lose, you'll get six o' my own. If I win, them three is mine."

"What's gotten into you?" Wang Bao asked, suddenly looking down.

"What's wrong with a little friendly bet?"

There used to be a time that people would do whatever they could to win Wang Bao over to their side, but those days were long done. Still, this humiliating move was something new to him. Besides, Mao Gen was still wet behind the ears. "Let's see what you got," he said.

The shotgun was loaded with pellets. Mao Gen didn't aim at any particular target, but in a general direction. Two chickens were finished the moment the trigger was pulled. The third, a rooster, fluttered, made five or six somersaults, twitched a few times, and then was still. Mao Gen kicked and made sure that all three chickens were dead. "I don't want 'em," he said to the bewildered Wang. "They're yours for the keeping."

The tale of this day became legend, and Wang Bao ate his fill of his own poultry. He ended up with a gastric ulcer after that.

Unfortunately, there weren't as many wild animals as there had once been. Gazelles had disappeared, though foxes were occasionally around. Mao Gen only really ever hunted hares, wild geese, long-tailed pheasants, and "half-winged" birds, also called sandgrouse. Mao Gen had a dream, like his legendary grandfather One-Gun Mao, to hang up all sorts of hides, but with the rarity of ever catching sight of a wild animal, the fantasy was a pipe dream. Mao Gen was never empty-handed, but his catch was far from enough to decorate his rooms. When the police confiscated shotguns, the gig was up. Mao Gen would have been content if he was allowed to keep the shotgun, but without it, a gaping hole formed in his heart. He had no appetite when eating, disliked whatever he saw, and had no interest in anything. He defied the ban by buying accessories and crafting a makeshift firearm of his own. He had a knack for this, too. Then he made a bow. At least archery wasn't banned. Armed with his quiver, Mao Gen would strut around the streets, but with a shotgun, he could only sneak out early and come home late. The bow provided cover for the shotgun. No one would examine the hares or half-winged birds for gunshot or arrow wounds, so he was in the clear.

All the young people around his age were married, but Mao Gen, aged twenty-five, had no luck in this regard. This put him on edge, which made it even more difficult to talk with people. He trusted nothing and didn't care about anything. If this were some advantage, it would also become a weakness. Mao Gen didn't believe in gods or spirits. In short, he didn't believe in anything. If anyone said that there were ghosts, Mao Gen would say, "Let the ghost come. I'll show it the end of my barrel." When it came to his grandfather's strange death, Mao Gen was disdainful. Eating a meal possesses risks of being choked to death, but a little puddle? Mao Gen's family was also poor. Colour TV was nothing new, but his family didn't even have a black-and-white one. This made him dismissive of the content. "It's all fantasy anyway. What's the point of even watching?" If someone tried to counter with any of it being "real life," he'd snap back with a "Get them to come to the other side of the screen, then, if they're so real." Very few people would talk to Mao Gen because of his tendency to quarrel on the matter.

One day in late autumn, Mao Gen bagged a wild goose with one of his arrows. He had waited in the naked oat stacks for it most of the day. Since he was using arrows, he didn't shy away from going back to the village in the light. When he met Zunai at the entrance of the village, she was picking up the bean pods that some careless man had dropped on the road. Zunai said that Mao Gen and his father were born in exactly the same way: neither opened their eyes until they got a slap. Mao Gen didn't believe that. After all the babies Zunai had delivered, how could she remember him and his father? He didn't refute her to her face, though. He knew where to draw the line.

Zunai sighed sadly when she saw the wild goose in Mao Gen's hand. Mao Gen asked Zunai what was wrong with her. "Been wanting to have a word with you for quite some time."

"Come again?"

"Don't go out like you do. It's not good." Anyone else saying this would have caused Mao Gen to strangle them, but this was Zunai. Mao Gen was unhappy, yes, but he wasn't brazen.

"Why shouldn't I?" he asked, smiling. Mao Gen thought Zunai would say things about gods and spirits. He had his own way to refute that, but Zunai didn't take that route.

"You didn't kill just one."

"Of course I killed just one."

"That one's got a companion. With it now gone, the other will soon follow from grief."

Mao Gen was stunned. "I didn't see any companion out there."

"Geese don't just show up out of nowhere. They're born somehow, and the cycle continues."

Mao Gen was almost persuaded by Zunai, but he didn't want to concede. Killing could prove that he was a real hunter. "So … isn't raising pigs for slaughter?" Mao Gen's voice wasn't loud, but the thorn in his words was very sharp.

"Pigs have been mandated for us by forces beyond our control."

Mao Gen thought he'd found the hole in Zunai's logic. "Severe drought this year, though. Where're your gods? Can't they see? Why no rain?"

Zunai wasn't angry at this, but said, "That stubbornness is why you don't have a wife."

"What's wrong with being single?"

Zunai shook her head and sighed. Mao Gen walked away. "Heed my words!" she shouted after him.

Mao Gen didn't turn a deaf ear to Zunai's words, and he didn't sleep well that night. A few days later, however, he went back to doing things his own way.

At the age of twenty-eight, Mao Gen finally had a family. The woman was from Meng Village, eight miles away. Her nickname was Lady Chub. Mao Gen didn't spend a penny when he got married to her, and her family sent them five sheep. Lady Chub weighed close to three hundred pounds and had a difficult time just moving around the house. She had two hobbies, eating and sleeping. There were no other disadvantages except those. Mao Gen had no right to be picky. Any woman was better than none. He said that to Zunai, but his heart still yearned somewhat. Still, he soon discovered the female advantage, or rather Lady Chub's advantage. Lady Chub didn't object to what he did. That was especially true when he came back with a hare or a wild goose. Lady Chub's face would shine then. Though the rest of her body had issues moving, her fingers were very flexible, and she was good at crocheting. Mao Gen went out wearing the sweaters made by Lady Chub, but no one believed such a woman could craft such a thing.

After Lady Chub became pregnant, Mao Gen visited Zunai once. Some people said that Lady Chub was old, too fat, and wouldn't have an easy time bearing children. Mao Gen didn't believe that only thin women could have children. He wanted to find Zunai to confirm. Zunai said that obese women encountered more difficulties, but it was not impossible. This time, Mao Gen believed in Zunai and thanked her for her kindness. Zunai was very interested in the pregnancy of Lady Chub. She came over once in a while to listen to and feel her belly. One month before the due date, Mao Gen asked Zunai whether it would be better to send Lady Chub to a hospital or to her. Although Zunai was a competent midwife, she was old after all. Some pregnant women chose hospitals, but there were others who lived far in the rural portions of the county who asked Zunai to help with the delivery. Zunai didn't answer directly, saying that it had to be decided by Mao Gen himself. It was troublesome to go to the hospital. Mao Gen thought it over and decided to stay in the village. On the same day that Mao Gen came to Zunai, she was heading to the neighbouring village to deliver some other new arrival. Because of Lady Chub, Mao Gen began to trust Zunai much more than in previous years.

The delivery of Mao Xiaogen didn't go very smoothly, but his life was saved. Zunai failed to save Lady Chub's life, however, and that shred of Mao Gen's trust in Zunai disappeared. Although the world was big, there was very little that Mao Gen could trust. Song Hui somehow found favour in his sight.

3

Song Hui and Mao Gen were next-door neighbours, and they frequently borrowed a broom or a shovel from each other. There were many exchanges between them, but Mao Gen never really considered her. Song Hui was more than ten years older than Mao Gen. She was the mother of two children when Mao Gen shot Wang Bao's chickens. The difference in age was just like a wall and moat between them. In addition, Song Hui had thick bones, a booming voice, and a dark complexion, not much different from a man. She never wore makeup and didn't use any facial cream. When Song Lihua, Qian Zhuang's wife, recommended something to conceal and remove her freckles, Song Hui said, "It can't cover the flaws on my face, and I don't want to waste the product." She didn't pay attention to her clothes. When Yang Bacha opened his flour mill, she'd get busy in work clothes as grey as dust. Her only concern was her hair. When she got married to Yang Bacha, she had long pigtails. She still had them. The flour didn't stain her hair because she always made sure she had it tightly wrapped when working. When Yang Bacha hit her, she always protected her hair and would rather let him hit her face. It was all a bit silly.

Mao Gen was a widower, but he was still a bit haughty. How could he like Song Hui?

The idea of taking care of Mao Xiaogen was put forward by Song Hui. "He's still a child. How can you leave him at home alone? You're a father like I've never known." She was rather outspoken. "Anyway, I'm available. Leave him to me. He needs someone in his life that can take care of him."

Mao Gen didn't believe that she would take care of Xiaogen without any sort of charge, though. "Name your price and don't beat around the bush. I have to think about whether I can afford it."

"You've *got* to be kidding me! Even if I were a penny away from destitute, I wouldn't ask for a mite! Just tell me if I can."

"Course you can."

"Shake the gunpowder out of that head of yours," she snapped, grabbing Mao Xiaogen and taking off with him.

Since then, Mao Gen usually sent Mao Xiaogen to the front yard where Song Hui lived when he was going out, and Song Hui would also take the initiative to take care of Mao Xaiogen when she was free. Once in a while, Mao Gen would bring Song Hui a hare. She would accept it, but she always said, "I won't take it the next time, though. I'll ruin it with my bad cooking. Give it to Xiaogen instead." She had a rough voice, but when it came to Xiaogen, she talked extremely softly. This softness made Mao Gen grateful, but that was all.

One day in midsummer, at noon, when Mao Gen came to

pick up Mao Xiaogen, Song Hui was washing her hair in the courtyard. She wore a large white vest with blue flower patterns. With her back to Mao Gen, she could hear his footsteps. "He just went to bed. You're just too late," she said while sprinkling water over her head. Mao Gen wanted to carry Mao Xiaogen on his back. "Don't worry," she said. "Just wait a bit. I'll send him back to you when it's dark. Maybe he'll wake up soon." Mao Gen thought for a moment and then nodded. When Mao Gen was about to leave, Song Hui piped up again. "Hey, do me a favour, will you, and pour the water on the street for me?" Mao Gen walked over and took the basin. Song Hui's hair was fragrant. He handed her the empty basin, glanced over her towering bosom, and immediately lowered his head. He remembered Lady Chub. He'd often help wash her hair when she was alive. Mao Gen didn't leave. Song Hui rinsed again and still needed the water to be poured. One third of her long hair was in the basin, and for the other two thirds, she needed to scoop up water with her hands to cover it all. She was very attentive and clearly enjoyed the whole process. Mao Gen stood in silence. A bee flew over and circled around his head several times before making its way to Song Hui. The bee didn't rush, but it seemed to be attracted by the fragrance. It circled several times but didn't fly away. It flew in a motion that curved outward, apparently trying to land on Song Hui's waist or back. Mao Gen felt something brew in his throat. He wanted to tell Song Hui, but he didn't know how. He stared at the bee with an ulterior motive until Song Hui straightened her waist and unintentionally drove it away.

Mao Gen sighed a long sigh. After Song Hui wiped her hair, she raised her head with a jerk, and the black hair that fell down on her chest was thrown behind her head. Mao Gen was struck by the enchanting swing, both physically and metaphorically, for it was then that he fell for her. When Song Hui looked back, she was like a nymph. Her round face was dark but red, and her eyes were like two pools of rippling water. She was plump, strong, and full of the smell of harvest. "I thought you were gone," she said. "I washed Xiaogen's hair this morning." Her voice was so beautiful that his soul was instantly taken away. "If you want to pick him up, I won't stop you." Her smile reminded Mao Gen of peonies.

"No … It's fine … No rush." Mao Gen fled in a hurry, but his soul failed to follow him home.

At dusk, Song Hui sent Mao Xiaogen back home with a naked oats dumpling in one hand. Mao Gen didn't dare look at Song Hui. He was bashful, afraid of being both noticed and ridiculed by her. It was fortunate she didn't catch on and left quickly. Mao Gen then became wrapped up by the thought that he'd never even asked her to sit down. He ran out, his throat suddenly blocked from uttering, let along shouting, a single word. She was long gone, but he was still standing in the yard. At night, he dreamed of washing Song Hui's hair and shaking it again and again. She asked him to pass a comb, but he couldn't find it. He was so anxious that he walked around searching until he woke up.

Taking Mao Xiaogen from the back yard to the front yard

became a happy journey. In order to extend the short distance, Mao Gen took great pains to saunter and find his way back at Song Hui's door. Of course, he had an excuse, like forgetting to lock the door or losing his lighter. He suddenly became "forgetful." Even if Song Hui picked up Mao Xiaogen, Mao Gen would still catch up with her because Mao Gen had forgotten either to make sure Xiaogen had socks on or to dry Xiaogen's insoles. He always "just remembered." Song Hui naturally laid in on him for his carelessness, sighing that the child still needed a mother figure. Mao Gen was willing to listen to her annoyance-driven words, for her voice was better than any silence. Should he neither see her nor her hear voice a single day, Mao Gen would feel he lost his soul and that the world was dead around him.

Because of Song Hui, Mao Gen's world had become colourful. Some of the changes that occurred weren't noticed by him at first until people told him. "How come your eyes have been so bright recently?" one said. Mao Gen looked in the mirror again and was surprised. For a moment, he was puzzled as to whether his eyes were bright or light was shining off his eyes. He was aware of some changes, though. As Mao Gen's finger tightened on the trigger, he suddenly remembered Zunai's words, and his hand relaxed. The goose walked away, not knowing that death was a mere step forward. Mao Gen finally understood the meaning of "companion." Lady Chub had lived with him for more than a year. Obviously, she was one of these companions, but in the bed only, not his mind or his heart. Mao Gen used to conflate the two, but no longer.

Of course, Mao Gen knew how to disguise himself. If Yang Bacha was at home, his eyes were only on Yang Bacha, not Song Hui. His ears were not idle, and they caught Song Hui's footsteps, breathing, and even heartbeat, whether she was washing a pot or sweeping the floor. Mao Gen always had cigarettes in his pocket. He hated smoking himself, but they were prepared for Yang Bacha. Having a conversation with Yang Bacha meant he could stay longer.

It wasn't every day he could stay, though, like when Yang Bacha was drunk. In the past, Song Hui's cries were just a sound. Like a trumpet, they were monotonous, boring. Now, Song Hui's shrieks were no longer a sound, but a knife which jabbed and jabbed, with each stroke either long or short, though each were directly into Mao Gen's heart, causing his blood to splash against the walls. Mao Gen couldn't let it go. Yang Bacha was a brute, a cruel beast to such a good woman. It crossed Mao Gen's mind to beat the snot out of Yang Bacha, and not just once, but he was still a little timid in his heart. Nothing happened.

One evening, when Song Hui was screaming, Mao Gen couldn't bear it any longer. Like a whirlwind, he blew into Song Hui's house. Yang Bacha swung the soles of his shoes at Song Hui's face. Song Hui was half curled up, neither avoiding nor fighting back. She was stronger and much taller than Yang Bacha. If she had fought back, Yang Bacha wouldn't come at her again. Yang Bacha was so plastered that his body was just a sick and frail representation of his sober self. Mao Gen held Yang Bacha with one hand and Yang Bacha's arm with the other. "Why are you like this, Bacha? Do fists solve anything?" Mao Gen's words were still gentle, but his hands were firm. Yang Bacha immediately grimaced in pain.

"Let … *go*!"

"Don't be the butt of people's jokes tomorrow."

"Fuck's sake."

Mao Gen half clamped and half hugged Yang Bacha, forcing him back onto the bed. A few minutes later, he heard snoring.

Song Hui had already climbed her way up from the ground. She sat on the stool at the door and continued stringing the beans. Mao Gen saw neither tears nor sign of despair.

"He asleep?" Song Hui asked.

"Yeah."

"Where's Xiaogen?"

"Been asleep since noon."

"Still got half the beans to finish. It's almost dusk."

Mao Gen was so desperate that he immediately squatted down to help and said that he just had nothing else to do.

"You shouldn't have tried to stop us from fighting. His bark is worse than his bite. His heart's heavy. It'll do him more harm not to let it all out."

Mao Gen was taken aback, then hurt. After being beaten, she had to defend the man. No woman could be as kind-hearted as her. "He shouldn't take it out on you, though."

Song Hui smiled. Smiled! "Who else, then? You? Would you let him do that to you?"

"What would give him the idea of even doing something like that to his wife?" He knew the mill had closed down and that Yang was cheated by a southerner and watched as everything around him fell apart. His life soon became only about drinking and fighting.

"I have my own issues, too. Crying helps with that."

"So you look forward to him hitting you?!"

"You think I do?"

Mao Gen felt a stone grow in his heart. "That's how it appears."

Song Hui hesitated. "Now that I look at it, I see what you mean."

Mao Gen was both distressed and angry. The distress made him even more angry, and anger aggravated his distress. "Why, though?"

"Haven't you ever been upset?"

"Sure, I have. It's not something I choose to experience."

"How do you drive your troubles away, then?" Mao Gen had never heard that phrase before and had to think. "Being upset is so horrible that the only way to get rid of the feeling is to drive it away."

"Still, even if I wanted to …" Mao Gen hesitated. He didn't dare say what he wanted to, but he hoped Song Hui would understand. As the night slowly descended, he felt closer to Song

Hui. She should understand, right?

"I don't pay others any mind. When I'm worked up, I find a way to howl."

"Well, I guess I shouldn't have stopped your fix."

"You unhappy?"

"No."

"Really?"

"Mm-hmm."

"I always offend those who try to 'help me out.' I'm always told I'm being ridiculous or what have you. You haven't said anything along those lines, but I can sense it."

What do you *know?* Mao Gen thought to himself.

Yang Bacha shouted for water. Song Hui immediately stood up. Having just finished with the beans, Mao Gen stood up and said goodbye.

After leaving the courtyard of Song Hui's house, Mao Gen's heart was in turmoil, as if he were having some inner battle with Song Hui, but when Mao Gen thought about it, he felt that nothing he said had offended her. It was not she, but Mao Gen himself who was unhappy. How could that possibly be, though? How could he be unhappy with Song Hui? True, there was no quarrel, but their conversation was even more awkward than having a quarrel. "When I'm worked up, I find a way to howl." Those were her words, but Mao Gen still had a biting remark. Mao Gen had heard something about her son. Song Hui never mentioned her son even though she loved to talk. She had her reasons, but if she didn't speak, she had to hold it in, which was painful. Yet, she was the one who called Mao Gen unhappy? That blew his mind. How could he be unhappy if he liked her so much? Mao Gen's heart was twisted every which way.

The next day, when Song Hui picked up Mao Xiaogen, Mao Gen apologized to her and said not to take his words seriously, especially if they had offended her. "What are you babbling about? I can't even remember what you said."

"I can't either."

"So, why are we talking about it?" She'd already forgot, or she didn't care. Otherwise, she wouldn't be … his Song Hui.

Mao Gen no longer tried to stop the couple from fighting each other, letting the sharp knife poke his heart, lungs, liver, and every muscle and sinew. That was the right thing to do. He had to bear it with Song Hui.

4

Mao Gen hung a string of small colourful lights on the back wall. Mao Xiaogen thought the eyes were too small, but he was still obsessed. These little eyes were all "being bad," open and closed, closed and open again. Still, Mao Xiaogen was no longer afraid of the dark night without the eye, at least not as afraid. The flashing eyes teased him, and he teased the flashing eyes, and in the midst of the playfulness, he fell asleep in peace.

Hospitalization was still useful, perhaps thanks to Dr. Zhao. She at least made Mao Gen understand that his son's illness was related to the brain, not the stomach. but the greatest credit was due to Song Hui. Mao Gen didn't dare tell Song Hui that he and his son escaped from the hospital. Naturally, he blamed himself for such deception and punished himself by slicing his leg with an arrowhead. The doctor was really competent, but Mao Xiaogen wouldn't get any better. "Thanks so much for the suggestion, Hui. It's been a while. You doing well?" Mao Gen greedily sniffed the aroma of sweat mixed with that of grass and beans on Song Hui's body as he spoke. He wanted to shake Song Hui's hand, which he had never physically touched before, but both of Song Hui's hands were busy, forcing him to mentally imagine himself taking her palm in his. "I can't repay you in this life, so I can be a bull or a horse for you to use in the next life," he'd often say.

This set Song Hui off. "Stop with all that groveling, will you?"

That's what family members say to one another!

The former school principal came and said that Mao Xiaogen shouldn't just be sitting around and needed to get back to his coursework. When he was still principal, he was forced to pull Xiaogen out. The school couldn't be held liable for a student as volatile as he was. In fact, the principal almost lost his job after an accident. He worked as a private tutor for more than three decades before becoming a formal teacher. He was about to retire, and he was afraid of making any mistakes. After Mao Xiaogen dropped out of school, his guilty conscience started to weigh on him. Post-retirement, he no longer needed to worry about taking responsibility. He planned to teach Mao Xiaogen how to read. He could teach Mao Xiaogen at his home, and Mao Xiaogen would be his only student. Why all this in the first place, though? To make up for what he had done? Mao Gen's suspicions were raised. The principal seemed to know what Mao Gen was thinking, saying that he had nothing else going on for him. He felt lonely amid the endless boredom, and his blood pressure had been rising. No "compensation" was needed. Mao Gen said he needed to consider the offer. Actually, he wanted an excuse to discuss things with Song Hui. "Why'd you do *that*? What's there to discuss?" Song Hui responded at once. "You should go and thank your ancestors for accumulating good fortune for you!"

Mao Xiaogen became the former principal's student, but Mao Gen didn't feel at ease. He had no excuse or reason to go to Song Hui's house again, and she rarely came over. Although Mao Gen intentionally passed through Song Hui's door when picking up and seeing off Mao Xiaogen, the chance for them to meet and talk was so small. Of course, Mao Gen could still hear her voice in the streets or at the store, which to some extent alleviated his inner hunger and thirst. He still "bore" things with Song Hui, and it would be better if the knife were to poke him harder so that he could feel comfortable. Compared to his tortured heart and his crazy yearning, however, her voice was a drop in the void.

At night, Mao Xiaogen could sleep long in most cases, but Mao Gen couldn't. On that day, Mao Gen didn't hear Song Hui's voice. They were neighbours and lived very close, but he didn't hear her voice all day. It was strange and unsettling. What was wrong with her? He couldn't figure it out no matter how hard he thought, but one thing was clear: her voice wasn't there. The "eyes" blinked so disturbingly that he almost jumped up and turned them off, but when he looked at the sleeping Mao Xiaogen, his hand was forced to withdraw. If he still couldn't sleep, he would get up and walk around Song Hui's yard. Song Hui had a high voice and snored loudly. It would be okay to listen in for a while. He was sure that he would hear it if she were there. After the inner turmoil subsided, he returned home.

Mao Gen once wanted to pull Mao Xiaogen out of his

classwork again, but he couldn't find a sound reason. The former principal treated Mao Xiaogen very well, often giving him walnuts, red dates, cakes, and the like. Although there were times he threatened punishment for not following directions by lifting a cane, he never struck Mao Xiaogen once. Of course, the more important thing was that the former principal worked hard, leaving homework every day and correcting every page. Except for the fact that Xiaogen had no other classmates, it was really like the brick-and-mortar school experience. Besides, would Song Hui agree to let Mao Xiaogen stop learning? The thought was laughable.

One day, Mao Gen went to pick Mao Xiaogen up and take him home, but the former principal was holding a flowerpot in tears. Mao Xiaogen had eaten the clivia that the former principal had been raising for sixteen years. Not only the leaves, but also the tubers were dug out and devoured. "This flower was just like my child," bemoaned the former principal, who with dishevelled grey hair suddenly appeared to be much older. Mao Xiaogen huddled in the corner, a trail of green juice dribbling from his mouth. Mao Gen grabbed him and raised his hand to hit him. The principal stopped him. "Doing that won't bring my flower back. This was my child. Mao Xiaogen is yours." Mao Gen slowly loosened his grip and repeatedly apologized to him. The former principal had suddenly come down with the runs and had to get some medicine. "I shouldn't have left him alone in the room. I should have taken him with me. It was all my fault." The former principal didn't blame Mao Xiaogen and shouldered it himself. The more the man said, the more apologetic Mao Gen became. One thing he didn't tell the principal was that every day when he went out, he had to put two handfuls of beans into Mao Xiaogen's pocket to ensure that he could have something to chew. That morning, he was negligent. At least half of this disaster had been caused by him.

Just after Mao Gen entered the yard, the former principal came out after him. He was afraid that Mao Gen would punish Mao Xiaogen. "These are flowers we're talking about. Nothing to beat anyone over." He then asked Mao Gen to send Mao Xiaogen to him on time the next day. If he saw Mao Xiaogen had been injured, he would never forgive Mao Gen. Apart from Song Hui, no one had been so good to Mao Xiaogen. Mao Gen felt that he had to compensate him for the clivia. Since Mao Xiaogen had eaten it, Mao Xiaogen would get him another pot. He thought of Ruhua. Mao Gen didn't have much contact with this woman, but she didn't seem like a difficult person to talk to. Unexpectedly, Ruhua refused. She said that Mao Gen could pick other flowers, but neither of the two pots of clivia she had. She didn't say why, but whatever the reason was, it was just a pot of flowers. Mao Gen said he had his reasons. He had come to buy one and let her offer a price. Ruhua said she didn't and would never sell flowers. She showed some unease. There was no room for negotiation. Mao Gen couldn't believe what he was hearing and angrily left, rushing into town to buy a pot for the former principal.

A year later, the former principal was taken to the city by his children. He'd fainted while giving lessons to Mao Xiaogen. After a thorough examination, no serious illness was discovered, but there was insufficient blood supply to the brain. The principal called Mao Gen and told him he would be back in a few days. In order to keep the former principal physically nearby, however, his son and daughter found him a job as a custodian in a private school. This immediately tied him down. On the phone, he guiltily explained the situation and apologized endlessly.

Mao Xiaogen returned to Song Hui, and Mao Gen fell into the honey pot again. His mouth was filled with honey, his tongue covered with sugar, and his eyebrows and eyes were smiling. He didn't want to be discovered, especially by Yang Bacha, so he had to feign feeling blue. "What's all the fuss about? I'll teach him how to count and write. I'm no egghead, but simple things are okay."

Song Hui wasn't just saying this just to say it, and she taught Mao Xiaogen attentively. One day, Mao Gen brought stewed bean curd with potatoes to the table and said, "Just hold on there, champ. It's hot," to Mao Xiaogen, who had been waiting for a long time. Mao Xiaogen knocked on the bowl.

"Goo-duh."

"What's up with you? What cat ate your tongue?" Mao Gen asked.

Mao Xiaogen hit the bowl again and said that he was speaking English. "Goo-duh. Good."

Mao Gen froze. "Who taught you that?"

"Mrs. Song!"

Mao Gen was incredulous. "She's been teaching you how to speak another *language*?" Mao Xiaogen nodded. Mao Gen was too excited to control himself. "How? What'd she do? How does she teach?!"

"No. Itch."

"I'll scratch your back later. Just answer my question."

"No!"

"No?"

"No eetch … eats … eat. No eat. *No eat!*"

"'No eat'? Do you mean," Mao Gen paused, "that you don't want to have anything?" Mao Xiaogen nodded. Mao Gen was so happy that he felt like he was about to fly and couldn't hold himself down.

He couldn't help running to Song Hui. "You know *English*? Not even the former principal does!" Song Hui's bosom trembled wildly when she laughed so hard that she had to catch her breath later. Mao Gen gave her a hand. Song Hui smiled.

"I don't know *that* much, just a few words and phrases."

"That's more than I know! Who taught you?"

Song Hui kept stroking her chest. "TV." Mao Gen couldn't believe it. "Really. You should get a TV for your son."

"Isn't that all fake?"

"What's it matter either way?" Mao Gen didn't reply. If someone else had said that, he would have found something to throw back, like how fake and real don't make a good couple, but he couldn't bear doing that to Song Hui.

Mao Xiaogen would always use the words "no" and "good" mixed with some others here and there whenever he could and replaced their Chinese equivalents entirely. Mao Gen became tired of this gig after a while.

Song Hui had helped out yet again. Mao Gen knew he ought to thank her as well as Yang Bacha. He bought a pack of Yuxi cigarettes for Yang Bacha and a bottle of Huangqi freckle removing cream for Song Hui. After waiting a few days, he finally had the opportunity to meet her alone. He took the bottle out from his inner jacket pocket, his heart beating like a drum.

"What's that?" Song Hui looked at the box, opened it, took it out, smelled it, and closed it again. "What's this all about?" She still spoke loudly, but her breath was a bit soft.

"I wanted to thank you for everything you've been doing. We wouldn't have made it far without you."

"What do you mean? I just—"

"No one's ever treated Xiaogen like a human being except you and that principal."

"No one has a perfect life. Xiaogen's issues unfortunately become visible for everyone to see. He likes sleep, but he's no freak."

"There really aren't many people like you, are there? Your kindness is something I can't ignore."

"Don't be so pessimistic. Of course there are kind-hearted people out there."

"None I'm aware of."

"Enough of that. Thanks, but I just can't take this." Mao Gen seemed to freeze as if hearing a judge utter his death sentence. "Money doesn't grow on trees. Don't spend it all on something like that."

She's thinking of Xiaogen.

Mao Gen finally came back to life and then said. "It wasn't anything outrageous."

"I never use the stuff. My blunt face isn't fit for it."

"Why do you always look down on yourself like that?!" Mao Gen exclaimed.

Song Hui was stunned. "There's no need to shout. Just about sent chills down my spine."

Mao Gen's gaze dispersed like a mist, and Song Hui suddenly became blurred. He shook his head, and she became clear again. She had a wound on her face, probably cut by the hard sole of some shoe. He'd noticed it long ago, but it stood out all of a sudden. "What do you mean it isn't fit? I'd say it's better than gold."

This was a brazen and reckless move. Mao Gen originally only wanted to give her the cream, but he didn't have the ability or courage to express his love to Song Hui until that very last sentence.

No matter how careless Song Hui was, she wasn't dim-witted. No one had ever said that her face was more precious than gold, not Yang Bacha, not Maixiang, not even her son. Not even she herself. The pores were big and the skin was dark. If exposed to the scorching sun for half a day, it would look like suede shoes and could contain four pounds of dust overtop. She didn't feel inferior because of this. Everyone has a unique appearance. The gods made her look like this, and there was nothing to complain about. Still, Mao Gen had said that her face was more precious than gold. After her initial shock, Song Hui felt awkward. She knew of Mao Gen's quirks, but she never took them to heart. He was just the strange type, already abnormal. When he said what he said, though, she couldn't even pretend not to understand it. Mao Gen couldn't really talk to anyone, so he would see her as a flower. He was really bad at praising people. Song Hui's mouth had already burst out into laughter. The whole thing was ridiculous. Suddenly, she felt something rushing and crashing into her chest. She wanted to stop and gritted her teeth, but instead of stopping, her body shuddered. "God!" She began to weep.

Mao Gen, having seen her distress, turned tail and ran.

5

This time he was in some big trouble, not just mere inconvenience. He ruined his own sky. Mao Gen fled for home, feeling butterflies in his heart, waiting for Song Hui to come and smash the box of facial cream on his forehead and to slap him in the face. He was like a toad that wanted to eat swan meat. What wishful thinking! Night had fallen, though, and Song Hui wasn't there. Neither was Yang Bacha. Yang was the definition of a bluff who liked to brandish a shovel. Mao Gen was never afraid of him, but the mishap he caused changed matters a great deal. He was ready for his comeuppance. In the end, however, it seemed as if Song Hui refused to tell her husband. She was never one to hide things. Why now? Mao Gen circled around Song Hui's yard like a donkey pulling a millstone. He tried to hear something, Song Hui's crying or snoring, but there was no sound whatsoever. He imagined Song Hui's eyes wide open. How could he sleep when his sky had fallen? Perhaps she didn't fully understand what he meant by his words and didn't choose to do anything about it. After the sky was long black, Mao Gen finally ran out of steam and dragged his stiff legs home.

Mao Gen didn't send Mao Xiaogen to Song Hui's house. It

was as if her yard was a field of landmines. He dared not step onto it. He was waiting. It was a long day. Mao Xiaogen was playing marbles alone. His left hand represented one person, and his right hand represented another. When the "two" quarrelled, one of the marbles would be swallowed. Of course, just like swallowing those coins, they would eventually find their way out the other side. His stomach was like an iron wall. Mao Gen couldn't do anything. He originally wanted to make several arrows, but after cutting his hand twice in succession, he had to give up. Mao Gen had been motionless for hours while hunting, but that kind of thing was much more appealing than this. As dusk approached, nothing had happened. He breathed a great sigh of relief, but he was also very disappointed.

On the third day, Mao Gen had an idea and let Mao Xiaogen go alone. No matter how many mines she had buried, none would blow Mao Xiaogen to smithereens. Mao Gen knew this very well in his heart. Song Hui herself said she would never leave Xiaogen. Perhaps he was the key to dismantling those mines. After a while, Mao Xiaogen returned with a bowed head. Mao Gen's eyes darkened, as if the eye in the sky had suddenly been plucked out. "She turn you away?" Mao Gen's voice was trembling. Mao Xiaogen shook his head. Mao Gen grabbed him around the shoulders. "What happened?"

"No wan dare," he attempted in English.

"She's not at home?"

"Door's shut."

"Where is she?!" Mao Xiaogen said nothing. Mao Gen realized he was being as thick as pig dung. He slammed his hands on the crown of his head. "That's right! She said she wouldn't be home for a few days. I'm losing it!" He never concealed anything from Mao Xiaogen.

The autumn harvest began a few days later. Two years prior, the combine harvester made its debut in Songzhuang Village. The iron beast was diesel-operated and worked much faster than any human. The wheat and naked oats were shaved off in no time. Seeds and stalks were separated, and people just needed to transport them via cart. The iron wonder was only good for huge tracts of land, though. Sickles were still the go-to for smaller plots. Mao Gen had three small ones to himself, one of which was adjacent to Song Hui's land. Mao Gen planted it with naked oats, while she grew flax. Mao Gen didn't let Mao Xiaogen go alone to Song Hui's house anymore, but he took Mao Xiaogen down to the field every day. The oats ripened early, which meant he wouldn't run into Song Hui, but every time he looked up, he would look into her field. He was slow with his sickle, taking his sweet time, but never once did he catch sight of her plump, sturdy figure. When the harvest was over, however, he still had an excuse to be out in the field. Rats packed food in secret "granaries" of their own to overwinter, but none could outsmart Mao Gen. He was the best rat-granary hunter there was. One year, he raked in four hundred fifty pounds of wheat, four hundred pounds of naked oats, and seven hundred pounds of flax, all from these critters' secret bunkers. People said the things were hard to find, but Mao Gen believed humans were smarter. Rats were lower on the food chain after all.

Finally, Song Hui appeared, but she came with Yang Bacha. She cut the crops and Yang Bacha tied them. Mao Gen also prepared a sickle in addition to the probe and bag, ready to help. This was a chance to approach her. She might welcome him, at least not show him a cold face. She was the only one who swept the field the previous year, so he thought it would be the same that year. What was the matter with Yang Bacha? Did he have nothing else to do? Mao Gen was perturbed. Still, Song Hui was back. He hadn't seen her for days. His wait was far from in vain. This thought alone brought a spark back to his spirits.

One rainy day, Mao Gen was lounging about. Mao Xiaogen was playing marbles on the ground when he suddenly cried, "Mrs. Song!" Mao Gen was unconsciously injected with a sharp dose of adrenaline. He turned his head and saw Song Hui standing at the door in a raincoat. Mao Gen wanted to sit up, but he was like a wild goose struck by a bullet, constantly fluttering and unable to support his body. Song Hui asked if he was sick. Mao Gen finally sat up, his face turning a deep shade of red.

"No!" he said. "No, just dozing off."

Song Hui lifted her hat and displayed the food bag in her hand. She had just cooked some corn and was offering a portion to Mao Xiaogen. Xiaogen reacted quickly, grasping the bag from Song Hui's hand, taking out an ear, and chomping down before husking it. The crop's aroma quickly filled the room.

"Watch it! It's still hot!"

"You're the one that always encourages him."

"It's just a few ears. I feel like I'm talking to a woman rather than a man, the way you hem and haw."

The familiar voice and tone were like the most beautiful melody, and Mao Gen suddenly felt refreshed. He was doing his best not to meet her gaze head-on, but he couldn't resist anymore. She seemed to have lost some weight, which must have been his fault. Her eyes were bigger, but deeper as well. He supposed it was also on his account. As the shadow over his heart passed, Mao Gen gave a dry smile. Song Hui was still Song Hui, her same carefree self, but something was different. There was a considerable gap between them.

"Look at those red eyes of yours. Sleepy head."

Mao Gen unexpectedly forgot to offer Song Hui a seat again. Mao Xiaogen tugged at her with one hand, the other still holding the ear of corn. Song Hui took a step forward, patted Xiaogen on the head, and said, "I can't stay. Got something to take care of." On her way out, she turned back. "Why don't you send Xiaogen over?"

The sigh that ensued was like that of a dead man walking being pardoned for the grizzliest murder. Mao Gen was delighted. Song Hui wasn't holding him to his words, meaning she decided not to think too much about what he had said. This was Song Hui's kindness. God only knows what would have happened had he fumbled like he did in front of some other woman. How could such a woman not pique his interest? As for that chasm between them, he believed it would melt away eventually. Song Hui was still his Song Hui, but he'd be more mindful in the future. He wanted to hide her in the bottom of his heart, where no one would ever find them out.

Song Hui had been gone for a long time, but Mao Gen could still smell her. The strong aroma of corn could not be concealed. The smell both enchanted and comforted Mao Gen, but there was a freshness to it he hadn't known before. He noticed it the moment she entered the door. At first, he thought it was the smell of a raincoat, but that wasn't it. Suddenly, his head opened like a skylight. The cream! It just had to be! Mao Gen was so excited that he was about to cry out in ecstasy. Yes, Song Hui had used the cream! She hadn't thrown it away, though that would have been better than smashing the bottle over his head. This small gesture was a win for Mao Gen.

The next day, Yang Bacha happened to be at home, and Mao Gen gave him the pack of Yuxi cigarettes and lit one for him.

"You win the lottery or something? Smoking something as expensive as Yuxi …"

"Just something special I decided to buy." He noticed the oil stain on Yang's sleeve and decided to lean in on that. "You do any repairs recently?" Sure enough, when it came to anything with an engine, Yang Bacha's eyes sparkled. He had a special fondness for gas-powered vehicles. Seeing one was better than seeing his mother, and he taught himself how to be an amateur mechanic. He could even figure out his way around a machine he'd never encountered before. If only he hadn't fallen to his drinking problem, he would have been some top-level power train expert. He was dull, yes, but not when it came to machinery. Songzhuang Village knew him well, but even people from other villages came to ask for his assistance. Yang Bacha didn't put on airs and never overcharged. Two packs of cigs and a spirit-paired meal was fair pay to him. It was no wonder he had constant access to booze.

Yang filled Mao in. Some guy in Li had been taken in and needed to sell his second-hand Dongfanghong tractor, three-bottom plough, and rotary tiller to cover his 40K bail. The four-wheel drive, 55 horsepower tractor was a Model 554 and was still in near-prime condition. His wife was in a frenzy trying to sell it, but she didn't know her way around. As long as the price was in the range of the asking price, she would sell it. "I had a look. Not a darn thing wrong with it, and the package was the complete deal!" His eyes were bulging so much in excitement that Mao Gen thought a school of fish was bound to pop out of his sockets.

Mao Gen didn't know anything about farm machines. Four-wheel drive and horsepower were like a foreign language compared to firearms. He never understood the fascination with motor vehicles, but he pretended to be all-in on the conversation, offering Yang another cigarette just as the first one was nearing its filter. "Course I had to look it over twice to be sure," Yang continued. Mao Gen didn't have the heart to listen to Yang

Bacha's rambling. He had a singular purpose for being there. Song Hui was teaching Mao Xiaogen addition and subtraction, and Mao Gen couldn't bear to miss out on hearing her wonderful voice. Mao Gen kept sniffing, the smoke far from a deterrent. The fact that Song Hui's scent was mixed in with it kept him rooted to the spot.

"I don't have any money, but I'd slap it down on the table if I did. What a deal!" Yang Bacha looked up longingly, as if the Dongfanghong tractor was hanging in the air. Mao Gen thought of someone painting cakes to satisfy a growling stomach. His shotgun was still hidden in the firewood room. Mao Gen had his desire. Yang Bacha was left longing for his. When Mao Gen thought of Yang Bacha beating Song Hui, Mao Gen's heart suddenly hardened. Mao Gen couldn't figure out how a mechanical genius could have been so fooled by some heavy-accented southerner, as Qian Zhuang put it. When the police handled the case, Yang was left without a single clue to provide them. Mao Gen couldn't fathom how the man failed to see just how much a treasure his wife was, but he kept his true feelings hidden as he handed him cigarettes and played into his sighs and woes.

Yang Bacha smoked the entire box of cigarettes in the blink of an eye. As for Mao Gen, he felt like his hunger was satisfied two times over.

In late autumn, Mao Gen welcomed another opportunity to accompany Song Hui.

Yang Bacha started to spit up blood after a nasty bout of drinking. He had already had a drink and engaged in yet another chat at Qian Zhuang's shop, but he couldn't refuse a toast, no matter how many he downed. That night, Yang Bacha was sent to the town hospital by Qian Zhuang. Song Hui called to ask Mao Gen to help feed their pigs, so that's how he found out.

The next day, Mao Gen took Mao Xiaogen to visit. Yang Bacha was like a cooked shrimp, curled up in a corner of the hospital bed and appearing half his normal size. Song Hui's eyes were red, and her face was sunken from exhaustion. Mao Gen's heart was punctured instantly. Song Hui said it was nothing serious and that Yang would be discharged in two days before laying in on Mao Gen for coming. Mao Gen said he was worried, so he had to come and have a look. He let her sleep while he took care of Yang Bacha. Song Hui later asked if he could stay longer as she went back to the village. "Of course," said Mao Gen, adding that he had fed the pigs. Song Hui said there were other things she had to take care of. She didn't explain; neither did he ask.

Song Hui returned to the hospital in the afternoon, her face covered with sweat. "Go ahead on back," she told Mao Gen. Mao Gen walked out of the ward, thinking about her sweaty face. He led Mao Xiaogen around the town, ate steamed buns, bought him a pound of peanuts, and returned to the hospital. While Mao Xiaogen was eating steamed stuffed buns, he went to the cosmetics store across the street. When he returned, he had something in tow. Mao Gen asked Song Hui to take Mao

Xiaogen back to the village, saying he would stay to take care of Yang Bacha and chat with him about tractors. Yang Bacha's eyes suddenly brightened. Song Hui refused, but Mao Gen's words were sincere. "You stepped in for Xiaogen. Can't I do the same with Bacha?" A standoff ensued.

"It'll be fine for a night," Yang interjected. "It'll help pass the time."

"I just got here and don't want to go all the way back."

"You don't have to. There are some empty beds here. I'm sure you can find a place tonight and can go back home tomorrow."

This was what Mao Gen had been planning on and hoping for for quite some time. Yang Bacha did all the convincing for him. Mao Gen's blood was rushing and almost broke through the top of his skull. He didn't believe in gods; they never gave him what he wanted. This time, though, he suddenly believed that someone or something was helping him. Gods also had eyes and saw into his heart. Mao Gen immediately agreed, remarking on how both the ward they were in as well as the next one over were empty. Song Hui looked at Yang Bacha and then Mao Gen and asked, "If Xiaogen doesn't sleep, how can we?"

"He stays up all Chinese New Year's Eve when he doesn't sleep well, but he always listens to you when you ask him to get some rest."

This sentence got inside Song Hui's heart. She grinned. "Got a point." When everything was settled, Mao Gen was willing to do whichever god had helped out a favour, even if it meant knocking some heads in.

Mao Xiaogen, who was used to sleeping with colourful eyes, refused to go to bed, but Song Hui had a way. She whispered in Mao Xiaogen's ear for a while and coaxed him into bed. She settled in next to him, held him in her arms, and asked Mao Gen to pull the curtain between the two beds. As he obliged, he had the daring, bold, and excited guess that Mao Xiaogen's hands had to be holding some part of Song Hui's body. The two were covered by a comforter, but Mao Gen knew he guessed right. No wonder Xiaogen was being so obedient! Mao Gen sat opposite to and chatted with Yang Bacha. When it came to tractors, Mao Gen rarely needed to utter a word edgewise. The curtain separated Yang Bacha from Song Hui. Yang Bacha couldn't see her, but Mao Gen could. Mao Gen's heart was with Song Hui, and he could sense any movement she made. Yang Bacha finally became drowsy and couldn't stop yawning. Mao Gen carefully tucked him in, had him lie down on an empty bed by the door, let him sleep, and turned off the light. The three beds were side by side, with Yang Bacha passed out on the far end. The curtain kept the slumbering Yang Bacha in his own separate space. While Mao Gen and Song Hui were on the same side of the curtain, although they weren't on the same bed, the space was integrated. Both were apart from Yang Bacha. This night belonged to Mao Gen, lying in the same room with Song Hui. It was no different from being together. Mao Gen's eyes were wide open, and his hard-earned time would be wasted if he slept. He couldn't! He wanted to enjoy it with each passing breath and savour each bite. Perhaps Song Hui would get up in the dark and lie down by his side, and he ... A shudder struck, and Mao Gen almost stopped breathing.

In late autumn, the house should have been as cold as water, but Mao Gen was getting hotter and hotter as he was lying over a brazier, almost melting. Shouldn't Song Hui be over the brazier, too? As he thought about this, he found Song Hui begin to rise. Mao Gen's breathing became rapid. Song Hui trod over lightly, but Mao Gen didn't dare move. He didn't know what she was going to do. Song Hui stood by his bedside for a moment, undoing her buttons one by one. Her skin was fair, and Mao Gen's eyes were shaking, his voice barely holding back from crying out. Song Hui promptly covered his mouth, grabbed his hand, and placed it on her plump bosom. Mao Gen gritted his teeth, but they were still chattering. She slid into the bed and covered him like a sack.

Mao Gen suddenly woke up. Damn it to Hell ... He'd fallen asleep! How could he do such a thing?! At least the god or gods had awarded him a dream. He had never had such a fantasy. Sensing moisture underneath, he realized the dream was a wet one. It was still baking hot. Song Hui had only illuminated his heart in the past, but on that hot night, Mao Gen was completely ignited by Song Hui, from top to bottom, from inside to outside. He didn't close his eyes anymore, trying to restrain himself from letting the hot magma within erupt through his mountain.

Early in the morning, Mao Gen was smoking in the hallway.

When Song Hui came out, he stuffed her hands with a container of facial cream, named Yumeijing, that had been held in his grip all night. He didn't say anything and also didn't give her a chance to speak. He then quickly walked into the ward. He had taken the plunge, and even if she hit him in the face, he would let her. After twenty minutes, Song Hui returned to the room. Mao Gen turned his back to her and avoided looking at her. Song Hui didn't hit him, but her voice was a bit special.

"Today's a bit cooler, don't you think?"

6

In the midwinter, the earth cracked like a mouth suddenly opening wide, and people had to raise their feet when walking to keep from being swallowed whole. Despite this, Mao Gen had been "bitten" several times, mostly when he was distracted. Since his second secret encounter with Song Hui, Mao Gen had circled around Song Hui's yard almost every night and refused to leave until dark. He gazed around and sniffed at the air, but as soon as he left, he thought the boiling magma was ready to burst yet again, poised to melt him at any given moment. Sitting and lying restlessly made it difficult to fall asleep. He had to turn over again and again, allowing his body to slowly cool. This was his homework as well as his medicine. He was beyond redemption at this point.

Although there were secrets, Mao Gen didn't dare make another mistake. A popular song went, "Eyes can meet, but two hands cheat." True, he hadn't officially taken Song Hui's hand. In the past, Mao Gen's wish had been vague, but he finally had a clear goal: to have her heart and body and to make her truly a woman of his own. Song Hui was still carefree, but there was something else in her eyes. Mao Gen was convinced that it came from their secret encounters. That day would come eventually.

Snow is the lover of winter, and winter without snow is boring and uninteresting. A heavy snowfall immediately brought vitality to the withered world. As a hunter, Mao Gen naturally liked snow because it helped him track his prey. An eagle flying high can not only see the hares hopping on the ground, but it is also said to be able to recognize their urine and feces. Mao Gen could, too, even if the urine froze. Hare urine was notably different compared to that of sheep, dogs, and humans. How so? Mao Gen couldn't say why exactly. He just knew. Even Mao Gen's grandfather might have lacked such an ability, but this spirit that possessed Mao Gen only manifested when it snowed. There were traces to follow. An approaching snowstorm also gave rise to other signals that Mao Gen had a magical ability to recognize.

A woman had been added to the chaotic mix for him this time around, though. Since becoming obsessed with Song Hui, he rarely hunted. She turned her nose up at the idea, so Mao Gen no longer needed the signs in the snow. More importantly, however, snow meant he couldn't circle Song Hui's yard anymore. He didn't want to leave messy footprints for others to track.

A bout of heavy snow drifted in to Mao Gen's great chagrin, falling for two days in a row as if on purpose. On the seventh or eighth day of sunshine, the ground finally hardened a bit, but in came another front. Mao Gen became worried. He had never believed in anything, and now he was thinking wildly. Was something stopping him? Why torture him in such a way?

A night without action in the house made him stir-crazy. That stubbornness of his resurfaced. He didn't believe that gods could stop him. He couldn't walk around Song Hui's yard, so he went around the village. Although it was a bit far from Song Hui's home, she was still in his heart. She was still his.

A few days before Chinese New Year, Song Hui's son, Yang Zhuangzhuang, returned for the first time. Yang Zhuangzhuang was like his mother, standing sturdy at five eleven. He hadn't come back in five or six years. This year, however, he brought back a "daughter-in-law" for Song Hui. She dressed ostentatiously in a leather skirt and long boots, a small red down jacket, and with hair that was mostly red like fire, but her bangs were blue. Her eyebrows were shaved off and replaced by two long, thin tattoos resembling eyebrows that stretched toward the temples. Her eyelashes were like two curtains that, when lowered, could cover the eyes. Her legs were like hemp stalks, the waist like a sifter. She looked like a goblin, which was fine because it was probably a popular style in cities. The problem was that her figure fell apart under careful scrutiny. She had no hips, and her chest was high, obviously the mark of some famous plastic surgeon. The most difficult thing to hide was "her" Adam's apple, though, which was the size of a walnut. Apparently, the rumours going around about Yang Zhuangzhuang were true.

The faces of Yang Bacha and Song Hui were unhappy, but Yang Zhuangzhuang was generous and introduced Wu Miaoran to Mao Gen. The name also seemed awkward. Wu Miaoran was actually a bit too cutesy. "Zhuangzhuang's told me so much about you." Wu Miaoran's voice was soft as if her throat had been pinched somehow, but it wasn't gentle at all. Mao Gen couldn't figure out exactly how things got that way. Yang Zhuangzhuang was tall and strong, so why not … find a girl? No wonder Song Hui never mentioned him. What kind of person Yang Zhuangzhuang preferred had nothing to do with Mao Gen, but he was the son of Song Hui, so Mao Gen couldn't turn a blind eye. The normal festive air of Chinese New Year was swept away, and Mao Gen felt as if some unknown stopper was blocking his heart.

The next day, Mao Gen went to the shop to buy some soy sauce. Five or six men were talking about Yang Zhuangzhuang and the "pretender," Wu Miaoran. To be precise, it was an argument about how the two could … Well … Some people said that Wu Miaoran had undergone surgery and had a hole carved out. The keyhole, one might say. Others argued that people's bodies were made by forces unbeknownst to humankind and it was a crime against nature to change them. Heart, liver, spleen, and kidney could be replaced, but bodies couldn't. What else could they do? When juices flowed, perhaps a backdoor was needed. How unsanitary and uncomfortable that had to be! The intestines and stomach were covered with soon-to-be excrement, but that seasoned the meat, perhaps. Some people said that using mouths was popular in cities. Immediately, someone objected, saying that Wu Miaoran's small mouth wouldn't be able to take it all in.

No one had a solid answer to the confounding riddle presented, though. Someone asked Qian Zhuang, who was balancing his sheets, what he thought.

"You guys really don't have anything else to do, do you? If it's eating at you that much, why don't you go ask Zhuangzhuang himself?"

The group stopped bickering at once, with one saying that they would be scolded for being so bold. In the end, they changed to another enigma: Wu Miaoran's background. It was said that this lad-turned-lady came from money.

Mao Gen couldn't listen anymore and quickly made his exit. He couldn't stop them, so he could only duck and cover. Only Qian Zhuang had said something decent. They only cared about the novelty. No one cared about Song Hui, and no one was willing to help her. Mao Gen wanted to help, but he didn't know how. When Yang Zhuangzhuang came back, Mao Gen kept Mao Xiaogen at home. He didn't see Song Hui for a whole day. He could only imagine how she … A massive pain gripped Mao Gen's heart, and his feet became heavier.

On Chinese New Year's Eve, Mao Gen and Mao Xiaogen sat in front of a TV. Mao Xiaogen was surrounded by a pile of food including melon seeds, peanuts, candy, fried dough twists, and apples. Every New Year's Eve, Mao Gen was generous and let Mao Xiaogen eat as much as he wanted. People like Mao Gen were gifted a bag of rice or noodles and a giant jug of oil by the local government. This year, Mao Gen asked Song Pin if he could have a TV set instead, but the only thing Song Pin said in return was that Mao Gen was being greedy. "You think the government is some big buffet you can just take what you want from?" Mao Gen turned and was about to leave. Song Pin stopped him again, giving him the village committee's TV set. Of course, it was merely lent to him, and Mao Gen had to return it after the two-week Chinese New Year celebrations were over. It was the first time Mao Gen and Mao Xiaogen watched TV at their home. Mao Xiaogen was as bouncy as popcorn. Mao Gen stared at the screen, but his eyes were empty, his ears not really taking in what he heard. Instead, he was planning his next move.

Mao Gen thought Song Hui would come, and she did. She'd picked up some food, which was obviously for Mao Xiaogen. Song Hui hadn't bought a new dress. Everything she had on was old and worn. The only thing new was the sadness in her eyes. Mao Gen's heart sank. "It's cold out. Why come here?" She simply snapped her head back in lieu of an answer.

Mao Gen followed Song Hui into the hall. "There's something I'm having difficulty with. I was wondering if you could do me a favour." She wasn't her normal self and was being strangely polite.

"What's this formality all about? Just ask, and I'll do it. I'd do anything for you."

"You're not a pig for me to direct around." The old Song Hui came back that moment before faltering again. "I just needed a space to cry. I feel like I'm suffocating and have no way to release all this pent-up emotion."

Mao Gen froze. "You want to cry?"

"Is that too shocking for you to handle?"

"No!" he replied hurriedly. "No, I mean … Zunai … Isn't that what Zunai's for?"

"It's New Year. How could I do that do her? Not to mention Maixiang wouldn't have it so randomly."

"I know you've been feeling up—"

"Don't dish it out like that, okay?"

Mao Gen pointed to the room west of his courtyard. "It's cold there, though."

Song Hui pushed through the indicated door, and Mao Gen pulled the lamp cord. The place was used as a storage unit for random things like grain, vegetable vats, and furniture. Hare skins were hung on the wall, and kang boards covered the windows on account of the grain, meaning artificial light was needed even during the day. Such an enclosed space was exactly what Song Hui needed. She sat on the ground. "Just turn those off and close the door," she requested. Mao Gen told her she'd catch a cold staying in there. "Are you *deaf*!" He was forced to back off.

Mao Gen wasn't far away, keeping watch over the door like a guard, but it wasn't long before he noticed that he couldn't hear anyone wailing. Afraid things might be taking a drastic turn, he gently pushed the door open but didn't pull at the cord again. From the light pouring in from outside, he could make out Song Hui's figure sitting exactly where he'd left her. She was like a clay sculpture.

"The tears aren't coming out!" Song Hui cried. "I have all this emotion, but it isn't finding an outlet. Is there anything you can do to help?"

"Wh-What?" Mao Gen didn't know what she meant.

"Hit me!" Song Hui ordered. "Use your shoe!"

"I ..." Mao Gen was like a deer caught in headlights. "I can't do that."

Song Hui began to get angry. "*Hit* me! Stop talking and *hit* me!"

Mao Gen bent down, grabbed her shoulders, and then kneaded them from top to bottom, over and over again.

Song Hui got even more upset. "I said *hit* me, not pamper me!"

Mao Gen grabbed her hand. "You're going to have to stand up for that. I'll do my best. With a jerk of his hand, Song Hui stood up, her legs and feet numb. She wasn't steady on her feet and fell forward, hugging Mao Gen around the neck. Suddenly, grief welling up, she cried like a flood bursting from a dike. Mao Gen closed the door with his foot. The two fell into darkness.

Song Hui was still holding Mao Gen's neck. She was taller than Mao Gen and rested her chin just above his forehead. Mao Gen found his mouth pressed right against her chest. At first, he didn't move, and something wet slid down his forehead, covering his face. It was her tears and saliva. Song Hui's chest vibrated rhythmically as her sobs changed length. Slowly, Mao Gen raised his arm and embraced her waist, which was pulsating at the same rhythm. This embrace made him almost one with her. The knife was still sharp and stabbing relentlessly through heart, but his happiness transported him away. It wasn't blood, but honey that flowed from his wounds. Finally, his bottled-up emotions burst beyond the cork. His tears freely mingled with Song Hui's and seeped into her clothing.

Song Hui's decision to come to Mao Gen's home had all been done in secret, so it couldn't last any substantial amount of time. Her wailing came and went quickly. For Mao Gen, it was too fleeting, but the preciousness of the moment had nothing to do with time. It was a historic breakthrough in their relationship. It was as if he had just taken a long, sweet drag of the best opium on the black market.

Mao Gen had despised and even resented Yang Zhuangzhuang. It was his return that had made Song Hui so unhappy, but most unexpectedly, Yang Zhuangzhuang became the catapult for him and Song Hui. Six days into the new year, Yang Zhuangzhuang and Wu Miaoran left. Mao Gen himself saw them off.

7

In early April, Yang Bacha left with his daughter, who lived in Baotou. Originally, Song Hui and Yang Bacha were supposed to go together, but Song Hui couldn't leave. The big pig had been sold, and she had just bought two piglets. Money was low, and the two piglets cost three hundred a pop. Song Hui stroked the pigs' backs each time she fed them so that the pigs would grow faster. She would also whisper to them, "Eat up and get strong and healthy. I'll take care of all your needs, so make good of what I give you." The piglets seemed to understand Song Hui's words and always nuzzled her arm or chest, their long snouts dribbling half-chewed fodder. After each feeding, Song Hui would be left with interesting stains all over her clothing. There were also sheep, chickens, and ducks to feed. They could be without Yang Bacha, but none could be without Song Hui. Her daughter and son-in-law performed traditional northeast Chinese song-and-dance routines as a duo and almost never had time to be at home. When other people would find time off, that's when their busiest season began. They were so busy that phone calls had to be dealt with separately, meaning one could do one call while the other would handle the next. Still, even with no time to be at home, a home base was always needed, so they had just put a downpayment on a house and were about to start the furnishing process. That was where Yang Bacha came in. He was tasked to be their interior decorator as well as temporary personal attendant over their possessions.

Mao Xiaogen was dropped off at Song Hui's three days after Yang Bacha's departure. Song Hui personally requested that he live with her for a while. Mao Xiaogen naturally liked the idea because her house had a big TV. Mao Gen didn't object at all. If Mao Xiaogen stayed with her, it might become possible for Mao Gen to stay, too. Mao Gen said he wanted to bring the colourful lights over, but Song Hui wouldn't have it. "Let me see what I can do with him." When Mao Gen remembered that night in the hospital, he suddenly felt both hot and parched. The next day, Mao Gen went over earlier than usual. The reason was because he had spent the whole night longing to see Song Hui. Seeing how Xiaogen slept and whether Song Hui's methods worked was merely an added bonus. Mao Xiaogen was still asleep when he arrived. Mao Gen's gaze fixed on Song Hui's face.

"He give you any trouble?"

Song Hui was busy and answered as she fluttered about. "Not in the slightest. He fell right to sleep after going to bed." Mao Gen was a bit jealous of this little boy of his.

In the evening, Mao Gen came over yet again. "You want him to stay another night, or …?"

"Stop hassling me, will you? Just go on and enjoy your own

time."

He was hoping she might say something else, but in the end, nothing else was said, not even after several days.

Evenings later, Mao Gen walked in. Song Hui and Mao Xiaogen were having dinner, fried potato strips and flatbread. Song Hui asked Mao Gen if he had eaten. He said that he hadn't yet. This was a lie.

"You came just in time, then. I baked too much flatbread."

Mao Gen refused, which he knew would agitate Song Hui. He asked Mao Xiaogen how many pancakes he had eaten. Mao Xiaogen shook his head, his gaze still on the TV.

"It's like I'm some stranger to him nowadays."

Song Hui glared at Mao Gen. "What? Are you saying he's been spending too much time with me?"

"Not at all. I should be thanking you. How you've managed to steer his habits has me blown away," he said. "Thank you. Really."

"Boy needs a mother." Mao Gen took the opportunity to stare at her. Her dark but red face, her thick and long braid. Those her age or younger didn't have long braids anymore, but she did. She usually wore two pigtails. That night, however, her hair was braided in one long plait, which was exceptionally thick. «You take issue with that?»

"Not at all." Mao Gen was a bit hesitant to be talking about the matter directly in front of Xiaogen, but that's when he noticed that Mao Xiaogen was getting sleepy and still holding half a flatbread in his hand.

"That TV has been frying his brain all day." She helped Mao Xiaogen lie down and pulled the comforter over him. The flatbread was still in his hand. She couldn't hold back a chuckle. "Just take that with you to your land of dreams."

Song Hui washed the pot and then fed the pigs.

"Anything I can do to help?" Mao Gen asked.

"No need." She wasn't overwhelmed and could even handle taking on three more pigs if she had to. She didn't drive Mao Gen away, so he didn't leave. Yang Bacha wasn't there, and Mao Xiaogen was sleeping. It seemed to be ordained by Heaven. Mao Gen's belief in the beyond rose once again. Something was brewing in the air, and the space suddenly became narrow. Song Hui walked in and out, always having something in her hand, but when she was finally empty-handed, Mao Gen couldn't contain himself anymore. He wanted to spring up and clamp her like an iron hook, but Song Hui's mouth was faster than his move to action. "Getting late."

This stopped Mao Gen in his tracks. This meant one of two things: either an invitation to leave or a request to hurry up and do what he'd been wanting to do for so long. He had no clue which one she meant. He hoped she would give him a hint, but Song Hui didn't. There was no expression on her face that could give him a sign. Mao Gen slowly stood up. "S'pose I'll be heading out, then." She didn't speak. Mao Gen was greatly disappointed. He walked very slowly, as if his feet were on thin ice, where one false move would plunge him into an icy abyss.

As he approached the gate, Mao Gen slipped a bit, causing the hot magma to roll inside him. He suddenly remembered something he'd heard once before in the shop: "Women like men who take charge." For the inexperienced Mao Gen, this sentence now emerged as both a lifeline and a signal. Song Hui was a straightforward person. Mao Gen shouldn't be so bashful, dawdling, or hesitant. He should be direct, spirited, and bold. He and she already had so many secrets, and her door was already open to him. It was he who didn't understand. Mao Gen's eyes were burning, and he took a few hurried strides. Song Hui was standing in the same place. She wanted to say something, but this time, Mao Gen didn't give her the chance. He rushed straight at her, pushed her against the wall, and touched the waist of her pant line. The fire within him turned him into a fumbling mess. It took him a while to find Song Hui's belt buckle. He tugged at it but couldn't pull it away, so he switched to the hand that was pinning Song Hui. He was both excited and nervous, but his hands weren't cooperating. He simply couldn't understand why everything wasn't just simply slipping off. He twisted the buckle, trying to snap the belt in two. Unexpectedly, Song Hui, who had been silent and trembling like he was this entire time, suddenly slapped his sweaty face.

Mao Gen was aghast.

Mao Gen was still in shock. His body was heaving violently, not only from the magma, but also with endless strikes from sickles, stones, and axes. Song Hui's scolding and wailing all rolled together and billowed. This wasn't how things were supposed to go. He and Song Hui had secrets. They had even hugged before! How much further could they go?! It was just as if only a layer of paper had been separating them, begging for something to break through. Mao Gen tried to smash his way through, but he'd been slapped for trying to get to the other side. What was wrong? How could this even happen?!

Mao Gen no longer circled Song Hui's yard. He picked up his long-unused, double-barrelled shotgun and rushed into the wilderness. He was about to burst. There had to be a way for him to calm down. No better place than the wilderness. He could walk with his eyes closed. At night, ears were more useful than eyes. He believed in Song Hui, but Song Hui didn't believe in him. On who's account had he refrained from hunting for so long? Mao Gen was both depressed and resentful. He didn't believe in anyone or anything anymore. He wanted … to kill … A hare, a squirrel, a kite, or a sparrow, whatever first crossed Mao Gen's path would be his for the taking. Listening with his ears, his mind was still wrapped up on what was going on between him and Song Hui.

By the time dawn arrived, Mao Gen had failed to find a single thing. There wasn't even a trace. It seemed every animal around knew he was approaching with malicious intent. Neither an animal nor a solution to his problem was discovered. Instead, the more he thought, the more confused he became. Mao Gen's heaving didn't disappear. His heart felt stoppered again.

As the sun rose, Mao Gen's eyes were red and swollen, and he wearily began to make his way back. Walking toward the side of Naobao Mountain, a murder of crows flew overhead. They cawed all the way, as if mocking Mao Gen for gaining nothing. That murder tipped him over the murderous edge.

He raised his shotgun and fired.

Chapter V

Zunai

1

The colossal ants' eyes were protruding, their heads and tails linked together like a robust chain. The opposite end of the chain was fastened to my ankle. The sun was scorching, and dust twirled in the air. I cried out and wrestled, but none of the grey shadows took notice of me. Helplessly, I reached around with my hands and attempted to grasp something, and at last, I seized onto something. Suddenly, the chain snapped.

I opened my eyes, finding myself lying beside achnatherum splendens. The verdant leaves were already a foot long, and the dried achnatherum splendens from last year were still reaching into the sky. Withered yellow and pale green, soft and firm, they clashed significantly with each other, yet constituted a singular entity. It felt as if I were beholding this for the first time, and uncertainty lingered. There were no clouds in the sky, which appeared as blue as if it had melded into one. Where was I? The itching sensation on my legs reminded me of my reclined position. I grasped the Bletilla and employed it to assist me in sitting up. The lower half of my body was unclothed, and several black ants were scuttling around my knees. A faint pain registered, and then I observed dried blood between my legs. I still hadn't fully grasped what had transpired, and my head began to throb. Amidst the discomfort, the scene unfolded like a cymbal hook.

I rose to my feet and determined my orientation. Once that was sorted, I found myself uncertain about the direction to take. The June breeze carried a warmth, yet it sliced through my legs like a razor blade. My gaze roamed for a while before settling on the achnatherum splendens, more than ten metres away. Something lay there. There they were—my red belt and black pants. My shoes were on the other side. It was surprising they had ended up so far away. As I dressed, I scanned my surroundings, fearing someone might suddenly emerge. My half-asleep brain abruptly snapped awake, absurdly alert. Father! Where was he? The sky spun, and my eyes darkened, but I managed to stay on my feet. The grass stretched expansively, and as I looked around, I spotted traces of flattened grass. Though not tall, the grass betrayed signs of disturbance upon closer inspection.

The grass imprints led me to my father's side, hundreds of metres from where I had collapsed. Whether the grass was flattened by me or my father was inconsequential at this point. I presumed my father had also fainted, and that belief persisted as I crouched down. He lay on his chest and abdomen, head turned to the side, slightly elevated as if fixated on something. His legs were bent, arms outstretched, and fingers spread like forks. I shouted and nudged him. My father felt as rigid as a rock. Summoning all my strength, I managed to turn him over. The image of that moment would haunt me for years, but at that instant, my mind abruptly ceased functioning. My father's chest was entirely stained red, yet it wasn't the blood-soaked and dried clothing that alarmed me, nor his pallid face. It was the swarm of ants scurrying around his chest. Red, black, and white, each exuding a sense of menace. For a moment, my thoughts turned to my mother. The ant colony, I speculated, was dispatched by her to bring my father to her side. My eyes remained wide, fixed, and unresponsive. To the left of his chest, a greater congregation of ants clustered around a hole. A sizable cavity in my father's body. Red ants, black ants, and white ants engaged in a frenzied struggle for the orifice. Ant colonies bit, shoved, and collided with one another. As the ant corpses piled up, some fell into the hole, while others were trampled by subsequent ants. Simultaneously, more ant reinforcements surged towards the hole from all directions. The ant colonies sought to employ it as a sanctuary, displaying madness, cruelty, and desperation. I was gripped by shock, taking a while before tears welled up. I removed the shoes I had recently put on and fiercely swatted at the ants. In my frenzy, I surpassed the recklessness of the ant colony. Their lifeless bodies accumulated like a mountain, but during brief respites, the surviving ants scampered away. Each moved with astonishing speed, yet as soon as they neared the hole, I perceived them as adversaries and promptly dispatched them.

Gradually, my strength dwindled, and my cries grew fainter. Eventually, I lowered my arm. I was no match for the ant colony, and even in my exhaustion, completely driving them away proved challenging. I scanned my surroundings once more, hoping for someone to pass by. The wind remained gentle, and a lark soared overhead. Not a soul was in sight. I relinquished any expectations. I had to handle it on my own. Unable to halt the ceaseless procession of ants, I needed to devise alternative solutions. I removed my tattered coat, rolling it into a cylinder like a rolling pin to seal my father's chest wound. Then, I plucked several Bletilla and clutched them in both my left and right hands to deter the frenzied ant colony. I harboured no fear, no hatred, and not even sadness, for I couldn't afford to concern myself with such emotions. This method proved effective; some ants fled, while others became disoriented and spun in place. In the June of the sixth year of the Republic of China, amidst the fierce battle with the ants, I learned a great deal, aside from my father's lifeless form. I remained Qiao Damei, yet I had undergone a profound transformation.

Li Fubo and Dawang sought me at noon. Yesterday, my father and I departed from Songzhuang Village, accompanied by Li Fubo's donkey. According to my father, we'd be able to return the same night. However, a night passed without any sign of us, causing Li Fubo to grow concerned. He summoned Dawang to help locate us. During that time, I was preparing to lay my father to rest. Lacking a shovel, I relied on my hands. I called out to Uncle Li, my eyes welling with tears, though they remained unshed. Li Fubo remarked, "If you feel like crying, just let it out. There's no need to hold back." Despite his advice, the tears refused to flow, and I repressed them. I reassured him, saying, "It's alright, Uncle Li." My composure surprised Li Fubo, but he chose not to comment further.

On the day I laid my father to rest, I fell ill. My entire body felt feeble, and my mouth was parched. Despite drinking several bowls of water, my throat still burned. Li Fubo sought the assistance of a town doctor. The physician examined my pulse and attributed my condition to excessive fear and yin deficiency. I doubted the doctor's diagnosis; while I might have been frightened, I wasn't terrified beyond reason. The doctor prescribed various medications, and Li Fubo enlisted Li Erni to prepare them for me and provide company. Li Erni's eyes were not level, and she rarely treated me with politeness, but her gaze unsettled me. Neither knives nor thorns, her eyes were soft and curved, resembling tiny whips. They didn't lash out at me, yet they hovered high, poised to descend at any moment. During the night, Li Erni suddenly let out a surprised shriek. I inquired about the cause, and she claimed to have seen a dark figure on the ground. My scalp tingled, but I remained composed. I remarked, "Erni, you had a nightmare." Erni pushed towards me, insisting she wasn't asleep and not dreaming. According to her, the dark figure touched her head. I fumbled to rise, lit a lamp, scrutinised the surroundings inside and outside, and warned Erni that I would dismiss her if she needlessly screamed again. Erni's face paled, expressing her discontent that I lacked conscience. She declared she didn't want to stay with me and that her father compelled her to accompany me. Even if I offered her two white steamed buns, she wouldn't agree. Unwilling to argue, I lay down, extinguishing the lamp. Erni curled up beside me like a child. Her fear was genuine. I reached for her hand. The next day, I took charge of my meals and medication, no longer requiring Li Erni's companionship. It was what Li Erni desired, but my words wounded her. She remarked, "I understand; you're an ungrateful house bird." Li Fubo also attempted to persuade me, claiming it was Erni who did a poor job, as he had already reprimanded her. I smiled and responded, "You misjudged Erni. She wasn't neglectful of me. I'm well now, so I don't want to trouble her any further." Li Fubo sighed, acknowledging that I exhibited even greater strength than my father.

Li Fubo had already reported to the police, but it took more than ten days for a uniformed official to come and interrogate me. Eventually, they mentioned that once the criminal was apprehended and brought to justice, they would verify the details with me before departing. Li Fubo tried to catch up with the official, uncertain of what to say, but the uniformed representative didn't slow down, displaying impatience. Despite his somber expression, Li Fubo entered the room feigning cheerfulness and remarked, "Bandits are not mightier than officials, and the earth is not mightier than heaven. Just wait, Damei, someone will settle your father's debt." The influence of the Qian Family was substantial. When the directive was given, my robbery case became unsolved. My father's misfortune held little significance for the government. The perfunctory questions from the uniformed official had already hinted at a grim outcome. While Li Fubo may not have been conflicted internally, he was merely offering consolation to me.

Li Fubo never broached the subject of the donkey, leaving it unspoken. However, I felt compelled to address it, though unsure how to broach the topic until I did. There was no room for further delay. I asserted that I would return the donkey to him as long as I remained alive. Li Fubo swiftly clarified that he wasn't discussing debt collection; it was simply about the donkey. Regardless of its significance, it paled in comparison to people. While he might not have had the intention of pursuing the debt, it didn't mean he didn't regard it seriously. Donkeys held equal, if not greater, importance than people. How could Li Fubo not feel distressed about losing his donkey? After all, it constituted a substantial portion of his property.

I had just made a promise to Li Fubo, though I was uncertain about its feasibility. A promise, by nature, carried no inherent weight. My father's box of curium pots and the meager few acres of thin farmland in Banpo were hardly equivalent to the value of Li Fubo's donkey. Unless Zhao Pangzi was willing to lend his assistance, or unless he still haboured hopes of his half-eared son marrying me. On the day I retrieved my father, Li Fubo sought my permission and spoke to Zhao Pangzi. However, there was no response from Zhao Pangzi, not even half a note. I had a premonition that if I were once a flower, albeit not very beautiful, now I wouldn't even qualify as grass. It wasn't worth the trouble, let alone nurturing extravagant expectations. After waiting for several days without any updates, I decided to take matters into my own hands. My aim wasn't to indulge in steamed stuffed buns; I simply wanted to return Li Fubo's donkey. If Zhao Pangzi assumed responsibility, I was prepared to comply with any request. In terms of audacity and thick-skinned resolve, Songzhuang Village couldn't produce another person like me. I wasn't afraid of becoming a subject of mockery. With the wilderness's stigma behind me, mere jests paled in comparison.

Naturally, I failed. It turned out that the Zhao family had returned my "Geng Tie"[1] five days before, which meant that the Zhao family had nothing to do with me then. Zhao Pangzi didn't humiliate me, but just scolded Hua Er Niang, a coquettish woman, for being useless, because the "Geng Tie" was returned by her.

I strolled a hundred and ten metres, and Zhao Jinyuan caught up. He was bent like a prawn in a wide arc. I declined his steamed dumplings.

Struggling to contain my annoyance, I'd stirred up a bit of trouble, and I was itching to escape this wretched town pronto. The outcome was predictable, yet I was merely affirming it. I held no grudge against the Zhao family and their lad, and they were quite civil towards me. Uncertain of the source of my vexation,

---

1 "Geng Tie" is a traditional custom in Chinese folk marriages. In ancient times, once a couple was engaged, they exchanged "Geng Tie," a piece of paper inscribed with eight essential details. This included their names, the eight characters representing their horoscope, ancestral home, and information about three generations of ancestors.

my thoughts were muddled, leading me down the wrong path.

It was already afternoon by the time I laid eyes on Songzhuang Village. My anger had dissipated, replaced by complete calmness. Yet, I discovered my feet were weak, my body felt weightless, and hunger gnawed at my stomach. I rested on the roadside for a while, contemplating why I had declined Zhao Jinyuan's offer of steamed stuffed buns. This anger seemed baseless. In the end, I still hadn't fully grasped the true "reason" behind it. The annulled engagement made sense; that chapter had been closed, and I wouldn't dwell on it any longer. Only Li Fubo's donkey occupied my thoughts. I couldn't rely on the Zhao family anymore. The question loomed: Where could I find money? Seeking respite, I sat down for a while and struggled to rise when dusk descended.

In the evening, I entered Li Fubo's house. Li Fubo seemed mildly surprised, perhaps due to the intensity in my eyes. He inquired, "What's the matter?" I shook my head. "It's nothing serious. I went to town today." Li Fubo turned around and retrieved the "Geng Tie." "Damei, I was worried you might take it hard. You shouldn't blame Hua Erniang; it was the 'Geng Tie' that I took from her hands." I smiled and assured him, "Don't worry, I won't act recklessly." Finally, I reiterated that I wouldn't do anything.

The following morning, I took up my hoe and ascended Naobao Mountain. Once, my father and I had tilled the land together, but now I had to tackle it alone. After cultivating the soil, I intended to make rounds with the curium box. Each person must carve out their own way of life, unique to them. However, they all proceed in that direction, unwavering and without fear of retreating. As one moves forward, the path widens. Glancing backward, the road narrows with every step backward. I couldn't burden the Li Fubo family any further.

When I reached the field, I was in a daze, and the ground had already been hoed. Initially, I had concerns about the weeds growing thick, resembling beards. Understanding the situation, my heart suddenly felt moist. Yes, it was the heart, not the eyes. I squatted and knelt between the ridges, extracting the agriophyllum squarrose sandwiched between the naked oats. Agriophyllum squarrose had a penchant for hiding amidst the seedlings. Once the soil on the back of the ridge was loosened, agriophyllum squarrose protruded among the seedlings and proliferated. It absorbed more water than the crops, and for every two times you hoed the field, it was necessary to pull out the agriophyllum squarrose. Later, Dawang arrived but walked to the other end of the field. At the centre, I remarked, "Dawang, you've worked hard." Dawang didn't look up; instead, he buried his head even lower. I continued, "There's nothing I can do to properly thank you. I'll treat you to fried cakes in autumn." Dawang remained silent. This quiet guy might still be upset with me.

My name bears a resemblance to Dawang's, but apart from that, there is no similarity between us. I hold positive sentiments towards him, even some curiosity, but he is by no means the husband I envisioned. That's why I didn't object to my father. However, Zhao Jinyuan doesn't fit the bill of my ideal husband either. Even though I have had no interactions with him, I am certain of it. To discern suitability, one doesn't necessarily need an extended period of time. Sometimes, a single glance suffices. I cannot articulate what my ideal husband is like, but I am certain that neither of them fits the description. Yet, I made a promise to Zhao Jinyuan. Is it the influence of my father's words, or have steamed stuffed buns charmed me? I cannot discern. Had I made a promise to Dawang, my father might not have lost his life, and I wouldn't be burdened with a debt that concerns me. Life is unpredictable, and I don't intend to blame my father. I habour no regrets. After all, no one can traverse backward, can they? Currently, I am solely interested in whether Dawang still wishes to marry me. On the morning of uprooting agriophyllum squarrose, I formulated a new plan when I unexpectedly encountered Dawang.

With God as my witness, I never intended to scheme against Dawang. My planning was for myself. I had already become a withered flower, not even equivalent in value to a donkey. By some standards, I might not even be as valuable as donkey skin. What about Li Fubo and Dawang? I'm uncertain; it might be worth it, or maybe not. If Li Erni were to express an opinion, I might be deemed as insignificant as a donkey dung egg. Li Fubo and Dawang may not think so, but how much influence do I really have? Let's start with Dawang. I didn't have many expectations; I just wanted to understand their perspectives.

At noon, I called Dawang over and handed him the parcel of wrapped dry food. It was undoubtedly not enough for a satisfying meal, and I hadn't prepared it for him. Dawang hesitated, "What about you?" I replied that I had already eaten. Dawang took my word for it; he had a straightforward temperament and didn't beat around the bush. I was familiar with his expressions. "I didn't see you eat," Dawang remarked. One of Dawang's advantages was his lack of pretence. "Huh? Were you peeking at me?" I shot him a slight glare, catching him off guard. Dawang immediately blushed and stammered, "No … I wasn't." I sighed at his innocence. "You just peeked at me. Don't you have the courage to admit it? Did you peek at me?" Dawang couldn't resist my gaze and confessed to peeking. Curious, I asked how many times. Dawang, being honest, stated it was nine times. Surprised, I remarked, "Nine times, so I'll have to punish you." Dawang grew extremely nervous. I decided, "Sour willow! You have to gather a bundle of sour willows for me today." Dawang's eyes lit up. "I'll go right now," he said. Before I could say anything more, he jumped up and ran away.

I sat slumped on the ground, unable to convey gratitude or sadness.

Dawang and I grew closer, and he assisted me with my tasks, digging and pulling out the sour willows. This inevitably stirred jealousy and discontent in Li Erni, even though each time Dawang brought back the willows, I would share half of them with her. Eventually, I discerned a somewhat gratifying aspect in the situation. Li Erni's heart wasn't malicious; it was merely consumed by vanity. A small heart tended to habour resentment, and vanity reveled in airs. She felt compelled to compete with others for survival, a trait ingrained in her since childhood. Someone destined to become a certain way might be predetermined. With the sour willow, if I didn't share it with her, she wouldn't be aware of it. By splitting it in half for her, she felt compelled to come over and check if I had more. If I did, or if she believed I did, words of jealousy would inevitably escape her lips.

I refrained from probing Li Fubo. Unlike Dawang, he was not someone you could size up right away. Nevertheless, Dawang's demeanour mirrored Li Fubo's attitude. Truthfully, Li Fubo was genuinely looking out for me. I couldn't determine whether it stemmed from pity for my vulnerability or if he believed in letting bygones be bygones, wanting to embrace me as a true member of their family.

Perplexed, Hua Erniang arrived at the door, dispatched by Li Fubo. Going with the flow, a hundred days after my father's demise, I wedded Dawang. According to the traditions of Songzhuang Village, weddings and funerals were not allowed in the same year. However, I couldn't wait.

2

I could sense the anxiety and confusion in Song Hui's narration. She was fearful and somewhat eager, her heart in turmoil with uncertainty about what to do. This wasn't inherently good or bad; it simply was. The concepts of good and bad were ever-shifting, contingent on individual perspectives. Not to mention, someone like Song Hui, with a simple mind, or even individuals with profound knowledge and precision akin to machines, couldn't formulate precise plans and measures.

"Zunai, what should I do?" Song Hui repeatedly asked.

I remained unable to provide an answer. Even if I were to sit up now, there was nothing I could teach her. This ability was beyond my reach, and even if I lived for another hundred years, I wouldn't possess it. Of course, Song Hui didn't anticipate a definitive answer from me. She simply wanted to converse. Much like Yang Zhuangzhuang's situation, talking to me seemed to provide solace for her troubled heart.

Ants were scurrying away.

3

Roosters heralded the first light of day, prompting Dawang to rise in the darkness. This practice was instilled by Li Fubo, my father-in-law. Even Li Erni, upon hearing the crowing of the cock for the second time, couldn't linger in bed. I heard Dawang carrying the urinal, and I urged him to put it down. Dawang whispered, "Nobody saw me." I insisted, "Put it down; it's my job!" Dawang earnestly placed it in the corner.

Mud needed to be moulded; if left unshaped, it wouldn't take form. Wood needed to be carved; there was no purpose in neglecting it. I didn't anticipate Dawang transforming into a different person, but at the very least, he had a way of conducting himself that wasn't deserving of contempt. For instance, regarding names, I taught Dawang, "If someone calls you stupid, you must ignore them. Remember, your name is Dawang. If the person doesn't address you by your name, they aren't worthy of engaging with you." Initially, he agreed. I warned, "If I hear or you inform me that you've responded to them, I'll impose a punishment, and you won't be allowed in my bed for three days." This approach proved to be highly effective.

Take, for instance, the task of emptying the chamber pot.

Having a chamber pot is a luxury for men, and not every man possesses one. Even in Zhangjiakou City, few people have the privilege of using silver chamber pots like Qian Guangwan. In most households, multiple individuals share a single chamber pot, raising the question of who should handle the task of emptying it. In Songzhuang Village, it was considered demeaning for a man to dispose of urine. I didn't permit Dawang to undertake this duty. As Dawang argued, no one would witness it, but that wasn't sufficient. To cultivate an image, one must first cultivate the heart. Without a well-formed character, creating an appearance is an unattainable endeavour. It's implausible to construct an image without a solid foundation.

Another example is sifting through the words of others and discerning whether they are genuine or meant to tease. The more attention you give, the more the teaser is inclined to persist, so it's preferable to disregard such teasing. Refrain from saying too much when you believe their words are genuine. Speaking excessively may lead to a loss. A simple smile suffices. Of course, if you struggle to distinguish between the genuine and the teasing, return and seek my advice.

I disciplined Dawang, and in the process, I disciplined myself as well. As the wife of the Li family, I made an effort to adhere to their customs. For instance, I ensured not to rise later than Li Erni. Dawang moved by my side, distancing himself from my father-in-law and Erni. If I overslept, my father-in-law wouldn't scold me, but I preferred not to receive special treatment. Dawang had previously roamed the village carrying a basket to collect livestock droppings from the streets. My father-in-law tended to the land, and Dawang excelled in his tasks. In one winter, Dawang even gathered half of the frozen wings near the village. I didn't have to venture outside, but there was plenty of work to be done both indoors and outdoors. I made a few modifications to certain customs, such as the ritual before meals. Before dinner, members of my father-in-law's family gathered around the table, each saying, "Respect for the land god." Dawang and I also respected the god, but I questioned the need to vocalise it. For me, keeping it in my heart held the same significance. The same applied to bowl licking. I prohibited Dawang from doing so; his tongue was already large, affecting his speech. If he continued stretching it this way, it would only get longer. Instead, I used clean water to wash the dishes, essentially adding an extra layer of cleanliness, superior to licking.

However, not all situations could be approached with calmness. There were always exceptions, and certain things remained beyond one's control. A notable example was when I found out I was pregnant.

This realization propelled me to expedite my marriage. Initially, I felt tremendous anxiety, uncertain about whom I could turn to for assistance or to whom I could disclose this shameful secret. I once considered confiding in Hua Erniang, but eventually, I abandoned the idea. Hua Erniang couldn't keep secrets. I tried various methods, such as binding my belly with a cloth strip, consuming lye, spending nights squatting on the urinal, and after marrying Dawang, I even rolled on the half slope of Naobao Mountain. At one point, I almost slit my belly with a sickle. However, heaven did not grant my wish, and I had subjected my unborn child to suffering in vain.

It became increasingly impossible to conceal the truth, and I decided it was time to stop hiding. There was no need for me to continue panicking and losing sleep over it. My father-in-law probably already knew about my pregnancy. If he couldn't face the situation, I would let Dawang leave me. In any case, it was just death, so there was nothing to fear. One day, after Dawang showed affection towards me, I disclosed to him, "You're going to be a dad." Dawang was genuinely surprised and asked if it was true. This fool should have noticed it already. I took his hand and placed it on my abdomen. "Really … really!" Dawang panicked and hastily tucked me in. This was Dawang's way; he may not have expressed himself eloquently, but his clumsy actions served as his language. His hand might not have felt it, but he believed in me. That was all I wanted.

One early morning in winter, before Dawang returned, I operated the bellows as Li Erni entered the room, carrying a golden pumpkin. It had been grown in the courtyard by my father-in-law and was a special seed melon. Placing it on the bellows board, Li Erni remarked, "Here you go! Don't eat the seeds!" I immediately grasped that my father-in-law had sent her over. The golden melon was his gesture. The weightiest burden on my heart was suddenly lifted, and I felt significantly more at ease. I requested Erni to take it back, conveying that the melon should be enjoyed by my father-in-law. Li Erni, habouring jealousy towards me, insisted, "How could you decline? You're a hero; it's meant for you." She held a bias against me, and I couldn't pinpoint when it had taken root. At every opportunity, she took pleasure in taunting me.

I didn't want to get frustrated early in the morning.

"Just leave it here," I said.

"Be careful when you eat it, the melon is ripe," said Erni. "Don't choke on it."

"Won't you go back to eat?" I asked.

"Dad sent me over to help you," answered Li Erni. "What can I do for you?"

"Nothing, you can go back."

"Then tell Dad, it's you who doesn't need me, it's not me who won't help you."

"I'll tell him later."

Li Erni, however, did not leave, leaning there, intentionally or unintentionally aiming at my abdomen. I figured she made up her mind again, accumulating anger and naturally venting it.

Sure enough, she couldn't hold it anymore, "Damei, how many months?"

Her curiosity was laced with landmines, and I wouldn't be fooled by her.

I smiled and said, "If I tell you, you won't believe me. You'll find out later."

"No wonder you love sour willows so much. If you had told me earlier, I would have given you all my half," said Li Erni.

I said, "If I eat too much, I will get a tooth ache."

Li Erni suddenly became mysterious. "Are you pregnant with twins? Your belly is about to catch up in size with the pumpkin," she asked.

I said, "You're very knowledgeable, who taught you?"

"Nobody taught me. I guessed. I like to guess," replied Li Erni.

I said, "Guess whether your husband-to-be has long legs or short legs, and if there are any pits on his face."

Li Erni's face changed. "Qiao Damei, I'm talking to you seriously."

I laughed, and said, "I am too, whether you guess it right or wrong, you will find out one day, right?"

Li Erni snorted, "I would rather marry a cat or dog than marry a fool."

I was not angry and said, "There aren't many people in the world who would call his or her brother a fool."

Li Erni said, "He's just a fool."

I cut her off and said, "Li Erni, you can insult me, but you can't insult your brother! If you say another bad word about your brother, I'll curl your mouth."

I yanked the shovel out of the stove. The fire shovel was emitting blue smoke.

Li Erni took a step back and squeezed out a dry smile. "Sister-in-law, he's stupid."

I exclaimed, "Don't insult him, no matter whether it's in front of him or behind his back!" Since I caught her weaknesses, I must let her have a longer memory.

Li Erni said, "I am not doing this on purpose."

I said, "You can't say it again even if it isn't intentional!"

Li Erni said, "If you don't need my help. I'm leaving."

I waved my hand. "Don't come again."

Following dinner, I brought the pumpkin to my father-in-law.

"It's not for you either. Don't carry it around everywhere." He remarked.

"I understand it's time to honour my father," I responded, "but it concerns him. How could I accept it?"

Let's split it up."

Just as Er Ni exited, my father-in-law inquired, "Er Ni didn't upset you?"

"No," I assured him, "she said she came to help me."

"If you need assistance, just ask her," My father-in-law commented. "She just has a sharp mouth."

"Don't worry," I reassured him. "She's kind to me. Her toughness is reserved for outsiders."

My father-in-law didn't say more; he understood his daughter's temperament. When meeting people, courtesy comes first, a lesson my father instilled in me from a young age. If I blamed Erni, my father-in-law might have scolded her. What good would that do? It would only foster resentment in Erni. Regardless of what happened, my father-in-law remained generous, earning my respect. I had no intention of making him angry.

There seemed to be nothing to worry about anymore. I really took it easy for a while. However, when my abdomen bulged, and the fetus kicked day and night, fear returned to me, and the level of fear increased day by day. It was a fear that is difficult to describe. I dreamed that I fell into a bloody river, my limbs twitching and struggling desperately. Finally, I climbed ashore, spitting blood and water crazily. Just as I was about to stand up, the mighty ants came over, some scratching my head, and some dragging my feet. I was dragged and couldn't help it. As soon as I escaped from the blood river and was dragged into the cave, I screamed with fear until I woke up. Another night, I was hung upside down on a tree by an ant colony. Ants were flying in the air, occasionally pricking my head and face with venomous needles from their tails, dripping blood, and smashing deep holes one after another. Another night, I saw my mother lying on the sand, ants coming in and out of her thighs. I tried to pounce, but my feet seemed to be tied and unable to move. One of the most terrifying dreams was during the day, when two half-human tall ants cut open my abdomen, grabbed the baby's arm, and raced along the way.

On a winter morning, I set out to gather firewood and spotted two ants with black bodies and red heads. It nearly took my breath away. What used to be a nightmare now felt like a clear blue sky with sunshine. Additionally, with every droplet of water turning into ice and chickens and dogs huddling in their nests, how could these ants possibly survive? I was on the verge of extending my hand when the ants suddenly darted along at such a high speed that I could barely keep up, eventually breaking into a trot. I swear, the ants didn't elude me, but in the blink of an eye, they vanished. Soon after, I heard a faint sob up ahead. I took a few steps, but the sound seemed to play hide and seek, jumping around. Perhaps there was an issue with my ear. Initially planning to retrace my steps, I found myself lost. If Dawang hadn't come to find me, I might have frozen solid. In reality, I hadn't ventured far. I suspect I had a hallucination and was chasing after it.

Li Erni came over every day, whether she liked it or not, or whether I welcomed her or not. "Do me a favour," I said, "If I die, tell Dawang to bury me with the curium pot box." Li Erni stared at me for a while and asked, "Who said you were going to die?" I said, "I guess I will." Li Erni asked, "Why don't you just talk to him?" I said, "I'm afraid to scare him." Li Erni was very angry and said, "Aren't you afraid of scaring me? I am even more timid than him." I said to her, 'You must help me with this, otherwise--" Erni was horrified by my expression and asked, "Are you really dying?" I said, "Maybe, this ... secret, you can't tell anyone." Erni nodded in horror. But she didn't keep the secret, as she turned around and told her father.

Three days later, my father-in-law summoned the midwife

from Dongpo. According to Erni later on, he had initially planned to invite the witch, but the witch had embarked on a long journey. Consequently, my father-in-law opted for a midwife as she also possessed some magical abilities. This marked the first time I encountered Master Huang. She was not of imposing stature, with a slender face, deep-set eyes, and an appearance suggesting she was in her fifties or sixties. Master Huang inquired about my condition, and I responded truthfully. After checking my pulse, she instructed me to lie flat on the bed. Placing her palm on my abdomen for a moment, she gently slid it across while chanting incantations. Next, she retrieved a yellow paper from her bag, cut two "8"-shaped symbols, ignited them, and mixed the ashes with water for me to swallow. Throughout this process, Master Huang's gaze was shrouded, creating an airtight seal that concealed her vision. At the culmination of the ceremony, she looked at me tenderly and with dignity, asserting that I had been plagued by a minor spirit. Now that the spirit had been dispelled, it would no longer disturb me. "The fetus is strong; you can rest assured." Remarkably, I have not been haunted by nightmares or hallucinations since then.

On an evening in early spring, I had just placed my meal on the table when a sudden ache gripped my abdomen. It had happened a few times before, but I had brushed it aside. I intended to rest after dinner. However, unlike previous occasions, the cramps didn't ease; instead, they intensified. I promptly instructed Dawang to summon Master Huang.

I have never been one to be coquettish. When my finger was cut with a sickle and a kitchen knife, I didn't even utter a sound. However, the pain of childbirth is incomparable to a mere cut; it's a pain that seems endless. Initially, it felt like being sliced with a blade, as if dense white bones were continuously being cut. Subsequently, the flesh clinging to the bone was cleanly severed. Then came the sensation of a drill, boring into the bones. Lastly, there was a biting sensation, as sharp teeth gnawed at the edge of the hole. This was the initial pain – a pain that one can comprehend, a pain with a form. Yet, accompanying this tangible pain was an intangible, shapeless agony, seemingly emanating from all directions, infiltrating the body through every pore. Eventually, I couldn't resist screaming until I lost consciousness.

The heavens and the earth seemed formless and void, shrouded in darkness, and my surroundings were unclear. I couldn't see anyone, but whispers, soft and gentle, filled the air. Slowly, I moved along with the sound, step by step, as the clouds parted, the sun rose, and birds soared while butterflies danced. When I opened my eyes, there was Master Huang – her slender face and deep eyes. She said, "The amniotic fluid has just broken, dear; it's not easy to have a baby. You have to endure, and I will transfer my strength to you." Master Huang cut the yellow paper once more, mixing the ashes into water. However, this time, she didn't let me drink it. Instead, she took a mouthful herself, turned three times on the ground, and suddenly sprayed it on me. Then, she grasped my hand. I was drenched and weak, yet in that moment, strength surged back into me. Not only did my body recover, but my trembling heart also steadied. I heard Dawang crying. "I'm not dead. Why are you crying?" I questioned. Shouting, "Dawang, if you cry again, I'll make you empty the urinal every day." The crying stopped abruptly. Amused, Master Huang remarked, "It seems that men are all afraid of emptying the urinal." I smiled too, feeling completely at ease.

Master Huang handed me a chopstick and instructed me to bite it. "It's not meat. Don't eat it." She directed me to follow her commands, applying force when necessary and refraining from using force when unnecessary. Additionally, she taught me how to leverage real strength versus virtual strength. When one's strength is wielded skilfully, pain can be transformed into a source of strength. Indeed, the pain seemed less intense than before. In that moment, I observed a light above Master Huang's head, akin to the sun's projection on the sky and clouds during a sunset.

Drawn to the light, I emitted a slight cough, and the hearty cry of the baby immediately filled the room.

4

I detected the scent of something burning. Song Hui was supposed to replenish the water, but her mouth seemed like an unyielding sluice gate that once opened, couldn't be closed. If I let her have her way, three days and three nights wouldn't be sufficient for her to finish talking.

Ants scurried away.

"Song Hui, you're going to stir up trouble!" I nearly shouted, though she couldn't hear me. How could she? I longed to see someone, anyone. This is how my aged bones would meet their end, fittingly submerged in a sea of flames. I'd lived too long. However, she was still young, not even half my age.

Someone arrived. I recognised it as Song Pin. His footsteps had a distinctive quality. Song Hui was roused by Song Pin's presence.

"Are you trying to kill Zunai? Foolish woman! It's all smoky. Can't you even smell it? Has your nose collapsed? My God, if I hadn't come in, the room would be on fire. You're about to give me a heart attack."

Song Hui wept in fear, incessantly berating herself and delivering self-inflicted slaps. It wasn't an act; she genuinely despised herself.

Song Pin scolded, "Wasn't it deliberate? I could have spared you."

Song Hui cried, "Secretary Song, you can beat me and kick me; I truly deserve it."

Song Pin's anger showed no signs of abating. "Damn it!"

Song Hui frantically exclaimed, "Let me die."

I clicked my tongue. Song Hui was truly capable of doing foolish things. Ants were scattering. Ants were scattering. Ants were scattering.

Song Pin questioned, "What are you doing?"

Song Hui replied, "Let me talk to Zunai."

Song Pin scolded, "Haven't you caused enough trouble? Get lost!"

Song Hui pleaded, "Let me bid farewell to Zunai before I meet my end."

Song Pin's tone softened, "Are you really going to die? What's the point of dying a thousand times?"

Song Hui's voice was akin to a water-soaked sponge, "Then what should I do?"

Song Pin exclaimed, "Open the door. I'm really choking."

Song Hui responded, "I already opened it."

Song Pin sniffed the air as if detecting other scents. "Is it coming from you?"

Song Hui explained, "Secretary Song, before I arrived, I changed my clothes and applied some facial oil."

Song Pin retorted, "Can you mask it by changing clothes?"

Song Hui questioned, "I'm your relative. Why are you treating me like this?"

Song Pin sneered, "What's wrong with me?"

5

When Li Chun turned one month old, I travelled to Dongpo. Carrying a wicker basket filled with twenty eggs and a block of tea that Dawang had purchased in town a few days ago, I set out. Master Huang's home was easily identifiable and quite unique. It wasn't the typical mud-skin dwelling that common folks resided in; instead, it was a cave excavated into the low slope behind the village, with a depth of seven or eight metres. On the northern table stood a statue of Bodhisattva Guanyin with an elevated handle. I couldn't discern whether it was crafted from wood or ceramic, and out of reverence, I dared not inspect closely. However, the incense burner in front of it was made of copper, and I could see that clearly.

Master Huang cast a gentle glance at my basket and remarked that she wouldn't repeatedly accept midwife money. I clarified that it wasn't midwife money but a special tribute for her. In response, Master Huang advised, "Take it back, and don't break my rules." I placed the eggs one by one on the ground and explained, "This is from both me and the baby. If you don't accept it, I'll be saddened. If you withhold my milk, the baby will suffer. You delivered the baby, Master Huang. Surely, you wouldn't want him to suffer." Master Huang smiled and continued, "You are young, but you can dig holes for me." Swiftly, I added, "You might not like to hear me speak. If I say the wrong thing, please forgive me." Master Huang replied, "I'll make an exception," for which I was deeply grateful. Master Huang then inquired, "Anything else?" Despite the smile on her face, her eyes grew sharp. Without beating around the bush, I openly told her that I wanted to learn from her as a teacher in delivering babies. She downplayed the significance of delivering babies, but I insisted, stating, "That's why I want you as my teacher." After staring at me for a moment, Master Huang declared, "I never accept apprentices." I countered, "That may be true for others. What if I were your daughter?" She responded, "You're not my daughter." Undeterred, I continued, "The first time you came to my house, I thought you looked familiar. Either we were family in a previous life, or I met you in a dream. We are destined for each other. This is no different from a daughter, and I will honour you like my own mother." Master Huang remained firm, saying, "You're very articulate, but it's of no use to me. Don't waste your time here. The child should be nursing now." My heart felt like it had been stabbed. Despite my pleas, Master Huang maintained her stance and refused to accept me as an apprentice. Filled with thoughts of Li Chun, I didn't dare stay any longer. Master Huang instructed me to take the things away, and as she picked up the eggs from the basket, I hurriedly departed.

The following day, I returned to Master Huang's house, this

time holding Li Chun in my arms. Naturally, I didn't expect Li Chun to be of much help. His voice had grown hoarse, and I couldn't leave him solely to Dawang anymore. Surprisingly, Master Huang had locked the door, with the wicker basket left outside—filled with plenty of brick tea and eggs. It was evident she was purposely avoiding me, demonstrating her extraordinary foresight. However, I wasn't one to retreat in the face of difficulties. I resolved to wait for Master Huang, standing guard at the door. As my leg grew numb, I stood up and walked around. Li Chun cried, so I fed him milk, and when he fell asleep, I seized the chance to take a brief nap. As the sun set in the west, and Master Huang had yet to appear, my suspicion deepened that she was deliberately avoiding me. Departing with a tinge of regret, I vowed to return.

On the third day, not only did I bring Li Chun, but I also packed dry food. My father's words echoed in my mind: "No matter how hard porcelain is, a diamond can drill through." Realizing it wasn't suitable to spend the night at her door without bedding, I came prepared for an extended wait. Even if my attempts proved futile, making a few trips in vain was a small price to pay.

On the sixth day, I prepared to go out, but my father-in-law halted me. Dawang had been conditioned to be obedient by me, so even if there was resentment, he wouldn't stop me. Only my father-in-law dared to intervene. His face bore a solemn expression as he declared, "If you acknowledge me as your father-in-law, you should listen to me." I replied, "Dad was joking. Unless you disown me, you'll always be my father-in-law in this life and the next. I'll still call you Dad." My father-in-law retorted, "I don't care what you want to do, but I need to look after your reputation. Master Huang doesn't want to take you as an apprentice. Why are you constantly running around?" I responded, "If she doesn't accept me today, she might tomorrow." My father-in-law argued, "There are no such apprenticeships. You can't take her as your teacher; you're obviously playing tricks." I insisted, "Whether it's reverence or aversion, as long as she accepts me." My father-in-law countered, "There's gossip outside, Damei, and it's not very pleasant to hear. Even if Master Huang teaches you, I'm afraid ... few people will seek you out to deliver babies." This statement carried a profound meaning, and I comprehended it. My father-in-law didn't mean to harm me; hence, he took such a circuitous route. I contemplated silently. My father-in-law continued, "We can still live, so why not stick to that? The war is chaotic. If we can go out less, let's go out less. If we can't go out, we can't go out. It's not pleasant to say, but it's inevitable to run into ghosts if you go out frequently. If ... how can I explain it to your father?" I replied, "You're protecting me, and I understand. But staying at home doesn't always make me feel safe." My father-in-law said, "It's better anyway." I stated, "I'm not afraid of anything. When disaster comes, I can't hide from it." My father-in-law was perplexed. Why did I want to be a midwife? The question was simple but challenging to answer. Was it the halo above Master Huang's head that enticed me, or was it her demeanour and posture that fascinated me? Perhaps I had fallen under some spell? I couldn't articulate it clearly. My father-in-law pointed out that none of the midwives in these three li and five villages were under fifty years old. "If you genuinely want to learn, you'll have to wait until you're that age." He hinted at delaying tactics. I promptly retorted, "If Master Huang accepts me, I might not even be able to learn it. I just want to see if I have this gift. If it's heaven's gift, so be it. But if not, I'll leave on my own." My father-in-law remarked, "Master Huang didn't accept you, so I doubt you're suitable." I suggested that perhaps, on the contrary, she feared that I might take away the job. My father-in-law was stunned by my statement, and after a while, he said, "Damei, you can't say this to anyone else. Master Huang wouldn't be pleased to hear it. She's half-immortal." I smiled and said, "Unless Dad goes and tells her." My father-in-law feigned anger, saying, "What did you say? I am your father-in-law." I teased, "I'm just joking; I know Dad is partial to me." My father-in-law retorted, "There's no daughter-in-law teasing her father-in-law. That would be a joke!" I remarked, "If Dad doesn't tell, I won't tell. Who would know? But Dad is standing in the doorway, inevitably seen by others. Aren't you afraid of someone spreading rumours behind your back?" My father-in-law appeared somewhat flustered and resentful. "I can't convince you, so I won't stop you. However, don't go alone; let Dawang accompany you." I silently breathed a sigh of relief. If my father-in-law had tried to stop me, I wouldn't have gone. I said, "Dongpo is not far away. Don't worry; Dawang still has work to do." My father-in-law suggested having Li Erni accompany me, but I rejected the idea, saying it would be worse. "This is not about showing her face. She hasn't even found her husband's family yet." My father-in-law nodded, "Alright, tell me what you need me to do!" I replied, "This is already enough!"

While this dramatic outcome couldn't substantiate anything concrete, it had the potential to foster growth.

On the eighth day, Master Huang finally lingered. As I knelt on the ground, she turned her attention towards me. Though she didn't engage in conversation as if I were a mere block of wood, the fact that she didn't dismiss me was enough to bring me solace.

Master Huang was sewing a coat, and I noticed that the one she was wearing had also been patched with several pieces. I made a mental note that I would buy her a piece of fabric the next time I visited. The baby delivery fee was neither too much nor too little. It was said that all the money she earned subsidised her son. Although the cave had doors and windows, the light was still dim. This may have been the reason, or it may have been that she was unwilling to look at me and buried her head very low. When threading, she looked up but couldn't get it in. Just as Li Chun fell asleep, I placed him on the ground and took the needle and thread. "Why did you put the child on the ground?" Master Huang finally spoke, albeit reproachfully. As I threaded the needle, she picked up Li Chun and placed him on a wooden bed. "You can't sew it," she said coldly, sensing my intention. I lowered the needle and thread and knelt down on the ground again. Master Huang sighed, "Get up, it's useless." I said, "I won't get up, even if I faint."

A gentle breeze swept in, causing Master Huang's hair around her ears and temples to flutter. The melodious call of a cuckoo bird echoed from a distance, gradually drawing near as if encircling the cave. On my way here, I had picked two Malan flowers, placing them in Li Chun's wrap. In this moment, it felt as if they were undergoing a transformation, emitting a potent fragrance.

"I saw it!" I suddenly exclaimed.

Master Huang's finger hesitated, and for a moment, I feared it might be stuck. "What did you see?" she inquired.

"Light!" I replied.

"Light?"

I continued, "I saw a red light above your head."

Master Huang exclaimed, "Rubbish!"

I didn't avoid her needle-sharp gaze, "I didn't deceive you, I genuinely witnessed it."

Master Huang stated, "That's the radiance of Bodhisattva Guanyin, not mine!"

I replied, "I don't mind whose it is; I still saw it!"

Master Huang fixed her gaze on me, piercing me with hundreds of holes before inquiring, "Did you truly see the light?"

I asserted, "I swear by Bodhisattva Guanyin!"

Master Huang paused for a moment and stated, "I must

establish some rules."

I managed to control my excitement, preventing it from overflowing, but my voice trembled as I urged, "Please proceed!"

Master Huang directed, "Get up, the ground is too cold."

"I prefer to listen on my knees," I insisted.

Master Huang remarked, "Firstly, shun greed. The host family ought to cover the delivery fee. If you receive more, don't let it overly delight you. If you receive less, refrain from complaining. Secondly, eschew irritability. Regardless of urgency or the pregnant woman's circumstances, maintain composure, as irritability can lead to confusion. Some women, in their discomfort, may not know how to exert themselves or may do so recklessly. In such instances, pregnant women may not heed your words, but it's crucial to understand that you remain the anchor and must guide them with a tranquil and composed heart. Thirdly, avoid anger. While assisting in natural childbirth can bring joy to all, accidents are inevitable. Often, it's not the midwife's fault. Some women leave without a word, just collecting their belongings, but confrontations can arise with those of a volatile temperament, leading to verbal or even physical assaults on the midwife. Have you seen the injuries on my face? There's more than one spot. In such situations, you must endure. You may see my reputation, but you don't see my grievances." Master Huang paused for a few seconds, stroking her chest. "Fourthly, steer clear of enmity. Delivery is a manifestation of accumulated virtue. Virtue knows no biases, regardless of the relationship. Whoever seeks your assistance for delivery, even if they're your foe, you mustn't turn them away. The words and actions of the midwife are under the scrutiny of Guanyin. Fifthly, banish fear. Pregnant women vary, and there are various forms of complications. Sometimes, both the mother and child may not be saved, and at times, only one can be rescued. You have to contend with the Lord of Hell. If fear resides in your heart, what should be saved may slip away, leading to a grave error."

I couldn't discern whether it was Master Huang's rules that subdued me or her countenance, frozen like autumn soil, that left me stunned. When Master Huang inquired if I remembered the rules, it took me a while to respond. She remarked, "Remembering is easier than adhering to them. Get up." "I prefer to listen on my knees, Master Huang," I insisted. Master Huang responded, "I merely hold the lamp, but you must walk on your own. No one is compelling you. You can choose this path or abstain; the power lies with you." I smiled, pouring a bowl of water for Master Huang. "I have already become your apprentice. You can beat, scold, and punish me. Tomorrow, even if you beat me, I won't leave." Master Huang remarked, "You have a kind face and a stubborn nature. You should be a successful person." She beckoned me over, examining my hand for a moment before asking me to raise and alter its posture. My fingers, long and slender like bamboo, didn't strike me as particularly remarkable. As Master Huang remained silent, the enigmatic mist in her deep eyes heightened my anxiety. Cautiously, I addressed her, and she responded, "You have a typical willow leaf hand. Out of a thousand midwives, only one has a willow leaf hand. The first time I saw you, I noticed your hand, and the more I looked, the more unique it seemed." As the mist dissipated, Master Huang's gaze resembled a deep well. She continued, "Perhaps you were born for this work." Expressing my gratitude, I promised to remember her kindness and vowed to share half of my delivery fees with her. However, my words unintentionally humiliated Master Huang. Panicking, I tried to explain, "You didn't accept me for this. I know, but I …" Master Huang sharply interrupted, "Stop talking!" I fell silent. Her countenance resembled ice cubes, taking a while to thaw. Eventually, she declared, "Master Huang is not envious of her disciples; you've been overthinking." I questioned, "Can you tell me more about that red light? What is it?"

6

Song Pin continued to scold Song Hui, who persisted in reflecting on her mistakes.

Song Pin's reprimands seemed unending, and Song Hui kept acknowledging her errors. What more did she need to do? I found it difficult to listen any longer. If I could cover my ears, I would have done so already. It occurred to me that Song Pin's tirade wasn't solely about the burnt pot; there must be underlying reasons. What could they be?

7

It was a humid and cool evening in mid-June, with the potent fragrance of wormwood and naked oats wafting through the air. I clutched Li Chun's coat, making my way home from the wellhead, continuously calling his name. For several consecutive nights, Li Chun had cried until dawn. According to Songzhuang Village beliefs, Li Chun's soul might be lost, possibly due to my repetitive night journeys with him. If a soul was lost, it needed to be called back promptly, as after more than a hundred days, it becomes difficult to retrieve. While the trustworthiness of this belief was questionable, no parent dared to risk losing their child's soul, and calling it back in time was crucial. Summoning a soul back wasn't a complex procedure. Circumambulate the wellhead three times, call the child's name three times, and the soul would supposedly attach itself to the jacket. The one invoking the soul had to be one of the parents, and Dawang followed me for soul protection. Upon entering the room, I covered Li Chun with my coat and breathed a sigh of relief. Li Chun was still peacefully asleep, and I hoped he would remain so this night. Li Chun's crying not only deprived Dawang and me of sleep but also disturbed my father-in-law and Erni in the neighbouring room. Tomorrow morning, Li Erni wouldn't be yawning and complaining anymore. Dawang closed the courtyard gate, although whether it was closed or not made no difference. He locked the door and arranged the bedding for both of us. "We can't go out today!" he declared, not explicitly stating that parents shouldn't venture out on a night of crying. I had assisted Master Huang in delivering babies three times, once in the daytime and twice in the middle of the night. The labour process could extend for a day and a night. As I ruminated on Li Chun, breastfeeding and at rest, I recalled obtaining Master Huang's permission to return midway and bring Li Chun along. Not every night saw a woman giving birth, and Master Huang should have been resting at home this particular night. I wasn't overly concerned about it until I unbuttoned the third button and stopped abruptly. I gazed at Li Chun, nestled in his dreams, and Dawang, already lying beneath the bed, and proceeded to rebutton the undone buttons one by one. Dawang stared at me dumbfounded, his bloodshot eyes betraying confusion. "Why?" he asked, his voice trembling. "I forgot to secure the chicken coop door," I replied. Dawang was about to rise, but I restrained him.

It wasn't because the chicken coop door wasn't blocked, but a sudden thought crossed my mind, "What if someone goes into labour tonight? What if Master Huang summons me? Changing clothes can consume time. If my delay impacts the delivery, it could lead to significant issues, and my apprenticeship might be put on hold. While I could voice my concerns, Dawang wouldn't oppose; even if he haboured objections inwardly, he would keep silent. I opted to lie. I didn't want him to endure the anticipation and anguish of waiting alongside me. For him, there was only hardship."

I removed the hemp ball blocking the chicken coop door and secured it again. Taking the shovel to the east wall and the broom to the west wall, I noticed the night growing darker. The wormwood ropes lay on the ground, and I picked them up one by one, hanging them on the clothes-drying pole. Dawang, a diligent and cheerful person, maintained the yard well. Surveying the surroundings, I couldn't find any more tasks and returned to the house. Dawang, sitting with his bare arms, questioned, "Why … took so long?" He didn't blame me but seemed concerned. If I stayed in the yard for an extended period, he would start worrying and searching for me. I assured him not to worry, and he could sleep first. Dawang insisted that if I didn't sleep, he wouldn't either. Reminding him of his lack of proper sleep in recent days and the upcoming work, I encouraged him to go to bed. However, Dawang claimed he wasn't sleepy. I understood the unspoken thoughts in his eyes. Dawang struggled with verbalizing his feelings, and his emotions were evident in his facial expressions and body language. Unable to resist his gaze, I quickly extricated myself and slipped into Dawang's quilt. It was the first time Dawang seemed bewildered. Urging him to act promptly, I refrained from letting him extinguish the light. Through Dawang's heavy breathing, my ears were attuned to the movements outside.

"God, not at this time …" I silently prayed. Dawang abruptly stopped, and I promptly pushed him aside, hastily donning my clothes. Dawang was taken aback. "What else do you need to do?" he inquired. I claimed I forgot to let the dough ferment. If only I had anticipated earlier, as now I had a premonition that it would be challenging to halt at this moment.

Just as I was finishing smoothing my hair, I heard an urgent and courteous shout. I said to Dawang, "Look after the children and try not to nap too long." Dawang inquired, "Where are you off to?" I replied, "Someone is about to give birth, so I need to hurry there." Dawang appeared to say something, but I didn't catch it clearly. If Li Chun's soul wailed in vain, there would be time enough to console it tomorrow. I didn't want to miss the chance to acquire these adept techniques.

That night, an ox cart arrived to pick up Master Huang. Due to her small feet and limited walking capacity, villagers from other areas often arranged transportation for her deliveries, either by oxen-driven carts or riding donkeys and horses. Xiyingzi Village, around ten miles southwest of Songzhuang Village, was Master Huang's destination that night. Whether due to the ox's difficulty in navigating the road in the dark or its fatigue and hunger, it didn't move as swiftly as a person, despite the constant urging and beatings from the drivers. I couldn't discern the man's face clearly, but it was evident he was an impatient person, continuously wiping and cursing. Master Huang abruptly stated, "Don't worry; it won't delay anything." Her voice held a certain coldness. The man, sensing Master Huang's displeasure and perhaps a touch of fear, mumbled about the pain starting in the afternoon and his anxiety. Master Huang reassured him, mentioning that the birth wouldn't happen before dawn, so they had time. The man insisted on the severity of the pain. In response, Master Huang calmly said, "I delivered the eldest child of your family. I know it well, and when we arrive, we will wait as needed." The man fell silent, ceasing to berate the ox.

I admire Master Huang's resolve and am even more astonished by her discernment. She didn't mention it casually; it was undoubtedly grounded in facts. I had been with her three times, and I could attest to it. However, what was her rationale? I wished to inquire, but I lacked the courage. On the day she accepted me as her apprentice, she informed me that she could only impart what was teachable, and everything else had to be comprehended independently.

We arrived at our destination around midnight. The 40-year-old pregnant woman, with a prominent belly and a swollen face, cried loudly every few minutes. Master Huang ushered the mother and aunt of the pregnant woman to the outer room, leaving me alone. As in previous occasions, Master Huang cut a few "8" character patterns, lit them, mixed the ashes with clean water, and sprayed them into her mouth three times while chanting incantations. The maternal cries immediately subsided. Master Huang then placed her hand on the pregnant woman's elevated abdomen, closed her eyes, and gently moved her hand. There was a faint light on the top of Master Huang's head. I didn't know if the pregnant woman noticed it, but I certainly did. Master Huang opened her eyes, her voice calm and soothing. "Don't be afraid," she reassured. The woman inquired, "Am I going to have the baby? It's killing me." Master Huang replied, "The child just fell asleep and woke up. Now it won't hurt. You can also sleep for a while and close your eyes!" The woman obediently closed her eyes.

Master Huang gave me a subtle wink, and I mirrored her actions, placing the palm of my hand on the pregnant woman's belly, moving with care. Master Huang explained that this was known as "touching the body," a practice requiring meticulous sensitivity. The child resided within the mother's womb, invisible to the eyes, yet their presence could be felt—the baby's head, feet, and even their five senses. The positioning of the legs, whether bent or not, and the extension of the arms could reveal the challenges of childbirth. In the initial three attempts, I hadn't truly mastered the technique. Master Huang emphasised that when touching the body, I shouldn't focus on anything else, including the pregnant woman, but solely on the baby in the placenta. Extraneous thoughts needed to be dispelled, yet it proved challenging for me to erase the pregnant woman or Master Huang from my mind. With Master Huang nearby, her hand on the pregnant woman's belly, how could I disregard and forget her?

This marked the fourth time I had accompanied Master Huang to engage in body-touching rituals. If I failed to do so correctly this time, Master Huang might have expelled me from my apprenticeship. With this thought, the top of my head felt faintly warm. "Don't be nervous, don't be anxious," Master Huang whispered. "He's your child, waiting for you in the dark. Slowly approach him and don't scare him. Yes, that's it. You have to call him."

The dense fog surrounded both the baby and me, rendering him invisible to my sight, and likewise, I to him. Yet, it felt as if he stood right in front of me. Holding my breath, I moved cautiously, softly calling out to him. Finally, the baby responded. I glimpsed the interplay of light and shadow within the thick fog as I took another step forward. The fog dissipated significantly, revealing the outline of the baby, bathed in light and shadow. "Child, my child, come closer!" The fog lifted entirely, unveiling the baby lying amidst a river adorned with pink lotus flowers. Standing on the shore, I waved to him as the lotus flowers drifted towards the bank. I gently placed my hand on the soft crown of the baby's head, stroking his pink arms and feet from top to bottom.

"Can you feel it?" Master Huang's voice brought me back from the river bank.

Opening my eyes, I couldn't contain my excitement. I was tempted to hug Master Huang, but her expression was not as warm as I had anticipated; in fact, it seemed a bit cold. She instructed me to describe the position of the baby's head and feet, and despite my surprised stammering, I was correct. Even without Master Huang's confirmation, I knew I was right. It was what I "saw."

Master Huang then remarked, "I have been learning this skill for many years, and you can do it four times." I wasn't sure if she was praising me or expressing a sense of sigh. I dared not feel any hint of complacency and quickly flattered her, saying, "It's all thanks to your guidance." Master Huang responded, "I don't have that much blessing for you. It's your own creation. She's asleep, and we should take a rest."

The mother and aunt of the expectant woman had readied a meal, consisting of scrambled eggs, fried yellow flowers, and noodles as the main course. Following our meal, Master Huang and I retired to the West Room for some rest. The pregnant woman's mother, with a hint of anxiety, inquired about when she should rouse us. Master Huang advised that she was weary and required sleep until dawn, suggesting that one person stay vigilant over the pregnant woman. The mother of the expectant lady remained somewhat unsettled. "If she goes into labour …" Master Huang emphatically reassured her that the birth would not occur before dawn.

Shortly after reclining, Master Huang emitted a faint snore. I remained engulfed in excitement, not the least bit drowsy, and even haboured the desire to linger beside the expectant woman. That sensation was truly delightful; I relived it repeatedly—dense fog, river water, lotus flowers, play of light and shadow, and a gentle summons. Early in the morning, Master Huang inquired, "Did you not sleep?" I replied that I had dozed off briefly. Master

Huang then asked, "Do you recall the guidelines?" I affirmed, "Yes," and promptly realised that I had been too restless. Master Huang remarked, "Engage in this manner, and you'll grow weary after a few instances." I assured him, "It won't occur again."

As foreseen by Master Huang, around noon, the expectant woman's pain intensified. She clenched her chopsticks between her teeth, refraining from shouting, but beads of sweat trickled down her forehead intermittently. Master Huang held a towel in hand, wiping her forehead periodically and guiding her on how to use it effectively. I stood by the bed, securing the woman's feet against the wooden edge. The candle had been lit, and after a while, I retrieved the scissors from the package, warming them over the flame. Master Huang instructed me to deliver the baby, with her as the assistant. The instructions were clear in my mind, yet I feared making an error, silently repeating the steps. While Master Huang would undoubtedly offer reminders, I was apprehensive about displaying any clumsiness. Despite my confidence, a hint of nervousness lingered. Fortunately, the maternal family remained in the outer room. Master Huang preferred they not enter, aiming to relieve any additional pressure on me.

The amniotic fluid went out, revealing the baby. That's who I touched, and suddenly my heart warmed. I guided the expectant woman on when to employ real strength and when to apply virtual strength. Occasionally, I cast a glance at Master Huang, who didn't issue any instructions or even glance my way. I refrained from looking at her any further; if she didn't correct me, that was the best confirmation and encouragement. The tension diminished, and there was no time for nerves to set in. The child's head and arms had already emerged, and I cradled them with my hands, aiding the woman in holding her breath and exerting all her strength. This was a crucial moment, with no room for a sluggish pause.

At three-quarters past the afternoon, the baby arrived—a seven-jin and eight-tael boy. After wrapping up the newborn, I summoned the family. It was only then that I realised my back was thoroughly wet, as if I had emerged from a river carrying a baby.

The eager husband of the expectant woman promptly escorted us back. The mother of the pregnant woman presented two red paper envelopes, one large and one small, as a token of gratitude for Master Huang and myself. During the meal, Master Huang informed everyone that I had delivered the baby, while she had assisted by wiping the mother's sweat. The pregnant woman observed it clearly, and Master Huang didn't need to underscore the point. When I saw those two red envelopes, a thought crossed my mind—I didn't want them. Once again, despite delivering the baby, the credit went to the master. The smaller red envelope from the pregnant woman's mother, intended for me, found its way into Master Huang's hands, and she, without a word, placed it in my arms. Familiar with Master Huang's disposition, I refrained from saying anything further.

Upon boarding the ox cart, I abruptly felt a tug on the rope.

Swiftly, I exclaimed, "Hold on a moment," leaped out of the cart without glancing at anyone, and darted into the room. The pregnant woman cradled the child, and I uttered, "Pass him to me." The pregnant woman remained unresponsive, her swollen face appearing bewildered. With a smile, I clarified that I needed to bid farewell to the little one. Not daring to procrastinate, I embraced the child, planted kisses on his forehead and crown, and then handed him over to the woman.

I cradled the child and announced loudly to Master Huang. She remained unresponsive, merely stating, "Let's go." Seated cross-legged, she maintained a perfectly upright posture even in the jolting cart. Tipping her face, she gazed at the fields and meadows. She was not one for verbose conversation, usually silent unless imparting wisdom to me. However, on that day, overwhelmed with joy, I yearned to converse with her. I fixed my gaze on her, anticipating the right moment. Yet, she never turned her head, as if I were invisible. The sunlight painted her cheeks and the corners of her eyes, wrinkling them like honey gold. A gentle breeze tousled her hair, causing it to flutter. Delivering and withholding, Master Huang seemed like two contrasting personas, and I preferred the version of her that was delivering. Her eyes would gleam with auspicious light, spirits soaring, movements nimble, and words resolute. But in that moment, Master Huang was akin to a statue.

"Don't fix your gaze on me like that," Master Huang remained facing away. "Is there something you need to express?"

she inquired. I cast a glance at the man beside the ox, puzzled as to why he didn't take a seat. He ceased hurrying, refrained from wielding the lash, and allowed the ox to slow down. My attention then returned to Master Huang's yellowed cheek, dispelling the doubts in my heart. "What's the basis for your predictions?" I asked. "Experience and intuition," Master Huang responded. Though I didn't quite grasp it, Master Huang offered no further explanation. After the passage of half an incense burn, I almost believed she had drifted into slumber when she finally turned around.

"As I mentioned, I teach only what can be taught to you. The rest, what can't be taught, you'll naturally discern if luck is on your side." After several years, I began to fathom the essence of Master Huang's words. A reporter named Chen Xiaolei posed a similar question to me, and I responded akin to Master Huang. Chen Xiaolei found it challenging to comprehend my meaning. Let me elucidate. I conveyed that intuition is just a feeling, inexplicable. Originally inquiring about Li Gui's tale, she suddenly took interest in my story midway. She interviewed me nine times and shared my bed for half a month. Back then, my legs and feet were robust, and I could still toil in the fields. This city girl wasn't distant from me; when I gathered firewood, she joined, and when I harvested vegetables, she toiled alongside me, pursuing me ardently. I wasn't attempting to conceal anything from her. It was genuinely challenging to articulate. Of course, she still made gains.

On that leisurely ox cart, in the warmth of a June afternoon,

I found myself habouring suspicions about Master Huang. Her gaze, keen and perceptive, caught on to my doubt instantly. "You need not doubt me. If I were narrow-minded, I wouldn't have taken you as my apprentice," Master Huang declared coldly. I blushed and stumbled through an explanation, but Master Huang had already turned her face away. Before her, an eagle soared through the air. In truth, I still haboured numerous inquiries about various topics, such as the eight-character patterns or incantations. Thus far, Master Huang had not disclosed any of these to me, and I hesitated to broach the subject again.

The thrill and elation waned, descending like faded petals to the dust. I attempted to mould myself into a sculpture, but the feat proved beyond my reach. Thoughts of Li Chun, who had lost his soul, crossed my mind. Guilt now permeated my being like artemisia. Despite this, I haboured no remorse for leaving him. This journey had yielded more gains than any before.

During the journey back, the ox cart halted for a quarter of an hour. The man ventured into the grass, gathering a bunch of bluebells. I assumed it was a gift for either Master Huang or myself, but he merely circled around us, sharing that the bellflower was his wife's favourite. Master Huang, unrushed, nodded patiently. Although my heart brimmed with anxiety, Master Huang remained silent, compelling me to endure the situation. Two or three miles from Songzhuang Village, I leaped out of the ox cart and instructed the man to take Master Huang directly to Dongpo, then hurried home on foot.

8

I, being mortal, knew that my aging body couldn't withstand the relentless passage of time, destined to crumble into dust someday. I couldn't discern whether that day would be in spring, summer, autumn, or winter, at noon or dusk, but I understood it would inevitably arrive. If given a choice, I'd opt for autumn. As dusk falls, the sky bathed in sunlight, mist rising, yellow leaves descending, and birds returning to their nests – a time when the soul might dance freely in the air. How serene and comforting it would be.

Yet, I had no say but to await the whims of fate. I thought I had already become clear, akin to lake water under the sun, seemingly undisturbed. However, from the moment an ant darted into my face in the morning, a sense of unease crept in. Instead of subsiding, this unease twisted me like a rope. "What's wrong with it?" I exclaimed loudly, not knowing whom to address.

9

Indeed, I was overly optimistic about the field of midwifery. Not all pregnant women undergo spontaneous childbirth, and occasional accidents make life more challenging than death. There are several types of births that instill fear in midwives, presenting the greatest tests of their skills and techniques. For instance, "Caidisheng" (footling breech birth) refers to a scenario where one foot is born first, while the other remains nestled inside; "Sadisheng" (breech with hand) involves one arm emerging first, seemingly testing the waters; "Zuodisheng" (buttocks breech birth) describes a situation where the baby sits on the ground with the buttocks emerging first, appearing intentionally playful; "Huadisheng"(frank breech birth with extended arms and legs) involves the baby emerging with one hand and one foot first, akin to a magician's act; "Hengdisheng"(transverse lie) describes a situation where the baby is positioned horizontally in the belly, engaging in playful antics; and then there's "Mendisheng,"(respiratory distress at birth) which denotes suffocation, signifying that the baby emerges without breathing, necessitating prompt attention from the midwife.

Master Huang shared with me various scenarios of dystocia,

always recounting them on rainy, windy, or snowy days. Coupled with her somber expression, the weight of the information pressed down on me, making it hard to breathe. Perhaps she intentionally exposed me to a sense of despair beforehand, aiming to etch the gravity of the situation deeply into my memory. As she emphasised, delivering a child was a virtuous act, but even a minor lapse in care could lead to dire consequences. Sometimes, a midwife could have been the difference between life and death, but panic could cause her to miss crucial opportunities to save lives. Master Huang detailed corresponding measures for each situation, such as "Mendisheng,"(respiratory distress at birth) which involves massaging, inverted drooping, back tapping, breathing techniques, and more. For instance, if a woman lacks or has insufficient amniotic fluid, she needs abdominal kneading, adjustment, and straightening to alleviate her pain.

Master Huang mentioned that there wouldn't be time for explanations on the spot, so I had to memorise everything in advance. She instructed me to recline on the bed and illustrate various techniques, including massage and alignment. Subsequently, she laid down and directed me to practice on her abdomen, guiding me on when to be gentle, when to apply pressure, when to proceed slowly, and when to be prompt. My usual routine involved making trips to Dongpo. If Dawang was at home, I'd entrust Li Chun to him. In instances when Dawang was occupied, I would bring Li Chun along with me.

At the end of winter, I accompanied Master Huang to

another residence for a childbirth. A man drove a carriage, a much faster mode of transport compared to the old ox cart. The snow had melted, leaving jagged but solid ruts in its wake. The carriage driver sported a black round felt hat, slightly small and disproportionate to his broad face. He was the pregnant woman's elder brother, and he eagerly briefed the family as soon as he arrived. A talkative fellow, he couldn't wait to share details, even revealing the location of his sister's chopstick holder. From his narrative, I learned that this was his sister's second child; the first had tragically passed away at birth. The previous midwife, found by his brother-in-law, didn't appear serious at first glance. "My sister's face was contorted with pain, yet she was leisurely sipping alcohol, insisting that it wasn't time and citing her experience with numerous deliveries. Eventually, my sister fainted, and the midwife, without missing a beat, stood up and remembered to drink the Chinese baijiu in her glass. I don't easily get angry, but my patience wore thin that day. If my wife hadn't pulled me away, I would have demanded she regurgitate everything she drank, letting some flowers bloom on her face. How could there be such a midwife? She didn't seem like a midwife at all; it was as if she had come to satisfy her own cravings. So, this time, I informed my brother-in-law in advance that I would never invite the previous one. After three inquiries, I ultimately chose Master Huang. I made the decision myself. My brother-in-law is always indecisive about major matters. I don't give advice to everyone, but in her case, I had to because she's my sister."

Master Huang appeared troubled, not necessarily due to the carriage driver's story but seemingly a common demeanour when boarding a carriage. She had a son who was indolent and had a penchant for gambling, often being pursued by creditors. I surmised that her son had likely approached her for money again the previous night. As the chilly wind blew, she yawned twice, covering the third one in time, evidently feeling very fatigued. It seemed she had endured a trying night. Master Huang and I sat on the shaft with the back of her felt cap turned towards me, unseen by the carriage driver, but visible to me. She gazed at the fields as if no longer entranced, her eyes wandering, skimming over the carriage driver, and settling on my face. I sensed she had something to express, but she remained silent.

"Can you pick up the pace? This is slower than an old ox cart," Master Huang suddenly remarked. The carriage driver promptly silenced and flicked the horse's buttocks with the whip, urging the chestnut-red horse from a brisk walk to a jog. The cart's wheels navigated the uneven ruts, jostling and rolling, causing Master Huang to sway back and forth. I seized the cart railing with one hand and held onto Master Huang with the other. The carriage driver turned around and advised, "Hold on tight." I assumed he would drive more cautiously, but a few minutes later, he resumed his chatter. "Don't worry, Master Huang, we'll definitely get there in time. My sister isn't in much pain yet. I picked you up early to be safe. You might have to stay for three or five days. The meat's been cut, the baijiu's been bought, and there's an unslaughtered rooster ready for you." "Why do you talk so much nonsense?" Master Huang responded curtly, making no effort to hide her irritation. The carriage driver, undeterred, continued his chatter. "When I'm happy, I'm just like when I'm drinking baijiu. My conversation box opens," he chuckled. Master Huang retorted coldly, "Don't throw us both into the ditch." "Rest assured," the carriage driver said confidently. Before he could finish, the right wheel sank into a deep pit, causing the cart to tilt suddenly. I panicked and managed to grab the railing, while Master Huang floated out of the cart like straw.

I leaped out before the cart came to a complete stop. Master Huang lay partially on the ground, mouth agape. I attempted to assist her, but she waved me off. Eventually, she slowly sat up, cheeks smudged with dirt and grey. The carriage driver, flustered, inquired, "Are you alright?" Master Huang paid no attention, stood up, and took a few steps. "It's my fault; I shouldn't have boasted," the carriage driver admitted, trailing behind her. Master Huang reached the carriage, and I helped her up. The carriage driver, now cautious, remarked, "Take it easy, take it easy this time. It was an accident, Master Huang. Just an accident." The carriage driver resumed his clamour. Master Huang threatened, "If you persist in chattering like a lady, I'll disembark." The warning had its effect, and the carriage driver finally closed his mouth.

Contrary to the carriage driver's assurances, we could hear shouts before even entering the yard. A young woman in her twenties greeted us with a petite and slender frame, a pallid complexion, and dishevelled hair. Master Huang sprayed rune water and recited incantations in the usual order. She assured the pregnant woman that, with the blessing of Bodhisattva Guanyin, the pain would be alleviated. However, this time, it proved less effective, and the pregnant woman's pain not only failed to decrease but seemed to intensify, prompting loud cries. Master Huang's wearied expression faded, and she regained her familiar demeanour—calm, serene, and confident. She advised, "Dear, you must trust in Bodhisattva Guanyin." The pregnant woman naturally held faith in Bodhisattva Guanyin, and though she didn't nod, her eyes conveyed unwavering belief. Nonetheless, the pain persisted, and within a minute, she shouted again. I swiftly placed my chopsticks across her mouth and ushered her family into the outer room. No family members remained on-site unless their assistance was needed, adhering to Master Huang's established protocol.

The delivery proved exceptionally challenging. Despite taking only two hours from the rupture of the amniotic fluid to the baby's emergence, the pregnant woman fainted three times. Master Huang, naturally, took charge of delivering the baby. I held onto the woman's arm, attempting to assist and provide support each time she lost consciousness.

The baby was born, and Master Huang quickly glanced at me. I immediately understood that it was "Mendisheng." (respiratory distress at birth) The child didn't cry; there was complete silence. The warm water had been changed three times.

Typically, the next steps would involve opening the Heavenly Gate—washing the baby's eyes, touching the dragon's nose and washing it, and opening the dragon's mouth to cleanse it. Subsequently, we would wash the baby's hands and feet from the head to the chest, removing any traces of the birthing process. Babies cry, a proclamation of their arrival in the world, and there is no sweeter cry than this. However, this baby remained silent.

Master Huang swiftly changed her grip, seizing the baby's feet, turning the baby's head downward, and delivering three slaps to the pink buttocks. Still, the baby remained silent. Master Huang laid the baby flat, performed a few mouth-to-mouth breaths, expelled the air, and then inhaled once more. In that moment, I witnessed the light above Master Huang's head again—not red, but multicoloured, incredibly enchanting. The light gradually descended, encompassing both Master Huang and the baby. Though they were physically close, it felt as though they were incredibly distant from me. I tried earnestly, but I couldn't bridge the gap.

The sound of crying echoed, and the light vanished. I snapped awake. Master Huang was vomiting, and I couldn't discern if it was her or the child. In haste, I picked up the baby.

On the journey back, Master Huang unexpectedly fell asleep amidst the turbulence. The pregnant woman's family suggested I stay with her for a day, but Master Huang insisted on departing. I still hadn't discussed payment for the delivery, and the family insisted I take the rooster as a token of gratitude. The carriage driver continued his incessant chatter, praising Master Huang's exceptional skills. Realizing she was asleep, he turned his attention to flattering me directly. "With a master like her, you're sure to be the right choice in the future. When my daughter-in-law gives birth, I'll definitely invite you," he remarked. I felt elated but refrained from responding. Surprisingly, his prophecy came true. I later delivered his three grandchildren and one granddaughter, and we became indirect relatives. Unfazed by my silence, he continued to share anecdotes about his wife and children. The rooster, seemingly not wanting to be left out, occasionally crowed, as if responding on my behalf.

I reclaimed the rooster, and Dawang inquired whether I intended to raise it or slaughter it. I explained that having two roosters would lead to daily fights, so I suggested sending it to Dad. Dawang then suggested killing it, mentioning it was just for show. I insisted on sending it to Dad, stating that I was still young and didn't require the nourishment. Dawang jokingly whispered, "You can nurse the baby." I retorted, "I can still get milk without a chicken, be sensible!" Dawang carried the rooster away. My father-in-law approached, having heard some gossip, and I intended to show respect to him while implying something else. Shortly after, Li Erni joined us with an air of discontent. "I thought you brought back a pig, but it's just a chicken," she remarked. I replied, "When I assist in delivering your baby, you can send me a pig." Li Erni snorted and retorted, "Even if you offered me a free delivery, I wouldn't consider using your services.

Don't think I'm unaware. You're just basking in Master Huang's favour." Li Erni reminded me that even if my maternal family compelled me to take the rooster, it was Master Huang's doing, and I shouldn't have brought it along. I called Dawang over, who seemed a bit embarrassed. I addressed my father-in-law, who was well aware of the situation, and Erni took the opportunity to make sarcastic remarks. I chose not to respond.

After breakfast the next day, I entered Master Huang's cave with the rooster in my arms. Master Huang's face still bore signs of fatigue and listlessness. "I cannot raise poultry, nor can I slaughter poultry. You'd better take it back," Master Huang's voice conveyed a weariness that matched her appearance. I apologised for my greed, and Master Huang shook her head, acknowledging that I deserved it. She mentioned that without my assistance the day before, she might have faced failure, and I earned the rooster as a reward. Master Huang expressed her anxiety, explaining that the pregnant woman's thin and narrow pelvis, coupled with the premature death of the first fetus, heightened maternal panic and weakened mental strength, increasing the risk of complications during delivery. "That's exactly what I expected. But the child is fine, and the mother is fine too," I remarked sincerely. Master Huang gave a faint smile. "If there was an accident, would they still gift you a rooster? Would I still receive this bonus? You haven't been beaten since you've been with me for so long, have you?" she added. I was taken aback and asked, "Is it true, Master …" Master Huang affirmed, "Do you think I was trying to coax you? I have seen so much that not every time can be safe; there are always unpredictable and unimaginable things." I reassured her that we had done our best and had a clear conscience. Master Huang shook her head, saying, "It's not as simple as you think. There's no big shame, there's no small shame. Sometimes I feel like a murderer." I was astonished and questioned, "Why do you say that?" Master Huang responded, "You may not understand now, but you will in the future." Her eyes grew deeper, and I couldn't see halfway through them.

After a prolonged silence, Master Huang spoke, "There's a situation that is the most perilous. I haven't informed you about it yet. If not handled promptly, it can jeopardise the lives of adults."

I gazed wide-eyed, "Something more severe than 'Mendisheng (respiratory distress at birth)?'"

Master Huang affirmed, "Certainly, there is, like stillbirths." She turned and retrieved the earthy yellow delivery bag, untying it. Alongside a copper bowl, candles, scissors, and yellow watch paper, there was also a fish-shaped leather bag. I was already acquainted with these items. In fact, I had seen the fish-shaped leather bags before, but Master Huang never allowed me to touch them. The rope binding the leather bag had a flexible buckle that could be pulled open. Master Huang extracted a blade about a finger's length from the bag. "Use this, when it is a stillbirth."

That day, dark clouds didn't shroud the sky. There was no rain, snow, or even a hint of wind. The sun radiated brightly, and upon entering the cave, I instinctively shielded my eyes to prevent the sun's glare. However, my heart felt burdened, as if weighed down by hundreds of stones, and the bright sunlight failed to penetrate the cave. It remained dim and suffocating, with only Master Huang's blade gleaming with a cold sheen. Surprisingly quiet, the cave allowed Master Huang's voice to flow unimpeded, each word hitting the ear like an arrow—precise and piercing.

"If you encounter a stillbirth, one method involves reaching into the lower body, aligning the placenta, and using your middle and index fingers to grasp the baby's upper jaw, gently pulling it out. However, achieving a smooth adjustment can be challenging. Once it becomes stuck, the chances of the pregnant woman surviving are slim. Therefore, it's necessary to use a blade to clear the womb. Although it's a difficult procedure, it is the most effective way to protect the pregnant woman. The blade should be placed in the palm of your hand, pressed with your thumb, and then extended through the lower body, gradually dividing the stillborn into several pieces. If there are numerous pieces, they can be easily left in the abdomen and subsequently removed one by one."

Master Huang demonstrated repeatedly before handing me the blade, reminiscent of the first time she noticed my willow leaf hand. She scrutinised it for a while; my fingers were thin and long, and my palms especially narrow. "One in a thousand, you can't be wrong," this marked the second time Master Huang praised me, but her words lacked warmth. Although nothing physical was present, Master Huang's guidance was remarkably specific.

"You must have the family hold down the pregnant woman and prevent her from kicking around! Keep an eye on her legs and stop them from kicking you! Otherwise, how will you withstand a maternal kick? Don't touch the candle, don't panic, break it off. Okay, that's right. Extend your hand into it slowly. Can you touch it?" I confirmed that I could touch it. Master Huang inquired, "Is the head up or down?" Initially stating, "It seems like it's down," "What do you mean by 'seems'? Be specific!" shouted Master Huang. I corrected myself, saying it was upward. Master Huang emphasised, "Start." Though my hand trembled briefly, I didn't hesitate. Slowly, I scratched and cut. "You're not killing people; you're saving them. Stay calm!" Master Huang whispered. My hand steadied, and I successfully cut open the baby. Blood flowed from the lower body of the woman. "Take it out, that's it!" I retrieved the meatball and stared at my bloodied hand, unable to believe that I had just completed a womb-cleaning operation.

Even though it was a simulation, I found myself drained of strength, unable to move for half a day. Master Huang handed me a glass of water, remarking that my nerves had been too tense. "Practice more, and you'll improve," she advised. It was my first time performing womb-cleaning surgery, and I had bitten my lips open. Master Huang remarked, "You should be better than me." I quickly responded, "An apprentice will never surpass the master." Master Huang suddenly turned serious and said, "This is not a matter of competition. Remember, the better you do, the more people you save. Have you rested enough? Get up!"

On that day, Master Huang also imparted knowledge about various prescriptions. "Maternal diseases are inevitable, and giving birth may exacerbate them. If not treated promptly, these diseases can persist throughout the mother's lifetime. There's a saying, 'Having a temporary illness for a lifetime,' which refers to this. Some patients don't originally have gynecological diseases, but rather, their conditions are purely a result of childbirth, such as red metrorrhagia and leakage. It is crucial to diagnose and treat them," she explained. Master Huang mentioned that the prescription had been passed down by her master, and she made adjustments to individual medicines. "Be flexible and not rigid in their use," she advised me.

Before parting ways, Master Huang gifted me a fish-shaped leather bag, seemingly understanding my thoughts. She said, "I still have one. Consider it a gift from me when you join me as an apprentice." I immediately comprehended and addressed her as Master Huang. A rare smile crossed Master Huang's face. "You can deliver a baby on your own now," she remarked. Feeling nervous, I admitted, "I'm still far from being able to do that, Master Huang. Have I done anything wrong?" Master Huang assured me, "I've taught you everything you need to know. If someone invites you to deliver their baby, gather your courage and do it." I expressed my apprehension, saying, "I still feel powerless. I'm afraid no one will ask me." Master Huang responded, "Without one, there will never be two. I'll keep you for another three months. After that, you can handle it on your own. It's not good to stay with me for too long."

During my three-month apprenticeship, I assisted in delivering fourteen babies, including one case of "Huadisheng" (frank breech birth with extended arms and legs) and one stillborn. I observed Master Huang's surgical operations firsthand. She remained calm, focusing on her work, and it felt like there was no one else present. After the procedures, she would look at me, conveying a silent message that seemed to say, "That's it. I'm not the executioner; I'm the rescuer."

As I completed my apprenticeship, I reflected on Master Huang's words: "Any accident can happen." In my 70 years of delivering babies, exceeding 10,000 in total, accidents were not uncommon. Yet, I was not afraid. Delivery was not just my profession but my life. My fear stemmed from the unexpected dangers hidden in life's journey, challenges difficult to anticipate and escape.

10

"Why hasn't Maixiang come back yet?" Song Pin inquired, "This wretched woman left Zunai without informing us. She must have lost her mind!" Although Song Pin's anger had abated, mentioning Maixiang caused his voice to escalate once more.

Song Hui pleaded, "She didn't leave Zunai alone; she entrusted herself to my care."

Song Pin sneered, retorting, "Take care of her? You're akin to a murderer!"

Song Hui asserted, "Zunai is compassionate; she will pardon me."

Song Pin's voice remained cold and unyielding, "Don't leverage Zunai against me. She might forgive you, but I won't!"

Song Hui, distressed, queried, "Secretary Song, I've been reproaching myself. What more do you want?"

Song Pin looked helpless, confessing, "Yes, what am I to do with you?"

Song Hui said, "You can do anything."

Song Pin suddenly smiled, "Song Hui, what do you mean by anything?"

Song Hui whispered, sounding a bit embarrassed, "Whatever

you want … it's fine."

Song Pin's tone lengthened, "Your attitude makes sense. Hmm, whatever it takes …" Then his tone suddenly changed, "Who do you think I am? Smell your body, do you take a bath once a year?" Song Pin said sarcastically.

Song Hui responded, "We are relatives."

Song Pin sneered again, saying, "Don't talk about this. So what even if you're my own sister? Does that mean we can be disrespectful to Zunai?"

Song Hui pleaded, "I didn't do it on purpose. Secretary Song, please forgive me."

Song Pin paused for a moment and demanded, "Where on earth has Maixiang gone? Tell me the truth!"

Song Hui hesitated, "Possibly … perhaps."

Song Pin snapped, "Can't you even utter a concise sentence?"

Song Hui hastily added, "Luo Bao! She went to the town to find Luo Bao."

Song Pin, evidently anticipating this, remarked, "I knew it!" Then he muttered to himself, "Why didn't I bump into her?"

Song Hui explained, "She left later than you."

Song Pin, with frustration, exclaimed, "On any other day, why today? Is her brain filled with grout rather than slop?"

Song Hui called to him, "Secretary Song."

Song Pin retorted, "Aren't you usually straightforward? Why the roundabout talk today?"

Song Hui pleaded with Song Pin not to disclose the incident

of the pot burning to Maixiang.

Song Pin queried, "What's the matter? Is she going to peel your skin off?"

Song Hui expressed, "I fear she won't want me to care for Zunai in the future."

Song Pin burst into laughter and remarked, "In the future? Do you think you still have a future?"

Song Hui responded, "Maixiang couldn't have stayed with Zunai. Someone had to fill in for her."

Song Pin mocked, "You have a good brain."

Song Hui explained, "I've already told you everything."

At that moment, Song Pin's phone rang, playing the duet tune of "*Hanging Red Lanterns*" with joy. However, the content of the call didn't match the festive tune. After hanging up, Song Pin cursed, "Damn it, I've just rested for a while, there's no end to it!"

Concerned, Song Hui asked, "Are you leaving?"

Song Pin explained, "Ruhua called the police and reported that Mao Gen shot and killed her crow."

Song Hui let out a cry.

In a cold tone, Song Pin asked, "What does it have to do with you? Take care of Zunai until Maixiang comes back. What's the stupor? Do you hear me?"

Song Hui responded, "I hear you." Her voice was trembling.

Chapter VI

Luo Bao

1

On an early morning in mid-August, Luo Shicheng was transferring tofu from a shelf drawer into a basin when he suddenly felt dizzy. It was as if leaves had been stuffed into his brain. Due to the dizziness, he stumbled a few times and accidentally poked his thumb into the tofu. Luo Shicheng gazed at the two irregular holes, feeling both pain and regret. Zhao Quezi (Cripple) was too picky, and Luo Shicheng didn't want to be careless. He replaced the damaged tofu with two new pieces and walked out with the basin in his arms.

The streets appeared desolate and empty, with the majority of shops shuttered. Before the foreign occupation of Beijing, shopkeepers liquidated their wares and fled to other locales. Only four establishments persevered, including Luo Shicheng's tofu shop, Wang Xi's grocery store, Wu Nu's tailor shop, and Zhao Quezi's restaurant. Among them, Zhao Quezi's restaurant fared slightly better, with most patrons being transient visitors. Luo Shicheng, who used to produce three cauldrons of tofu daily, had reduced his output to two cauldrons about half a month ago. Just three days prior, he further scaled down to a solitary cauldron, and half of the production went to Zhao Quezi's restaurant.

Luo Shicheng encountered only a wandering thin dog, the madman Niusan, and the Ma Fu couple who were working in the field as usual. Perhaps the Ma Fu couple's nonchalance eased Luo Shicheng's concerns, and his footsteps became much lighter. However, before reaching Zhao Quezi's restaurant, Luo Shicheng's heart cramped again. The doors and windows were closed, with no sign of life inside. Luo Shicheng hoped Zhao Quezi was just sleeping in. Due to the late closing time, Zhao Quezi had a reason to sleep in. Approaching, Luo Shicheng's eyes darkened once more. The door was not bolted from the inside, but a rusty lock hung from the outside. Disbelief filled Luo Shicheng as he stared at the door. The black silk in his eyes waved away, and Luo Shicheng glanced at the door again before banging on it. It seemed that Zhao Quezi was still inside. Feeling teased, Luo Shicheng lost his temper in anger, kicking the door relentlessly.

Luo Shicheng panted heavily, but the door stayed shut, almost offering a frigid indifference by refusing to budge even slightly. The previous day, Luo Shicheng had gifted some tofu to Zhao Quezi, and in return, Zhao Quezi had solemnly sworn never to flee. "Foreigners are known to steal items when they spot them, and to rape women when they encounter them. Jimingyi[1] is only 300 miles away from Beijing, so they could arrive quite soon if they wanted to," Luo Shicheng inquired again, "Aren't you afraid of them?" Zhao Quezi responded, "I'd be dishonest if I said I wasn't scared, but I'd never abandon Jimingyi. Our fate rests on destiny. Where else could we escape to?" Disdain marked Zhao Quezi's face, and it was his tone that convinced Luo Shicheng. Surprisingly, overnight, Zhao Quezi vanished without a trace. He still owed Luo Shicheng half a year's worth of tofu money. Perhaps Zhao Quezi had no intention of settling the debt and lied to him. According to Luo Shicheng's policy, customers couldn't owe him more than a month's worth of tofu money, but he had extended the deadline for Zhao Quezi due to their planned familial ties. Who would have guessed that Zhao Quezi would deceive him?

Despite his anger driving him to the edge, Luo Shicheng didn't lose his composure. Early in the morning, he started grinding tofu, recognizing its value and unwilling to let it spoil in his hands. After venting his frustration for a while, he returned to the store, divided the tofu into buckets, hoisted them onto his shoulder, and began peddling his tofu in the nearby villages.

---

1 "Jimingyi" is an ancient historical city, named after its location against Jiming Mountain. Situated in Jimingyi Village, Jimingyi Town, Huailai County, Hebei Province, it stands as the remnants of a courier station established during the Ming Dynasty (1368 – 1644). It holds historical significance as the poignant site where Empress Dowager Cixi and Emperor Guangxu faced homelessness and destitution. Additionally, it served as a watering hole for Genghis Khan during his Western Expedition. The Flying Horse Posthouse, on the other hand, symbolised the depths of despair for Zhao Xiangzi and acted as the crucial lifeline for Emperor Taizong during the Northern Expedition of the Tang Dynasty.

In the evening, Luo Shicheng returned to Jimingyi with three tofu pieces remaining in the bucket, which was a decent outcome. The family consumed one piece, while the other two, the ones with holes poked by his thumb, were lowered into the well. This method helped preserve his unsold tofu. When Luo Shicheng's wife inquired whether he would continue making tofu, he snapped, exclaiming, "All the villagers have left. Who can I sell it to?" She probed further, asking if he intended to stay or flee like everyone else. Luo Shicheng did not provide an immediate answer. He possessed a cautious and thoughtful nature, especially when it came to significant matters. Making major decisions was a challenge for him. He had contemplated for days, repeatedly weighing the pros and cons of whether to escape, yet remained indecisive. "Let's wait a couple of days and see," he eventually responded to his wife. Perhaps Zhao Quezi would return, he mused. It appeared that Zhao Quezi was his lifeline.

As the couple was turning off the lights to sleep, a hurried tap on the door echoed, clearly not from one hand but several. Luo Shicheng's wife was frightened, her face turning pale. Luo Shicheng was no less scared. Could the foreigner devils have arrived in Jimingyi so quickly? As a man, Luo Shicheng couldn't curl up into a ball. He couldn't hide. Regardless of who was outside, the door had to be opened. If it was smashed open, there would be no room for negotiation.

Outside the door stood three individuals, lacking the deep-set eyes, fair skin, and high noses, and they were neither officials nor soldiers, let alone bandits. Nevertheless, they were not ordinary passersby either. Despite their seemingly commonplace attire, their eyes and gestures set them apart. One of them inquired, "Are you a tofu maker?" Without waiting for Luo Shicheng to respond, he demanded, "Do you have any fresh tofu now? How much do you have? Bring it all out!" Though no knife was at Luo Shicheng's neck, the tone was authoritative. Luo Shicheng breathed a sigh of relief and guided the three people to the courtyard's centre. He retrieved the bucket from the well, explaining that there were only two pieces left. The man queried if there was any fresh meat available, be it chicken, duck, or pork. Observing their hunger, Luo Shicheng mentioned having a chicken. Another person swiftly captured the Plymouth Rock chicken in its nest. The chicken, sensing danger, emitted a particularly mournful cry. The man handed the chicken to Luo Shicheng, instructing coldly, "Kill it!" Cautiously, Luo Shicheng asked, "Now?" The man's response was succinct, "Now!"

Luo Shicheng quickly killed the chicken, removed its feathers, and stewed the chicken and tofu together. The three people urged Luo Shicheng to work swiftly, but they also insisted he be careful. In Jimingyi and the surrounding villages, the Luo Family's tofu garnered abundant praise. It was exquisite, tender, and fragrant, especially suitable for being stewed with meat. After simmering, the tofu would resemble a honeycomb, earning it the name "honeycomb tofu." It required slow simmering; otherwise, the holes would be too small for the soup to penetrate adequately, resulting in a less flavourful taste. Luo Shicheng valued his tofu's reputation. Although he was stewing bean curd for several unknown people, he remained calm. Though appearing anxious, he ensured the cauldron's fire was not too intense. At midnight, the chicken pieces were finally simmered to perfection. The room was filled with the delightful aroma of incense, and even Luo Shicheng's appetite was stirred.

Luo Shicheng anticipated that the three individuals would consume their meal and depart the same night. However, to his astonishment, after he filled a bowl with chicken and tofu, two of them departed with the bowl, leaving one behind to guard the door. Evidently, this person aimed to prevent Luo Shicheng from leaving the room. Luo Shicheng suspected they had an accomplice, surmising that the chicken and tofu were likely delivered to their leader. Any attempt by Luo Shicheng to act deviously would likely not go unpunished.

Luo Shicheng and his wife remained awake all night, uncertain of what would happen. Later, the guard ordered Luo Shicheng to follow him to a nearby location. It turned out to be the Yuelai Inn, which had been closed for several days. Before entering, the guard instructed him to bow his head when passing through the doorway, and he had to kneel on the ground immediately upon entering. Luo Shicheng's heart pounded like a drum, his legs trembled, and he knelt as he stepped across the threshold. A woman with an old and dignified voice asked him questions. Although her inquiries lasted only a few minutes, it felt like an eternity for Luo Shicheng, and his back was almost soaked with sweat when he left. He was questioned about tofu, and later, when trying to recount the events to his wife, he couldn't recall the specifics of what the woman had asked. Along with his black porcelain bowl, Luo Shicheng brought back a white porcelain plate with blue patterns and a silver ingot.

After a few days, Luo Shicheng learned the identity of those people—they were Empress Dowager Cixi and the accompanying officials fleeing westward. The dragon pattern on the plate indicated its royal origin. This adventure solidified Luo Shicheng's resolve. If Cixi was fleeing, why should he hesitate?

A hundred years later, Luo Bao reclined on his soft bed, reminiscing not about the legend of his great-grandfather and the missing royal porcelain plate, nor the tales his father used to narrate, "When my grandfather was …"—speaking of the illness of boasting that his cautious father succumbed to a few years before death. Instead, his memories focused on the dark, narrow room filled with beans. The hangers' original colour wasn't clear, and the pattern of the stone mill could only be discerned by careful touch. A circular groove on the ground, formed by the steps of his father and himself, stood as a testament to the room's history. His mother, frail in health, seldom turned the millstone, but she didn't idle; she held a lamp high, its small, bean-like flame preventing young Luo Bao from stumbling in the dark.

On nights when tofu grinding was on the agenda, Luo Bao was often roused by his father before three in the morning.

Occasionally, he would turn over and attempt to fall back asleep. While his father was not generally irritable and wore a smile during the day, at night, he transformed into someone stern and austere. If Luo Bao accidentally dozed off, his father would tug at his ear to jolt him awake. On one winter day, his father penalised him by covering Luo Bao's face with a chilled, wet towel. His mother consistently shielded Luo Bao, ensuring he woke up before his father could intervene. Despite his young age of five or six, Luo Bao couldn't actively assist his father in grinding tofu. Yet, his father's intention wasn't to make him physically exert himself; instead, the focus was on learning the procedures, understanding water temperature, heat, and the firmness or tenderness of the tofu. The goal was to commit these aspects to memory, study diligently, and, of course, practice with his own hands. Although it seemed straightforward, the more he learned, the more nuances he needed to master, making the initiation even more challenging. "There is no best, only better," his father would say. "This is not just about making tofu; it's about earning a living," he emphasised. At that time, Luo Bao might not have fully comprehended these words, but they etched themselves firmly in his memory.

Father would leave the village right before dawn and return right after nightfall, adopting a stealthy demeanour reminiscent of a thief. This was in the mid-1970s when Father had his "tail cut"[1]

---

1 Tail Cutting refers to the elimination of what is termed as private ownership residue. It was once a widely adopted "leftist" slogan in rural areas. In reality, it constituted a constraint and assault on the lawful economic pursuits of a substantial number of farmers.

once and he was frightened. Instead of heading to Yingpan Town, he consistently ventured to villages and towns further away, where inspections were less frequent, occasionally reaching the borders of Inner Mongolia. Most often, Father undertook these journeys solo for convenience, but a few times each year, he brought Luo Bao along. Father would shoulder a pole, with a bucket brimming with tofu dangling from one end and Luo Bao snugly nestled in a basket on the opposite side. Eventually, Father innovated by crafting a unicycle, maintaining the tofu on one side and keeping Luo Bao on the other.

On the journey, Luo Bao swiftly drifted into a dream. In rainy weather, Father would wrap the basket with a plastic cloth and insert a bamboo tube diagonally inside. Even during a light drizzle, it would produce a sound akin to beans being fried on the cloth, while a downpour resembled the crackling of firecrackers. However, no sound could rouse Luo Bao; instead, it became his lullaby. The muddy terrain caused Father to furrow his brow, but secretly, Luo Bao was delighted. This meant that Father wouldn't wake him up at every stop. Although there were occasions when Luo Bao was tasked with removing tofu from the bucket during light rain, more often than not, Father allowed him to indulge in sweet dreams within his cave-like shelter, akin to a hibernating animal. As soon as the rain ceased, Luo Bao would no longer receive such treatment. It appeared that, without Luo Bao, the tofu couldn't be sold, or perhaps tofu was his cherished treasure. Father ensured that Luo Bao didn't miss any aspect related to tofu, whether it was handling bowls or counting money. While Father would count the money, he always asked Luo Bao to count it again, or rather, to "touch it." It seemed that only when Luo Bao touched the money did it truly become the possession of the father and son. During that time, counterfeit coins were nonexistent, so Father didn't make Luo Bao authenticate the money's authenticity. Instead, he aimed to let him experience the satisfaction of earning money. "Is it all right?" Father's eyes gleamed, casting light upon his face, almost as if seeking affirmation. Luo Bao promptly nodded without hesitation.

Selling tofu brought challenging and monotonous days, but it also introduced unexpected events and delightful surprises. There were several places Father visited once a month, including school cafeterias, supply and marketing cooperatives, and veterinary stations. Most of the time, these trips resulted in little success. The horse station was another regular stop for Father. Situated far from the village, it lacked proper roads and comprised several adobe houses and a horse pen resembling a football field in size. It wasn't a stable but an open-air pen, stacked with soil and standing about three or four metres tall. On one side of the ground near the top of the enclosure, there was a two-metre-wide and one-metre-deep trench, serving the dual purpose of water drainage and preventing energetic horses from leaping over the enclosure. The outer wall was sloped, and Luo Bao could climb to the top without Father's assistance.

There were around two to three hundred horses in the pen,

and they didn't exhibit the energy for galloping on the grassland; instead, they strolled leisurely. Occasionally, some more aggressive ones would engage in kicking and biting skirmishes with their companions. After two or three bouts, the submissive horses would flee to avoid giving the aggressive ones a chance to assert dominance. Although conflicts occurred on the racetrack, the overall atmosphere was generally calm and uneventful. However, during the breeding season, things were different, and that was what Luo Bao enjoyed the most. Later, he discovered that Father was even more captivated by it than he was.

Elsewhere, there were eight stallions kept for stud services, and they were treated with special care. The mares could only see the stallions on the days of mating. Before entering the arena, the stallions' breath would be smelled by the mares, making them restless. The stallions, in turn, became even more agitated, hissing, raising their hooves, and swinging their tails. The stableman, who regularly bought tofu, quickly loosened the ropes, and the stallions charged into the herd. Inexperienced and young mares were pushed forward, while the experienced ones, who had already become mothers, sought opportunities to get close to the stallions. The stallions, faced with an array of mares, didn't spend much time choosing and often pounced on the nearest one. A robust stallion could be paired with two or three mares simultaneously. When paired with a second horse, the stallion became less irritable and usually chose the younger ones. Cooperation was crucial, as inexperienced mares might not know how to align, and the stableman had to ensure the stallion's genitals were inserted into the mare's body to avoid potential harm. Every year, there were instances of small mares being pressed and bent over, as the stableman couldn't intervene in time. Some people from afar came to watch, and those with experience explained the process to the spectators. Luo Bao, still young, could understand a bit of this through the indoctrination of the experienced audience. The sounds and smells of fecal odour, foul urine, snorting, and hissing suddenly disappeared at that moment, leaving only the visual impressions. One night, Luo Bao mentioned this experience to Maixiang, who commented that Luo Bao wasn't decent in nature. Luo Bao fell silent, refraining from discussing it further, but the scene often replayed in his mind, akin to withered leaves that couldn't be ignored when autumn arrived.

Usually, regardless of whether all the tofu had been sold or not, Luo Bao and his father would return to the village right after nightfall. However, there were exceptions. If they ventured too far and the weather suddenly changed, they would seek shelter in a nearby village household. Luo Bao was often confused and didn't have a deep impression, but he remembered one household in particular. The woman there was a distant relative of his father, and Father asked Luo Bao to call her aunt. Aunt's husband worked as a cart driver and was away for most of the year. Father frequently stopped at Aunt's house, and every time, she made pancakes for them. If there were one or two pieces of tofu left in Father's bucket, they were surely reserved for Aunt.

On a late autumn evening, cold rain was in the air. As they dined, Aunt brought out half a bottle of baijiu to share with Father. After two cups, Father's face turned as red as a cockscomb, but the more Aunt drank, the paler she became. With no sign of the rain letting up, Aunt suggested that Father stay overnight. Father, still chewing his food, replied with a voice as hazy as the meal, "Let's wait and see." Luo Bao's eyelids felt like blankets, so heavy they couldn't be lifted. Aunt took out her pillow, saying, "Look, you need to do this for your child." What Father said remained unclear to Luo Bao. It resembled distant fog—thin and light.

When Luo Bao woke up, it was already the next morning, and Father and Luo Bao hurried on their way. Father's face was pale, and as he walked, it seemed that he had caught a cold. Father had never discussed anything with Luo Bao, but on that day, he asked him if he wanted to go to Yingpan Town. Yingpan Town was a big town, so Father's offer tempted him. Luo Bao did not know Father's intention, but the result was that they lost all the money from selling tofu. They returned empty-handed and didn't buy anything.

After that incident, Father never went to Aunt's house to rest, and her name was seldom mentioned again. Later, as the first household in Songzhuang Village to reach 10,000 yuan, Father attended the county's award ceremony, adorned with a red flower the size of a bowl. Although the flower was crafted from paper, its four leaves were made of cloth. Father proudly hung it on the wall of the tofu workshop. After clearing the mud that had blocked the windows, the entire workshop became brighter, and the stains in the corners became exceptionally clear. Two days later, Aunt suddenly appeared at the door. Though years had passed since they last met, her face remained round, and her eyebrows still curved in a perpetual chuckle. Aunt and Mother met for the first time, and Father introduced them to each other with a smile even more forced than the one on the paper flower. Aunt had come to borrow money due to significant difficulties. Her husband, suffering from a debilitating illness, couldn't survive without treatment. Wiping away tears, Aunt expressed gratitude for having close relatives like them, stating, "Otherwise, my husband and I would have to hang ourselves."

Mother's expression remained frozen, and she uttered no words. Father wore a smile tinged with apology, directed at both Mother and Aunt. He clarified that the 10,000-yuan household title was not genuine. While he had earned some money, it had been spent on beans and equipment. Father detailed his own challenges, and Aunt shared hers, the two narratives running parallel without interference. Aunt's eyes looked as if a "Dragon King[1]" was living therein, and the more she wiped them, the more tears flowed, wetting her chest. Father was about to hand her a towel but was halted by Mother. It took him a while to

---

1　In Chinese legend, the Dragon King is responsible for controlling rainfall. He possesses the ability to summon clouds and rain, ward off disasters, and bestow blessings.

comprehend her intention. He promptly exchanged the towel with the one he was using, rough edges and all, unsoaked by water, placing it stiffly into Aunt's hand.

Mother had prepared dinner for Aunt, but she claimed she couldn't eat it. Eventually, she ceased crying but made no move to leave until the following morning when Father handed her three hundred yuan. Mother, infuriated, snatched the red flower from the wall, where it had adorned for just three days, and thrust it into the stove.

2

Luo Bao was as weak as tofu: timid and easily intimidated. Anyone could bully him.

At the age of three, while trying to feed a few grains of rice to a furry chick, he was knocked down by an angry old hen. The hen, pure black with golden eyes, a red crown, and white claws, had hatched 25 chicks. Witnessing a cat devour one of her chicks, the hen tried to fight back but failed as the cat leaped onto a tree branch. Furious and considering Luo Bao an accomplice, the hen pecked at him relentlessly. If it weren't for Mother intervening, Luo Bao might have ended up pockmarked, with his face and hands bearing seven or eight peck marks. At the age of four, a rooster jumped onto Luo Bao's shoulder and pecked at the cold steamed bread he had half-chewed. Unresisting, Luo Bao threw it away, yet the rooster still scratched his neck. By the time he was five, while passing by a house, a recently-birthed sow rushed out of the yard. Towering over Luo Bao, with bristles standing on end and fierce eyes, the sow grabbed his leg and dragged the crying Luo Bao into the yard. It took the host clubbing the sow a few times to make it release Luo Bao. Being bullied by children of the same age or even younger inflicted even more suffering on Luo

Bao. A scar, the size of a bean, adorned his forehead, a result of being struck by another child with a stone.

Every time, Luo Bao and his parents received apologies or compensation, such as candies and apricots. The most substantial compensation they ever got was 20 eggs from the sow's family. However, regardless of the apologies or compensation, nothing changed, and Luo Bao continued to be labeled as a coward. It seemed the entire world knew that Luo Bao from Songzhuang Village would get leg cramps before facing a sow.

His mother would often sigh and furrow her brows. If only she could somehow send Luo Bao back into her womb and give birth to him again, she would do it, enduring the suffering. Meanwhile, his father, while teaching Luo Bao how to grind tofu, also worked on toughening his courage. This included leaving him alone in the dark mill or applying the whip for training. His father even contemplated raising a sow, but this idea faced rejection from his mother.

Father was the inheritor of honeycomb tofu, but in Luo Bao's heart, his father seemed more like a mould, consistently contemplating how to shape Luo Bao into the desired form. In some ways, Father succeeded. For instance, initially left-handed, Luo Bao changed after his father repeatedly whipped him. However, when it came to calculating on an abacus, his father demanded Luo Bao to use both hands, subjecting him to a hellish training regimen. During that time, Luo Bao often trembled before his father, who seemed more cruel than the devil, feeling as if he stood on eggshells that could break with the slightest error. Luo Bao's exceptional numerical and calculation skills were somewhat a result of his father's intimidation. Luo Bao had a habit of licking his lips, unintentionally. It was a reflex with no conscious intention. He couldn't help it, especially when hungry, as if there were grains of rice or sugar stuck there that could alleviate his hunger. Whenever Father caught Luo Bao doing that, he would pinch him, leaving bruises on Luo Bao's face until he managed to break the habit of licking his lips.

Despite Father's efforts, Luo Bao remained timid, and his cowardice proved resistant to change. Frustrated by repeated failures, Father, seething with anger, began to believe or accept that Luo Bao's life was akin to that of tofu. Another aspect of Luo Bao that Father failed to reshape was his slowness.

When Luo Bao's parents finished their meal, each of them drank a bowl of water boiled for steaming rice, but Luo Bao only ate half of his meal. Whether it was rice, steamed bread, noodles, or porridge, Luo Bao chewed it over and over again. This was especially true when eating oat noodles; it seemed as if the oat noodles had thorns, and he bit them with great caution to avoid being stabbed. "Can't you eat faster? Is it poisoned or what?" Father would always reprimand. Instead of picking up the pace, Luo Bao would stop chewing, anticipating Father's palm to fall. Father wasn't initially so angry, but Luo Bao's seemingly insensible eating habits frustrated him, leading to slaps or the bowl being snatched and poured out. Father believed that Luo Bao, who had experienced famine like him, shouldn't eat so slowly. People who are extremely hungry would find tree bark delicious; eating slowly meant missing out on even the leaves. If the bowl snatched by Father seemed like it belonged to someone else, Luo Bao showed no interest, displaying no signs of fuss, anger, or grievance. Though he could be pinched like dough, no one knew that a small, hard bone fragment was hidden in the middle. It was small enough to be ignored but undeniably present. Even after not eating for half a day or an entire day, when Luo Bao had his next meal, he still didn't eat as fast as Father expected, let alone gobble it down. It appeared that Luo Bao was never hungry enough, prompting Father to continue starving him. Strangely, the hungrier Luo Bao became, the more slowly he ate, as if his strength to hold the chopsticks had waned. Father's face twisted in anger. How could he be worse than a fool? If he were a fool, would you dig his brains out? Perhaps it was due to Mother's influence that Father refrained from breaking Luo Bao's bowl anymore. Nevertheless, every two or three months, Father still punished him for his perceived slowness.

Certainly, if Luo Bao was just slow in eating, it might have been acceptable. However, he exhibited a sluggishness in everything he did, consistently lagging behind others. While other children had already reached the end of the field when picking wheat ears, Luo Bao ambled along, only halfway through. When grazing his donkey, he was always led by the animal. At times, the donkey would break free and go off on its own, munching on green wheat seedlings instead of heading to the grassland by the water. This prompted the owner of the wheat fields to visit Luo Bao's house. In an attempt to make amends, Luo Bao's parents had to plead for him, offering two pieces of tofu as compensation.

"Are you doing this on purpose?" Father once asked, expressing suspicion even though Luo Bao's face didn't show any stubbornness or determination to act against him. While doing accounting, Father read the numbers aloud, and Luo Bao swiftly manipulated the abacus, fingers racing and beads clattering. However, after completing the calculations, Luo Bao seemed to solidify and became sluggish. When Father asked him to report the result, he would often scratch the root of his ear first. Father, suspecting that Luo Bao had made mistakes, would calculate it himself to confirm Luo Bao's accuracy. "Are you afraid to say it?" Father questioned, but Luo Bao insisted he wasn't afraid. Father persisted, "Then why don't you just quickly tell me?" However, Luo Bao remained silent.

Father and Mother brought Luo Bao to Zunai, suspecting that he might be cursed. It was a spring day, and Zunai sat on a small stool, washing sow thistle. Although Mother offered to help, Zunai insisted, saying, "No, I can manage on my own." Zunai meticulously dried the washed sow thistle in a sieve, waiting for them to wilt before pickling them. Having previously given tofu to Zunai, Luo Bao had witnessed the vegetable-pickling process. Zunai's method differed from his mother's; she didn't just throw the vegetables into the vat, add a few handfuls of salt, and press them down with a stone. Instead, Zunai placed sow thistle one by one, arranged even more orderly than when they grew in the ground. She used a small wooden spoon to scoop salt, a dark red spoon with a cracked handle. This particular spoon captivated Luo Bao, though he couldn't quite articulate why.

The parents hesitated to confess their doubts, worried about affecting Zunai's mood or making her feel embarrassed. However, when Zunai noticed their hesitation and grabbed Luo Bao's hand, she asked what was wrong. Father then shared his suspicions about Luo Bao with Zunai. His face twisted with anxiety as he stressed how anxious they had been. Zunai, seemingly unperturbed, touched Luo Bao's head and picked up a feather by her foot. She instructed Luo Bao to blow on it, and as he did, the feather floated into the air, drifting towards the outside of the courtyard. The parents couldn't contain their excitement, as if the perceived spell on Luo Bao had been carried away by the feather. Zunai then asked Luo Bao to pick up a stone and throw it into the air. When the stone fell to the ground, she raised her head and said, "See. The stone fell, and the feather went up. Each person has their own character. Why do you want to alter it? The child is normal. What could I say about you? If there were a curse, it is you two who put it on him."

Following that incident, Father refrained from scolding Luo Bao, although he still couldn't appreciate the slow pace at which his son did everything, akin to a snail. Luo Bao could discern this sentiment from his father's expression.

Upon completing primary school, Luo Bao discontinued his education and began working at his family's tofu workshop. He suggested this idea himself, and his parents raised no objections. Despite his lively mind and proficiency in academics, particularly in mathematics, Luo Bao consistently failed exams. No child could outdo him in solving problems like the "cage of chickens and rabbits" or the "lair of cows and ducks,"[1] classic brain teasers often found in math classrooms. However, Luo Bao's struggle lay in his slow writing and the meticulous mental calculations he performed before jotting down his answers. While the teacher empathised, Luo Bao's parents were relieved that he no longer had to compete with other children. Making tofu proved to be a better fit for Luo Bao.

Although Luo Bao could already make tofu by himself, Father still taught him a lesson. The legend of his great-grandfather, the silver ingot, royal porcelain plates, Jimingyi, the origin of honeycomb tofu, and so on. Father's eyes shone like inlaid silver. Father's gaze barely left Luo Bao's face, as if he were about to apply the silver light to Luo Bao's body.

"Got it?" Father asked repeatedly.

"Got it!" Luo Bao's voice was loud, although he didn't respond so quickly.

---

1 The scenario of chickens and rabbits in a cage or cows and ducks in a circle constitutes a classic problem-solving challenge frequently encountered in mathematics classrooms and brain games. This particular problem serves as a litmus test for students' logical reasoning and problem-solving skills. While it may appear straightforward, it intricately incorporates various techniques for effective problem resolution.

Father patted Luo Bao on the shoulder, which was his way of expressing his approval. Luo Bao was fourteen years old that year.

No one, including Father, knew the relationship between Luo Bao and tofu. Neither was it necessary to inherit one's ancestral heritage, nor was he just a helpless person suitable for this profession, nor was his temperament like tofu. That was his secret. When the bean aroma pounced, his body would grow countless nostrils and mouths.

3

On a winter evening, Luo Bao purchased a piece of soap from the grocery store, stepped outside, and turned the corner. Suddenly, a peculiar fragrance caught his attention. Unlike the robust scent of beans, this aroma was light, soft, and delicate, yet it possessed the power to permeate his chest. Although Luo Bao had initially turned away, he reversed his steps to try and identify the source of the scent. The bitter wind had chafed his cheeks, and his Adam's apple was increasingly swollen. As he sniffed, he encountered the smells of cattle and horse dung, mingled with the pungent aroma of fried vegetables, undoubtedly cooked with lard. However, the chest-piercing fragrance eluded him. In the winter, when everything lay dormant and the earth was cold and rigid, Luo Bao pondered what flavour could be more fragrant than beans in this world. Ultimately, he considered the possibility that his nose might be playing a small trick on him.

The streets of Songzhuang Village weren't particularly lengthy, yet they were full of twists and turns. Some paths appeared passable but led to dead ends. One might think they had reached the conclusion, only to discover a small gap serving as the beginning of another street. Over the years, numerous houses had been constructed, some on the original foundations, others near the Butterfly River, causing the village to expand. For a stranger, navigating the village during the day could be challenging, let alone at night, with the labyrinthine layout making it easy to get lost.

Certainly, Luo Bao had an accurate knowledge of the interconnected streets and the neighbouring households because Father regularly took him along to sell tofu. Rather than taking a direct route out of the village, they navigated through several corners and streets. From childhood, Luo Bao had become intimately familiar with the streets of Songzhuang Village, akin to knowing the back of his hand. While passing the grinding wheel (now collapsed), the peculiar fragrance wafted into Luo Bao's senses once more. Luo Bao abruptly stood up, surveying his surroundings. There was nothing unusual; only the dim houses and trees occupied the space. The fragrance had vanished entirely, leaving no trace. Scents had roots and didn't randomly waft in the night sky. Where was its origin? Luo Bao shifted his gaze and fixated on the exposed grinding wheel for a brief moment. After covering several dozen metres, the fragrance emerged again, playing a game of hide-and-seek.

Luo Bao rose at three o'clock in the morning, guided not by Father's ear-pulling or the blare of an alarm clock but by an automatic spring in his head. His early bedtime routine was a result of this internal clock. Despite the growth of his Adam's apple and beard, Luo Bao's courage remained unchanged. He wasn't afraid of the dark but feared the possibility that the pen's door might not have been securely closed, leading to sows wandering into the streets. In the darkness, the sow's behaviour could be even more unruly, and Luo Bao had no desire to be devoured alive. He seldom ventured out at night, and when he did, he promptly returned home after completing his tasks. However, on that particular night, Luo Bao strolled through the streets without a hint of nervousness or concern, replaced by an indescribable surge of excitement coursing through his veins. He chased and sniffed, following an aroma that flickered and broke, like a thread in the darkness that could be sensed but not grasped.

If it weren't for Father's call, Luo Bao might have continued to pursue the elusive scent. Father remarked, "I thought you were lost," a blend of concern and sarcasm in his words. At this point, Luo Bao and Father had assumed distinct roles. Luo Bao managed the entire tofu grinding process, while Father focused on selling it, now aided by a bicycle instead of a wheelbarrow. As the primary labourer in the family, Luo Bao had gained the authority to disregard his father. It would be several years before he openly challenged Father, and his preferred mode of confrontation was often silence. Father inquired about Luo Bao's whereabouts, and this time, Luo Bao could not remain silent. However, his response lacked warmth: "Nothing, just hanging around." Father stated, "Your mother is extremely worried about you." Luo Bao retorted, "I'm not a three-year-old child." Father shared, "Your mother had a headache again." "Did you buy her medicine?"

Luo Bao inquired. Father affirmed, "Yes." The conversation ended there. The strange fragrance that had penetrated Luo Bao's heart and lungs was no longer present. Feeling unwilling to let it go, he turned around once more but failed to find it. He stood still in the cold wind for a moment, eventually returning with disappointment.

Following that encounter, Luo Bao intentionally or unintentionally walked through the streets at night, but the elusive fragrance never graced him again. Luo Bao kept this experience to himself, a personal treasure he had no intention of sharing with anyone. Besides, he had no one to share it with— no playmates, no close friends. Once, he had a younger sister who passed away prematurely at the age of three. However, he couldn't even recall what his sister looked like. As for his parents, Luo Bao was only willing to engage with them in conversations about tofu.

On a spring morning, while Luo Bao was washing soybeans, Maixiang entered carrying an enamel basin. In Songzhuang Village, residents would come directly to Luo Bao's home to purchase tofu. Each day, Luo Bao would prepare a cauldron of tofu in the workshop. Initially, Father wanted to reserve only half a cauldron for the villagers, thinking that even if only a few people bought it, there wouldn't be any leftovers. However, Luo Bao insisted on providing a full cauldron, and rather than arguing with Father, he would promptly make a new cauldron if all the tofu was taken away. This approach succeeded, and Father eventually gave in to Luo Bao's preference. Luo Bao didn't reveal the true reason to Father. It wasn't because he feared the people of Songzhuang Village wouldn't have enough tofu, but rather, witnessing their disappointed expressions would make him uneasy.

Maixiang's mother was a frequent customer when it came to buying tofu. While others might purchase one piece, she typically bought two because her daughter, Maixiang, had a particular fondness for tofu, especially when consumed raw. "She breaks off one piece when heading out, another piece when coming back," Maixiang's mother would share. "Luo Bao, the tofu you make is more delicious than your father's. Maixiang has become greedy for your tofu." Maixiang's mother was quite talkative and always spoke about her daughter when purchasing tofu. Luo Bao lacked male friends and had minimal interaction with girls, leaving him with little understanding of them. The sole girl he was aware of was Maixiang, and all his knowledge about girls came from Maixiang's mother. Naturally, he had glimpsed Maixiang from a distance without uttering a word to her.

Luo Bao gazed at Maixiang in astonishment, his eyes resembling copper bells, as if she had descended from the heavens unexpectedly. He even entertained the thought that Maixiang's mother might be wearing a mask, playing a deliberate prank on him. The enamel basin held by Maixiang was recognizable to him, adorned with two red carp on its side, one of them featuring a glazed tail. The person who should have held it had a physique reminiscent of a carp. However, standing before him now was another individual, simultaneously familiar and unfamiliar, with a round face, red lips, and gracefully curved eyebrows that seemed to have been skilfully crafted.

Maixiang turned around and noticed there was no one behind her, only to find Luo Bao staring at her. She felt a mix of shyness and anger, unable to discern which was genuine. "People say you are just like a girl. It's incredible that you really look like a silly girl!" Maixiang teased. This sudden comment made Luo Bao blush and left him perplexed. Maixiang then casually ordered, "Tofu, two pieces!" As Luo Bao picked up the enamel basin from her hand, a strange fragrance hit him abruptly and rapidly, catching him off guard. Trembling, the basin slipped from his grasp, prompting Maixiang to exclaim, "Look at you!" After checking and confirming that it wasn't broken, Maixiang insisted on compensation, jokingly suggesting at least three pieces of tofu. In this unusual encounter, Luo Bao found himself conversing with a girl for the first time. Uncertain if Maixiang was joking or serious, he sincerely asked her how much compensation was needed, given his lack of experience. Maixiang, amused, responded, "At least three pieces of tofu." Relieved, Luo Bao washed the basin twice and filled it with three pieces of tofu. However, Maixiang confessed that she was just joking. Luo Bao, feeling obligated, insisted on compensating her, and Maixiang, after studying him for a while, broke a piece of tofu and stuffed it into her mouth. She expressed her love for Luo Bao's tofu but requested him not to disclose it. Promising to keep it a secret,

Luo Bao assured her that he wouldn't tell anyone. Pleased with his honesty, Maixiang said, "You are an honest person. I believe you."

Maixiang had been gone for a while, yet Luo Bao retained vivid memories of her mannerisms while consuming bean curd and the delightful fragrance that permeated his heart and lungs as if from a needle. The source of the fragrance lay with Maixiang. Was it in her hair, her eyes, her mouth, or her pores? Luo Bao was eager to ask but lacked the courage. Nevertheless, he ultimately discovered it, a revelation both unexpected and fortunate.

Three days later, Maixiang returned to buy tofu. Luo Bao was speculating on whether it would be Maixiang or her mother this time. Without any apparent reason, he secretly hoped for Maixiang and offered a silent prayer. Surprisingly, Maixiang did come, perhaps a result of his prayer. Radiant like a lottery winner, Luo Bao's face beamed with joy. Maixiang, as before, broke off a corner of the tofu and put it into her mouth, paying no attention to Luo Bao's direct gaze. In a haughty tone, she remarked, "Don't laugh at me, you make such delicious tofu!" Although Maixiang's tone was contemptuous, Luo Bao didn't feel excited; instead, he regarded it as an indescribable pleasure. As they conversed, her fragrance pierced through his senses. Luo Bao wished Maixiang would stay a bit longer but lacked the courage to keep her. As she turned around to leave, an idea struck Luo Bao. He suggested that if she came the next day, he would prepare a bowl of jellied tofu with sauce for her in advance, emphasizing that it was better than regular tofu. Uncertain of her reaction, his heart pounded wildly. Maixiang seemed taken aback, and a shadow crossed her flat, round eyes, hinting at a gathering cloud of darkness. "What do you mean?" she asked, revealing her displeasure. The feared anger had surfaced. Stammering, Luo Bao retreated, "Nothing … nothing … just …" Then, like the clouds giving way to sunlight, Maixiang burst into laughter, bending at the waist. "Look at you. You've got guts thinner than a needle," she teased. Dumbfounded, Luo Bao wondered which version of Maixiang was real. Maixiang straightened up and inquired, "You aren't lying?" Luo Bao vigourously shook his head. Maixiang chuckled, "Okay, stop shaking, just shake it again, and it will fall off. I agree; I'll come over tomorrow."

Luo Bao rose earlier than usual, despite it being unnecessary, as sleep eluded him. Uncertain of Maixiang's arrival, despite her agreement, he pondered her capricious nature. Before Maixiang even entered the room, Luo Bao, pacing anxiously, abruptly halted. The distinctive fragrance enveloped him, piercing through like needles.

While Maixiang tasted the tofu jelly, Luo Bao watched her silently, his entire fate seemingly hanging on her verdict. Finally, she declared it was great, and Luo Bao's anxiously suspended heart finally found its resting place. Maixiang then asked if this dish was also a tradition passed down from his ancestors, to which Luo Bao nodded, although it was actually his own invention. But Maixiang had a surprising twist to her next words. Instead of expressing any dissatisfaction, she mentioned that she couldn't afford it.

Taken aback, Luo Bao immediately blurted out, "I don't want any money." Maixiang, staring at him intently, questioned his motive, suspecting he might be up to something. Luo Bao's face turned red as he made a detailed confession about his plans to expand the variety of foods he sold, seeking her opinion on different dishes. In response, Maixiang asked, "That is your plan. You want me to taste it? Why me?" Luo Bao found her suitable for the role. Inquisitive, Maixiang asked, "Am I a glutton?" Luo Bao replied, "You understand!" Maixiang, seemingly satisfied, said, "You are just saying nice words. Is that all?" Hesitating, Luo Bao confessed, "There are more … Don't be angry." Calmly, Maixiang replied, "Look how shy you are." Gathering courage, Luo Bao expressed, "I like your fragrance." This admission stunned Maixiang, who asked, "Did you smell it?" Luo Bao nodded, prompting Maixiang to show him two matching cloth bags—one pink, containing morning glory, and the other with white flower patterns on a blue background, containing henbane. She explained they were sachets she made. Maixiang, seeming doubtful, asked if Luo Bao could really smell them. Before he could answer, she concluded, 'You really have a dog nose. I've been wearing it for two years, and there has been no one … There's no better appreciation than this." Impulsively, Luo Bao shared the story of that strange winter night and his repeated searches. Maixiang chided him, saying, "You should feel ashamed," but Luo Bao insisted, "I really … like it." Maixiang questioned, "Can I really help you?" Luo Bao affirmed, "You can! No one is more suitable than you." However, Maixiang posed a hypothetical, "What if I refuse you?" Luo Bao looked at her helplessly. After a brief contemplation, Maixiang nodded and said, "Okay." Overflowing with gratitude, Luo Bao thanked her repeatedly, as if he had won a grand prize. Teasingly, Maixiang said, "No wonder I could eat it for free. I fell into your trap!" Luo Bao struggled, "I'm really …" But Maixiang interrupted, "Don't quibble. You look honest and timid on the surface, but you have a lot of ideas in your mind."

4

It resembled a butterfly delicately alighting on a flower, closing its wings, or a feather gently brushing the earth—too weightless to touch. Luo Bao, sensing a cue, promptly opened his eyes. Instead of immediately illuminating the room, he gazed upwards, fixating on a window or the ceiling. Maixiang's appearances emerged from the shadows, engaged in activities like breaking tofu, pulling bean skin, or pouting while serving tofu jelly with sauce—her expressions a theatrical performance that was both familiar and unfamiliar. The peculiar fragrance didn't waft through the air but lingered beside his ear. She crafted it for him. The robust bean aroma remained distinct, unmarred by the fragrance, ensuring the purity of the bean scent. At least, that's how Luo Bao perceived it. Observing the girl in the darkness became a source of delight for him. After sufficient contemplation, he would secretly smile before leaping out of bed.

That night, something unusual disrupted Luo Bao's peaceful slumber. A mysterious spring seemed to have malfunctioned and emitted a clicking sound. Abruptly awakened, his eyes widened, and he frantically scanned his surroundings, trying to make sense of the disturbance. He felt a deep conviction that something significant had occurred. Breathing heavily, as if he had just sprinted, Luo Bao strained his senses to detect shouts and shuffling footsteps that seemed to be fading away. While others in Songzhuang Village were still immersed in the quiet of the dawn, Luo Bao was already busy with his tofu, the steam rising from it on a wooden board. After a moment of squatting at the door, savouring the fragrance, Luo Bao usually took out his sachet. However, on this particular morning, there was no need—the enticing aroma lingered around him wherever he went. As he continued to relish the scent, the noise from the street grew louder. Puzzled, Luo Bao wondered what was happening. Had the commotion reached him, disrupting his usual peaceful morning routine?

Luo Bao found himself in a daze as the approaching steps grew nearer. Unconsciously, he switched on the light, and a knock echoed at the window. Despite the unexpected disturbance, Luo Bao was already neatly dressed. This habit traced back to the Tangshan earthquake[1], where families, affected by the calamity, slept fully clothed in tents. Unlike the adults and children who had adapted to this practice, Luo Bao, even in his sleep, preferred to be unclothed. Having been frequently roused from sleep by his father, he developed the skill of dressing quickly and maintained the habit throughout his life. Known for his unhurried pace in

---

1 Tangshan earthquake: On July 28, 1976, an abrupt 7.8 magnitude earthquake rocked Tangshan, Hebei Province. The burgeoning heavy industrial city of Tangshan endured a catastrophic calamity and was reduced to ruins.

most matters, Luo Bao, as a blacksmith once remarked, wouldn't be flustered even if a wolf bit him. However, the exception to this was his remarkable speed when getting dressed. Except for his parents, no one had witnessed Luo Bao's swift dressing routine, making it a fact that was hard for others to believe.

The arrival was none other than Song Tai, Maixiang's cousin. He seized Luo Bao without preamble, stating, "Follow me!"

A decade senior to Luo Bao, Song Tai was known for his idleness, nonsensical banter, and jesting with everyone, including his parents. At thirteen, he once asked his mother for money to buy a hat, leading to a bizarre exchange where he questioned his lineage and demanded funds from his supposed biological mother. His mother, incensed, vehemently asserted her role in his birth and criticised his lack of conscience. Despite the refusal, Song Tai managed to buy the hat by locating hidden money his mother stored in various places every other month. Despite his penchant for mischief and laziness, one day Song Tai transformed into a seemingly successful and refined individual, donning sunglasses, smoking filtered cigarettes, and wearing glossy leather shoes. His mother, alarmed, inquired about his sudden change. To her shock, Song Tai claimed to have robbed three American banks and become a millionaire's son-in-law. Perplexed and concerned, his mother resorted to daily prayers with burning incense. It was only later revealed, upon Song Tai's police detainment, that he had stolen a cow. Upon his release from prison, Song Tai persisted in his idle and boastful ways. While others his age were raising families, he remained single, surrounded by a constant stream of women. Women frequently visited Songzhuang Village in search of him, some even arriving pregnant. His mother, on one occasion, hosted a pregnant woman who appeared skilled in housework, only to have her reclaimed by her husband three months later. When questioned, Song Tai, nonchalant as ever, would reply, "Which one are you referring to? I have a lot of women."

Of course, Luo Bao had heard various stories about Song Tai, but distinguishing the real from the imaginary was challenging. Yet, he paid little attention to them. Luo Bao and Song Tai belonged to different realms and had scarcely interacted. It was Song Tai who apprehended Luo Bao one dark night, instructing him to follow without offering any explanation.

Luo Bao, though timid, was not foolish. He inquired of Song Tai, "W-what are you doing?"

Song Tai declared, "Maixiang ran away with someone!" Luo Bao felt as if his head had been struck by lightning, a thunderous reverberation coursing through him. Were it not for Song Tai's grip, he would have crumpled.

"Hey!" Song Tai exclaimed, "It's not an earthquake. Why are you shaking?"

Trembling, Luo Bao queried, "With … who?"

Impatiently, Song Tai retorted, "You are really annoying. Anyway, she didn't go with you. Don't ask. Hurry up and put on your shoes. Or else we won't be able to catch up with them."

Struggling to put on his shoes, Luo Bao found assistance from Song Tai, albeit accompanied by a string of curses. As the door locked behind them, Luo Bao suddenly recollected Song Tai's identity, the legends surrounding him fleeting like dust in the wind.

"You're not lying to me, are you?" Luo Bao hesitated, retreating as if melding into the wall.

With a forceful shove, Song Tai scoffed, "Lying to you would insult my IQ. Let's go!"

Luo Bao stumbled and plunged into the obscurity. Song Tai hastened his pace, leaving Luo Bao struggling to keep up. Eventually, Song Tai paused, prompting Luo Bao to hasten. The duo ventured westward, departing from the village. However, Song Tai tripped and tumbled to the ground. After rising, he cursed vehemently, spitting out sand. "What did I do to deserve this? Damn it!" he exclaimed in frustration.

The fall appeared to have shaken Song Tai, tempering his impatience as he now walked alongside Luo Bao. Song Tai, acknowledging Luo Bao's disbelief, urged him to keep his eyes wide open, cautioning that Maixiang might be concealed behind bushes. Luo Bao, still grappling with the incredulity of Maixiang's betrayal, voiced his doubts once more. In the darkness, Song Tai's sneer resembled that of an owl, sending shivers down Luo Bao's spine. Song Tai, in a tone both mocking and sinister, remarked, "Pretty boy. Why do you have to be so inquisitive?"

The person who kidnapped Maixiang was someone with a

southern accent named Qiu Houzi (Monkey), who often visited the village to collect medicinal materials. Qiu Houzi was of average height, with slender arms and a soft-spoken demeanour. He would come every summer and leave after autumn, renting a house in Yingpan Town and hiring helpers. On the day of the abduction, Qiu Houzi and Maixiang were conversing in the street when Song Tai spotted them. While he couldn't hear their conversation, Song Tai's keen eyes immediately led him to conclude that Maixiang and Qiu Houzi were involved romantically. Although the details of their connection were unclear to Song Tai, he trusted his instincts. Song Tai approached Maixiang's father, expressing concern about her and warning him about Qiu Houzi. Despite Song Tai's efforts, Maixiang's father didn't believe the information and mocked Song Tai due to past events. Unfazed, Song Tai decided to distance himself from the situation. However, about half a month ago, he encountered Qiu Houzi again in town. Given the late autumn season with no medicinal materials to collect, Qiu Houzi should have left, but he was still lingering. Song Tai suspected this was related to Maixiang and once again cautioned Maixiang's father. This time, Maixiang's father took his words more seriously, though still habouring doubts. While he prevented Maixiang from leaving the village, he didn't exercise strict control over her movements. In the middle of the night, Maixiang's father heard a disturbance from the West Room. Upon investigation, he discovered that Maixiang had disappeared.

Maixiang's father rallied his family and relatives, pursuing in three directions – north, south, and east. The shuffling footsteps, Luo Bao surmised, belonged to them. Despite Song Tai's assurance being validated, Maixiang's father remained sceptical of Song Tai's conclusion that Qiu Houzi and Maixiang had fled west.

"Fools didn't believe me. I wanted to catch Maixiang and Qiu Houzi and show them I was right. I can't do it alone. Suddenly, I thought of you. Maixiang often comes to your tofu shop. You do care about her, right?" Song Tai stated, adding, "I'm too talkative, but I never misjudge people."

The autumn wind carried a biting chill, yet within Luo Bao, an internal fire raged like burning charcoal in his chest. The emotions—whether anger, grievance, shame, or despair—remained a turbulent mix. What he did know was that the burning charcoal sensation intensified, threatening to consume him entirely. Just yesterday, Maixiang had visited the tofu shop, their intimacy evident, only for her to betray Luo Bao overnight. And all for a Southerner!

With the approaching dawn, the contours of woods, fields, ditches, and villages became discernible. As far as the eye could see, no human figures appeared, only cows, horses, and birds gracing the landscape. Their journey encountered a man driving a carriage, and Song Tai queried him about a man and a woman, specifically highlighting the man's likeness to a monkey. Despite receiving a negative response, Song Tai leaped onto the carriage frame, peering into the covering woven with achnatherum splendens. "He has been dealing with the police a lot, and he has learned a lot of tricks," speculated Luo Bao. Further along the road, they encountered a funeral procession. A teenage boy at the front held a funeral flag, followed by a drummer and a four-wheeled cart pulling a coffin. The uneven road caused the four-wheeled cart to bounce, creating the illusion that the coffin was jumping along. Behind the cart, a dozen men in mourning garments looked solemn and fatigued. Luo Bao and Song Tai stood in the farmland beside the road, making way for the funeral procession. As the end of the procession approached, Song Tai unexpectedly seized one of the mourners, startling both Luo Bao and the man. However, Song Tai had no intention of opening the coffin. After gesturing to smoke, the man handed Song Tai half a box of cigarettes and a lighter. Song Tai lit one and waved at Luo Bao, who declined. Voicing his frustration, Song Tai swore, "It's really cold! Damn Qiu Houzi!"

As the morning wore on, there was still no sign of Maixiang and Qiu Houzi. Luo Bao and Song Tai reached the intersection of the provincial and national highways, a location Song Tai deemed suitable for hitchhiking. This intersection provided routes to Zhangjiakou to the south, Inner Mongolia to the north, and Kangbao to the west. As fatigue began to set in for Song Tai, he inquired if Luo Bao had any money. Luo Bao produced a crumpled one-hundred-yuan bill, originally intended for buying a scarf for Maixiang. Song Tai used the money to purchase beer, ham sausage, bread, pickled vegetables, and peanuts from a nearby store. The two of them sat on the floor, watching the constant flow of passing vehicles, including buses, trucks, and cars. Some vehicles revealed their contents, such as pigs, cows, or coal, while others were covered with cloth and appeared bulging. Occasionally, Song Tai glanced as if he could discern what Luo Bao was thinking, remarking, "Maybe we were a bit late. If they don't show up soon, we'll head back."

During the journey spanning dozens of miles, the expanding charcoal bag in Luo Bao's chest gradually dissipated. It felt as though it had burned out, leaving behind only a thin layer of fog and dust, and a sprawling fire of steel needles that remained untouched. These needles persisted, bare and unrestrained, resembling an additional row of ribs. While his chest no longer swelled, the row of steel needles proved unavoidable with every movement. Hungry and thirsty, Luo Bao struggled to swallow as easily as Song Tai. His cautious approach made each swallow an arduous task. Hoping to catch up with Maixiang, he haboured no intentions of harming her but sought answers to the deception. Despite the absence of tangible progress, Luo Bao experienced a sense of relief. Perhaps Song Tai's actions were merely a prank, utter nonsense. Yet, his intuition insisted that Song Tai likely spoke the truth.

After consuming the last drop of beer, Song Tai suggested they return, as if their nocturnal journey had culminated in reaching this particular intersection for a substantial meal. Luo Bao raised no objections, clutching the partially eaten bread in his left hand and following Song Tai with a bottle of unopened water in his right.

Even though he had just eaten, Song Tai didn't let his mouth idle.

"Never tried smoking before?"

"No."

"Have you ever drunk alcohol?"

"No."

"Have you ever had sex with a woman?"

Luo Bao remained silent.

"What's the point of your life then?"

"Making tofu!" Luo Bao's response was swift and resolute.

Song Tai didn't anticipate Luo Bao's swift response. After a brief pause, he smiled once again. "Making tofu? That can be fun?" His disdain irked Luo Bao, who retorted, "Of course, it can!" Chuckling, Song Tai challenged him, "Then tell me how." Coldly, Luo Bao replied, "You wouldn't understand even if I told you." Song Tai, feigning cleverness, suggested, "Because it's an ancestral tradition you're continuing?" His tone carried a hint of arrogance, but Luo Bao ignored him. Song Tai remarked, "After all, living in a tofu shop all your life is a bit of a loss." Unfazed, Luo Bao countered, "It's better than staying in prison!" This triggered Song Tai, who abruptly turned and delivered a fierce kick, catching Luo Bao off guard. He tumbled, and mineral water and bread scattered in the distance. Song Tai scolded, "You want to humiliate me? You're still tender!" Despite the fall, Luo Bao remained defiant, not retaliating. Song Tai swaggered off.

Luo Bao remained seated, almost hoping that Song Tai would continue kicking him. Observing Song Tai's departure, Luo Bao felt a sense of letdown. When Song Tai returned and offered his hand to help Luo Bao up, Luo Bao comprehended the gesture but didn't fully grasp it until Song Tai physically pulled him to his feet. "Don't compete with me. I'm shameless like this," Song Tai remarked.

While Song Tai continued his incessant chatter, Luo Bao remained silent. Song Tai, seemingly aware of how to coax Luo Bao into speaking, inquired about what he liked about Maixiang. Instead of asking if he liked her or not, Song Tai probed into the specifics of what attracted him to her. Luo Bao's face betrayed surprise, as if Song Tai had already been privy to his feelings for Maixiang. Pride evident, Song Tai remarked, "When I talk about Maixiang, you expose your secret. Even if your parents didn't know about it, I already knew. What are you ashamed to talk about? This is quite normal." Luo Bao lowered his head, prompting Song Tai to assert, "I'm sure you didn't hold her hand. A touch doesn't count, it has to be seriously holding it!" Luo Bao's head sank even lower. Song Tai continued, "This isn't acceptable! Even if you're a piece of tofu, you can't be shy about this. No woman likes shy men. However, Maixiang isn't a good match for you. She's two or three years older than you, right?" Luo Bao responded, "She is two years older than me, but I don't care if she's older than me." Song Tai, seemingly satisfied with the response, commented, "I've finally pried your mouth open. I thought you were going to be dumb the whole way back." Luo Bao confessed, "I just like her." Song Tai probed further, asking, "Does she know?" After a moment's hesitation, Luo Bao replied, "Maybe …" Sympathetically, Song Tai remarked, "You're too honest. Your woman will be taken away by someone else before you realise it … Look at my mouth; now I should shut up. I don't want to hurt you!"

By the time they reached the village, it was already noon. The other two groups, like Song Tai and Luo Bao, returned empty-handed. Exhausted and frustrated, they gathered in the courtyard, pinning their hopes on the last group of pursuers. After all, Maixiang didn't possess wings and couldn't fly away. However, Luo Bao sensed that their words were merely a form of solace for Maixiang's mother, and certainty eluded them all. Uninterested in staying for the discussion or the meal, Luo Bao found himself engulfed in the sea of wheat fragrance. Tossed around from the surface to the depths, he struggled to open his eyes or mouth, only able to perceive the cacophony of noises and roars. The experience was almost suffocating. Unnoticed by anyone, Luo Bao slipped away.

At dusk, the final group of pursuers returned, successful in capturing Maixiang and Qiu Houzi. When Luo Bao heard the news, the faint candlelight, almost extinguished, suddenly flared up.

Unlike others who ran, Luo Bao, burdened with the weight of

seawater, felt his legs heavy. Despite the sluggishness, he managed to navigate through the crowd that had gathered. There, tied to a tree, was Qiu Houzi. While Luo Bao recognised him, it was the first time he laid eyes on him. Qiu Houzi's face was discoloured and swollen, bearing several blood marks on his thin, elongated neck, showing distinct signs of strangulation. His physique and appearance were unremarkable, even somewhat unsightly. How could Maixiang elope with such a person? What feature of his captivated Maixiang's affection? What on earth made him appealing?

Unnoticed by the crowd, Luo Bao's expression betrayed no hint of his grief, anger, or pain. They remained oblivious to the fact that this unremarkable face belonged to Luo Bao's romantic rival, the one who had forcibly snatched Maixiang from his grasp. Though Maixiang had been brought back, Luo Bao's heart lay shattered.

5

For over a month, Maixiang confined herself indoors, engaging in only two activities: eating and sleeping.

Similarly, it appeared that Luo Bao was also bound, spending his entire day within the tofu shop. Two years prior, Luo Bao had convinced his father to acquire an abandoned vinegar shop close to collapse. The vinegar shop, formerly owned by someone surnamed Liu, had remained idle since the owner's stroke. With the villagers resorting to obtaining vinegar from outside Songzhuang Village, Liu had long sought to pass on the ownership to someone else, but there were no takers. Luo Bao extended an offer, which they didn't refuse. He demolished the vinegar shop and erected his own tofu shop in its place. Initially, Father disagreed, asserting that the West House could still be utilised, and there was no need for unnecessary expenditures. Luo Bao didn't argue but instead went on strike against his father. After a week, unable to withstand the standoff and faced with customer complaints about the absence of Luo Bao's tofu, Father, fearing the potential risk to the established brand, reluctantly yielded. It couldn't be said that he was persuaded; rather, he was coerced.

In this manner, Luo Bao established his own independent realm. He toiled and slept within the confines of his kingdom, only returning to his original home to partake in meals. Even then, he would swiftly depart after dinner, occasionally forgoing the meal altogether, even though it was only a few steps away. If he didn't return, he would either figure something out himself or receive food sent over by his mother. Luo Bao didn't purposefully engage in conflicts with his father or mother; rather, he sought an autonomous space for quiet contemplation. He preferred pondering over exploring. For instance, with the beehive tofu, he contemplated whether enlarging the holes in the beehive would be more appealing since people enjoyed eating it. He experimented and achieved it, only to encounter a new challenge: the enlarged holes made the tofu more prone to breakage. Diligently addressing the issue of firmness, after numerous trials, he succeeded in creating honeycomb tofu with ample holes yet maintained firmness. He never disclosed this to his father, knowing that sharing the information might hinder his ability to continue making it.

Luo Bao's deliberate pace suited his penchant for contemplation. Whether standing or walking, he could immerse himself in thought. It could be argued that his love for pondering contributed to his unhurried demeanour. Within his self-established kingdom, he wielded autonomy and recklessness, impervious to external influences.

However, since Maixiang's failed elopement with Qiu Houzi,

Luo Bao's mood had darkened, and he was no longer the same. His focus had waned, and he no longer displayed the intense concentration he once did. When engrossed in thought previously, his attention was unwavering, akin to a tightly twisted rope or two inseparable cows. Now, his once-vibrant mind resembled withered straw, unable to withstand even the slightest breeze. Though Luo Bao's tofu-making process remained unaffected, having become routine and almost mechanical, it lacked the depth of thought. Distracted and haunted by Maixiang's unpredictable appearances, his attempts often led to repeated setbacks.

Despite intense contemplation, Luo Bao struggled to comprehend why Maixiang had betrayed him. Her role in tasting tofu samples was merely an excuse for her to be close to him. Otherwise, how could she linger around him for half a day? Even without her assistance, he continued his experiments. He shared a different kind of connection with her. Although he never confessed, never seized her hand, and accidental touches were dismissed, she had once embraced him. This was a secret Luo Bao kept from Song Tai; it was a shared intimacy between him and Maixiang.

Just a month before Maixiang eloped, a sow and six piglets infiltrated the tofu shop. Luo Bao, typically engrossed in his work, suddenly found himself bewildered. Despite having grown beyond his childhood years, the memory of a sow's bite still haunted him. He usually avoided sows, particularly those who had recently given birth. His cowardice left him feeling ashamed, perhaps contributing to his tendency to withdraw into his kingdom. Although the invading sow demanded attention, Luo Bao couldn't simply ignore it. Armed with a broom, he attempted to drive it away. To his dismay, instead of fleeing, the sow charged at him with a fierce expression, as if it had discerned his cowardice. In a panic, Luo Bao tossed aside the broom and leaped onto a beam, leaving the sow to assert dominance. Maixiang entered the room and burst into laughter upon witnessing Luo Bao discarding his broom in a moment of confusion.

Maixiang took charge and chased the sow away, prompting Luo Bao to descend from the beam with a pale, shrinking face. As Maixiang passed by, she gently embraced Luo Bao, providing comfort and helping him regain his composure. When Luo Bao attempted to explain, Maixiang playfully remarked, "You must have been tofu in your previous life, so the sow bit you." She warned in a teasing manner, "You can't bully me in the future, or I'll let the sow eat you alive." Later, she actually led the sow to find Luo Bao, seeking playful retaliation. Could this be a hint for the future? Luo Bao wasn't oblivious; Maixiang belonged to him, and he had already begun contemplating proposing to her. Despite the failed elopement, it felt like he had been poisoned, almost to the point of demise.

Maixiang's mother occasionally visited to buy tofu. She remained silent, avoiding any mention of Maixiang's well-being— whether she had gained or lost weight, whether she was sitting or lying down. Maixiang's mother simply purchased tofu and departed. One day, unable to contain himself, Luo Bao inquired about Maixiang's condition. Maixiang's mother glanced at him obliquely, as if assessing whether his intentions were malicious, and then replied solemnly, "She's very well!" The response was succinct and clear, yet it carried a sense of vagueness and ambiguity. Luo Bao grasped the message but struggled to decipher the profound meaning behind the words.

In late autumn, amidst heavy rain that brought a standstill to both chickens and dogs, Maixiang entered the tofu shop with an umbrella in hand. Luo Bao had been experiencing frequent hallucinations lately, brief and fleeting, but this time the illusion persisted, leaving Luo Bao wide-eyed. Maixiang greeted him, saying, "Don't you recognise me?" It dawned on Luo Bao that it was indeed Maixiang. Beneath the grey-green umbrella, Maixiang's face appeared gaunt and slender, as though it had been shaved down. She wore loose-fitting clothes and black high-top rain shoes that almost covered half of her legs. The shoes might not have been hers, but the clothes were familiar to Luo Bao— an ensemble of grey and blue coat. She had worn it on multiple occasions, looking fitting, respectable, and generous. However, it now seemed oddly out of place, as if she had borrowed it hastily and draped it casually around her. Luo Bao understood; she had become one size thinner. The ice lodged within Luo Bao's chest suddenly melted, and tears streamed down like rain. No anger, no confusion, no grievance—only heartache.

Maixiang remained composed, curling her mouth into

a smile, albeit a slightly melancholic one. She addressed the situation, saying, "Is this how you welcome me? Who has been bothering you?" Overwhelmed with tears, Luo Bao struggled to speak. Maixiang teased, "Alright, the sky is crying, and you're crying. It's so annoying! If you keep crying, I'll just leave!" Determined to cease his tears, Luo Bao accepted the handkerchief Maixiang offered. As he wiped away his tears, Maixiang sniffed and inquired about who would taste the tofu samples for him. Luo Bao explained that he hadn't found anyone suitable for the task. Maixiang probed, "Did you even look for someone?" Luo Bao admitted he hadn't. Maixiang sighed and asked, "If you didn't look, how can you be so sure there's no one suitable?" Luo Bao simply replied, "I just know." Maixiang declared, "Alright, I'm on duty. Bring your sample." Feeling embarrassed that he didn't have any ready, Luo Bao quickly mentioned that he had soaked beans and could prepare a sample now. Maixiang encouraged him, saying, "What are you waiting for?"

Luo Bao was engrossed in his work, and Maixiang offered her help. Despite Luo Bao insisting that she take a break and let him handle it alone, Maixiang insisted, mentioning that her bones felt crisp when she rested. Reluctantly, Luo Bao allowed her to assist him. He had no knowledge of what transpired during the past month and one day, how she endured being cut into bamboo throughout the day and night. Nonetheless, she survived and did not succumb to the fate of another woman in Songzhuang Village who took her own life. This was a stroke of fortune. Perhaps

Maixiang had found a new sense of purpose, or maybe she still haboured thoughts of Qiu Houzi. Qiu Houzi had pledged to stay away from Yingpan Town, let alone Songzhuang Village, for his own sake, ensuring that Maixiang would not encounter him again. Regardless of the circumstances, Luo Bao didn't care. Having nearly lost her once, he couldn't bear the thought of losing her again. The pursuit that lasted half a night and one morning had yielded positive results. While he didn't particularly like Song Tai, some of the things Song Tai mentioned that night were etched into Luo Bao's heart.

"Marry me!" Luo Bao declared abruptly. Maixiang casually sampled a piece of bean skin and commended him on improving his skills. In Luo Bao's mind, the realization struck: "I can't wait any longer. It has to be today. Now."

Maixiang, in the midst of counting sheets, paused upon hearing the proposal. While not displaying surprise, her expression took on a peculiar quality. She asked, "How old are you?"

"Twenty!" Luo Bao replied.

Her gaze focused on his upper lip. Maixiang took a moment to react and remarked, "You're not joking, are you? You're even more tender than your tofu! Look at you! To be precise, it's not called a beard yet; it's just fluff."

Initially, she treated him like a child, and Luo Bao felt an indescribable frustration and despair. However, he wasn't overwhelmed by her thoughtlessness; rather, it fuelled the anger that was already smouldering within him. He exclaimed, "I'm not a child. Don't treat me like a child!"

"Oh," Maixiang responded, "You've grown up, and you know how to scare people."

Luo Bao's heart felt as if it were dripping blood. "I'm not trying to scare you. What I said was real. I like you! I've liked you for a while!"

Maixiang smiled and asked, "What do you mean by 'like'? Huh?"

She no longer implied but smiled barefaced and unrestrained, as if Luo Bao weren't even qualified to say the word "like," as if the word was patented by her. Unable to tolerate it any longer, Luo Bao wanted to show her and make her understand that he was already a man. He lunged at Maixiang, attempting to hug her, but his movements were too forceful. Maixiang retreated and fell, and then he also fell.

For a while, it felt like Luo Bao was rolling around with Maixiang in his arms. It seemed like he touched something, but it was also possible he hadn't touched anything. She seemed to have shouted, but it was also possible that she had not shouted. They hugged tightly, or maybe they didn't hug at all. He kissed her, or maybe he didn't kiss her. He may have torn at her clothes, or perhaps not at all. They rolled around like a duck on a grill, constantly flipping and turning, unable to stop. Luo Bao had already fainted, his mouth dry, yet he couldn't stop. It wasn't until dusk, and a cold wind came through the open door, that the tumble switch was finally turned off.

Luo Bao sat up, feeling the heat on his face. He left the door open, allowing the chilly wind to cut through the wound. By not closing the door, they avoided kicking it and creating a loud noise in the dusk. If the door remained open, Maixiang's family, relatives, and possibly even Song Tai wouldn't rush in, tie him up, and drag him through the mud. That was how they treated Qiu Houzi, his back and shoulders worn, flesh exposed. It would be easier to drag him through the mud and water, and they wouldn't have to go too far. They would pass through two streets and three alleys to reach the courtyard of Maixiang's house. There, they would tie him to the tree where Qiu Houzi had been tied and then discuss ways to punish him.

Nevertheless, it was midnight, and the stillness prevailed. No footsteps shuffled, no cries or shouts pierced the air. Only the occasional ominous cries of an owl echoed briefly before being swallowed by the vast darkness. "They haven't reached a resolution," Luo Bao speculated. Rather than fleeing or seeking refuge elsewhere, he patiently waited in the shop. Maixiang had conveyed that he deserved this retribution.

Throughout the day, Luo Bao waited, but the anticipated event did not materialise. Could it be that nothing had transpired? Whenever this notion surfaced, he swiftly dismissed it. Although he refrained from turning over, sporadic bouts of dizziness and the lingering pain in his face served as constant reminders of the events that had occurred. Perhaps Maixiang was grappling with indecision. But what was the cause?

On the third, fourth, and fifth days, as Luo Bao soaked the washed soybeans in a bucket, a sudden itch tingled his nose. Even amidst the commotion of a bustling market, he could discern that fragrance, let alone in his tofu shop. Turning cautiously, he feared that any sudden movement might dissipate the delicate scent. There, leaning against the door frame, was Maixiang—much thinner, almost excessively so. "It's my fault," Luo Bao thought. She was seeking retribution, and he was prepared to let her do as she pleased.

"You're a fool!" Maixiang spoke slowly.

Luo Bao took off his gloves and threw them on the worktop.

"You can't be more stupid!" Maixiang said very slowly, evidently not having thought about what she wanted to say beforehand.

Luo Bao looked around and remembered that there was a rope that could be used to tie cattle and horses.

"How am I worth your love?" Maixiang raised her voice, as if suddenly angry.

Luo Bao immediately withdrew his gaze and faced her anger, coming up to her with difficulty and determination. "Everything about you is fine!"

Maixiang said, "I'm three years older than you."

Luo Bao said, "Two years old. It's better to be three years old. If you were three years older than me, I would have felt like holding onto a golden brick.[1]"

Maixiang said, "I eloped with someone."

"I don't care," said Luo Bao.

Maixiang asked, "Do you really like me?"

Luo Bao said, "The gods can testify!"

Maixiang said, "You've really grown up. Ask my parents for a proposal. If they don't object, I'll marry you."

Even though he had a suspicion, Luo Bao still found this rather unforeseen and abrupt. He was akin to a wrongdoer, tightly bound on the path to the execution grounds, when he suddenly got lured by a wedding sedan chair and swiftly hopped into it. "Do you … truly … consent to this?" Luo Bao felt it imperative to verify.

"You're nothing but a fool!" Maixiang appeared to have lost all strength, gradually descending onto the doorstep.

---

1   In Chinese culture, there's a saying that if a woman is three years older than her husband, it's like the man is holding onto a golden brick. This ancient metaphor implies that if the wife is slightly older, possessing more maturity and stability, she is better equipped to nurture and manage a family. Additionally, with her life experience, she becomes adept at taking care of others. In times of challenges, the wife can offer valuable advice to her husband. Furthermore, in moments of disagreement, the older wife tends to be more tolerant, fostering a harmonious atmosphere within the family.

6

In the following year, just as the grass was beginning to bud, Luo Bao married Maixiang, and she took up residence in his abode.

The union encountered some difficulties. Luo Bao's parents were opposed. Age wasn't a significant issue, primarily because Maixiang had a questionable reputation. Rumour had it that before eloping with Qiu Houzi, she had also been involved with Banshan, a vendor of seasonings. If she behaved this way as a daughter, how could she manage in matrimony? Luo Bao was a benevolent person, and he couldn't restrain Maixiang at all. Furthermore, Maixiang had an insatiable appetite; it wasn't that they feared she would consume too much herself, but rather that she might devour others. Numerous instances had proven that women with voracious appetites couldn't resist temptation, and cracked eggs were inevitably attractive to flies. Suddenly, Father became loquacious, as if he weren't a tofu seller but a specialist in discourse. In simple terms, he scrutinised Maixiang's shortcomings from a historical and global perspective. Mother merely uttered a few words, "Luo Bao, this isn't right" or "She's not deserving of you."

Luo Bao refrained from retorting, maintaining his consistent style. He would always be akin to a lamb. Even if kicked or swung at, he never retaliated. However, convincing him to change his mind proved challenging. Short of locking him up in a pigpen, there was no way to uproot the stake in his heart.

The situation with Maixiang's family wasn't progressing smoothly either. Maixiang's mother was agreeable. She comprehended Luo Bao's nature, assuring that Maixiang wouldn't face mistreatment if she married him. Luo Bao's family was reputable, and it suited the gluttonous Maixiang, who desired culinary indulgence. Maixiang's father objected. Having toiled in the blacksmith's shop for half his life, he earned the moniker Second Blacksmith. He preferred robust men over Luo Bao, who, as pale as a scholar, possessed a womanly demeanour and trembled at the sight of a sow.

Luo Bao garnered support from various quarters, including Song Tai, who claimed to be his matchmaker. Despite the challenges, obstacles were gradually dismantled. Engaged in April and married in May, the unhurried Luo Bao orchestrated a swift miracle in the annals of marriages in Songzhuang Village.

Following the nuptials, Luo Bao ceased urging Father to venture into villages and peddle tofu, redirecting him to procure beans instead. Luo Bao enlisted the services of Xishun, a person who stammered, to transport tofu, bean skin, bean cubes, dried tofu, and bean sprouts to greengrocers in various towns and snack bars in sizable villages. All it took was a phone call specifying the quantity and variety desired. Luo Bao even went the extra mile to purchase a tricycle for Xishun. Father was a tad irked, but he headed to work before he could voice his complaints. Soybean products boasted significant sales, necessitating a substantial amount of beans. Failure to procure the beans promptly could lead to shortages in the associated products. The quality of the beans was paramount; without top-notch beans, excellent tofu couldn't be produced. "I just can't trust handing this task to others." One evening, over dinner, Luo Bao spoke with Father, making an exception by sipping half a glass of baijiu. Father's eyes welled up, unable to fathom what occupied the taciturn Luo Bao's thoughts all day. He might have swift legs, but keeping pace with Luo Bao's thoughts proved elusive. For instance, if Luo Bao hadn't mentioned the bean collection initiative, how would he have known about this hidden idea or the depth of Luo Bao's trust? Once a member of a 10,000-yuan household, he had adorned himself with a large red flower only to be sent away by his son for thousands of miles. It was a surprise and also a source of sadness. If not for his attempt to maintain composure and preserve his paternal authority, tears might have welled up in his eyes.

Maixiang no longer made a daily visit to the tofu shop since Luo Bao had diversified the food offerings. Luo Bao had no plans to expand the menu, so there was no need for her to sample anything. The request for her to taste things had originally been an excuse. Now that she was his wife, he no longer had to concern himself with such matters. Unless, of course, she wanted to witness him at work. Yet, what was so fascinating about watching him work? Maixiang didn't have to toil in the fields or assist in the shop. Besides cooking, she also crafted sachets. It wouldn't be an exaggeration to say that Maixiang was the first full-time wife of Songzhuang Village. In times when there was no cooking or sachet-making to be done, Maixiang, along with a group of mostly older women, enjoyed playing games. The game involved sticks, dots, characters, and symbols similar to Mahjong, but they were playing cards. Winning or losing only amounted to eight or ten yuan, as it was purely for amusement. Luo Bao never inquired whether Maixiang had won or lost, but she would share, "Oh, I lost 3 yuan today." She seemed despondent, as if she had lost 300 or 3,000 yuan. Alternatively, she would excitedly boast, claiming she won eight yuan. "Today, luck was on my side, and I swept them all away." Luo Bao refrained from commenting, simply smiling, embracing her, and savouring her scent. Occasionally, Luo Bao would mention, "There's a whiff of cigarette smoke." Maixiang would reply, "So-and-so was watching us play, and their smoke practically choked everyone to death." Luo Bao remained indifferent. His fascination extended not only to her breath but also to her. At night, the aroma of her fragrance enveloped the air.

7

In Songzhuang Village, if there were a ranking for those who relished Luo Bao's tofu, Li Guixian would undoubtedly secure a place on the list.

Li Guixian, known by her stage name Red Peony, was taken from Datong, Shanxi Province, to learn Jin Opera at the tender age of six under her uncle's guidance. In Songzhuang Village, Jin Opera was locally referred to as Shanxi Bangzi. By the age of 18, she gained fame in Zhangjiakou, standing at the forefront among the four renowned huadan, a key female role in Jin Opera during that era. In Zhangjiakou, a popular saying went, "If you look at Red Peony, the hair of the old crane is still young." One of her most enchanting performances was as Dou E in *Snow in June*, evoking deep emotions that resonated throughout the theatre, accompanied by cries from the audience, while snowflakes danced outside. Despite being September, Zhangjiakou had never experienced such heavy snowfall, leading some to believe that Red Peony sang the tears of God. Jin Opera artist Ding Guoxian, known by his stage name Guozi Hong, specifically travelled to Zhangjiakou to dine with Red Peony. Red Peony, a talent destined to soar, unexpectedly returned to Songzhuang Village in the late 1970s and remained there for the rest of her life. Despite her fame, she remained unmarried and adopted a boy named Tudun. His countenance was fair, yet his eyes lacked lustre, and he drooled incessantly. Rumours circulated that Red Peony made a gender-related mistake during a performance, leading to her dismissal and return to the village. Some claimed she served a prison sentence for stabbing a man with a fruit knife. There were whispers that Tudun wasn't adopted but rather born to Red Peony and the mentioned man. Others believed Tudun had a destined connection to the earth, with a fortune teller predicting his safety in the countryside. Tragically, at the age of thirteen, Tudun met his demise from a horse kick, leaving Red Peony to live a solitary existence thereafter.

Red Peony had forfeited her graceful posture and the melodious, lark-like singing voice that once defined her. Afflicted by rheumatism, she adorned herself in a cotton coat even during the summer. Though her posture remained upright, her waist had noticeably expanded. The name Red Peony was no longer in use; instead, everyone referred to her as Tudun's mother. Tudun navigated the world in this manner. Her actual name, Li Guixian, was remembered only by Song Pin and the accountant.

Luo Bao had never actually heard Tudun's mother sing, yet for some inexplicable reason, he haboured an affection for the name Red Peony and silently addressed her as such in his heart. Tudun's mother consistently purchased only half a piece of tofu, and although Luo Bao charged her half the regular price, he always handed over a full piece. "I can't eat a whole piece," she would explain. "This is half a piece," Luo Bao blinked, and she remained silent. Never in debt, she unfailingly prepared her money in advance, wrapping a few cents in a handkerchief. She seemed to own many handkerchiefs, and even if the colours faded, they were consistently washed clean and carried the scent of soap. When receiving the box of tofu from Luo Bao, instead of standing upright, she would shake her wrist, as if her boneless wrist were still adorned with long sleeves. It was not a deliberate action; rather, it was a habit. This seemingly simple yet difficult-to-replicate gesture always stirred a pang in Luo Bao's heart. He refrained from speaking much or asking her questions. On one occasion, when she came to purchase tofu, the village loudspeakers played Shanxi Bangzi. Tudun's mother's eyes suddenly lit up, radiating like the bright sun, and she exclaimed, "This is *Three Bridges Up.*" Luo Bao was taken aback, not because she identified the play, but because of the brightness in her eyes. He thought her gaze had been clouded for a while, yet he hadn't expected it to shine so brightly. Seizing the moment, he inquired, "Did you sing before?" In that moment, Tudun's mother transformed into Red Peony and recounted a lengthy list of songs she had sung, such as *Dajinzhi, Wujiapo, Yutangchun, and Qinxianglian.* Then, just as swiftly, she reverted to being Tudun's mother—aged and solemn.

The initial clash between Luo Bao and Maixiang occurred, with Tudun's mother serving as the catalyst.

Luo Bao purchased a sizable colour television for Maixiang,

a luxury in Songzhuang Village during the early 1990s when only a handful of households owned such sets. It boasted a 29-inch screen, making Luo Bao the proud owner of the first one in the village. Qian Zhuang followed suit six months later. Every evening, Luo Bao's house teemed with people eager to witness the marvel of a colour television. Maixiang basked in the attention, and her demeanour gradually shifted. Amidst the envy-filled crowd, Tudun's mother remained unenthused. Her pivotal entrance that night was prompted by news of a theatrical competition, although she missed the opportunity to watch it. The remote control firmly rested in Maixiang's hands, who had a penchant for TV series. After a brief stay, Tudun's mother departed.

When the house was vacant, Maixiang discovered that the five yuan she had hidden under the bedcloth had vanished. That amount represented Maixiang's earnings from an afternoon's work. She immediately suspected Tudun's mother and was on the verge of heading to her house to confront her. Before this incident, nothing had gone missing, but Tudun's mother had visited today, and now the money was gone. Luo Bao intervened, suggesting there was no concrete evidence to blame Tudun's mother. Maixiang argued that Tudun's mother had sat in that corner, often placing money under the bedcloth without any previous losses. The money disappearing on the day Tudun's mother visited seemed too coincidental. Luo Bao proposed that Maixiang might have misremembered placing the money there. Angrily, Maixiang retorted, "Do you think I have a pig's brain?" Luo Bao emphasised that, regardless of who took the money, she shouldn't let five yuan disrupt the harmony with others. Maixiang insisted it was not just about the money; it was a matter of disrespect. She couldn't tolerate thieves; if Tudun's mother stole five yuan today, who's to say she wouldn't take ten yuan tomorrow? Luo Bao pointed out that Tudun's mother was an elderly woman, and it wasn't suitable for Maixiang to take matters into her own hands. Maixiang sneered, "She's old but doesn't understand respect, so she deserves what she gets." Despite still wanting to go, Luo Bao held her back, suggesting they address it tomorrow since it was almost midnight. Maixiang relented and didn't insist any further.

Maixiang remained upset and somewhat distant. In an attempt to lift her spirits, Luo Bao embraced her, employing all the techniques of grinding tofu on her. He gently rubbed and caressed Maixiang, aiming to bring a smile to her face. Eventually, Maixiang couldn't resist warming up to his efforts. She drifted into a peaceful sleep, and by morning, she playfully teased Luo Bao. He mused to himself that she had seemingly forgotten about her unhappiness from the previous night. After all, it was only five yuan—not a substantial amount.

At dusk, the moment Luo Bao stepped through the door, Maixiang proudly informed him that her guess was correct; Tudun's mother had indeed stolen the five yuan. Luo Bao felt a sudden discomfort, as if something had snapped inside him. "You went to see her?" he inquired, surprised. Unperturbed, Maixiang replied, "How could I know if I didn't ask her?" The pain radiated from the point of discomfort throughout Luo Bao's entire body, making it difficult for him to stand. He didn't lose his temper with Maixiang, but his voice turned icy. "You shouldn't have done this to her." Maixiang's eyebrows shot up. "I shouldn't have done this to her? Am I in the wrong?" Luo Bao uttered, "That's a shame." Internally, he lamented how beautiful she used to be. Maixiang retorted, "Her face is a face, but my face isn't a face anymore? Are you with her or with me?" Luo Bao responded, "You hurt me by saying that. I let you do whatever you want." Maixiang snorted, "If I was in your heart, you wouldn't have said such nonsense." Luo Bao couldn't help but feel a pang in his chest. He pleaded with her not to go because he cared about her. The word would spread, and her already tarnished reputation would suffer even more. Maixiang argued, "It was Tudun's mother who stole my money, and my reputation is bad? What kind of absurd logic is that? Yes, I have a bad reputation, and I've had it for a while. You already knew! Who was crying about marrying me? Luo Bao, it's only been two or three years, and your heart has been torn by wolves already?" As the argument escalated, Luo Bao attempted to diffuse the tension, asking for forgiveness. He acknowledged that he had said something he shouldn't have. However, Maixiang refused to let him off, accusing him of finally revealing his true colours. With Maixiang maintaining her combative stance, Luo Bao decided to retreat to the shop around midnight. He estimated that by then, those watching TV would have left, and Maixiang's anger should have subsided. Unexpectedly, Maixiang locked the door, and after a brief pause, Luo Bao quietly left.

Maixiang chose not to prolong the conflict with Luo Bao. The following day, she visited the tofu shop, expressing a sudden craving for tofu jelly. Naturally, Luo Bao prepared it for her. He didn't mind when she locked the door, doing his best to move past their disagreement. Luo Bao also paid a visit to Tudun's mother. She asserted that Maixiang had falsely accused her, clarifying that she hadn't taken the money but still gave Maixiang five yuan to appease her anger. "Five yuan, I can afford it," Tudun's mother stated with a subtle but not insignificant pride evident in her wrinkles. Luo Bao's eyes welled with tears as he expressed that he would feel sad if she didn't continue buying tofu. Tudun's mother smiled, replying, "Of course, I still want to buy it, as long as you're willing to sell it to me."

A few months later, another conflict erupted between Luo Bao and Maixiang. It wasn't as intense as a full-blown war, but the smoke that billowed was enough to suffocate anyone. This time, the source of the disagreement was Song Tai. Song Tai needed 2000 yuan and borrowed it from Luo Bao. Despite Luo Bao's dislike for Song Tai, he acknowledged that Song Tai had helped him and owed him a favour. Moreover, Song Tai was visibly distressed. Luo Bao, having just finished counting his profits, handed over two thousand to him. Song Tai expressed gratitude for his kindness and asked Luo Bao to take care of Maixiang. Luo Bao handed the money to Maixiang casually, even with a tone that carried a sense of achievement. Maixiang had been in charge of their finances since the day of their marriage. It was Luo Bao who had appointed her to this duty, making her feel like she had suddenly been plunged into boiling water. "My God," she exclaimed, waving her arms as if attempting to climb out but lacking a sense of direction. Dizzy from the heat, her mouth askew, she could only utter, "My God." Unaware that he had made a mistake, Luo Bao offered a hand, but Maixiang pushed him away, seemingly accustomed to the scalding sensation. "Maixiang!" Luo Bao shouted out boldly, fearing that she had taken ill. Maixiang stopped waving and stared at him, saying, "You're a pig!" Perplexed, Luo Bao didn't understand what he had done wrong. Maixiang accused him, "My God," and either calmed or became discouraged. Eventually, she said, "Okay, I'll tell you." Luo Bao learned that Song Tai had initially approached Maixiang for the loan, but she had refused. Maixiang accused Luo Bao of pretending to be a good person and a hero. Luo Bao pleaded ignorance, stating that he didn't want to trap her in an injustice. Maixiang sneered, "You know who he is, right? Just a liar!" Luo Bao pointed out that Song Tai was her cousin. Maixiang responded, "Even if it was my father, I would consider whether I should lend to him or whether he can repay me." This made Luo Bao resentful, but he didn't want to engage in conflict with Maixiang. He tried to smooth things over by assuring her that Song Tai would repay the loan. Maixiang questioned, "How can you be so sure he'll repay it?" Luo Bao lowered his head and mumbled, "But if he doesn't return it, I will admit I was wrong."

Maixiang demanded, "Luo Bao, what did you say?" Ignoring his reluctance to explain, she forced him to repeat what he had said. Maixiang finally heard him clearly but didn't understand. She asked him to explain. "Who doesn't meet with some difficulties at times?" said Luo Bao. Maixiang retorted, "It depends on whether it's worth it. There are too many people in need all over the world. Can you give generously to all of them? Who do you think you are?" As the argument progressed, Maixiang slowed down her tone and said, "We're just tofu grinders. We're not philanthropists. You don't have principles. That's your biggest problem." Luo Bao lowered his head, avoiding confrontation with her as her anger subsided. Maixiang believed Luo Bao had heard her opinion and seized the opportunity to assert herself. She said, "It is more important to be principled when having good intentions. If you help a bad person, you're just an accomplice." Though Luo Bao endured, the term "accomplice" was too harsh for him to ignore. "I have principles," he asserted. Maixiang hissed, her teeth tingling cold. "If you were alone, you can do whatever you want. Now that you're not alone, it's like two strands of rope can't be twisted together. How are you going to live your life? You don't want to live with me anymore?" Luo Bao retorted, "Don't talk nonsense!" Maixiang argued, "If we want to live our lives, we can't improve. We must live our lives well, and if we live our lives well, we must agree on our ideas." Luo Bao nodded in agreement. Maixiang continued, "It's not too much to ask that you make sure you discuss such matters with me first, is it?" Luo Bao honestly said,

"It's not too much."

From then on, Maixiang decided whom they would lend money to and to whom they wouldn't, marking a positive change in their situation.

"I'm not much like a husband, more akin to a seamster," Luo Bao contemplated on more than one occasion. Despite his careful efforts, issues inevitably arose, be it a tear here or wear there. He certainly wouldn't exacerbate the gap or enlarge the hole. He stitched and stitched, enduring pricks and bleeding fingers, refusing to stop until the clothes were fully mended. However skilled the technique, there remained a distinction between sewn clothes and new ones. A discerning touch could always detect the undulation of stitches and irregular patches. Even if one couldn't feel it physically, they still sensed it in their heart. No one would choose to live with closed eyes; doing so would only deepen one's sense of despondency. The initial damage might have been a small hole, easily ignored, known only to the owner. However, when stitched, what was once a minor flaw became a more prominent seam. Initially, a small hole could be overlooked, its existence known only to the owner. But when a significant hole appeared, it became visible to everyone.

When viewed from behind, what Luo Bao and Maixiang left on the ground resembled not footprints but holes and pits.

In December of that year, Luo Bao, as was his routine, carved out a piece of meat and prepared ten blocks of tofu for Mao Gen and Mao Xiaogen. On that day, as Luo Bao was about to depart, he learned that Xishun had veered into a ditch. The path was obstructed by heavy snow, making travel exceedingly challenging. Attending to Xishun's situation, Luo Bao entrusted Maixiang with delivering the food. Upon his return, the tofu was nowhere to be found, but the meat remained untouched. Maixiang informed him that she had sent the stewed meat a few days earlier. Despite Luo Bao instructing her to discard it, she hadn't complied. Shocked, Luo Bao exclaimed, "What if you accidentally poison someone to death?" Maixiang brushed off the concern, stating, "It was just a little burnt. How could it be deadly?" She assured him that nothing untoward would happen. Luo Bao, dismayed, muttered to himself, "How could you do this?" Maixiang's expression finally hardened as she retorted, "What's wrong with me? Do I have a heart as malevolent as snakes and scorpions?" Attempting to diffuse the tension, Luo Bao said, "It's nothing. I just feel we shouldn't give away anything we wouldn't eat." Maixiang countered, "We only give away things we don't like. Who gives away things they enjoy?" Luo Bao found fault with her logic, stating, "We should give away things we like. If something doesn't seem right, why give it to others?" Maixiang argued that the purpose of giving was to bring oneself joy, not to please others. However, her anger flared up again. "Why do you always try to please others?" she demanded. Luo Bao clarified that he wasn't attempting to please anyone. Maixiang pressed him, asking why he consistently sided with others.

The fire did not subside; instead, it burned more vigourously, and Luo Bao felt uneasy, retreating to hide himself away. He regretted initiating the conflict, not intending to quarrel with Maixiang. How had it come to this?

A sturdy dam couldn't withstand the gradual erosion, even if it was just ants gnawing away. There might not have been a significant change on the surface, but numerous internal holes had formed. Some could be patched, while others resisted all efforts. When it came to dealing with others, Luo Bao could endure and conceal. However, later, their arguments erupted without a clear trigger, like an unlit fuse suddenly igniting. This was mostly due to Luo Bao's own issues. Maixiang suddenly couldn't bear the smell of raw beans on Luo Bao's body. During their intimate moments, she looked down upon him, stating, "The heavy bean odour makes my head choke." Luo Bao hastily cleaned himself, but the scent had permeated his flesh and bones, becoming an integral part of his body. Despite repeated washings and soap applications, it lingered stubbornly. Summer posed no issue, but in the cold winter, bathing was a challenge. Shivering, Luo Bao rubbed himself while bathing, unable to shake off Song Tai's words, leaving him further disheartened. Did Maixiang change, or did he fail to see her clearly? He pondered. Everyone had flaws, he reasoned, and as her husband, he should tolerate them. Harmony required mutual concessions. Maixiang, who also enjoyed making sachets, devised a solution to mask the bean odour. She crafted a thick sachet resembling a cotton vest, placed it on Luo Bao, and added two more to the waist of his pants. The peculiar aroma initially fascinated Luo Bao. He was captivated by the fragrance and, in turn, by Maixiang. While he still appreciated the scent, the sachets had become a source of torment. Many types of cages existed—iron chains, stone walls, and others. Despite his business thriving, Luo Bao found himself personally imprisoned.

During that time, Luo Bao remained unaware that a woman named An Min would soon rewrite his life.

Chapter VII

Zunai

1

I have lived through famine, hunger, war, and plague. Naturally, I've also endured the profound trauma of losing family members. Yet, I've managed to survive without being torn apart by wild dogs or attacked by crows. However, it's akin to a deep wound; even if it heals, it inevitably leaves scars. Each segment and every locale carries a story, reminiscent of the branches of an ancient tree. They wake up in the morning fog, rest in the evening mist, day after day, year after year.

During my apprenticeship year, the weather exhibited extreme abnormalities. Following the seed sowing, only one instance of rain occurred. The parched ground cracked, and the scorched wheat seedlings disintegrated upon touch. Birds accustomed to soaring through the sky suddenly plummeted, and hungry squirrels, resorting to feeding on the remains of their companions, burrowed into the grassland. As the long summer day drew to a close, a sudden rain shower ushered in overcast and rainy conditions that persisted for more than ten days. Though it was too late to scatter buckwheat, any rain was preferable to none.

On a night when the rain showed no signs of letting up, Dawang and I retired early. Li Chun, too, slipped into bed as darkness fell. However, simply lying down didn't make falling asleep any easier. Dawang mentioned that Father had tasked him with buying autumn cabbage seeds in town the next day and inquired if there was anything I needed him to get. I figured my father-in-law had already devised a plan for remediation and was merely awaiting the cessation of the rain. I replied, "No," and Dawang remained silent. Dawang and I were not accustomed to whispering to each other, let alone uttering frivolous or nonsensical words. He would touch me, at times with his arms or feet, and I understood the unspoken message. It was akin to our approach to farming—focused, diligent, and devoid of distractions. When he rose from bed, he unfailingly ensured my quilt was neatly tucked in. Our conversations were rare and centreed on practical matters. Occasionally, upon hearing a rumour, he would briefly mention it. It was never a complete narrative, but I could deduce the truth from the fragments. If I found it intriguing, I would inquire with Li Erni. She had a penchant for gossip and seemed to be privy to everything.

In the almost hypnotic ticking of the eaves' water, I suddenly heard an abrupt sound. The noise, produced by big feet trampling through the mud, approached from a distance to near. It was heading towards my yard. I nudged Dawang, urging him to light a lamp while I fumbled for my clothes in the darkness. Dawang illuminated the lamp and saw me dressed neatly. Startled, he stammered. I explained, "Someone might be giving birth, didn't you hear it?" Dawang shook his head, displaying concern. This had occurred twice before. In the dead of night, I heard a knock on the door and implored Dawang to light the lamp, only to find no expectant family awaiting me. It was I who had succumbed to hysteria. Yes, I yearned to deliver a baby, and it was driving me mad. No one had requested my assistance in delivering their baby. Four or five months had elapsed, and I had been waiting anxiously. I was losing my sanity, tormenting Dawang in the process.

But this time, I genuinely heard it, and there was no issue with my ears. Dawang was on the verge of extinguishing the lamp, but I halted him. "Listen carefully, are you deaf?" I hadn't been this exasperated with him before. After two or three minutes, Dawang's face reflected astonishment. There was no need to inquire about his thoughts, as he too had heard the noise.

The individual approaching turned out to be Liu Zhuanyun, who sought my assistance in delivering his daughter-in-law.

Without hesitation, I swiftly seized the package that had been opened numerous times but never put to use. Liu Zhuanyun suggested I wear a plastic rain poncho, but I insisted, "There's no need." However, after a moment's consideration, realizing I couldn't appear completely drenched in front of the pregnant woman, I took the poncho from his hand. Liu Zhuanyun's house was situated in the northwest corner of Songzhuang Village, a bit further away. I inquired about when his daughter-in-law started experiencing pain, and he informed me that it had just begun. He and his wife slept in the East Room, while his daughter-in-law rested in the West Room. Disturbance emanated from the daughter-in-law's room, prompting Liu Zhuanyun and his wife to rise. "There was no time to ask Master Huang, so I have to trouble you to help us deliver the child," Liu Zhuanyun admitted, straightforward about the situation. If not for the incessant rain and the slippery road, he wouldn't have sought my assistance.

Liu Zhuanyun, originally known as Liu Ergou, was a migrant who had escaped from Datong, Shanxi Province. He specialised in raising cattle and horses in the Qian Family, treating them as dearly as his own son. One day, the Qian Family was on the verge of selling an old, critically ill cow. Liu Zhuanyun approached Qian Guangwan, insisting that the cow should not be sold, as he would regret it. Normally, Liu Ergou would lower his head in Qian Guangwan's presence, but this time, he didn't avert his gaze. When questioned by Qian Guangwan, Liu Ergou mentioned there was bezoar in its tripe, emphasizing his eight years of experience raising the cow. Skeptical, Qian Guangwan inquired about how Liu Ergou knew, and he confidently asserted, "I have been feeding this cow for eight years, and I know." Despite some doubt, Qian Guangwan ordered the cow to be slaughtered. To everyone's surprise, there indeed was bezoar in the tripe, weighing six kgs and seven taels, and it was valued more than several cows. Delighted, Qian Guangwan rewarded Liu Ergou, who subsequently built a house and moved away from the rat kiln he previously resided in. Qian Guangwan also changed Liu Ergou's name to Liu Zhuanyun, symbolizing a positive change in luck.

True to the name change, Liu Zhuanyun's luck took a turn for the better. His son, Liu Wang, worked for a few days at Song Aizi's Wanlongyong Fur Shop and unexpectedly gained favour from the Silk Shop owner. Liu Wang became a delivery person for Yuchengtai, the reputed largest Silk & Satin Shop in Zhangjiakou. Consequently, Liu Zhuanyun earned a notable reputation in Songzhuang Village.

As I entered the room, Liu Zhuanyun's wife clutched my sleeve tightly. Sweating profusely and trembling like chaff, she seemed greatly disturbed, likely unsettled by the howls of Liu Wang's wife. The latter, facing the wall, gripped her hands as if attempting to carve a hole into it, as though hoping the pain of childbirth could escape through such an act. Amidst her cries, she pressed her mouth against the wall, displaying a yearning to bite off a piece. In her anguish, she kicked the quilt, mattress, and pillow into disarray.

I reassured her, saying, "Don't be afraid. If I cast a spell, you won't feel any more pain." Liu Wang's wife certainly heard me. Although she didn't look at me, her body shuddered. Unwrapping my bundle, I suddenly froze as I had forgotten to bring my yellow joss paper, prepared a few months ago. My head stopped for just a few seconds, and I woke up, asking Liu Zhuanyun's wife to scoop up half a bowl of water. Holding it in my mouth, I sprayed three mouthfuls at Liu Wang's wife and then recited a mantra—or rather, my mouth was just moving. I didn't know what I should recite; Master Huang hadn't taught me and left me to figure it out for myself. I really couldn't figure it out. Pretending, Liu Wang's wife's pain unexpectedly subsided, and she turned her wet face toward me. At that moment, I suddenly grasped the profound meaning of Master Huang. Confidently, I asked, "Is the pain not so severe now?" Liu Wang's wife's voice was weak, and she said, "It's a little better." Liu Zhuanyun's wife's jaw almost dropped in surprise. She looked at me as if she thought I was a fairy. Not indulging in complacency, I asked her to boil water immediately. Then, I grabbed Liu Wang's wife's hand and instructed her to follow my lead. She nodded weakly.

The pain surged once more, and Liu Wang's wife could no longer contain herself. However, she refrained from howling and clutching the wall as before. The "spell" had not failed; it was still effective. After a while, she let out a sigh and inquired if she was in danger. I sternly composed my face and replied, "Bodhisattva Guanyin is watching over us. Don't speak nonsense." Liu Wang's wife instantly regretted her words, wishing she could retract that sentence. I reassured her, explaining that Bodhisattva Guanyin wouldn't hold it against her. While some, like the journalist Chen Xiaolei, might find my words absurd, I had to emphasise that, at that moment, they served a crucial purpose. Trust between a pregnant woman and a midwife was essential for a successful delivery. As I comforted Liu Wang's wife, I mentioned Liu Wang, highlighting potential opportunities for him to work in Zhangjiakou or at a renowned silk and satin factory. I stressed the promising prospects he might have in the future, urging her to uplift his spirits. Liu Wang's wife's eyes lit up. Truth be told, since this was my first time delivering a baby solo, I was quite nervous. Sharing these thoughts not only provided her encouragement but also helped to calm my own nerves. Another valuable lesson I gleaned from Liu Wang's wife's experience was that casual conversation could serve as a means of comfort and act as a soothing balm to alleviate pain.

Liu Wang's wife was usually talkative, but when I mentioned it, she couldn't seem to stop talking. I interrupted her, explaining that excessive talking could also deplete energy. Assessing her pain and examining her lower body, I estimated that she would give birth sometime between midnight and dawn. Therefore, I advised her to rest and conserve energy for the upcoming labour.

As I had anticipated, at midnight, the amniotic fluid ruptured, and an hour later, the baby's head emerged. Initially, I considered enlisting Liu Zhuanyun's wife to assist in holding Liu Wang's wife, but I feared that her anxiety might transfer to Liu Wang's wife. I found Liu Zhuanyun's wife's reaction perplexing; she appeared as if she was witnessing childbirth for the first time. Consequently, I asked her to wait outside for further instructions. As long as Liu Wang's wife cooperated, I could manage the delivery on my own. She exhibited good behaviour, although the pain caused her to bite off the chopsticks in her mouth. She grasped every word I whispered in her ear without requiring repetition. With no one holding her and nothing to grip on the bare bed, she didn't thrash around. It was not the pillows supporting the sides of her body; rather, it was her sheer determination. The pillows were merely auxiliary, underscoring the decisive role of our communication. "You're Liu Wang's wife, so try to make a good showing!" I occasionally offered these words, providing a momentary relaxation. Just like withered flowers absorbing rain and dew, she quickly regained her composure.

Come on! At this point, I felt no panic; I was calm and confident. A loud cry resonated, and Liu Wang's wife opened her eyes, gazing at me intently. Understanding her unspoken question, I informed her that it was a boy. Encouraging her once more, I said, "You're making a valuable contribution to the Liu Family." Liu Wang's wife grinned with an extremely faint smile.

After drinking a cup of brown sugar water, Liu Wang's wife resumed experiencing pain. "Is there any problem?" inquired Liu Zhuanyun's wife. I smiled and reassured her that the delivery was progressing smoothly. The child had already been born, so what other issues could arise? The pain persisted, and Liu Wang's wife panted as if her intestines were about to rupture. I comforted her, saying, "It's okay. I'll help you change your posture." Some pregnant women also endure pain when the placenta descends. As I spread apart her legs, I was nearly taken aback. There were indeed twins on the way. The birth of the second child went incredibly smoothly, and Liu Wang's wife later mentioned that the child emerged effortlessly, requiring no exertion on her part.

I didn't depart from the Liu Family until the chimney smoke

wafted in the drizzle. Carrying with me a mix of joy, pride, and, undoubtedly, vanity, I strolled at a leisurely pace. Despite having regained my strength with the Liu Family's rice porridge and steamed buns, my steps were slow, not due to the slippery road but by deliberate choice. Eventually, I encountered someone carrying water. As we exchanged greetings, I casually mentioned that Liu Wang's wife had given birth to twins. He inquired, "Did you assist in delivering the babies?" My surprise was evident despite the rain and fog, and I responded with a deep hum. On another street, to my surprise, I came across Hua Erniang. She was already bustling about early in the morning. Hua Erniang was a talkative individual who enjoyed spreading news to a wider audience.

The triumph in the initial battle served as an auspicious sign. Consequently, I found myself gradually being summoned to assist in delivering more babies, extending from Songzhuang Village to neighbouring villages. Surprisingly, it wasn't overly troublesome; the act of delivering itself served as the most effective form of publicity. Additionally, both expectant mothers and their families were known for their loquaciousness, proving more impactful than any self-praise from midwives. Each word spoken had legs that carried it in all directions. For instance, Liu Wang propagated my name all the way to Zhangjiakou. While it was unlikely for a pregnant woman to journey from Zhangjiakou to Songzhuang Village specifically for my services, the mere mention of such a skilled practitioner could lead them to consider me over others.

The apprentice's daughter-in-law of Song Aizi (dwarf) in Chongli was expecting, and he requested my assistance. Naturally, he had learned about me through Song Aizi. His wife, dealing with a congenital disability in both legs resembling the thickness of shovel handles, haboured fears of potential mishaps. She had already made inquiries, and Song Aizi, abiding by the counsel of his father, Song Guaizi (cripple), recommended me. I didn't disappoint the apprentice, even though it proved to be a more challenging case. Of course, this happened a few years later.

When my daughter Li Tao was born, I opted to deliver her on my own. Dawang suggested calling Master Huang, but I declined, considering it too late for him to arrive anyway. I kept the news from Dawang until my amniotic fluid ruptured because I had already made the decision to handle the delivery myself. It wasn't just a test for me; I wanted to experience the entire process. During Li Chun's birth, I only felt the pain and neglected to "communicate" with my child. While babies can't speak, they can sense emotions, and there exists a connection between positive and negative emotions and how they perceive them. When assisting in the delivery for Zhao Xiaopu, I attempted to communicate with the fetus and was astonished to discover that the baby could sense the language of my hands. This revelation greatly surprised me. Not every fetus was willing to engage in communication, but I attached immense importance to this connection. It wouldn't be an exaggeration to say that, in certain aspects, I had surpassed Master Huang. Given the opportunity to have children of my own, I certainly wouldn't miss the chance to communicate with them.

From the leakage of the amniotic fluid to cradling Li Tao in my arms, the entire process took less than two hours. Li Tao emitted a cry and then drifted into a peaceful slumber, seemingly making up for lost sleep in my womb. Dawang, under my directives, sought guidance on the next steps. I instructed him to inform my father of the news initially and then return to prepare porridge for me.

2

Song Pin walked away for a while, but Song Hui remained in a daze. She feared that the news from Mao Gen had startled her. Although this straightforward woman couldn't clearly articulate her relationship with Mao Gen, or her secret desires and worries, it was evident that she cared about him.

Suddenly, a stool fell with a thud. Song Hui rushed out and closed the door, the impact of the bolt nearly shaking my eardrum. Without hesitation, Song Hui entered and grabbed my hand, her strength causing me pain. I couldn't bring myself to say I couldn't move, but the discomfort was palpable. "You silly child, always in such a hurry," I sighed inwardly.

"Zunai, please help him!" Song Hui wailed, shaking Zunai's hand.

Ants were scurrying away.

"Zunai, please!" She shook her hand again.

Ants were fleeing. Ants were fleeing.

"My dear Zunai, please help him, only you can help him!" Song Hui pleaded and wailed.

This was my dilemma—an ordinary person, half-dead, yet worshipped as a god. I could sense the sorrow of everyone seated before me, but I couldn't offer a comforting word. All I could do was silently transform into a receptacle, absorbing their grievances, sadness, anger, and inexplicable mental burdens. Yes, I wasn't a saint, nor a fairy; I was merely a receptacle. I had repeated it a thousand times, but who could hear me?

"You're a foolish woman," I silently reproached Song Hui. Maixiang would be returning soon.

"Did she catch my subtle hint?" Song Hui abruptly applied the brakes. I could almost envision her expression, mouth half-agape, facial muscles frozen. Eventually, she slowly released my hand. "What's happening to me?" she mumbled to herself.

"Zunai, did I hurt you?" Fear tainted her voice. "I didn't mean to. Please forgive me."

Ants scattered in panic.

"Zunai, you have the right to punish me. My cursed paw … Alas, just please ensure Mao Gen is safe. What would Mao Xiaogen do if anything happened to him?

"Oh, you're such a naive child!" I sighed once more.

3

Even at that time, I held deep respect for Master Huang. May she rest in peace in the heavens. Without her, my future might not have unfolded as it did. However, concurrently, I haboured a profound sense of guilt towards her.

I pledged to God that I had no intention of competing with her, even though it took only two or three years for me to attain a level of fame comparable to hers. In some aspects, I even believed I had surpassed her. I wasn't boasting; I only showcased my abilities after assisting Liu Wang's wife during childbirth. Overwhelmed by excitement, I found that the word-of-mouth spread had its own magic. For instance, my skills were deemed superior, and the pain of pregnant women seemed to subside as soon as I entered the threshold. The oversight in my first delivery sparked inspiration. Without uttering a mantra, a mouthful of clear water served as a psychological cue. Some claimed I could speak the language of the fetus, and that babies could understand my commands. While I didn't command them, my judgment of the time of birth was remarkably accurate. Numerous mysterious legends circulated about me, suggesting that in my previous life, I was a child of Bodhisattva Guanyin, and my willow leaf hands bore mysterious annotations and stories. Such legends proliferated endlessly, and all I could do was let them spread.

Initially, I didn't fully comprehend the significance for Master Huang of a constant stream of people seeking my assistance in delivering babies. One day, two families of pregnant women arrived simultaneously, leading to a dispute. I suggested that the person who arrived later ask Master Huang to deliver his wife's baby, but he refused. He insisted that his wife, being as tall as a wheat stack with a stomach resembling an inverted cauldron, required my assistance. I emphasised that I was Master Huang's apprentice and that her delivery skills far surpassed mine, but the man remained adamant, fixated on having me perform the delivery. I then approached the first man who had initially sought Master Huang's assistance, but he too refused. Furthermore, he had made a prior appointment and had already come a few days earlier. After a brief assessment of the situation, I decided to visit the latter man's house first and then proceed to the first man's house. The first man objected to this plan and grabbed my arm. I reasoned with him, explaining that the two villages were not far apart, and it wouldn't be too late to visit half a day later. He eventually relented and released his grip. Upon my arrival at the latter man's house, the baby was already showing its feet, explaining the man's urgency. After the delivery, I rushed to the other village, where the man waited outside the courtyard. The pregnant woman's amniotic fluid had not ruptured, and the baby was not delivered until late at night. Before departing, the man grabbed my arm again and, in addition to the payment, also gifted me a hen.

Early the next morning, I visited the cave-dwelling to see Master Huang. I had promised her that I would give half of the money to her, and I kept my word after the first delivery. However, Master Huang refused to accept it and seemed a bit angered. Despite my repeated pleas, she rudely drove me away, exclaiming, "You're insulting me!" Her eyes, as sharp as a knife, seemed to cut all over my body. From that point forward, every time I visited her, my hands were empty.

This time was a bit different. After assisting the woman who was "as tall as a wheat rick" in delivering her baby, her husband informed me that they had initially arranged the delivery with Master Huang. However, his relatives reminded him that I was more agile, so he changed his mind. "This wasn't so good," I thought. "I not only took away Master Huang's job but also embarrassed her." I consoled myself by thinking that this time, I was like filling in for Master Huang. Of course, all the payment money had to be handed over to her.

Master Huang's countenance remained impassive as I nervously recounted the delivery process, ensuring no additions or omissions. Afterward, I carefully presented the payment money on a small table, feeling Master Huang's gaze flicker across my face. Suddenly, she threw the money across the room, and I realised it was a bad sign. She seemed prepared, like a loaded bullet awaiting discharge. "Are you mocking me for being old?" Her voice, though not loud, carried a chilling, icy tone. Panic set in, and my words stumbled, "Master Huang, that's not what I meant." Anger simmered in Master Huang, but it didn't erupt like a machine gun. She paused and spoke in an indescribably gentle tone, "Damei, your delivery skills are excellent, but there is one thing you've forgotten. We are guides for babies entering the world. You lead, I lead. As long as things proceed smoothly, it's the same. Good deeds come first, and payments come second. Although I may feel disheartened at times, I don't envy you. You surpass me; it's natural! How can I defy the laws of heaven?" Master Huang's words left me feeling ashamed.

Master Huang spoke earnestly, imparting a piece of golden and precious advice that I would carry with me throughout my life. Nevertheless, it couldn't be denied that midwifery was Master Huang's sole means of livelihood, and with her son, addicted to gambling, adding to her struggles, life became even more challenging when no one sought her services.

By that time, I had already begun delivering babies for the Mongolian people. Despite the presence of many midwives, most were too old to travel long distances. The Mongols sought my assistance not only because of my growing reputation but also because of my ability to ride a horse. Initially, I had to share a horse with others, but as I learned to ride, I ventured alone. When the Mongols approached, they rode a horse and also brought one for me. In the 10th year of the Republic of China, after the government permitted the Chahar District to convert pasture lands into farmland, a considerable stretch of grassland transformed, prompting a substantial migration of herdsmen to the north. Despite the changes, many herdsmen still sought my help in delivering babies, and I never turned them away. It was challenging; even with horseback travel, it took an entire day to reach some locations. In adverse weather conditions like wind, rain, or snow, the journey could extend beyond a day. I navigated many nighttime paths, where hardships and fatigue were secondary; the main concern was the danger. For instance, I had to contend with wolves on the grassland and steer clear of bandits who preyed on people travelling the roads. Sometimes, to ensure my presence, they would send three or four people to manage transportation. Having interacted with herdsmen extensively, I learned Mongolian and, of course, their customs. The Mongolians didn't offer money, but they would bring a variety of gifts, such as cheese, milk sticks, beef jerky, lamb jerky, and baijiu. During those years of famine, these offerings helped me overcome one difficulty after another. Naturally, there were also lasting regrets. I shouldn't have sent Li Chun to the pasture. However, I haboured no blame for anyone. If blame were to be assigned, Li Chun should shoulder it himself. There was a path, but he chose the cliff.

Upon returning from the pastoral area, I would bring some milk curd and milk skins for Master Huang to taste, something rare for her. I made it clear that these items couldn't be bought. After several occasions, Master Huang subtly conveyed that she had grown tired of these treats. Understanding her sentiments, I returned empty-handed.

The world was descending into increasing chaos. Today, Tom and Dick fought, tomorrow, Harry and someone else fought, and the day after tomorrow, everyone fought each other. Those engaged in business or serving as soldiers kept bringing back information from the outside to Songzhuang Village, whether true or false, leaving people bewildered. However, in any chaotic world, women still had to bear children. Perhaps, it was precisely because of the chaos that women felt compelled to contribute to their families. Poor families needed children, and so did wealthy families. To midwives like us, there was no distinction between the rich and the poor, noble and humble. As Master Huang once said, "Even if they are enemies, we should deliver children for them."

On a cold, moonlit night, another group of bandits targeted the Qian Family and infiltrated Songzhuang Village. However, the Qian Family was already on high alert, reportedly equipped with newly purchased guns. Following a fierce confrontation, the bandits retreated, leaving only one servant of the Qian Family injured. That night, while delivering a baby in another village, I returned to Songzhuang Village much later. Before entering the yard, I was summoned by the Qian Family's housekeeper.

The Qian Family did not suffer financial or property losses, but Qian Guangwan's pregnant third wife experienced severe abdominal pain due to intense fear. As the old saying goes, perfection is unattainable, and there are always unforeseen challenges. Although Qian Guangwan possessed immense wealth, the family's size didn't match his expectations. Two wives had given birth to two sons and two daughters for the Qian Family. One son was named Qian Bairi, and the other was named Qian Baiyue. Unfortunately, Qian Bairi remained mute. This third wife was carefully chosen by Qian Guangwan, possessing ample breasts, buttocks, and wide hips. Qian Guangwan had even pre-selected names for his future sons, including Qian Baixing, Qian Baichen, Qian Baijiang, Qian Baihai, and more. Half a month ago, I had examined Qian Guangwan's third wife, and there were still at least forty to fifty days until delivery. Experiencing abdominal pain at this stage was not a favourable sign.

Qian Guangwan was unexpectedly waiting outside his third wife's room. Observing his expression, it was clear that his heart was in turmoil. "Do your utmost to save the child," he urged, his anxiety mingled with dignity, "I will reward you generously!" By now, the initial nervousness of meeting him for the first time had dissipated, and I responded politely, "Even if you don't give me a penny, I'll do my best to save the child." Qian Guangwan seemed to have more to say, but I interrupted him, stating, "This is not the time for conversation. I need to go in now."

Once I entered the room, the third wife ceased her moaning. She lay beneath the quilt, her hair dishevelled, her face pallid, and the mole on the lower corner of her mouth growing more pronounced. As I prepared to lift the quilt, she reached out and grabbed my hand, pleading, "Please! Even if I ..." Her words were cut off as I swiftly reacted, halting before she could continue. "Don't think like that. I'm here; everything will be okay," I reassured her. I couldn't discern whether she doubted my words or if she haboured some ominous premonition. She muttered, "If ..." In response, I raised my voice, "Listen to me, don't let your mind wander!" The third wife was so shocked and rendered speechless by my firmness that she simply clung to me tightly.

Soothing the emotions of the third wife proved to be no easy task. As I lifted the quilt, it became apparent that the child, named Qian Baixing, was on the verge of being born prematurely. Upon informing the third wife, panic seized her once more, as if a knife were at her throat. Her slightly red face turned pale, and she exclaimed, "No, the pregnancy time is not sufficient." I reassured her that some children are impatient and cannot be stopped from being born. Adding, "The fetus is in the correct position, so the birth will likely be smooth," I tried to alleviate her fears. Yet, she continued to plead with me to save her. Among the women I had delivered babies for, each had a unique personality, but none displayed the level of fright exhibited by the third wife, bordering on despair. Despite her fear, I maintained a calm demeanour. "Do you not believe in Bodhisattva Guanyin?" I inquired. She replied, "Yes, of course I do." I assured her, "Bodhisattva Guanyin is blessing the child, so you can rest assured." The third wife's eyes, curved like crescents, were exceptionally beautiful but resembled withered branches—grey and hardened. Under my guidance and comfort, finally, green buds of hope emerged.

Qian Guangwan, with his myriad experiences, appeared flustered yet composed. He suggested that, given the imminent birth, we should follow the standard delivery procedure. He gestured towards several women standing outside the house, instructing, "If there is any need, just give them orders." Turning to them, I said, "Boil two basins of water." The process of delivering a child remained uncomplicated, even for the wealthy.

At noon, Qian Baixing was born safely. Despite being premature, he weighed 2.3kg.

Qian Guangwan gave me a small ingot of silver, and the third wife wished to present me with her silver hairpin, but I politely declined. I had earned enough gratification and was not overly greedy. Regardless of Qian Guangwan's wealth, I adhered to my own principles. I may not be a saint, but I abided by my self-imposed rules. Thanks to Master Huang, her "Five Commandments" had gradually shaped my virtue and reputation. It wasn't just the skill of delivering babies that had spread.

During that time, I limited myself to delivering babies in rural areas and on the grasslands. Following the birth of Qian Baixing, I started receiving invitations from families in Zhangbei City. Life resembled the weather outside the Great Wall, constantly changing, with a clear sky before noon and rolling dark clouds in the afternoon. Just as I reached my peak—perhaps it was inappropriate and somewhat presumptuous to say so—I encountered the first hurdle after my apprenticeship.

4

Ants were scurrying away.

5

Zhao Jinyuan entered the door, his face green, and the lump on his forehead dark purple, an extremely peculiar sight. His mouth and nostrils were wide open as he breathed heavily, resembling a mule horse that had run a long distance. Without waiting for him to speak, I quickly picked up my baggage and prepared to leave. Although he attempted to speak, the effort seemed so strenuous that his neck appeared almost choked. Zhao Jinyuan caught up with me and yanked my arm fiercely, uttering only, "Save her." I retorted, "Release my hand. How can I save your wife if you don't let me go?"

Zhao Jinyuan had arrived riding a donkey, incessantly whipping its buttocks in the hope that the animal would swiftly carry him to Songzhuang Village. However, he ended up being knocked into a ditch by the donkey. Unfazed, Zhao Jinyuan didn't attempt to catch up with the donkey but instead trotted toward Songzhuang Village. Half walking and half running, he followed me, and eventually, his tongue proved useful, even if he could only speak intermittently.

Let's start from Li Erni.

Li Erni's marriage once concerned my father-in-law. Blessed

with a beautiful appearance, she could have been even more stunning if she didn't squint. Li Erni always looked down upon others, and given her pretty looks, she found it challenging to develop feelings for anyone. She believed that the men she encountered either had short legs or hailed from poor families. Refusing to let my father-in-law make the decision for her, she insisted on choosing a husband for herself. Hua Erniang tirelessly arranged countless blind dates for Erni, but she didn't develop feelings for any of them. If it weren't for my father-in-law's discreet promise of benefits for Hua Erniang, she wouldn't have accepted the responsibility. Eventually, Li Erni fell in love with a descendant of Zhao Xiaopu. The prospective groom was a decent-looking camel traveller, but not all camel travellers shared Song Aizi's good fortune. Within six months of getting engaged to Li Erni, the camel traveller was fatally stabbed while attempting to intervene in a fight. Although Li Erni hadn't officially married him, her perceived value dropped significantly. She seemed indifferent, at least on the surface, but my father-in-law fell seriously ill. The marriage seemed doomed, and both Hua Erniang and I tried to comfort him with this reality. During my father-in-law's illness, Zhao Jinyuan's newly wedded wife succumbed to diarrhea. After a series of unexpected events, Li Erni ended up marrying Zhao Jinyuan, the same person who had been engaged to me. Li Erni was content with this marriage. Despite Zhao Jinyuan having a previous wife, who was still partially deaf, his family was well-off, and he had assets to showcase. Every time Li Erni returned, she carried a bag of steamed stuffed buns, reminiscent of that wet morning when I did the same. Erni would sigh at me and express her worries, saying, "My destiny is tied to eating steamed buns. Even though I don't want to eat them every day, I can't help it," or "I eat meat every day. I'm tired of it."

After Li Erni became pregnant, my father-in-law sent me to visit her. I understood his intentions, but Erni refused to let me examine her baby. She mentioned that a doctor had already checked her pulse, emphasizing that it was a certified physician. Since my father-in-law sent me for this task, I felt the need to relay the situation to him. "Erni wouldn't let me check her baby," I reported, avoiding direct confrontation with her. My father-in-law, being a sensible person, understood when I mentioned the certified doctor that Erni had declined. He criticised Erni for not being reasonable and advised me not to argue with her. While I didn't appreciate Erni's attitude, I haboured no envy towards her. There was something accumulating in Erni's heart, some of which I could sense, while some remained perplexing. Instead of unraveling over time, it solidified, akin to white pebbles on a riverbed.

I made several more trips until the delivery was imminent, and the Zhao Family decided to appoint a midwife, neither me nor Master Huang. The Zhao Family's intentions remained unclear, but I chose not to dwell on it. When my father-in-law mentioned this, I understood that it had nothing to do with me. I felt a bit adrift, with a few strands of hair light enough to be overlooked. Perhaps I could still be of assistance, maybe she still needed me. There was a hunch deep within me. I would prefer if she didn't need me and the birth went smoothly. However, what if she required help? I didn't even step outside the yard that day, simply waiting. Unexpectedly, the moment I was anticipating truly arrived.

Autumn was fading away, with grey and yellow hues dominating the scenery. The only exception was Zhao Jinyuan, appearing out of breath, his face displaying an untimely green tint. While my words offered comfort to him, my heart sank. From Zhao Jinyuan's sporadic words, I had already inferred that something was amiss.

As Zhao Jinyuan and I entered the door, darkness had already descended. The faces of the Zhao family seemed blurred, resembling wriggling pieces of dough. The dough appeared eager to let me pass, yet in different directions, it sought to separate and collide with other pieces. Disregarding politeness, I maneuvered through the dough and went straight into Li Erni's room. A strong smell overwhelmed me, an indistinguishable mixture of fishy, spicy, sour, and despair. The lights flickered, as if fearing the volatile atmosphere might extinguish them at any moment. Li Erni lay in the middle of the bed, with the midwife kneeling between her legs, sweating profusely from her strenuous efforts, yet appearing helpless. Before I could fully stand still, she recoiled, as if anticipating this moment. "She isn't cooperating with me. I have never seen such a delicate woman before," complained the midwife. I remained silent, unaware of when she left. Li Erni was so feeble that her eyes struggled to open. However, she made a concerted effort to keep them open, and the thin gap seemed more like when her eyes were closed. She uttered two words, which I could hear clearly or infer from the movement of her mouth. "Relax!" I exclaimed, but my heart had descended into an ice cave. The amniotic fluid had broken last night, signifying almost a day and a night had passed, and the baby's chances of survival were nearly nonexistent. Despite holding onto a sliver of hope and silently praying, Erni wasn't favoured by luck.

...

I addressed the gathering of onlookers, emphasizing that surgery was imperative. Without timely removal of the deceased fetus, Erni's life would be at risk. This was not a discussion with these bystanders but rather an informational statement. Li Erni was my sister-in-law, and I couldn't stand by and watch her perish. Seeking assistance, I scanned the room, and one person stepped forward to accompany me back to Erni's room. I instructed her to hold Erni down to prevent any resistance. Then, I retrieved the blade that Master Huang had given me from my bundle. It had never been used before, and I hadn't anticipated that its first application would be with Erni.

Li Erni's gaze resembled withered petals, tired and drooping, with only her eyelashes fluttering in a struggle. She seemed to have something to say, but lacked the strength to open her mouth. Nonetheless, she could hear for sure.

I reassured her, saying, "Erni, you can't sleep. You're going to be a mother; you have to cooperate with me."

I continued, "It's going to be okay. You can rest assured."

And finally, "I touched the baby; it's a stocky fellow."

I confess, I was deceiving her. I couldn't allow her emotions to fluctuate, and I especially couldn't let her drift into sleep. While speaking, I gripped her leg and, with a razor blade in hand, reached into her lower body. Indeed, I touched the baby— a tender infant. However, even though he remained within Erni, he had already departed from her and was distant. "Sorry, kid," I whispered. My fingers moved swiftly, and my ears were filled with the grinding sound, akin to a sharp knife cutting through rock. Blood oozed from Li Erni's body, belonging to both the baby and Li Erni. Her leg twitched briefly, perhaps in response to the sensation. I raised my voice, "Ernie, it's almost out. Bear with it." I extracted a mass of tissue, promptly discarding it into the basin without a second glance. Taking a deep breath, I reached in once more. There was no room for pause or hesitation.

After completing the cleaning of the uterus, I suddenly collapsed, sitting there unable to lift my hands or move my legs, letting the sweat flow freely. Li Erni, almost unconscious and cold, inquired, "Boy or girl?" Her voice wasn't loud, but it marked her first words. Still not fully conscious, I subconsciously responded, "Boy." Li Erni abruptly sat up, pushing aside the attendant, "Give him to me," she demanded. A thunderous roar resonated in my head, "Erni, there was nothing I could do. Don't blame me."

Erni's eyes widened, and she shouted, "Where is he? Give him to me!" The trembling attendant reacted, tightly hugging Erni. Zhao Jinyuan poked his head in, and I instructed him to take the basin outside. "You can't see him now, Erni," I insisted. However, Li Erni had already caught a glimpse. A mouthful of blood sprayed onto my face, and Li Erni fainted. I pinched and shouted, and Erni finally regained consciousness. Her hair was dishevelled as she yelled, "Qiao Damei! Qiao Damei!! Qiao Damei!!!" Without a barrage of insults, she repeatedly shouted my name, which was more unsettling than being scolded. If she had a knife, Li Erni wouldn't hesitate to stab me. I had personally dismembered her child, her first child. She had every right to scold me.

Late at night, Li Erni seemed to be fine, and just as Dawang came to pick me up, I left. It seemed she might be better off without seeing me.

Three days later, I went to see Li Erni. She was huddled in the corner of the bed, her face pale. I called her name, but she didn't move, her eyes fixed on me like nails. After a while, she cursed, the words cutting like a dagger. "Murderer!"

I shuddered, struggling to contain my emotions. I tried to explain, "It was not my fault. If I didn't clean up the deceased baby in your uterus promptly, your life would be in danger." However, Erni couldn't listen, and it felt as if she were repeatedly stabbing me with a dagger. I didn't dare to stay for long, so I quickly left.

Half a month later, I visited for the third time. During

this period, I successfully delivered two babies, both without complications. Unfortunately, Erni experienced a rare stillbirth. Her eyes weren't as filled with nails as last time, but her demeanour was icy. "What are you doing here again? Haven't you hurt me enough yet?" She launched the first strike.

Understanding her resentment, I knew explanations might be futile, but I couldn't remain silent. "You can scold me, but heaven is above me. I swear, I didn't have any evil intentions. At that time, there was no time to discuss it with you, but I made it clear to the Zhao Family."

Li Erni retorted, "What do they know?"

Feeling a pang, I said, "Erni, you are Dawang's younger sister and my sister-in-law. Despite our disagreements before, I wouldn't harm you either."

Li Erni's eyes lifted upwards, her gaze piercing as if she had seen through me. She asked, "I married Zhao Jinyuan, dare you say you're not jealous?"

I was momentarily taken aback. "Why would I be jealous?" I responded.

Li Erni insisted, "Of course, you don't want to admit it."

I retorted, "Okay, if that's what you think. Even if it were true, I wouldn't harm your baby. I have delivered so many babies—"

Li Erni cut me off, tears welling up. "You delivered so many babies without an issue, but when it came to my baby ..."

How could I make it clear that nature plays a role in these

situations? When she stopped sobbing, I said, "You have a prejudice against me. If I were there at the beginning, maybe it wouldn't have …"

Li Erni interrupted, "I fear that you might even harm me."

I asserted, "I have a clear conscience; think whatever you want."

Li Erni accused, "What are you doing here without shame? To take credit for your achievements?"

I took out the piece of silver I had in my possession, a gift from Qian Guangwan. It was meant as a goodwill gesture.

I was not a murderer, but an uneasy feeling lingered within me. Li Erni gave me a cold glance and turned her head away. That was good. I was afraid she would throw the silver at me.

I never anticipated that this silver ingot would lead to disaster. Li Erni and Zhao Jinyuan sought to use it as a pretext to sue me, claiming that if I had no guilt, why would I attempt to reconcile with a silver ingot? To exacerbate matters, the woman who had assisted Li Erni during childbirth asserted that despite the difficult delivery, her baby still had signs of life when she left. A potential lawsuit loomed on the horizon. Fortunately, my father-in-law stepped in to mediate. In the evening, Dawang picked me up, and I explained the situation to my father-in-law. He was a sensible person and wouldn't allow Li Erni to falsely accuse me. Perhaps, Li Erni merely wanted to frighten me and vent her anger, with no intention of escalating the issue. After my father-in-law persuaded her, she relented. Another contributing factor was the return of

Li Gui, who had been absent for many years, bringing great joy that managed to dispel the gloom. However, Erni's resentment remained, temporarily buried. Several years later, another storm brewed.

6

Someone rapped on the door, a sound I immediately recognised as Maixiang's. Others wouldn't dare create such a commotion. Song Hui, lost in her sorrow and concern, seemed oblivious to the noise. Maybe she heard it but chose to seize this rare moment. Perhaps she understood that after today, she could no longer be alone with me, sensing or anticipating that Song Pin would no longer cover up for her. She ignored it, as there was nothing more important than her prayer. Kneeling beside me, her breath ebbed and flowed like waves. Though her voice was gentle, I detected impatience in her tone. Not for her own sake, but for Mao Gen.

"Zunai, he might not have come to pay his respects to you, but he held deep respect for you in his heart. Please don't hold it against him," she implored. Then, she presented a litany of reasons explaining why Mao Gen hadn't come to worship me.

A naive woman, convinced that I was penalizing Mao Gen. She attributed Mao Gen's perceived punishment to this so-called "retribution."

"Zunai, please pardon him for his transgressions. I assure you, he will present himself before your bed to pay his respects. Despite his slightly warped disposition, he is not a bad person.

You brought him into this world, and you know him, don't you?"

Alas, the more she spoke, the more outrageous it became. I was not Bodhisattva Guanyin. I've delivered more than 10,000 babies. How could I understand everyone? How could I predict their future? Everyone was born as pink meatballs; the difference lay in the smoothness of the birth, in the loudness and hoarseness of the crying, in the differences in weight, and in the presence or absence of birthmarks. None of this portended anything. Although they later walked on different paths, some became police officers, some became thieves, some were wealthy, some were impoverished, some lived as smoothly as a boat in still water, and some lived lives that were as bumpy as climbing over mountains. I guided them out of the womb, and they did not bear any distinctive signs. There might be a password, but I couldn't explain it clearly. Of course, one thing that was evident was that the beginning of the road was actually the end of the road.

Good men and faithful women – let me call them that for now. They treated me like a fairy. They didn't know that the clarity in my heart was not because my hands were like lotus flowers, making life bloom, but it was because I had witnessed death after death, or rather, I guarded life and witnessed death. I thought I had seen it through, but I hadn't. The return of Qiao Shitou made me realise that I was just a witness to life and death, akin to a mirror.

Ants were scurrying away.

Song Hui's prayers upset me.

$$7$$

People were no different from kites, some soaring high only to be pulled back, while others' strings snapped and were lost. Every year, some folks left Songzhuang Village to engage in trade, join the army, or seek their livelihood through other means. Living away from home was no easy feat, and only a few, like Song Aizi, transformed from being a camel puller to a shopkeeper. Most found themselves bouncing back to Songzhuang Village after several years, only to live out their days until old age took its toll. Some departed without a word, as if existing in another realm, such as Ji Family's third son, Ji Laosan. It was rumoured that he served as a soldier in Zhangjiakou and met his end in a mutiny. The upheaval was real, with hundreds of individuals plundering shops and homes in broad daylight. Song Aizi's shop nearly went up in flames, but no one could confirm if Ji Laosan was counted among the casualties. The Ji Family remained sceptical. Without seeing their son's remains, they refused to entertain grim thoughts. However, even as Ji Laosan's mother passed away, and his two brothers met their end, there was no word about Ji Laosan—he had vanished without a trace.

Li Gui's situation was somewhat peculiar. After more than

ten years of silence, he suddenly reappeared.

My father-in-law often spoke of Li Gui, especially when my father was alive. It was one of their recurring topics. Li Gui was restless and inclined to cause trouble in his youth. My father-in-law couldn't fathom why, despite his advice to stay in the village and farm, Li Gui ended up in his current predicament. With dozens of sheep under his care, even if we sold Li Gui, we couldn't afford those sheep! My father-in-law was angry and anxious. My father consoled him, suggesting that perhaps Li Gui could find a solution. My father-in-law remarked that when a scholar encountered a soldier, there was no need for explanation. "As a shepherd, what could he do?" My father said, "Maybe he encountered a kind officer." My father-in-law gazed into the distance as if envisioning Li Gui standing there. "I suppose so, as long as he doesn't provoke others," my father-in-law stated. Originally discussing another matter, the conversation between the two turned towards Li Gui. Li Gui seemed like water in a dam, and my father-in-law was the one digging the dam. Each time, he dug a big hole, and my father filled it. The dialogue between the two was not easy. When my father blocked all the holes my father-in-law had dug, and my father-in-law could no longer dig, silence fell. After my father's demise, my father-in-law ceased mentioning Li Gui. One day, when Li Chun was two years old, my father held him, and he peed on my father. My father suddenly brought up Li Gui, likening Li Chun's mischievousness to his second grandfather. I was tending to the bellows and didn't respond to my father-in-law because I didn't know how to answer him. "Don't you wonder where your second grandpa vanished?" my father-in-law inquired. I sensed it was for my benefit. My father-in-law was finally going to dig; perhaps he couldn't hold back any longer. Still hesitant, I didn't know what to say. My father-in-law directly asked me, "Damei, do you think he is still alive?" I couldn't feign ignorance and silence, so I mentioned that he was a good person, and God would protect him. My father-in-law sighed, "God sometimes dozes off. I dreamt of him a few days ago, riding a white horse. He didn't respond when I called out to him." I pretended surprise, "Really? That's a good omen." My father-in-law's face betrayed worry, stating that dreams were ominous. I smiled but couldn't assure him. Dreams could be positive or negative, and we could only hope for the best. My father-in-law felt a bit embarrassed, hoping Li Gui was fine, but worry lingered. I remarked, "Indeed, my second uncle might miss you too." My father-in-law shook his head, "No way, he would have returned by now if he did." I suggested, "Wait, perhaps one day he'll come back, riding a big and tall horse." My father-in-law's face relaxed a lot. "Damei, you are sensible. I can chat away with you." I expected my father-in-law to bring up Li Gui frequently, as he did with my father, but he didn't. It was only occasional, not digging or filling the holes he had dug himself. "When your second uncle returns, he should get married. Or, maybe your second uncle is brave and was born to venture out into the world." My father-in-law could hope for the best, but his eyes grew darker and thicker. I realised he haboured ominous suspicions or premonitions but was unwilling to disclose them. He contemplated positive scenarios to mask his inner pain.

My father-in-law later mentioned that he almost didn't recognise Li Gui. If it weren't for Li Gui addressing him as elder brother, he might have assumed it was someone from the government inquiring about me and silently scolding Erni for being foolish. My father-in-law had likely envisioned Li Gui's return many times, imagining a pale and emaciated face, tattered clothes, and a beggar's bag on his back. Perhaps leaning on a stick, limping, or speaking in a strange manner. The grand horse, however, was only present in dreams. The actual scene differed significantly from my father's imagination. My father-in-law trembled for a moment, and the firewood in his arms tumbled to his feet. Though my father-in-law recognised Li Gui, he still inquired about his identity. Li Gui hadn't become a beggar, but he didn't seem to have struck it rich either, judging by his attire. His once-round face now bore edges and corners, with cheeks that were shriveled and sunken. He might not have been able to eat well every day, but he appeared surprisingly well, showing no signs of misfortune. My father-in-law didn't dwell on it much; the important thing was that Li Gui had returned alive.

A few years ago, I huddled in a corner of the shack, eavesdropping on my father's conversation with a stranger. I was still a tinker with dreams of entering the palace. Today, I am a midwife with three children. Li Gui seemed like a connecting thread, drawing my father and me back to Songzhuang Village. Was it fate? I didn't know. Li Gui was equally astonished to discover that the wife of his nephew was the daughter of the tinker. He bantered with his father-in-law, "I wasn't at home, but I'm still a hero." And jokingly with Dawang, "How will you thank your second uncle for marrying such a capable wife?" The reserved Dawang scratched his neck, just laughing. During the meal, my father-in-law inquired about Li Gui's experiences over the past few years, but Li Gui found it challenging to encapsulate it in a single word.

That night, my father-in-law and Li Gui chatted until almost dawn. Li Gui persistently inquired about the family, the village, the town, and even Zhangjiakou City in Zhangbei. My father-in-law patiently shared details about his own family, explaining the intricacies of his wife's and Sanbao's burials. However, when it came to matters beyond our family, my father-in-law kept it brief. He was keen to learn about Li Gui's experiences over the years, but every time he paused, Li Gui posed new questions. Eventually, my father-in-law couldn't contain himself and said, "What's this got to do with you? Tell me about yourself." Li Gui claimed he had nothing to share because he couldn't find his sheep, so he didn't dare to return and instead wandered aimlessly. My father-in-law expressed his dissatisfaction with not receiving any messages, but Li Gui smiled ruefully and explained, "I'd like to send messages back, but who would send them for me?" My father-in-law then inquired about Li Gui's experiences over the years. Li Gui mentioned facing both difficulties and advantages outside. Disagreeing, my father-in-law asked, "If it's tough outside, why aren't you coming back home?" Li Gui retorted, "I go outside to see the world. Staying in the village is like a toad at the bottom of a well; you can only see a small piece of the sky." My father-in-law found Li Gui's dismissive behaviour distasteful. He sneered, "It seems you've developed skills. Your brother hasn't even been to Zhang Beicheng; he's the toad at the bottom of the well." Li Gui sensed my father-in-law's displeasure and quickly corrected himself, "I mean, I'm the toad at the bottom of the well." My father-in-law snorted, unimpressed, and remarked, "Of course, I don't want to argue with you. Tell me what you've seen in the world." Li Gui was unwilling to share, saying, "I can't explain it in a few words." My father-in-law insisted, "I'm not interested in the outside world. Regardless of how well Song Aizi's business is doing, it's not our concern. I just miss you." He then asked Li Gui about his means of support. Li Gui evaded the crucial details and focused on trivial matters, claiming he had done a bit of everything. My father-in-law scoffed, "You've done everything, yet you can't stick with anything for long, can you? You're almost forty, and you're still like this!" Li Gui responded, "It started that way, but things changed later on." My father-in-law pressed, "What did you do later on then?" Li Gui yawned, "I'm sleepy. Can I sleep first? I'll tell you later." Irritated, my father-in-law pushed him, saying, "I haven't heard from you for so many years. I was worried sick, walking into walls. I've been asking you questions, but I can't get a truthful word." Li Gui claimed he was genuinely tired. Seeing through his tactics, my father-in-law remarked, "When it comes to the important points, you just laugh, just like in the past." Li Gui argued, "Some things have changed, and some haven't. If I become a different person, would you still recognise me?" My father-in-law affirmed, "Let me ask you, have you gotten married yet?" Li Gui grinned and teased, "You've wanted to ask that since I got here, haven't you?" My father-in-law retorted, "Don't interrupt me. Have you gotten married?" Li Gui remained silent for a moment, then honestly admitted, "Not yet." My father-in-law snorted, saying, "I knew you weren't married. Dawang has three children now. You, Dawang's uncle, are still single. Talking about seeing the world?" Li Gui chuckled and said, "Hey, hey! Dawang is a fortunate person. How can I compare with him?" My father-in-law, furious, stated, "Don't joke with me. Be serious." Li Gui asked, "What is serious? Getting married and having children?" My father-in-law retorted, "What? Isn't that serious?" Li Gui grinned, "Don't be angry, brother. It's true. I just don't care. However, I do have a crush." This made my father-in-law even more unhappy, and Li Gui's words nearly pushed him over the edge. He demanded, "Can you be serious? Why can't you say something serious?" Li Gui quickly responded, "I'm kidding with you. With my situation, who would take an interest in me?" My father-in-law sighed, "Not a serious word from you." Li Gui complained, "The roosters have crowed. Can't you let me sleep for a while? You aren't kicking me out, are you?" My father-in-law remained silent.

What began as a casual chat later transformed into an interrogation of Li Gui by my father-in-law. The subsequent nights unfolded in a similar fashion. My father-in-law was eager to extract some "serious" information from Li Gui, but Li Gui skilfully avoided divulging anything substantial, making a mockery of the situation. My father-in-law gained nothing concrete from him, except the certainty that Li Gui was still single.

On the fifth day after Li Gui's return, my father-in-law went to visit Hua Erniang. At that time, Li Erni had already settled down, and my father-in-law's thoughts were wholly consumed by Li Gui. The other party, seven or eight years younger than Li Gui, had two children. My father-in-law, always busy and determined to see Li Gui settled, arranged a blind date for him the next day. Li Gui became anxious upon learning this and complained that my father-in-law hadn't consulted him. My father-in-law retorted, "It's just a blind date; what is there to discuss with you? I can handle this. If only you had listened earlier, maybe you would be a grandpa by now." Li Gui responded, "I don't have time for a blind date. If you want to go, you can go in my place." My father-in-law's expression darkened as he threatened to tie Li Gui up to ensure he went on the blind date. He even theatrically produced a ball of rope from under the kang mat[1] and put on a show for Li Gui. Li Gui accused my father-in-law of being unreasonable, to which my father-in-law retorted, "I'd be tying up my younger brother – what are you talking about?" Li Gui chose not to argue further. He compromised, stating that he would go on the blind date, but he had to be genuinely attracted to the woman. This irked my father-in-law, who retorted, "What gives you the capital to be so picky?" Li Gui asserted that he was a man of principle, not a mule or horse to be paired casually. My father-in-law, conceding, remarked, "Perhaps the woman might not like you either."

My father-in-law accompanied Li Gui on the outing. Hua Erniang led the way, Li Gui walked in the middle, and my father-in-law followed behind. Initially, he had intended for Dawang to follow as well, but he worried it might embarrass Li Gui. This decision haunted my father-in-law for a long time. Li Gui was in high spirits, engaging in conversation with Hua Erniang about family matters. Upon encountering Zhang Jiaying, Li Gui claimed he needed to urinate. My father, ever watchful, accompanied Li Gui away from the sidewalk to the ditch. My father-in-law also felt the urge to relieve himself, and while his action was genuine, Li Gui's was a ruse. With a quick feint, Li Gui sprang out of the ditch and made a swift escape. Since that day, my father-in-law

---

1   Kang mat: In rural areas of northern China, it is common to sleep on a hot kang, made of adobe or bricks, with the surface typically consisting of sand and soil. To clean it, a layer of mat "kang mat" is laid on the surface.

never saw Li Gui again.

"If only he had settled down with a family earlier, he wouldn't be wandering aimlessly." Half a year after Li Gui's departure, my father-in-law frequently spoke about him. It seemed that Li Gui was inherently restless; the more he ran, the less inclined he was to return home. At dusk, my father-in-law would sit on the stone at the door, continuously smoking his long-stemmed pipe, as if waiting for Li Gui's return. The night grew darker, and the fireworks continued to flicker. My father-in-law's old smoking habits intensified. Dawang and I advised him to smoke less, but he paid no heed. Only Li Chun could persuade him. Li Chun seized his long-stemmed pipe, and my father-in-law relinquished it. He always yielded to his grandson, allowing him to play around as he pleased.

"Damei, what do you reckon Li Gui does for a living?" My father-in-law queried me six times on various occasions. Either he forgot he'd already asked, or my responses didn't satisfy him. I couldn't provide a clear answer. Since Li Gui remained tight-lipped about his livelihood, I was left in the dark when it came to making educated guesses. Naturally, my father-in-law only confided in me; he avoided discussing it with Dawang or Erni, knowing he couldn't rely on them. He also refrained from sharing his concerns with others. One night, my father-in-law recalled Li Gui mumbling in his sleep, sparking worries that he might have turned to banditry and robbery. On another occasion, he suspected Li Gui of committing some crime, speculating that someone might be pursuing him, explaining his tendency to run. My father-in-law discussed this with me, a mix of seeking my opinion and contemplating aloud. Until his passing, my father-in-law never unraveled the mystery of Li Gui's secret.

There was one thing I dared not disclose to my father-in-law. One evening after dinner, Li Gui and I had a conversation at home. He commended me for being sensible and capable. When discussing my father-in-law, Li Gui mentioned that his brother had endured hardships throughout his life and urged me to take better care of him. At that moment, I had a premonition that Li Gui would eventually depart. It felt like a farewell request from him. Of course, even if I had shared this with my father-in-law, it wouldn't have stopped Li Gui. Nonetheless, a sense of guilt lingered within me, especially when my father-in-law and I discussed Li Gui's secret. I couldn't shake the feeling that I had colluded with Li Gui in deceiving him, leaving my heart filled with emptiness.

8

"Are you deaf? My throat is about to burst!" Maixiang angrily demanded.

Song Hui nervously explained that she hadn't slept well the previous night and had taken a nap.

Maixiang's anger escalated. "What's wrong with your eyes? Did you doze off, making your eyes turn red?"

Feeling uneasy, Song Hui's voice wavered. "I just rubbed them."

Maixiang was not easily fooled, and Song Hui wasn't adept at lying. Her expression had long betrayed her. Maixiang, now composed in her interrogation, stated, "Come on, what were you doing?"

Song Hui insisted, "I was really sleepy."

Maixiang leaned down, scrutinizing Zunai from head to toe. "You didn't touch Zunai?"

Song Hui asserted, "No."

Maixiang pressed further, "You didn't get close to her?"

Again, Song Hui denied it.

Maixiang sneered, "Then how did the mark on Zunai's hand appear? Did the cat do it?"

Regardless of how strong Song Hui's hand was, it wouldn't leave marks on mine. I secretly signalled to Song Hui, "Don't be deceived." However, Song Hui couldn't sustain the deceit and confessed to briefly touching Zunai's hand … a few times.

"Just a moment?"

"Three … four times."

Ants were scattering.

Maixiang's voice suddenly escalated, yelling, "Why is your memory so poor? Who gave you permission to touch Zunai? Did you even touch Zunai's hand? What did I instruct you? Have wolves taken away your memories?"

Song Hui remained silent, seemingly knocked unconscious by Maixiang's relentless barrage.

Maixiang had crossed a line. Even if Song Hui had made a mistake, the severe scolding was unwarranted. I knew Maixiang was upset with Luo Bao, and every time she returned, her mood was sour. Song Hui had unwittingly become the target of her frustration.

Maixiang demanded, "Why aren't you saying anything? Are you mute?"

After a prolonged silence, Song Hui finally found her voice. "Zunai wouldn't blame me."

Maixiang retorted, "Zunai is under my care. Whether you can touch Zunai is my decision!"

Song Hui responded, "I didn't initiate it, but I don't know what happened afterward. My hands were out of control. If you can't get over it, just chop off my hands."

Maixiang sneered, "Do you think I wouldn't? Try touching her hand again!"

Song Hui replied, "I don't want to try; my hands are still useful."

Maixiang suddenly smiled and remarked, "You're a silly fool; you're driving me crazy."

Song Hui advised her to avoid getting overwhelmed by anger.

Maixiang claimed she was already furious. Then, Maixiang sniffed and asked, "What is that smell?"

"Yes, can you detect that aroma?" Song Hui was greatly alarmed.

"Of course, I can perceive such an unusual scent." Maixiang was an expert in crafting spices and was highly sensitive to odours. Anger had clogged her nostrils, but now her nose was in operation. "You didn't do anything else, did you?"

Song Hui confessed everything. At one point, she had hoped Song Pin would cover for her, but now she abandoned her wishful thinking and resistance.

Maixiang stamped her feet in anger. "You made Zunai endure this scent, you foolish elder sister! Good heavens, you've caused a great deal of trouble!"

Song Hui retorted, "I timely opened the door and window, and Zunai didn't choke. If you doubt it, ask Secretary Song."

"Huh?" Maixiang's voice wavered, "Did Song Pin find out? What's going on?"

Song Hui disclosed the truth.

"You fool, you've betrayed me!" Maixiang cried out.

Song Hui stammered, "I … didn't … do it on purpose."

Maixiang yelled, "Are you still dwelling on this? Get out!"

9

One afternoon in September, the sky was overcast, giving the impression that rain might be imminent. There had been no sunlight for two days, yet not a single drop of rain had fallen. It was merely a false alarm. A large saloon car arrived at the entrance of the village, paused for two minutes, and then proceeded into the village. Children, along with seven or eight adults, chased after the car, with the swiftest among them even reaching the front of the vehicle. The four-wheeled behemoth acted like a colossal magnet, drawing them in and captivating their attention. Perhaps they had heard about it, but not many had actually seen it. They speculated that the vehicle was heading to Qian's house, and there were rumours that Qian Guangwan was unwell. Some also suggested that the vehicle might be going to the residence of Song Guaizi. Song Guizi had already mentioned that his son would have him stay in Zhangjiakou for a while. He chose not to go because Zhangjiakou was too chaotic, and he feared getting lost. Moreover, his legs and feet were not in good condition, unless his son came to pick him up. No one seemed to consider Liu Zhuanyun. His son, Liu Wang, was just a messenger, and he had never been involved in such a grand spectacle before.

To the surprise of onlookers, the monster halted at the entrance of Li Dawang's courtyard instead of proceeding to the Qian Family or the Song Family. Subsequently, two individuals, one tall and one short, pushed open the courtyard door. After a moment, I, Qiao Damei, followed them, carrying my baby delivery bag. The tall man opened the car door, and I accidentally bumped my head while entering the vehicle. The tall man raised his arm to shield me and said, "Be careful." Some people were still in pursuit, including my son Li Chun, until the monster drove out of the village, disappearing, leaving only lingering footsteps in the dust.

"Where are we heading?" I asked cautiously.

The tall man kept his gaze fixed ahead and replied, "You'll find out when we get there. Don't inquire too much!"

While they were outwardly polite, using the word "please," their actions were somewhat unreasonable. They instructed me to pack up within five minutes and follow them, allowing no room for casual questions. It felt akin to being escorted to prison, minus the torture gear, yet I wasn't afraid. They selected me to deliver the baby, and I was merely curious about the pregnant woman whose representatives had such distinct mannerisms.

Upon entering Zhangbei City, the hefty gentleman informed me about the county mayor's wife being in labour. He turned towards me, his expression grave, and his tone low. "Do you comprehend?" he pressed. I replied, "I understand." He not only stressed the county mayor's wife's identity but also emphasised the need for utmost diligence. "Utilise all your capabilities; the county mayor will surely reward you. If there is any mistake, there's no turning back!" He believed that a stern warning would ensure my best efforts. I refrained from expressing its futility; after all, cattle and horses couldn't feed from the same trough. I simply affirmed, "I've got it."

It was a spacious courtyard with five main rooms and three western rooms. The tall man shouted twice, and a woman in a large grey coat with a double-breasted front emerged, guiding me into one of the rooms. The pregnant woman was reclining against the quilt, munching on melon seeds. Upon spotting me, she didn't cease and merely cast her loose, lazy gaze my way for a moment, as if by chance. "Are you the midwife?" she inquired. Despite having a youthful face, if not for her swollen figure, one might believe she was fourteen or fifteen years old. I responded, "I'm from Songzhuang Village, and my name is Qiao Damei." The county mayor's wife remarked, "The name is correct. I thought … You're not much older than me." I smiled and said, "You're so young; I'm already the mother of three children." The county mayor's wife then asked, "Did you deliver for Qian Guangwan's wife?" I nodded. The county mayor's wife said, "Yes, that's you. Sit down." Surprisingly, it seemed more like an invitation for a casual chat than a preparation for childbirth. I suggested, "Lie down and let me examine you." The county mayor's wife responded, "Don't worry, it's windy. You should warm up first."I assured her, "It isn't cold; I came here by car." The county mayor's wife then asked the woman who had guided me into the house, "Is there any water in the basin?" The woman made a sound of acknowledgment and promptly brought a basin filled with water to me.

While I rubbed and washed, the county mayor's wife continuously observed my hands. After finishing, I stood up, wiped them clean, and she gestured for me to come closer. She seized my hand, inspecting it for a moment. It was indeed a skilful, dexterous hand! She seemed partly curious and partly interested in ensuring cleanliness. As she reclined, she cast a glance at the attendant woman, who silently exited the room.

The county mayor's wife experienced pain last night, but it was short-lived. After the examination, I informed her that there were still ten or eight days left until delivery. Surprised, she said, "How's that possible? The pain was severe last night." "I wouldn't make mistakes in judgment," I assured her. "Are you sure?" inquired the county mayor's wife. I replied, "I live in this business, and my reputation is not built on deception. Even with a ton of courage, I wouldn't dare deceive you." The magistrate's wife fixed her gaze on my face for a moment and said, "So, you can stay here." I responded, "No." The county mayor's wife's expression darkened, "Why? Are you afraid I won't take care of your meals?" I smiled, my words neither humble nor arrogant, "Li Xia, my son, is not yet two years old, and he cannot be left alone." Of course, the real issue was that she didn't currently require my services. I continued, "I can come by myself a few days later." There was another unspoken reason – if I stayed here, what if someone else needed my assistance in delivering their baby? However, the county mayor's wife's demeanour didn't soften, and she coldly stated, "I didn't tie your feet, so you can do as you like."

Gaining entry into the county mayor's residence was no easy feat, and naturally, leaving wasn't any simpler. Following dinner, I was ushered to meet the county mayor, and the sight startled me to the point where I nearly exclaimed. Despite a few additional wrinkles, the face still resembled a wax gourd, the corpulent figure threatening to burst out of the grey-blue coat. Indeed, the former police sergeant Lu had ascended to the position of county mayor. More than a decade had elapsed, and County Mayor Lu had completely forgotten about the tinker's daughter. Given my current identity, I feared he wouldn't recollect any significant events.

"Are you planning to leave?" The county mayor got straight to the point. I may not have seen much of the world, but I had experienced more than a few things. Though a bit nervous, I wasn't afraid of him. I explained that even though it was his wife's first delivery, she was in the correct position and had sufficient fetal air. There was no need for him to worry. Staying here until the onset of labour wouldn't be beneficial. I planned to come over the day before labour commenced. "What do you need to do? I'll send someone to take care of it," declared the county mayor. "You stay here and look after my wife!" He left no room for negotiation.

I had no choice but to stay. As the saying goes, "Arms cannot bend thighs," and I wasn't even an arm in this scenario. There were numerous rules, each demanding strict adherence. In the daytime, I stood by the county mayor's wife, and during the night, I remained in the adjacent room. Fortunately, my companion was the woman in the grey coat, and she was quite talkative. I pondered why the county mayor chose not to send his wife to the hospital in Zhangjiakou City and instead invited a midwife from the countryside. The woman explained that the county mayor followed his wife's wishes.

Late on the ninth night, the county mayor's wife successfully delivered a baby boy, aligning with the time I had inferred. Despite being petite and particular, she cooperated when it mattered. County Mayor Lu's first wife had passed away two years ago, and he remarried after her death. Despite his age, he still had a son. Both his wife and son were in good health. Every wrinkle on County Mayor Lu's winter melon face seemed to radiate a smile. The reward for my assistance was three silver coins, along with soda, mooncakes, and tea. This wasn't a secret, and there was no need for secrecy. County Mayor Lu didn't instruct me otherwise.

I returned to Songzhuang Village in the big saloon car, much like how I had departed, with a crowd of children and adults trailing behind, fascinated by the unusual spectacle. Since then, I gained some fame in Zhangbei City, making twenty or thirty trips each year, but I never used the big saloon car again. The latent danger had been eliminated, and in some branches of time, it had morphed into an attempt to harm me. Of course, what choice did

I have, even if I were a prophet?

Among the women whose babies I delivered, the highest-ranking wasn't the county mayor. Later, I also assisted in delivering the baby of the wife of the Deputy Lieutenant-General of Chahar Province. She was an actress, and despite being pregnant, she maintained an appealing appearance. If her clothing were looser, few could tell she was expecting when she walked down the street. So, I claimed she was pregnant with both a boy and a girl, and few believed it until the twins were born. The Deputy Lieutenant-General of Chahar Province remarked that my eyes were too prophetic, unaware that observation was just one aspect. The key lay in listening and touching. Additionally, I aided in the delivery of Feng Yuxiang's division commander's wife, whose husband only had one arm.

I didn't intend to boast. Maternity knows no distinction between high and low status, and there's no such thing as painless childbirth. I wouldn't show favouritism based on wealth, alter my procedures, intentionally make things difficult, or act haughty with ordinary people. Even beggars received the same treatment. A beggar couple overheard me somehow, and when they came to my door, the woman was already struggling to walk. She gave birth to a child on my bed and left my house after a month.

Certainly, people held different attitudes towards me. County Mayor Lu detained me for ten days without many complications, and he was quite considerate. There was a particular soldier whose rank I couldn't discern, and he had a volatile temper. I speculated that he might have suffered a defeat. While I was attending to a fetus that had swallowed filth, he held a gun to the back of my head, berating me as worthless. Fortunately, the fetus turned out fine. If there had been an accident, he might have killed me. During those years, bandits were prevalent, with reports of seventy or eighty bandit nests, large and small, outside the North of the Great Wall. Some farmed during the day and plundered at night, labeled by officials as "The Second Bandits." Some were anxious about going unnoticed, raising flags on mountaintops. When bandits visited my house, I had to comply. Refusing meant risking the lives of my entire family. Dealing with them was akin to walking on a tightrope, much more challenging than dealing with soldiers, especially those with poor temperaments. I had entered and exited bandit dens multiple times, which were not the caves and woods as some people described. They were all villages, with loess and grey walls. I feared them, but when I saw a pregnant woman, my fear dissipated. Birth and delivery simplified the relationship. I had witnessed the light on top of Master Huang's head more than once. Whether others saw it or not, I would also have it on top of my head. It was the virtue, blessing, and confidence bestowed upon the midwife by God.

Rumours about me became increasingly divine, suggesting that I could not only predict the day but also the exact hour of a birth. Some even claimed that I possessed the ability to use incantations to change the gender of a fetus. While the former was exaggerated, the latter was pure nonsense and absurd. Those who added these untrue details might not have haboured any ill intentions. People accustomed to gossip often excelled at fabricating stories. However, many of my troubles stemmed from these false rumours, and a single individual, Li Erni, had caused numerous disturbances.

Even though Li Erni withdrew her complaint for some reason, her jealousy persisted. She haboured a significant bias against me, always assuming that my actions were intentional. Little did she know, I felt no better than her. Two years later, Li Erni became pregnant again, but I wasn't the one to deliver the baby, despite being prepared. Fortunately, the delivery went smoothly, and she gave birth to a baby girl. I didn't hasten to visit her, so I requested my father-in-law to bring her something.

Li Erni returned to Songzhuang Village and stayed with my father-in-law for half a month when her daughter Zhao Fenghuang was one year old. Despite just a partition wall separating us, Li Erni never visited me. I was the one who went to see her. If my father-in-law was in the room, Li Erni would exchange a few words with me. If my father-in-law was busy in the yard, she would be as cold as ice. Initially, I didn't feel the need to explain. She carried a hard rock, and I couldn't hatch a chick with any enthusiasm, but her perpetual coldness made the situation uncomfortable. Considering she was Dawang's sister, I decided to revisit the old story and make another attempt to thaw her frostiness and resentment.

Li Erni remained silent initially, her expression frozen. Later,

Zhao Fenghuang accidentally peed on her, and as if she had been watered down, her demeanour softened, and her eyes narrowed. She asked, "Did you assist the magistrate's wife in childbirth?"

I nodded.

Li Erni inquired again, "Did you also assist in the delivery for the lieutenant-general's wife?"

I nodded once more.

Li Erni's tone remained unchanged, "I heard that you also helped bandits' wives give birth."

I replied, "I don't concern myself with what their men do; a midwife can't handle so much."

Li Erni remarked, "That's it. You're so powerful and capable, why did you only give me …" The corners of my eyes suddenly dropped.

I said sadly, "I've already explained, how can you believe me?"

Li Erni raised her voice, flames in her eyes, then shouted, "Bring my son back to life. Then I will believe you. If Zhao Jinyuan also had a gun, you wouldn't have haboured traitors. If it weren't for Dad protecting you, or you enjoying good fruits …"

I tried to contain myself and refrained from saying anything more. Words were futile.

My eyes were blurred, and I didn't know how I left. That night, I stayed awake, unable to shake off the misunderstanding. Since I couldn't escape it, I wouldn't attempt to. When the rooster crowed, my resolve solidified. This misunderstanding had to be addressed; I secretly pledged to do so.

10

"I thought Luo Bao had allowed you to stay with him. Why did you come back again?" Song Pin sneered.

Maixiang said angrily, "He is my husband, can't I see him? Why do you keep blabbing on?"

Song Pin suddenly lost his temper, and his muted voice turned serrated. "If I hadn't arrived in time, Zunai would have choked to death!"

Maixiang retorted, "Song Hui isn't usually like this, I didn't expect … a brainless woman. It pissed me off!"

Song Pin hissed, "Do you have a brain? If you have a brain, why do you want to see Luo Bao at this time? Can he flee abroad after just a few days?"

Maixiang defended, "Just for a moment.."

Song Pin said, "If there's any accident with Zunai, Maixiang, don't say you can't explain it, even I can't escape it."

Maixiang said, "You've been a secretary for so many years, no one can do anything to you."

Song Pin sneered, "Don't flatter me. In Qiao Shitou's eyes, I'm nothing. It's a trivial matter to dismiss me. You think too simply about the consequences. Don't you know who Qiao Shitou is?"

The ants scattered, not just on my face but also within my heart. In their eyes, Qiao Shitou seemed like colossal tusks. I had heard rumours about Qiao Shitou, and perhaps they held some truth. I no longer had the opportunity or the possibility to personally inquire about him, and even if I did, there was no guarantee that I would get any answers. He had always been adept at keeping secrets, a skill he had cultivated since childhood.

Maixiang was evidently frightened, pausing for a while before saying, "Zunai is a fairy, and nothing will happen."

Song Pin remained cold and remarked, "You said it's okay, so it's okay?"

Maixiang asserted, "I promise."

Song Pin retorted, "You're quite a braggart. Even if Zunai is safe, have you ever thought that if Qiao Shitou saw today's incident, would he easily let you and me off?"

Maixiang mumbled, "He won't know anything unless you tell him."

Song Pin raised his voice, "What I'm talking about is just in case! What if?"

Maixiang said, "My incense is very smoky, and when Qiao Shitou comes back … He will never smell it."

Song Pin remarked, "Maybe he'll be home tomorrow morning. How do you get rid of the smell?"

Maixiang was surprised, "Won't he come back in a few days? Why is he returning so suddenly?"

Song Pin explained that he had already reached the county,

and upon his return to Songzhuang Village, he would have just stepped on the accelerator.

Maixiang inquired, "Did he call you?"

Song Pin, a bit annoyed, replied, "Do you think he always reports to me? Town Mayor Yang said so. The county mayor called him."

Maixiang's reaction was a bit slow as she whispered, "This is too sudden."

Song Pin snorted again, "I told you a long time ago that you couldn't leave Zunai, but why did you still go to town today?"

Maixiang explained, "Zunai loves fresh tofu."

Song Pin responded, "Stop your tricks; there's still one night left. You should get ready."

Maixiang asked, "What should I prepare?"

Annoyed, Song Pin said, "Do you need me to teach you? Everything has to be prepared. You can't let Qiao Shitou find fault."

Maixiang assured, "I didn't neglect Zunai, you know."

Song Pin retorted, "Don't say these useless things. Zunai may not care, but that doesn't mean Qiao Shitou doesn't ... By the way, have you found that ant?"

Maixiang chuckled, "Your eyesight must be getting worse, absolutely not."

Song Pin emphasised, "I don't care if my eyesight is getting worse; you must check again!"